Cathy Kissinger

D0018855

Advance Praise for
he Widow's Husband

Novelist Khaled Hosseini, author of *The Kite Runner* and *A Thousand Splendid Suns,* says, "Tamim Ansary's book is a lavishly detailed and unfailingly engrossing story of loyalty, custom, honor, and love… There isn't a false note in this account of the doomed British campaign in Afghanistan and the intertwined lives that unravel, in unexpected ways, as civilizations collide. This is historical fiction at its page-turning best…"

Playwright Charlie Varon, author of *The People's Violin* and *Rush Limbaugh in Night School,* says this book, "…kept me up later than I'd planned, I had to finish it! A fascinating immersion into 19th century Afghanistan, its village life and its invaders. It will change the way you think about this part of the world…"

Novelist Erika Mailman, author of *The Witch's Trinity* and *A Woman of Ill Fame* says, "This book is an incandescent lamp I will return to again and again, to bask in the marvelous language and the unforgettable characters… a beautiful and moving work of fiction. Ansary proves himself an extraordinary novelist…"

THE WIDOW'S HUSBAND

TAMIM ANSARY

VOX NOVUS
A NUMINA PRESS BOOK
SAN RAFAEL, CALIFORNIA

The Widow's Husband

Copyright © 2009 by Tamim Ansary

All rights reserved. No part of this book may be reproduced in any form or by any electronic or mechanical means, including information storage and retrieval systems without permission in writing from the Publisher, except by a reviewer who may quote brief passages in a review.

This novel is entirely a product of the author's imagination. All characters, events, and places in it are fictitious or are fictionally re-imagined historical events and persons. Any similarity to real persons, living or dead, is coincidental and not intended by the author.

Library of Congress Cataloging-in-Publication Data

Ansary, Mir Tamim.
  The widow's husband / Tamim Ansary. -- 1st print ed.
     p. cm.
  ISBN-13: 978-0-9753615-0-4
  ISBN-10: 0-9753615-5-4
  1. British--Afghanistan--Fiction. 2. Afghan Wars--Fiction. 3. Villages--Afghanistan--Fiction. 4. Kabul (Afghanistan)--Fiction. 5. Afghanistan--History--19th century--Fiction. I. Title.
  PS3601.N5553W53 2009
  813'.6--dc22
                              2009032695

A *Vox Novus* Book
Published by NUMINA PRESS
www.numinapress.com

Cover art and design © 2009 by Elina Ansary.

An e-book edition of *The Widow's Husband* is available on www.scribd.com

Printed in U.S.A.

Every writer should have a writers' group like mine, the San Francisco Writers' Workshop, in all its protean diversity, unending flux, and unfailing support. I also wish to thank the San Francisco Arts Commission for a grant that gave me the time to set other cares aside for a year and write this novel.

Historical Note

In 1839, Great Britain sent an army into Afghanistan to replace the country's ruler with a more compliant king. The "Army of the Indus" completed its assignment easily. Soon wives and retainers followed husbands and lovers and a vigorous British community began to thrive in Kabul. Three years later, that entire community tried to flee the country over the Hindu Kush mountains; but out of 17,000 men, women, and children who left the city on a stormy January day, only one man made it out of the country alive.

1

Let me take you across the miles and down through the years to a tiny village in Afghanistan, some hundred miles north of Kabul, in the year 1841. The village was called Char Bagh, which means Four Gardens, and it's still there, although it has changed a little since those days. A paved road runs within ten miles of it now, flanked by poles carrying electric wires. The malik of Char Bagh owns a television set, as is only proper for a headman, and one day, when power reaches the village, he means to turn it on. In 1841, of course, there was no electricity anywhere, not even in England.

The village nestles at the bottom of a valley shaped like an elongated gravy bowl. The sides are steep and boulder-studded. From the valley floor, one can see the flat, blue silhouettes of gigantic mountains ringing the high hills on every side. A river enters at one end, tumbling down from the upper reaches in a series of cataracts. It makes a lazy loop through the flat part of the valley, then picks up speed flowing south, acquiring choppy rapids just before it squeezes into a crack between two walls of granite. There is no getting into the valley along the river bank at this lower end, nor at the upper end either. The only entrance is from the side. Today, a gravel road just wide enough for a single car winds down from Red Pass, and until recently government officials from Kabul came here occasionally for rustic vacations: the headman kept a tidy little inn before Soviet carpet bombing took it out. But in 1841, the only way to reach Char Bagh was on foot, coming down the western slope on a goat track worn into the hard soil by generations of hooves and human feet.

Late one morning in that spring of 1841, the malik of Char Bagh was sitting in one of the second-story rooms of his clan compound, inspecting his beard and moustache in the lid of his snuff tin, hoping to find a white hair or two. Unfortunately, all he saw in the little mirror was his usual black beard, his usual smooth skin, virtually the skin of a boy. With a sigh, he took a pinch of snuff. A headman without a single streak of white in his beard—how was such a man to exert authority? All of Ibrahim's cares these past six months, all the weight upon his shoulders since his brother's death elevated him to the leadership of the village had not gained him so much as a single wrinkle. His was a hard lot.

A clatter sounded. The young headman cocked his head. Did it come from downstairs…? No: it was only Asad's donkey braying away in the compound down the street. Ibrahim opened the shutters. A chill breeze blew in, but he didn't care. He wanted the air and the light, but most of all, he wanted to see if *she* was coming. With the window open, the donkey sounded even louder. Beyond its irritating noise, Ibrahim detected the chitter of children, a sound he adored, and beyond them the rumble of the Sorkhab River running into Needle's Eye, another sound he savored. But no one was coming down from Red Pass.

The malik packed another small pinch of snuff under his tongue and settled back into his book. Rumi's mystical masterpiece was a precious legacy handed down from his father's grandfather's great, great grandfather. The Qur'an in Farsi, some people called it. Ibrahim read a couplet out loud, running his finger below the line to keep his place: *The moment my intoxication wanes* … Intoxication—how was a man to interpret that word? *I erupt a hundred heads of lamentation…* What did the poet mean, 'erupt ?' And what were these 'hundred heads of lamentation'? If only he could discuss such mysterious words with somebody, anybody, but alas: no other man in his village could read.

Then Ibrahim heard another sound. This one definitely came from somewhere inside the house. It had to be his sister-in-law. Khadija must be back from Sorkhab. Ibrahim straightened up, not wanting her (or anyone) to see him slumping. By the time the door swung open he looked suitably sunk in his studies.

The widow entered noiselessly. Ibrahim didn't look up but he didn't have to: her strong features rose up in his mind's eye, vivid as a dream: those dark green eyes, those high cheekbones. Although she was nearly Ibrahim's age, she looked almost as girlish as his wife. When he did glance up at last, she was coming toward him barefoot, the end of her gray scarf drooping over her breast. She was still wearing her floral visiting dress.

"Oh, what a journey," she exclaimed. "Oh, what a journey, brother-jan, I'm dying of exhaustion, simply dying." She paused to refill his cup, but when she touched his teapot she frowned: "Cold? Hajji-sahib, why do you allow yourself to suffer this way? When you have so many people to serve you!" She tipped her head back and let out a melodic keen: "Naheed!"

A girl clattered up the steps. "Auntie?"

"Get some hot tea for your father, my dear. Hot, I said! Bring a cup for your auntie too. All that way in the blazing sunlight! It's not good for a woman of my age."

The girl went helter-skelter back downstairs.

"Your age," Ibrahim scoffed. "Of your hundred petals, not one has blown." He issued the ritual compliment lightly but felt the danger of saying such a thing to his sister-in-law when they were alone, and so he buried it quickly with the patterned chatter of a well-mannered man: "You're back, safe and whole, Allah be praised. May you not be tired. Tell me about Sorkhab, your people: all in splendid health *inshallah?*"

"Oh! Let me catch my breath! Please!" She released several sighs to dramatize her fatigue, but she was just building suspense. The village of Sorkhab was only three hours away, she was strong, and she was riding a donkey. But she knew how anxious he was for the news she bore, so she was holding it back, just to tease him. Khadija the tease.

"Your people," he persisted. "Were they well?"

"Yes, Hajji-sahib. Bless you. They all asked about your health."

3

Khadija then launched into a list of relatives who were well and had asked about his health, reporting their inquiries in a ritual sing-song.

"Good," he interrupted, before she could list every man, woman, and child in Sorkhab. "Excellent. But tell me." He tilted toward her. "Have they started plowing?"

Just then, Naheed bustled back with the tea service. She set her tray down, brushed her bangs back, unloaded two pot-bellied teapots, two cups, a bowl of brown-sugar nuggets, and two wooden spoons with painted handles. She poured a cup for each adult, piled the used dishes onto her tray, and scurried out again.

"The plowing?" Ibrahim prodded.

"No," said the widow. "The soil is still too muddy ..."

A fly banged into the wooden shutter. Ibrahim gazed at his sister-in-law through the steam from his tea cup, waiting.

"Hajji-sahib, it's not good," she said. "Mustapha Khan's daughter-in-law dropped twins last week, boys this time. Allah smiles on the man, but he has twenty people living with him now. His daughter-in-laws are fighting, his eldest son is whining for a house of his own—you know where this ends."

"It can't!" he cried out. "They must not!"

"They intend to," she said. "They will. They've already laid out new fields. They're going to plow new land east of the river."

"Where will the water come from?" the headman of Char Bagh lamented.

Khadija said nothing. He did not expect her to. They both knew the situation. Char Bagh was situated in a cul-de-sac, cut off from the country downstream by cliffs. Its water came entirely from the Sorkhab River, and the river flowed through Sorkhab before it reached Char Bagh. If the bigger village wanted to divert all the water and let none reach Char Bagh, it could do that..

"Has it gone beyond mere talk?"

"Yes," she said. "The Sorkhab elders were out there last week, marking where to put in new irrigation ditches. They plan to water a thousand more *jireebs*, I heard."

"A thousand!" Ibrahim paled. "Do they think they're a city now?"

"It's not just Mustafa Khan. Mullah Yaqub has big plans too. His son is building a house. And then there's Saifuddin …and Jamal…That whole village is growing, Hajji-sahib. Something must be done about that village."

"That village is *your* village," he reminded her gently.

She cast him a reproachful look. The fly banged against the shutters again, buzzed for a few seconds, and then settled somewhere. "How can you say such a thing?" she said in a husky thrum. "*This* is my village, Ibrahim-jan. My place is here. I am *yours* now."

Ibrahim struggled to keep his face still. She was his. Well, he did have the right. Any honorable man does the decent thing and marries his brother's widow, especially if he's a headman with responsibilities: a beautiful widow can turn a village upside down. One morsel of meat and all the men turn into cats, as they say. Better such a widow were somebody's wife, and Ibrahim after all had only one wife at the moment. He could certainly afford two. If Khadija were his wife right now he could lock the door…He allowed his eyes to graze over those breasts, that rounded waist… lock the door and undo that first button…

He blinked back to the present moment. His mother-in-law would never allow it. Any second wife but *this* one. What was he thinking? How could he dream of overturning the harmony of his household with such a move, reckless of the discord it would sow? Out loud, he said, "You're ours, it's true…" nodding solemnly. "You've been ours for … what? Eleven years now?"

"Twelve," she murmured.

He knew that, of course. Knew exactly how many years had passed since the night his brother married her, the night Ibrahim first set eyes on her. He was a boy then, she was a girl, they were of an age. But Khadija belonged to his brother who was twenty years older. Ibrahim remembered that moment better than anything in his life except his trip to Mecca with his father and brother as a little boy.

"But you have kin over there, Khadija-jan. Your dear mother …I will never allow enmity to grow between us and them. We are one village."

"Please, Hajji-sahib. We're not one village, never say such a thing on *my* account. If they take more water, we'll have less. You're our malik, you must put our needs first."

"How?" He looked into her eyes. "In your opinion, how should I proceed?"

"In *my* opinion?"

"Yes. You know all the men of Sorkhab, you know how they think. Advise me."

"Oh. Dear Hajji-sahib!" she said breathlessly. "I am only a woman. But if I were you? I would take their malik aside and warn him. I would make him tremble! He thinks he can toy with you because you're young? Teach him, Ibrahim. You're twice the man he is!"

Ibrahim raised haunted eyes to his sister-in-law. "Oh for God's sake, Khadija, what am I to say? Eat less, drink less, stop your women from having babies? What am I to offer?"

"Why should you offer anything? It's too late for striking bargains, Malik-sahib. It's time to make that jackal know the taste and smell of fear."

Ibrahim shook his head. "I can't start a fight. You can't really want me to. They're still your kin. They're still our neighbors. If God forbid someone gets killed, we'll never see the end of fighting. Our children's grandchildren will still be killing each other. And besides there are so many more of them."

"But you're strong," she pleaded. "Don't be afraid."

"Afraid!" Color leapt into his cheeks. "Who said anything about 'afraid?' I only want to be prudent. If a battle breaks out, seven hundred of them against three hundred of us—what kind of malik leads his men into such a battle? This whole village depends on my decisions. I can't be reckless."

She receded then into womanly modesty. "Your decisions will be wise, I'm sure." She set her cup in its saucer upside down. "We all look up to you, Hajji-sahib. I only wish you trusted yourself as much as we trust you. They're the bigger village, but you're the bigger man. If I've worried you, I'm not sorry. You need to know what Sorkhab is up to. And how would you know if you didn't have your little spy, eh?" She poked at him playfully. "Eh?"

The contact made him shiver. He frowned to hide his arousal.

"You've done well," he gruffed. "If you want to go again in a few weeks, let me know: I'll send some boys along. Take Soraya next time."

Did her features tighten for a second at the sound of his wife's name? He couldn't tell. "I will," she assured him. "Malik-sahib, I think of her as my own sister, you know. I'm grateful for your protection."

"It's my duty," he declared. "Respect for my dear brother comes first."

"If you need anything, just command me. A widow must make herself useful," Khadija murmured.

He wriggled in place. "Widows see the worst of things, I know, but I promise you, no one will ever harm my brother's widow, so long as I live, *inshallah*."

Khadija rose to her feet, never allowing her skirts to fall away from her pantalooned legs, and yet the grace of her body somehow showed through all the garments. For a moment, Ibrahim allowed his mind to dwell on the pleasures his brother must have taken with this woman. They were famously noisy behind closed doors. His own wife made no noise at all when he took her. She just lay still in the dark and succumbed to his embraces; and yet how could he complain? Delicate, haunted Soraya had given him a son, a wonderful son, bright-eyed little Ahmad—not to mention two beautiful daughters. His brother's wife, by contrast, had remained tragically barren throughout the years of her marriage to Ashraf. Well, every man had his own special burdens to bear. Allah knows best.

2

That same spring morning, shortly after the widow Khadija returned from her journey, a stranger came down the goat track. Sunlight slathered the rocks that day, crocuses had bloomed and columbines dotted the hillsides with bits of blue, but a stiff breeze was blowing from the north and the upper passes were still choked with snow. No one traveled to distant places at this time of year, not even on the big highway visible from the peaks. Here in Char Bagh, at this season, most people still huddled in their houses at night, keeping warm around charcoal-burning braziers and eating through last year's stores as they told and retold the ancient stories.

And yet, on this particular morning, here came a total stranger trudging down from Red Pass wrapped in a shabby cloak, an odd old man with a thicket of a beard, a vagabond by the looks of him. He was walking along empty handed and alone without even a dog along for protection. Where could he have come from? Where could he be going on a path that led only into a cul-de-sac?

No one asked those questions because no one spotted him except two young boys, Ahmad and Karim, who happened to be sitting high on the hillside that morning. They were supposed to be watching their families' flocks, but instead these bad boys were playing knucklebones in a clear patch among the weeds, letting their heavy-jowled dogs do all the herding. When the little fellows saw the vagabond trudging over the crest of the hill, they stopped their game to watch the big-boned old man leave the path and traverse the hillside and climb over a ridge and then come down to the base of the rock known as Baba's Nose. They watched him shove in amongst the gray weeds and settle next to one of the rock's "nostrils," where no one could see him from the path, nor from the village below. The old man took off his turban and from its green folds produce a boiled egg, which he peeled and consumed. Then, for a long while, he simply sat motionless, eyes closed, arms outstretched, hands open.

The boys scratched their heads and snuffled back snot. This wanderer certainly trumped any game of knucklebones, for how often did a fellow get to see a total stranger? Ten-year-old Karim had seen total strangers only once in his life, and that one time probably didn't count because it was the time the marauders came, and he had mostly kept his eyes shut. Nine-year-old Ahmad, the headman's son, was more sophisticated; he had been way upstream in Sorkhab, the bigger village north of Red Pass. His aunt Khadija came from there and he had been with her several times when she went home to visit her family. But even he had never seen a stranger like this.

Suddenly the vagabond stood up, folded his turban lengthwise five times until it was just the length and width of a prayer rug and spread it out on a patch of bare earth. He stroked it smooth with scrupulous care, brushing away twigs and stray insects, then stepped out of his slippers and onto the folded fabric. Facing west, he lifted his hands to his ears, and began to chant softly, "Allaaaaaaaaaaaaahu...!"

"Who is he?" Karim demanded.

The younger boy shrugged.

"Is he from Sorkhab?"

"I never saw him before."

"Look at that!" Karim spat with disgust. "You can see his skin." He pointed and both boys stared at the holes in the man's threadbare shirt. "Well, I'm going to throw a stone at him," Karim declared. "Help me find a good one, Ahmad-jan. I'll make that old dog move. You'll see."

"Don't do that," Ahmad cautioned. "Your mama will get mad."

"Drrt! Why should my mama get mad? My papa always says, protect the village from strangers—that's what he says. Remember that time the marauders came?" The ten-year-old puffed out his chest and then sneered, "Oh! You don't remember, you weren't here. *You* were in Sorkhab. Well, you listen to me, Ahmad-jan. Strangers are bad. When you get to be my age, you'll know."

"You have to shelter travelers though. That's the rule," said Ahmad.. "That's what my papa says."

"Hmm." Karim knew this rule. In fact, he knew both rules: never trust a stranger, always take in travelers. Which one applied? "What if he creeps down and looks at our women?" Karim frowned. "I bet that's what he's up to. I can hit him from here. Want to bet?"

"I don't gamble," Ahmad retorted, rolling onto his belly to look at the beggar some more. The man had finished his prayers and was wrapping his turban around his skull cap. And now he was settling himself cross-legged in front of Baba's Nose and starting to thumb a string of prayer beads, taking no notice of the boys, even though they were well within his sight.

"You don't gamble?" Karim snorted. "You donkey-butt! What's knucklebones if it isn't gambling? Well, I'm going to crack his skull open." Karim had found his weapon, a round, black stone the size of his fist. He rolled it in his palm.

"Stop that.," Ahmad whispered angrily. "What's wrong with you? The poor man is just resting!"

"Let him rest somewhere else. This is our village, by Allah." Karim took a two-step running start for momentum and flung his stone. The stranger still paid no attention; he just kept flicking his prayer beads, his thick lips moving in some chant. Karim's rock rose into the sunlight. The trajectory was good. It looked like it would land near the stranger, maybe right on his head. Just at that moment, however, the stranger swung his arm casually and something left his hand—a clod of dirt. Even though he flung it up without aiming or looking, it banged into Karim's rock at the tip-top of its arc. The clod shattered, but the rock dropped directly down to the earth and from the spot where rock and dirt clod had banged together, a lark swooped away.

The boys gaped at each other. Each one saw the terror in the other's eyes. Suddenly Ahmad jumped to his feet and went scrambling down the hillside, with Karim only inches behind him, both boys running for the safety of Char Bagh, that cluster of cob huts and houses that was their home.

3

Lost in the turmoil of her thoughts, Khadija started across the courtyard. At the gateway to the women's yard, she paused, however. Over by the kitchen, she saw Soraya's daughter scolding the headman's great-aunt once-removed. "Get your paws out of there," the girl was yelling. "Who said you could gorge?" The poor crone had been scooping mutton fat out of the urn to lick off her fingers. Always the last in the compound to eat, she was always hungry.

"Shakila!" Khadija cried out. "You be nice!"

The girl saw Khadija advancing upon her and cast quick glances right and left to see which way she might bolt, but she was not going to get off so easily. An eight-year-old child shouting at a white-haired crone! What was Soraya teaching her children?

At that moment, however, the crone herself intervened. "This darling?" she grinned, displaying several missing teeth. "She's always nice!" and the humble old woman gave the child a hug. That's how it was, Khadija thought, when you were living on the charity of a distant relative and you got old and weak and no one needed you for anything. You could never let your smile slip, you could never be less than loving, and if someone stepped on your toes, you could never fail to thank them, as if a bit of pain was just what you were hoping for. Who were you to complain or make anyone feel guilty? In that relentlessly cheerful crone, Khadija saw her own eventual self, unless Ibrahim made her his second wife.

"Auntie-dear," she said gently to the old woman. "Go rest now. You must be tired." Then she addressed the girl severely. "Shakila, take those two big water jugs to the river and bring them back full. Hurry now. We need water for dinner."

The girl scuttled off to do as she was told. Khadija's husband might be dead, but her authority had not faded—yet.

ॐ

Soraya sat next to a vegetable bin with a cutting board on her lap, peeling and chopping onions. A *djinn* was lurking nearby. She could tell because her head was throbbing in that special weird way. She just hoped the nasty spirit hadn't gotten into the kitchen. She tended to sense them wherever it was dank and dark—those were the sorts of places djinns preferred. She heard them at night quite often just outside the windows, skulking in the rain, scratching at the sills, noises no one else could hear.

The kitchen had no windows, only smoke holes and a doorway to augment whatever light the fires cast. Decades of cooking had turned the walls and ceiling black. The holes above the fire-pits worked well enough on ordinary days, but on feast-days, when all the fires were going at once, the room filled with so much smoke, the women had to work with their head scarves pressed over their mouths. Today was no feast day, but the soot had formed a permanent crust that suited djinns perfectly: against that soot, the dreadful creatures could quite disappear.

A shadow suddenly darkened the room, and Soraya looked up fearfully, but it was only her sister-in-law stooping to enter through the low doorway. The widow set a bucket of water next to one of the fire pits and crouched beside Soraya.

"Salaam aleikum," the slender girl murmured.

"Waleikum a'salaam, my precious," said the widow Khadija.

"May you not be tired."

"May you be healthy."

"When did you get home? You must be exhausted? Sorkhab is so far away."

"I had a chance to catch my breath," Khadija assured her. "I just had a quiet cup of tea with Hajji Sahib. Are you cooking dinner already?

Good girl. Let's get some rice soaking."

"Rice!" Soraya exclaimed, her forehead wrinkling. "Are we having rice? Are there guests tonight?"

"Not tonight."

"Are we celebrating something?"

"No, little one. It's just that Hajji-sahib has some big worries right now. He'll need some cheering up." Khadija leaned a little closer and dropped her voice. "Sorkhab is going to plow extra fields."

She spoke as if this were ominous news but Soraya couldn't see the danger "Let them plow," she shrugged. "So what?"

"So what!" Khadija rocked back on her heels a little, laughing. "You innocent little sugar cube. That's what I love about you. If they plow more land, they'll take more water. Don't you see? More for them means less for us."

"But the river is so big!"

Khadija smiled. "Big now, but what happens to it in the summer?"

Soraya muffled a giggle. "Shrinks like a man's thingie?"

"Yes, dear, like a man's thingie, and once it shrinks, there won't be enough for all of us." Khadija stared into the coals. "It's a strange world, isn't it?" she mused. "A man is so small, and yet there's enough of him for two, three, even four wives. A river is so big, and yet there isn't enough of it for even two little villages."

"Hmm." Soraya pondered this analogy dubiously. "Ghulam Haidar has only two wives, but they exhaust him. That's why he's so pale, they say. That's why he faints."

"Oh, pfft!" Khadija dismissed Ghulam Haidar with a snort. "He's pale because he's thin blooded, and he faints because his wives quarrel. Wives don't have to quarrel. Take us, for example. You and I would never quarrel, would we, Soraya-jan? If my Ashraf had taken a second wife—someone sweet-tempered like you—I would not have cared a bit, not one bit, and I don't even have a son. A woman with a son has nothing to fear from a second wife. The mother of a man's first-born son will always be the queen of his household."

"But I'm his wife now and I don't even get to decide if we'll have rice."

"My precious! Of course you get to decide, you just don't want to. It's easier to let me go on managing things, isn't it? But surely you don't want to deprive your husband of some tasty rice tonight, with all his worries. Oh, believe me, if the river runs dry, we'll all have cause to worry. We might have to fight Sorkhab for water. That's why Hajji-sahib is anxious, you see? It's difficult for a man so young to be malik and bear all that responsibility. You and I must ease his life, so let's give him a feast of spinach rice tonight, shall we?"

But Soraya was not listening. Out in the courtyard, she saw her darling little Ahmad wrestling with his friend Karim. That big brute had one arm locked around her darling's neck and he was twisting about wildly, making the younger, smaller boy thrash and yelp. A horrid picture filled Soraya's mind, of her son's head ripping right off his neck. "Karim!" she shouted, rising.

Khadija caught at her green skirts. "Leave them alone. They're learning to be men."

"Karim!" the mother cried out again. "You bad boys stop wrestling! Come indoors or Auntie Khadija will take a whip to you!"

The boys stopped wrestling but even as Soraya turned back she felt the twist in her gut. A shiver ran up her spine and flashes filled her eyes. She knew what was coming, and sure enough, as soon as the flashes faded, there was the horrid thing, right in the corner, squat and evil, merging with the shadows. Khadija's voice came to her from far away. "Soraya-jan? Is something wrong?"

"Don't you see it? Look!"

"Look at what? The cat?"

Instantly the darkness resolved into a feral gray cat skulking in the corner, but Soraya was not fooled. "That's no cat," she whimpered. "That's a djinn. See how it stares? Don't leave me, Khadija!"

"I will never leave you." Khadija snatched up a spoon as if to threaten the cat-shaped djinn, but the boys tumbled into the room just then, scaring the creature away.

"Mama," the little fellow blurted. "There's a man on the hill."

"Is there," Soraya managed to say. Thank God for her son: the sight of him made her heart bloom. Already the stench of djinn was subsiding

15

and the aroma of warm bread was filling Soraya's senses. "Come over here, Ahmad-jan. You too, Karim, let me give you both a bit of bread with clotted cream. Would you like that?"

The boys sidled in, but Ahmad kept talking about the man on the hill. "Should I go tell Papa?"

"Your father has a lot on his mind," Khadija scolded.

"But Auntie, a stranger's sitting right next to Baba's Nose and Karim says he's come to gawk at our women."

"I tried to move him along, by God!" Karim boasted.

"But the man just waved and suddenly this clod of dirt flew up and poof," said Ahmad. "A bird flew away. I'm not lying. He's a wizard or something."

"A wizard! Well, well, well," Khadija twinkled. "We haven't had a wizard in this valley since…How long since we've had a wizard in these parts, Soraya-jan?"

"Not since that flying monkey-man…" said Soraya. She closed her eyes and let the pictures fill her mind. "The one with the beard made of fire," she recounted, "and the tail that stretched all the way to Kabul." The story started taking shape. "That was before you two were born. He came into the village right after sunset prayer and sitting on his shoulders was an old woman with a lump on her back. When she sneezed, the lump exploded into birds, thousands of birds!" She paused again to let the story grow details. Friendship, she thought… between the monkey and the man … a bag full of stones that turned into … turned into jewels at night—

But Khadija broke the story-dream with a laugh "Soraya, the things you say!"

"It's not a joke!" Ahmad cried bitterly. "it's not a story. There's a man up there."

The women smiled. "Perhaps we should put this sorcerer to work on Ghulam Haidar's two wives," Khadija suggested. "He might end their quarrelling."

"Stop laughing," Ahmad pouted. "There *is* a man, he turned a stone into a bird, Auntie. He's all raggedy and strange."

"What stone?" Khadija's sudden sharp tone made Soraya look up.

"The one Karim threw at him."

Soraya pushed her work aside. "You threw a stone at a traveler passing through? A *stone*, Karim?"

"He's not passing through," the boy protested. "He thinks he lives here now. He's just sitting next to our rock like it's his rock. He made a prayer mat out of his turban and said *namaz* right in front of us."

"What's wrong with that?" Khadija demanded. "He fears God."

Ahmad and Karim shuffled in place, trading guilty glances. "But he's a stranger!" Karim insisted and then seemed to remember another point in his defense. "He criss-crosses his turban in front. We don't do like that. He's probably a bandit, he's probably got a gang coming to steal women, just like those other ones. Well, I have to go. My mother needs me at home." He jumped to his feet.

"Sit," Khadija commanded. "What was this stranger doing when you left?"

Ahmad answered. "Counting his prayer beads."

"And walking in circles," Karim added.

"And chanting," said Ahmad.

"Chanting what? Qur'an?"

"No, not Qur'an, Auntie. He was just sort of humming. Like this." Ahmad began buzzing out an aimless, tuneless hum.

Khadija looked at Soraya "Chanting, walking in circles, counting his prayer beads—make up a plate of food." Her green eyes were gleaming. Soraya had never seen her sister-in-law so excited. "I think a *malang* has come to Char Bagh!" Khadija exulted.

4

Karim and Ahmad came out of the headman's compound, carrying a heavy basket. The main path through the village was a dusty track that meandered among scattered fruit trees and across occasional irrigation ditches. Here and there, smaller pathways branched away to lose themselves among the compounds of the humbler clans, but the boys kept going past the big communal well, past the bridge, past the mosque, until they reached the mouth of the steep path leading up to Baba's Nose. Here, Karim paused.

"Go ahead," he said to his friend.

"You first," Ahmad shot back.

Karim grimaced but led the way. It was only right: he was the bigger boy, the older boy...As they approached the stranger, however, he balked again. "Please, Ahmad-jan. You take his tea to him."

"Why me? You threw the stone." The climb had left Ahmad wheezing for breath.

"I know, but he might put a curse on me. He's a malang!"

Ahmad crept around a cistern built to collect rainwater. He could see the vagabond sitting against Baba's Nose, humming away. Ahmad crouched down among the weeds, and Karim hunkered next to him. Both boys watched the vagabond thumb his green prayer beads round and round.

"Run up," Karim whispered. "Run up, set it down, run back— nothing to it." He gave Ahmad a push.

"Don't push," Ahmad complained. "You made me spill!"

"So go before it cools!"

"Should I unwrap the bread? Auntie might be angry if I leave the cloth behind."

"Dummie! You think he'll take the cloth when he goes? He's a malang! He might not even take his clothes!"

"Okay, okay." Ahmad drew a breath. "Here I go then." But just as he clenched the basket, he went into one of his coughing fits. Karim waited patiently, knowing it might take a while to pass. Finally Ahmad wiped his brow and took hold of the basket again. Under the cloth was a potful of steaming tea, a cup already half-filled with sugar, a stick for stirring, a loaf of this morning's bread re-heated over the dinner-fire, and a bag of date-and-walnut leather. Squaring his shoulders, Ahmad climbed the last few paces.

The malang didn't stop murmuring, but he looked up and nodded slightly. From this close, Ahmad could see the man's broad features, his prominent nose, his full, fleshy lips. A bushy gray beard sprouted not just from his chin but from his cheeks to his cheekbones. His forehead bore a wreath of wrinkles, yet his eyes looked young.

"My aunt sent this." Ahmad set the tray beside the man's knee and tried to remember the words he'd been told to say. "Your road has been long, sahib. May this tea warm you."

"God bless you, little boy. Nice of you. Thank your good aunt."

Ahmad was startled. He had heard of malangs so lost in ecstatic worship they let insects inhabit their beards and moss grow around their feet. He had heard of malangs who survived in the worst weather without shelter, because they thought so constantly about God that nothing could harm them. Ahmad knew all this about malangs, but he never knew malangs could speak and say ordinary things like "bless you" and "thank-your-aunt".

Should he say something in return? Questions surged in him. *Who are you? Where did you come from?* Oh, how he longed to ask. What lay beyond the mountains? A traveling man must have seen great things: giants— who could tell? Dragons. Battles. Even, perhaps, the great city of Kabul.

The malang slipped his beads into his vest pocket and peeped under the cloth. Then he tore a chunk off the loaf of bread, filled and stirred his cup, dipped his bread in the sweet hot tea, and began to chew with gusto, taking no further notice of the boy. Karim, lying flat against the ground waved at Ahmad through the weeds, an urgent irritated gesture that meant: what are you waiting for? Run back!

But Ahmad could not leave without asking at least a question or two. "Malang-sahib, did you come from far away?" His breath rasped.

The vagabond glanced at the boy. "Why do you call me 'malang'?"

"Aren't you one? What are you, then? Just a traveler, sir?"

"Yes, my boy. Just a traveler."

"Well a traveler is a great thing to be," said Ahmad. "I'll be one myself when I'm grown. I'll travel so far away, so far, you wait and see! My father went all the way to Mecca with his papa when *he* was a boy. One day…" Ahmad groped for a place inconceivably distant. "I will go to Kabul."

"If God wills it," the malang agreed gently.

"But where did you come from, sir?" Ahmad stopped to cough, then dared to add, "And where are you going?"

The malang drew his prayer beads out again. "Yesterday, little man, I was with my beloved. Tomorrow, *inshallah*, I will be with my beloved."

"Oh." So this was a suitor going somewhere to claim his bride. But wait: if he was with her yesterday, why was he here now? And where were his people, why had they left him without so much as a donkey, even? "How long will you stay here, sir?"

"Until The Friend calls to me," the malang replied. "I have yielded to The Friend, like the leaves and the birds and the stars and the worms. How about you, good lad? Have you yielded to the stars and the worms?"

"Maybe," Ahmad stammered. Was the man talking about Allah in some strange way? Just to be on the safe side, the little boy recited his Testament of Faith: "*La illaha il-allahu wa Mohammedu-rasullilah.*" No god but God and Mohammed bears His Message.

A hornet came circling down in a great swooping spiral, moving not like a bee or a wasp, but slowly, very slowly. The hornet moved so slowly that Ahmad could see the big orange-banded body swaying and tilting as it swung below the supporting wings. The boy sucked in a scared breath. Hornets could hurt you bad, kill you even! But this one bypassed Ahmad, alighting instead on the malang's hand, which in turn was resting on the man's knee. The malang did not move. After a moment, the hornet lifted off and buzzed around his head. Ahmad went on holding his breath. The malang caught his eye and winked, then opened his mouth and stuck out his tongue. The hornet landed on that flap of flesh. The malang closed his mouth and smiled. A moment later, he opened his mouth and the hornet soared away, shaking droplets of moisture off its tiny legs. Ahmad rubbed his eyes, feeling dizzy.

A thud sounded to his right—Karim had thrown a stone to get his attention. The next one might hit the malang.

"Entrusting you to God, Sahib," Ahmad blurted, jumping up to go, so his friend wouldn't throw another stone.

"God protect you, sugar cube," the malang replied, his eyes suddenly sad. Ahmad trotted back to his friend.

"You *talked* to him!" Karim chittered. "What did he say? What did he say?"

"He said he's on his way to claim his bride," Ahmad said thoughtfully.

"Where did he come from, did he say?"

"From his bride."

Karim snickered. "He can't be doing both, donkey-butt."

"You're the donkey-butt. God made him crazy, but he's still got powers." At that moment Ahmad realized he had to tell his father. His father the malik needed to know about this man on the hill. The thought of breaking into his father's mighty presence made the boy feel sweaty, but someone had to tell him, and who else could do it? Ahmad started up the stairs.

൭൱

Ibrahim heard the knock but didn't look up from his book. *My beloved can tie water into knots...* There it was again, the poet's favorite word: *beloved...* An image of Khadija flickered into the malik's mind, but of course when the great poet Senayee said Beloved, he meant … another image flared up in Ibrahim's mind—that moment in Mecca, standing before the black stone, when the sound of the crowds had died to a whisper and he had almost felt—but just then his father had squeezed his shoulder and the spell was broken. So he had never completed a connection…to Allah… yet he never forgot either. Ibrahim jotted *Mecca* near the word "my beloved," writing carefully because the page was thin. He didn't hear the door opening until he heard his son's voice.

"Agha-jan?" the boy squeaked. "There's a stranger in the village."

Ibrahim set his pen down and rubbed his eyes. The poem dissipated around him like a dream. "What sort of stranger, Little Fellow?"

"The kind that swallows hornets. He can turn stones into birds, papa!"

The village headman closed his book and put it on the shelf, then twisted the cap back onto the ink bottle, making sure not to spill any ink on his book, for ink was precious and books irreplaceable. Then he patted the spot beside him on the mat, his eyes doting on his heir. "Stones into birds, eh? Sit down and tell me about this man. He comes from Sorkhab, you say?"

"No, Papa. He's a traveler. He comes from his beloved, he says."

"His Beloved?" Ice formed suddenly in Ibrahim's veins.

"Yes, sir. He's on his way to meet her. Only—he just came from where she was—he said. It was confusing! But he said—"

"His Beloved?" the malik repeated. "He used that word exactly? You're sure?"

"Yes, Agha-jan." Ahmad took a breath. "Then he talked about worms. Then he started humming. No, the humming was first. And the bird was this morning. This afternoon a hornet landed on his tongue, but he just swallowed it. Then it came out and flew away. I bet he can cure snakebites. Karim says he wants to kill us and steal our women, but I don't think so. He doesn't even have a donkey, Papa. He walked over the hill. It's true!"

Ibrahim's pulse was racing now. Through the open window came the aroma of wet pebbles and cattails. "Where is he now?"

"Next to Baba's Nose. He's been there since morning. Auntie Khadija made us take some food to him up there."

"Since morning! Oh no." Ibrahim scrambled to his feet. "Run away and play but don't tell anyone about this man. Not till I've seen him." He patted the boy's head and hurried out.

5

Halfway up the slope, Ibrahim paused to pull his cloak tighter, then kept climbing into the shadow of the cliffs. Soon he discerned the figure hunched in the deeper shadows of Baba's Nose. "A'salaam aleikum," he called out.

"W'aleikum a'salaam," the voice sang back.

Ibrahim picked his way around the rainwater cistern. "I am Ibrahim," he said. "Malik of the village you see below."

"I am Vagabond Alaudin, occupant of the body you see before you."

So he had a name! Vagabond Alaudin. Ibrahim thought about the Malang of the Sixty Steps. He too was a vagabond before he found a perch above Gardez, where he lived on leaves and twigs until the weather wore his clothes to rags. The people cut a staircase up to him, sixty steps hewn into solid rock, so that pilgrims might bring food and drink to the God-crazed man, so that people in need might touch his rags for healing grace. Miracles were reported after that around Gardez—miracles! What if Char Bagh had acquired such a hermit?

But then Ibrahim remembered the Howling Malang of Gulabad, who sometimes hit people with sticks. And what about the famous Slapping Malang? He could only hope Char Bagh had not acquired one of those!

"They tell me you've come a long way, Traveler. Come down to the village tonight. It may rain. Spend the night under my roof."

"Long life to you, Chief, but I prefer to stay up here," said the vagabond. "It won't rain till Tuesday, God willing, and I've promised to let the stars take a look at me tonight. You can't break a promise to that crowd. Unless your house has no roof, then it would be okay. Or if the roof has holes. Does your roof have holes, Chief?"

Ibrahim shook his head. The man certainly sounded like a malang. What if pilgrims started drifting in … ? "My roof has no holes, but as for rain, sahib, you never know in these parts. It can be clear at sunset and pouring by midnight. I can't have a traveler spending the night in a downpour so near my house. Be my guest, I insist. My people are cooking a feast."

"Your people have already given me bread and tea and sugar and more. My contentment is complete. You can hear the river from up here. Listen! Can you hear it?"

"Yes."

"Can you hear it down below, from your house?"

"Not from inside unless you open the windows."

"What about the frogs? Up here, after nightfall, they sing louder than people. How loud are they down there?"

The malik smiled. "Down there I'm sad to say the people are louder than the frogs." Actually, the man did not seem as strange as a true malang. Aside from his peculiar insistence on staying outdoors, he seemed quite approachable. He might even be…but no: Ibrahim shut out that hope. A Sufi sheikh does not wander about in rags. "Frogs aside, sahib, I'm sure you will be more comfortable under my roof. Really, as malik of Char Bagh, I can't have people saying that our hospitality fell short. Never!"

"No one will say such a thing of you, Malik-jan. If they do, I'll get a big stick and beat them on the head. Who owns this patch of ground I sit upon?" The malang lifted his butt and patted the soil just beneath it.

"Who would claim this?" Ibrahim scratched his head. "It's too steep. You can't water it, you can't farm it. This land is worthless."

"Well, then, do I have your permission to sit up here and ponder God?"

"Certainly. But you can ponder God anywhere, can't you?" Ibrahim moistened his lips. When the malang made no reply, he said, "Let me ask you one question, if it would not be rude to ask. Where are you going?

South toward Kabul? North perhaps? Which way are you headed?"

The malang laughed. "South, north, east, west, what does it matter. My Beloved awaits me everywhere." Then he shook his head ruefully. " In short, I have decided to stop moving and wait for my Beloved to embrace me right here."

A couplet of Rumi's suddenly popped into Ibrahim's mind. *All you tribes who went to Mecca! Where have you been? All along, the Beloved was right here …Come in.* For so many years, reading such lines, Ibrahim had longed to know what those poets knew, to feel what they so obviously felt. Even as a child, when his father had taken him along on that epic journey to Mecca, he hungered for the actual warmth of Allah in his heart. At the Ka'ba, he had performed all the rites in tremulous hope; but when his turn came to stone Satan, he hit another pilgrim instead, and everybody laughed. Everybody forgave him, of course. He's just a little boy, they said, as if for him the pilgrimage was just some sort of game. It was never a game for Ibrahim, not even then. He could not remember a time before the hunger gnawed at him. Even now, no one knew how it gnawed at him. No one knew the loneliness of a man who could read and had twenty-two books of his own, filled with mystical verses that he couldn't fathom, a man who had no companion with whom to share his books or any master who could help him puzzle out what they contained.

"Traveler," he choked out. "I think I know what you're talking about. I too would open my arms to the Beloved. I too…" But he had lost the thread. "Like the poet says…" he ventured hopelessly. Then another couplet from the lyrics of Maulana Rumi flashed into his mind— he knew so many thousands by heart—and it burst from his throat spontaneously. *"Your heart brims from rim to rim with Me… Exile, break in. Break into the prison of love! Be free!*

The malang nodded, staring out across the slope and toward the river far away, and then said, *"Ever the sky whirls, the elements reel and stew. Earth, air, fire, water—all are drunk on You."*

Ibrahim breathed out. Oh, this was no mere malang, turning stones into birds and doing magic tricks. "Sheikh-sahib," he croaked, tears stinging his eyelids. "Sufi-sahib!"

"Sufi?" the traveler laughed. "What is that? Don't exaggerate, my lord. I am merely a Drunkard, that is all. Out of my gourd. Too besotted to leave this perch lest I stumble and fall. Here I am, and here I'll stay. Good day, malik. Good day, my dear. Good day, good day."

6

The rice would turn sticky if he didn't come soon. And yet she had to keep it warm. Biting her scarf to keep it in front of her mouth, Khadija heaped more live coals on the pot lids. Where was that headman? Where was he?

The outer gate rattled. Fifteen women flooded into the courtyard to bombard Ibrahim with questions. "Did you see him? What did he say? Is he really a malang?"

Followed by his women, young Hajji Ibrahim entered the house and discarded his cloak. "Brr." He stamped his feet. "One thing I can tell you, the man intends to stay up there all night under the stars. To hear the frogs sing, he says. To hear the crickets. Isn't it wonderful? I hope he doesn't freeze." The headman sniffed the air. "Do I smell a feast? Soraya, my rose, you have outdone yourself."

Soraya ignored her husband, because one of the girls had put something in her mouth. She was tapping the child on the chin, coaxing her with, "Open… Open…"

"I hope it pleases you." Khadija felt shy about taking ownership of the meal, but she said the words anyway. "Since winter is over, I thought why not celebrate? After all, we have a surplus and if a malang has come to Char Bagh—"

"He's not a malang."

Khadija felt slapped.

"He's more than that. He's a poet," said the headman. "A poet and a

Sufi sheikh! Yes! And a learned scholar, I believe."

Soraya snickered. "Since when does a learned scholar sit on a rock all night listening to frogs?"

"Since when are you qualified to judge what learned scholars do?" the headman flashed. "How many scholars do you know?"

His unruffled wife cocked an eye at him. "Just you," she said.

Khadija had to admit, it was saucily well done. Ibrahim stared at his wife for a moment, his cheeks and cheekbones still ruddy above his sharp black beard. Then he said, "Send him a plate of dinner, heaped high, swimming in oil. He must want for nothing!" He hurried upstairs without a backward glance.

Khadija called after him, "What about your dinner, Ibrahim-jan?"

"I'll eat later," he said impatiently.

But the malik did not come down again that night, and when the women sent Ahmad up to check on him, the boy heard nothing behind the door but the rhythmic muttering that either meant his father was reading books again or that he was reciting extra prayers.

☙◌◖

The next day Khadija decided to go see the headman without warning or permission. After knocking she waited till she heard a muffled grunt and entered. He was crouched over his writing board, carefully copying words from one of his books onto a sheet of paper. He'd already copied at least fifteen of his twenty-two books, she knew, some of them twice. She waited for him to finish working, but he just kept at it.

"Hajji-jan."

"Yes?" He set his pen down and sat up. No matter how distracted he was, his voice was always courteous. She waited for him to wrap his book in cloth and set his papers out of harm's way. It struck her that Ibrahim had never looked so deeply happy.

"You said you wanted my advice..." she murmured.

"I do. I want it. Have you thought of something?"

"Yes. About the water? I should have brought this up the other day."

"It's fine. Tell me now."

"First, tell me: are you planning to consult the other men about this?"

"Of course. It's my duty as malik. I will call a meeting."

"Before the meeting: will you speak with Ghulam Dastagir?" She could picture Karim's grim father as she spoke his name.

"I thought I might. A leader must seek advice, even if he doesn't need it. That is what my brother taught me. He said, never let people think you proud."

"Well, just be careful how you do it," Khadija said softly.

"What do you mean?"

"Do you know what Ghulam Dastagir says to his wife?"

"Of course not. How would I know. What does he say?"

"That you are untried and inexperienced, that you won't be able to make decisions on your own, that you will come to him for advice as a boy comes to his father."

The malik rubbed his cheeks hard. "He said that?"

"To his wife, who told Akram Gul's wife, who told me. Ghulam Dastagir thought the village should have chosen him as leader, and it still gnaws at him."

"That's no secret," muttered Ibrahim.

"Well. I am only saying. If you ask Ghulam Dastagir for advice, make sure he knows you don't actually *need* his advice. Make him feel that you are asking purely as a show of respect. That way, you do what's proper, you leave him nothing to criticize, but you give away none of your strength."

"Sometimes, Khadija-jan, I think Allah really should have made you a man."

She closed her eyelids to let her long lashes lie against her smooth cheekbones. "But alas, no...he made me a woman. What have you decided about Sorkhab? Will you talk to Malik Mustapha? When will you go?"

"I haven't decided. I have other things on my mind right now. This sheikh on our hillside, we must take good care of him so that he'll have no reason to wander off."

"The malang, you mean?"

"Everyone is calling him 'the malang', yes, but I tell you, Khadija-jan, when people hear about this man, we'll have pilgrims coming to the village. We'll have to build a place for them to sleep, somewhere over the hill, away from the village, so they can visit the sheikh as they wish."

"We could charge money," said Khadija. "We could sell them food."

"Just what I was thinking—if it's lawful. I'll have to ask Mullah Yaqub about it."

"Mullah Yaqub lives in Sorkhab. He'll tell you no. He'll want the malang to grow dissatisfied with Char Bagh and move to Sorkhab. Then Mullah Yaqub's opinion will change, that rascal. Don't trust him. You know more about religion than he does."

Ibrahim stroked his beard. "Well, perhaps you're right. How could the holy law forbid feeding pilgrims? I don't need to consult him. It can't be necessary."

"What would you do with the money, if any comes our way?" Khadija wondered.

"We could build a water mill," Ibrahim mused. "We could get Ghulam Haidar some carpentry tools—oh, what he could do with a big saw! Or enlarge the mosque, perhaps! We could send someone to Baghlan to shop."

"They could bring back some cosmetics," said Khadija. "Some of the younger women, you know, the merriment of a good wedding...It lifts everybody's spirits."

"Indeed, indeed, I will consider all these things," the headman said. "I'll give it plenty of thought. You see what I'm dealing with, though. I have a lot on my mind! I'll remember what you said about Ghulam Dastagir, though.."

"See that you do, Hajji-sahib. It's for your own good. Well, I will leave you to your thoughts now." She turned to leave, but at the threshold, she spotted a crumb of dirt, and with her back to her brother-in-law, she bent over to pick it up. Feeling the headman's interested gaze on her backside, she cast a glance over her shoulder, flushed with embarrassment, and straightened up abruptly. Their eyes met and the look between them was a short, fiery flash of flirtation. Khadija hurried out.

7

The moment Ibrahim stepped out of his compound, his cousin Asadullah hailed him from down the street. "Hajji-sahib," the squat man shouted. "Did you hear? We have ourselves a malang!"

"I know," Ibrahim shouted back. "I know. Have you sent him food?"

"Do you want me to? I'll do it, Hajji-sahib, a thousand times," Asad grinned.

"I shouldn't have to ask you. It's not for my sake," Ibrahim clucked. "Do it for your own sake. He's a man of God, you'll earn credit with Allah. In fact, I'm thinking of building a shelter for our guest. How would you and your boys like to help me?"

"What guest?" Asadullah came limping toward him, still grinning.

"The man on the hill! Who else? He won't come down to the village. What if people see him up there and say we don't know how to treat a guest!"

Asadullah spat and swore. "Who says so? My boys and I'll beat him till he squeals."

"You miss my point, Asad-jan. I'm saying, let's be sure to treat our guest handsomely. Will you help me build a shelter for the sheikh?"

"What sheikh?"

"The malang, as all of you call him! The man on the hill!" Ibrahim made an effort not to roll his eyes. "Will you help me?"

"Faster'n a five legged horse, Hajji-sahib. You're the headman, ain't cha?"

"That I am," Ibrahim sighed. "Meet me up there this afternoon, then." He left his cousin still bowing and grinning and headed down to his fields. The soil was too wet to plow, but he could inspect the irrigation works today and see what needed repair. Next week, God willing, he would bring his buffalo down and cut some furrows.

He took a shortcut across this year's fallow fields. The headman enjoyed ambling barefoot under a blue sky, feeling the mud squish between his toes. It was a cloudless day and the sun was finally shedding some real warmth. The snow on the higher peaks looked wet, and all the slopes were sweating rivulets. The trickle of water sounded on every side.

When he reached the bend in the river, he spied Ghulam Dastagir standing mutely on a field that bordered one of Ibrahim's, peering at the ground. In the further distance, over a series of low partition walls, Ibrahim saw two other farmers gathering stones. The elm trees along the river still sparkled with this morning's dew. Ibrahim waved to Ghulam Dastagir but the latter was staring at something by his feet. The headman climbed over the wall and picked his way over the scorched stubble of last year's wheat. "Salaam aleikum, dearest Ghulam Dastagir. How are you?"

"Peace be on you, young fellow," the other responded.

Young fellow! Oh, the scoundrel couldn't resist! "Thank you, Farmer-sahib. May you be vigorous. How is your household?"

"Very well, thanks be to Allah. Good health, good health. How's your great uncle? I hear he complains of back pain."

"Old age, my brother. God provides. What do you study so earnestly there?"

"The milk weeds, lad. They're very tall. The rains have been heavy this month! Heavy rain now means a dry summer later. You may not know this, but don't worry, a man learns from experience and you'll have that in time. I just want to warn you, though, a dry summer means the river might run low by the month of Mizan. As malik, this is something you should start thinking about now."

"In God we put our trust," the village chieftain murmured uneasily.

Ghulam Dastagir gave him a wolfish look. "Truly. We are always in God's hands. So all is well with you, Malik-sahib? Your mother-in-law is...?"

"Better, sahib. And your children?"

"Oh, my youngest, you know, that knave! Too much spirit in the rascal. Too much spirit!" Thus did Ghulam Dastagir frame his boasting as complaint. "I vow I'll take a stick to the little tiger. He must be tamed before he swallows a plum bigger than his anus. Have you heard the story he's spreading lately? Some stranger on Baba's Nose!"

"It's no mere story. There is a man up there. Our sons discovered him together."

"Yes, they're inseparable, your son and mine. Your great brother and I were like that as boys!" The memory brought a wistful smile to Ghulam Dastagir's lips, but it faded. "What do you make of this hillside stranger? Folks say he's a malang, but he might just be some vagabond, looking to lure our women up there. They'll want amulets, you know, women always do. What's your opinion, young fellow?"

Ibrahim tried to keep the irritation out of his features. "I went up and spoke to him myself. He's no fool, I can tell you that much. He's wide awake. If he's a malang, he's a new kind—not that I disrespect malangs, but this fellow might be something even greater, not less, as you seem to think. A real sage, he might be. A Sufi sheikh."

"Sheikh!" Ghulam Dastagir let out a guffaw. "Is that what he told you?"

"He didn't say it. I just noticed that he can quote the poets."

"Oh—quote the poets." Ghulam Dastagir dismissed this evidence. "My brother-in-law quotes the poets. Two months in Baghlan and he quotes the poets. You'll never find a bigger fool."

"Your brother-in-law *parrots* poets. This man understands what he's reciting."

"I see." Ghulam Dastagir leaned on his shovel, his forearms bulging in his sleeves. "This one *understands* the poets. Why didn't you say so?" His dry voice let Ibrahim know where poets rated in the scheme of things for Ghulam Dastagir.

Ibrahim remembered a long ago day when he was one of a dozen little boys watching Ghulam Dastagir stick-fight some brute from Sorkhab. He remembered his quick moves, his agile strokes. He remembered the crashing blow that sent Sorkhab's champion sprawling, remembered how he and all his little friends had cheered! Certainly Ibrahim owed this man some deference: Ghulam Dastagir was at least twenty years his elder.

And yet! On this issue of respect for poets and scholars, Ibrahim could not back down. His family name was at stake. "A man who understands Rumi and Sa'di is a boon to any village. I hope to God he'll choose to live among us."

"Perhaps you'd like to invite this vagabond into your women's quarters, Hajji-sahib?" Ghulam Dastagir grinned.

Ibrahim held his ground. "Don't worry about the womenfolk. He won't come down from the hillside, even if you ask. I know because I've asked. Nonetheless, we must take care of him. He might be an angel sent to test our generosity, you know. At the very least, he's a malang and that's a great deal right there. If he prefers to stay outdoors, I think we must build three walls around him and put a roof over his head."

"Three walls! What about the fourth? Will this be like Mullah Nasruddin's tomb, padlocked against thieves on three sides, gaping on the fourth?"

Ibrahim tolerated the jibe with a smile. "What can thieves steal from a man with no possessions? He enjoys looking at the river, let's leave him a view. What do you think?"

Ghulam Dastagir merely shrugged. "Whatever you wish, Hajji-sahib. People have entrusted such decisions to you." He left the rest unsaid: if the village woke up one day to find all their horses and daughters stolen by the vagabond, the blame would fall entirely upon Ibrahim. "I'll bring a few good men up there this afternoon if you want."

"Excellent," said Ibrahim, "Let's show him some generosity before Sorkhab lures him away."

"Speaking of Sorkhab, Ibrahim-jan." There was condescension in the shift to the intimate *jan*. "They used too much water last year.

There's an agreement between us, you know. Unspoken but it's there, and they broke it. Your late, lamented brother intended to confront them about it before the planting started this year. Now, with the river in danger of running low, it's all the more urgent they cut back. Do you plan to pay them a visit soon and deliver the message? Don't worry, there's nothing to fear. I'll go with you."

Ibrahim glanced over the garden walls at the other two farmers. If the conflict with Sorkhab exploded into a fight, people would be hurt. Ibrahim longed to share the burden of the responsibility he bore.

"Actually," he said, "I have had some word from Sorkhab."

"Good," said the older man. "They're offering to cut back on their own? Good, good. They know when to be afraid."

"Actually...no. The word is: they're planning to put more land under cultivation."

A sharp grunt escaped Ghulam Dastagir's lips. "More?"

"At least a thousand *jireebs* more. Mustafa Khan has new twin sons, Mullah Yaqub—"

"Fuck his new twin sons! They think they can drain the river and get away with it? Steal our water just like that?"

"Well, it's God's river, and it does flow past them first, that's a fact."

"The more they take, the less they leave! Have you missed *that* fact, Malik-sahib?"

"I have missed nothing, brother." Ibrahim drew himself up to his full height, which still left him inches short of Ghulam Dastagir. "I am only telling you what a judge would say. We have to negotiate with these people."

"Fuck negotiating. They'll take bargaining for weakness. We have to draw a line."

"It isn't that simple."

"Of course it's that simple! They plan to steal our water. And who are these castrated donkeys? *We're* descended from Babur's own men. Who are *they*? You, Malik-sahib—descended from the great scholar Ahmad Wali, the most learned man of his age! Are *you* going to let these upstarts place themselves above you? Who are *their* people?"

"It's true that when—"

"When our forefathers built Char Bagh, they were nothing but a bunch of starving peasants, that's what! The emperor put *us* in charge, gave *us* dominion over this valley—"

"That was three hundred years ago. That emperor is gone. His whole dynasty—"

"—and *they're* going to drain *our* river? We must pay them a visit, a group of us—men, not boys! You'll come too, of course. You'll deliver the ultimatum: *take more than your share and you will live to regret it!* That's what you'll say."

"Well spoken, Ghulam Dastagir, but they're over seven hundred people, and we're not even four hundred. This is a delicate business."

"Delicate! I'll cram a stick up their delicate butts. I bested their best boy in a stick fight twenty years ago! Your cherished brother—God pardon him—your brother would never have talked as you are talking now, Ibrahim."

"How am I talking? I bow to no one, Ghulam Dastagir. I only say, let's not start with swords. Let's start by showing respect and expecting the best. That's how honorable men behave. For God's sake, let us not squander the hard-earned honor our forefathers laid in store for us."

Ghulam Dastagir absorbed these comments sullenly. "Well, I bow to your judgment," he said without conviction, "You are, of course, 'malik,' but let's see what the elders say—"

"I'll call a *jirgah*," Ibrahim interrupted. "Nothing you and I say here has any force anyway. Let the question ripen for a few days, and then I will call the men together at the mosque. There you can make your views known to all—"

"When and where did I ever flinch from making my views known? I may never have been to Mecca, but a man learns a thing or two from experience over the years."

Ibrahim held his tongue. Scoring points in verbal sparring would only harden Ghulam Dastagir against him and make working with the man more difficult later. "I will look to you for the wisdom that experience brings. Now, about the sheikh—"

"Yes. The malang, you mean."

"I call him sheikh. Will you meet me at Baba's Nose about mid-afternoon?"

"I said I would, didn't I?" Ghulam Dastagir pulled out his snuff box and took a pinch. "Ghulam Dastagir keeps his word." He popped the snuff under his tongue and pursed his lips to keep it where the flavor would permeate, then fixed flint-gray eyes upon Ibrahim. "Accept some advice, Malik-sahib. People are nothing without land. Land is nothing without water. Protect our water and everyone will respect you, despite your tender years. Lose our water and even our children's grandchildren will curse your name."

"I treasure your advice, dear friend." Ibrahim spoke with just enough enthusiasm to meet the minimum requirements of good manners.

8

Picture the steep slope west of Char Bagh bathed in light shortly after a cold, bright noon. Picture thirty men, seven or eight from each clan, trudging uphill behind Ibrahim, presumably to help him build a shelter for the vagabond. Even Ghulam Haidar's father was among them, hobbling along on his elephant feet. What could he possibly do to help? Not a thing. He just wanted to see the vagabond for himself. This was understood. In truth, this was what they all wanted, what drew them all up the mountain after Ibrahim: to judge for themselves who the stranger was up there and what he might be up to.

The malang was sitting cross-legged among the weeds, his eyes closed. In a hushed voice, Ibrahim asked the men to begin their work uphill a bit so as not to wake the God-intoxicated hermit. After all, there was plenty of work to be done before actual construction could begin: soil would have to be dug and crumbled and mixed with straw. Water would have to be stirred in and kneaded smooth with bare feet to make wet clay that would harden into tough sun-baked cob—

But scarcely had the men started digging when the malang turned his head, his eyes wide open. He had not been sleeping after. He had only been meditating. He rose to his feet, and what a big man he was! Real meat on his bones, real weight on his belly, not by any means a starving beggar. A smile curved the crease between his thick lips and his eyes glinted with merriment—a crazed merriment, some would say later. He shoved in amongst the men, snatched up a shovel, and boomed "Y'allah khair!" *God bless!*

"He talks," someone whispered.

"Why should he not?" Ibrahim scolded. "Sheikh-sahib, forgive my kinsmen's manners."

The malang waved off the apology and set to work, pushing his spade into the earth with a powerful foot, his soles protected by calluses as thick as sandals. The men could not stop to gawk, for the malang's industry shamed them into effort. All worked vigorously until the sinking sun dipped just below the poplars lining the hilltops in the direction of Mecca. Then the malang stepped back, leaving his spade stuck in the earth. "What are we building here, boys?"

"Why—why, a shelter. For *you*, sir!" the village headman declared. "Since you won't come down to us, we bring our hospitality up to you. We'll put three walls around you and leave the fourth direction open so you can gaze over the river. Nothing to shut out the sound of frogs and crickets."

"Excellent." The malang clapped like a child. "This pleases me, dear hearts. But three walls? I'm a simple man, two walls will do. Let the rock form the third wall. Then again, what am I thinking? Put up a fourth wall if you wish, just don't put a roof over it. Make a waterproof box around me. When the rains come, *inshallah* it will fill with water, I will float to the top, and *then* I will hear frogs and crickets."

"No!" Ibrahim protested earnestly. "What do you mean? We intend to put a roof over your head! Never will I let rain wet your head. We want to shelter you."

The malang clapped a hand on his shoulder and squeezed. Ibrahim saw ruefully that he had been joking. "Sheikh-sahib, is all this acceptable to you?"

"Is it acceptable to grass when a tree grows?"

Ghulam Dastagir rolled his eyes, but Ibrahim frowned, trying to decipher the man's deeper meaning. "I believe it is," he ventured.

"Well, then, have at it," said the malang, waving at the ground. "An idle shovel is a waste of iron. Dig, dig, dig, my boy! While you work, I will listen to the frogs."

"Later, the boys will bring you rice and spinach *qurma*." the malik assured him.

"Oh, bread and tea, plenty for me. Your open hearts enthrall! Your homes be green, your eyes be bright, Allah bless you all." The malang bowed to Ibrahim, then to the next man, and then to the next, turning in a circle, bowing every few inches, bowing to every man present and then continuing to turn, shuffling in place and bowing, bowing to the rocks, bowing to the slope above, bowing to the trees, turning and turning, fast and faster until he was dancing and spinning in a glee no one could call anything but mad. At last he stopped whirling, pushed his turban-wrapped skull cap back and wiped his glistening forehead. "Listen! Can you hear them?"

The men all cocked their heads and listened intently. "Hear what?" Ghulam Dastagir complained. "I can't hear a thing."

"You can't? Neither can I. Send for an ear doctor! Do you have an ear doctor in Char Bagh? Or must we send to Sorkhab?"

Ibrahim paled. "Not Sorkhab!"

"He's a lunatic," Ghulam Dastagir whispered.

"Or touched by God," his brother-in-law frowned. "If we don't understand him, it might be our fault."

"Well, he's no malang. He never mentions Allah."

"He said 'Allah bless us all.' He said 'y'allah khair'."

"Anyone can say y'allah khair."

"He quotes the poets, I hear."

But this only made the big man flush.

Meanwhile, the malang had withdrawn from the group to wash his face and limbs with water from one of the buckets. The time for sunset prayer had come, the men realized, and they all clustered around the buckets to perform their ritual ablutions. But the malang, who had started first, finished first. While the others were still washing, he rose to his feet. Along the ground, where the slope formed a level shelf, he spread his turban, a long swath of drab green fabric, some twenty paces long and two paces wide. This was for the men. For himself, he retrieved a bit of cloth from a bundle stashed near the rock and laid it down in front of the turban. He took his place on this little mat, facing west, without hesitation or discussion positioning himself as prayer leader for the entire group. No one questioned this at the time, and no one could remember feeling one way or another about it later. The men of Char Bagh simply lined up behind the malang, facing west like him. After a contemplative moment, the malang raised his hands to his ears and chanted, "Allaaaaaaaaahu akbar!" The men followed suit, moving through the prayer ritual in tandem, repeating the syllables to themselves but responding to the cues set by the malang for bowing, going to the ground, and bending forward in supplication to touch their foreheads to the earth, guided into unison by the malang's intermittent chant of "Alaaaahu akbar!"

When the prayer was finished, the malang picked up a shovel and went right back to work. The men had intended to knock off for the day, but the sight of their guest laboring so vigorously made them pick up tools again too.

Surprisingly, they got the two walls built by the time lights started twinkling from the women's fires in the village below. They had accomplished much because so many of them had pitched in, and because all of them had worked so hard, and because the malang had done the work of two. Where could he have gotten the energy? No one could fathom it. Each of the villagers was quite aware that his own household had sent up nothing but bread and sweetened tea and perhaps a few dried figs or nuts. Had the man been surviving on crickets and the like? Malangs were said to eat such fare and yet—the whole thing was a mystery.

Asad and his boys had hauled along some poles for the roof, and they helped Ibrahim lay these across the two walls. Next , straw was packed between the poles, but it was too late now to plaster cob over the straw. That would have to wait till morning. At least this first day's construction had provided the malang with shelter from the wind and the rudiments of a roof.

On the way down, Ghulam Dastagir glanced back over his shoulder. What he saw made him pause, and seeing him pause, Ibrahim pulled up too. "What is it?"

"Look up there!" Ghulam Dastagir pointed toward the malang's shelter. "What's that on his roof?"

Ibrahim squinted at the bulky mass atop the shelter they had just built. "It's him," he said finally. "He's sitting on the roof."

"Not under it?" Ghulam Dastagir fumed. "Then all our work was for nothing. He's just mocking us. "

"We've pleased him. Pleasing him was our intention, so it was a good day's work," said Ibrahim. "And once we've sealed his hut, I'm sure he'll use it to get out of the rain."

They trudged a few more paces down the hill. Then someone let out a little cry of laughter. Again, the men stopped and looked back. Ghulam Dastagir, who had poor eyesight at night, demanded anxiously, "What now? What's he doing? Is he still on the roof?"

"He's still on the roof."

"What's he doing?"

"He's dancing," said Ibrahim.

9

Khadija pulled up short at the sound of voices. Women were packed into the room at the end of the hall, clucking and gossiping. "The way she was combing her hair—"

Cold coils tightened around Khadija's heart. She moved closer, feeling her way by touch through the lightless corridor.

"Just before she went to him," a voice cut in venomously.

In the black space surrounding the compound, crickets roared.

"Combing away!" the first woman cut back in. "Oiling every strand right to the tip—oh, she wanted to shine for him, she did!"

The women must not have heard Khadija's footsteps yet. The widow set one hand against the wall to steady herself. The straw embedded in the cob scratched against her palm. Fury began to bubble inside her, but she quelled it. She would need cool strength for the work at hand. Strength and charm.

"My dear!" The first voice again, speaking almost in a whisper now. "When you fuss with your face like that just before you go see a man, it can only mean one thing." Khadija recognized Soraya's half-cousin Khushdil, visiting from the compound down the street. A malicious little woman with eyes always squeezed half-shut by fat!

"Snare him into marriage? Not always!" This was Soraya's mother. "She might—"

"Why shouldn't he marry her?" This protest came from Ibrahim's paternal aunt. "She's his brother's widow, after all—alone in this world, alas! A man has obligations! What if you were in her place?"

"Well, taking her in, that's honorable, but marriage—"

Here, however, Soraya's mother cut in again, determined to finish her point. "Who says she's looking for marriage? She *might* just be craving—"

"That poor woman! One day, the wife of the greatest man in all the valley—the next day bereft, alone, widowed! Childless! My heart weeps for her, my dears." Ibrahim's aunt again? Khadija bit her lips, leaning against the wall for support.

"I was there the day she came back from Sorkhab," said a deeper voice: the Crone—even *she* felt qualified to offer an opinion! "—huffing and puffing and sweating! Well, if you have something to tell Hajji-sahib, I thought, why not go to him just as you are? But no! She had to wash her face! Comb her hair! Put rouge on her cheeks—"

"Rouge! You saw her putting on rouge?"

"I saw it on her cheeks, I'm sure—"

"Where would she get rouge? She might have been flushed from the journey—"

"Still flushed after washing with well-water? Oh, you're a trusting one. I don't know where she got rouge, but she's got it, that's all I know."

Khadija touched her cheeks. She had pinched them that day to bring up the blood—that was her "rouge." Tears stung her eyelids.

"She must have gotten some from the nomads last year. God knows what she traded for it. And kept it hidden somewhere. I tell you that woman is trying to tempt Hajji-sahib. I wonder how you stand for it, Soraya-jan."

"Khadija has always been kind to me," Soraya murmured.

I should break in now, thought Khadija; but her heart was thumping too wildly. She couldn't be sure of controlling herself.

"Kind to you! Well, I hope you'll appreciate her 'kindness' the day she marries your husband!"

"And what if she does?" Ibrahim's aunt persisted. "Soraya-jan will still be his first wife, first in his heart—and mother of his first-born son."

"And younger too," another voice declared reassuringly. "You're surely younger, Soraya-jan. I remember the winter you were born, we went to Sorkhab for a wedding, and there was Khadija, already walking, talking, making mischief. Before you were even born."

"How would you remember one pebble among so much gravel, Auntie? You're teasing!"

"No, by Allah, Khadija stood out. Such eyes! A lovely child! And mischievous? Oh, you never saw such sauce. You couldn't help but notice that one. I said to myself—yes, all those years ago, I said: that one will be a devil. Even then I knew it."

"I will always be Ibrahim-jan's favorite," Soraya insisted bravely.

"I thought the same about my husband before he took Malia," came Khushdil's querulous complaint. "I was your age then and just as silly. Oh, when we're young and well-made, our husbands favor us, and we think it's our God-given nature to fascinate, just like the flower gives joy and the wolf makes people afraid. Then the new wife comes along and we learn. We learn." Khushdil released a long, moist sigh. "You're inexperienced, girlie. Let me tell you what the world has in store for you. The new wife is *always* the favorite. Mice like to come back to the same hole every night, but men? Men are not mice, they'll stick it into a watermelon just for variety. Imagine what delight they take in a second wife, even a used-up widow with a dry womb."

"Hush. You should be ashamed of talking that way," someone scolded.

"Oh! Your ears are too delicate? Never seen cows do it, have you? Never seen donkeys do it? Dogs? Sheep? It's all around us, why should I be ashamed to talk about it?"

"I meant about Khadija's womb."

Khadija hunched against the wall. The cricket-sounds had died away. Some insect dropped from the ceiling, and she brushed it off her shoulder, hoping it was not a scorpion. A hectoring voice broke the silence.

"I tell you, I don't think she's trying to get Ibrahim-jan to marry her." Soraya's intimidating mother was pushing to finish her point. "Virginity gone, womb dry—what's to hold her back? She's a widow. Women like that are beyond shame, they'll take their pleasure as they please. They'll do anything. Just anything."

"If only I had been a widow at her age," half-cousin Khushdil lamented.

"With a handsome brother-in-law to play with," someone laughed.

"Don't listen to them," Khadija's aunt counseled Soraya. "You and Khadija get along like sisters. If you become co-wives, all the better. The first year or two will be difficult, but after that, my dear! After that, it will always be two of you against one of him. Work together and you can rule this house. You get along, don't you?"

"She's bossy, but I don't mind."

In the hallway, clench-fisted Khadija considered slinking away—no, running as fast as she could, away from all this judging and sneering, but run where? She had nowhere to go. She could only stand and fight for her place, right here. She steeled herself, cleared her throat, and began moving bumpily down the hall, making noise to announce her presence, so the women could change topic and save face.

By the time she turned the corner, they had all put on cordial faces. "Khadija-jan," they beamed brightly. "Where have you been? We were just talking about how hard you work. Must you keep track of every last potato? Sit down, you take on too much responsibility. Only six months widowed, you're still grieving, you should be letting us take care of you."

Khadija's eyes searched out Soraya. The younger woman blushed and said nothing, but nothing needed to be said. Amidst all the nasty gossiping, she had stood up for Khadija. Even in her mother's presence, she had said a few kinds words about the widow. Khadija swept into the room and settled regally next to her nervous young sister-in-law. Why did these women conspire against her? Why should most of them care whether Khadija secured a high place or sank to servant-level in the house where she had once been queen? Only Soraya had a stake in this matter. What did that sour-hearted Khushdil stand to gain or lose? It was only spite that drove her, nothing but spite!

Khadija knew what she had to do, she had to distract these women from their petty jealousies, by rallying them around some excitement. Then it came to her. "Which of you has seen the malang?"

"Are you asking me?" Khushdil tittered.

"Any of you. Who has seen the malang? Anyone?"

A flurry of voices rose up to protest her question. How could they have seen the malang? He was up on Baba's Nose, he would not come down to the village.

"Well, then, we must go up there," Khadija trumpeted. "We see the malang for ourselves. Which of you has sent him food?"

"I sent him some raisins," Khushdil said sheepishly; and several others then declared their charities but with a penitent awareness of how meager their offerings had been.

"It's not enough," Khadija said. "Sorkhab has sent him dried meat, fruit-and-nut leather…we must take him something wonderful. Warm pudding! Yes, that's just the thing—*halwa*! And we must take it to him in person."

The women burst into argument at the audacity of Khadija's plan. Leave their compounds? Leave the very village? Climb the mountain? Absurd! But Khadija insisted. They would be wearing their ankle-length *chadaris*. There would be nothing to reproach in their conduct, it would be a pilgrimage. She herself had been to see the Howling Malang of Gulabad once. Her late husband had taken her—didn't they all remember? To quicken her womb, had been the hope. If she could see that malang, why not this malang, their very own malang? They might get amulets from the mystical man. Gradually, she won the women over. They talked themselves into it, really, for all were burning with curiosity to see a man who had seen Allah, saw him every day if the stories were true.

The visitors slept over that night, and the next morning, after the first spate of chores, Khadija directed the preparation of the halwa. They heated up real clarified butter, not sheep's fat, they stirred sugar and wheat-flour into it, and ground pistachios, and water and essence of roses into it, making a cauldron of the warm pudding, and they ate quite a bit of it themselves while they cooked—just to make sure it was acceptable: licking the grease off their fingers and smacking their lips with satisfaction. Khushdil ate twice as much as the others, and Khadija wanted to slap her fat face. Stop gorging on another household's scant food, she wanted to scold. But officially this was Soraya's household, and so Soraya had to take the lead, and Soraya, of course, remained oblivious to the tubby locust despoiling her husband's stores.

At last the *halwa* was thick and hot. They left it in the pot while they got properly dressed, putting on their loveliest dresses and blouses—the women from the other compounds ran home for their finest fineries and came back quickly with their clothes stuffed into bags. Some decked themselves out in jewelry taken from private dowry boxes. Much chattering took place, many witty back-biting jibes were exchanged during the commotion, the ceremony, and the excitement of dressing up.

Finally they put on cloth coats that covered their plumage. Over the coats they dropped their *chadaris*, pleated sacks that covered them from skull to ankle, so that no one could see the glamorous garments under their body-veils. The women had dressed up for one another alone.

Khadija ladled a healthy portion of the rice-flour pudding into a bowl. The rest would be distributed to other households as celebration. She wrapped the bowl in cloth, and set the cloth in a basket on a layer of straw to keep the pudding warm. Now they were ready for their expedition.

"W'allah!" Soraya's mother cried out suddenly. "What are we thinking? We can't go up there without an escort."

"But we're wearing *chadaris*. What's the harm?"

"The harm! As if anyone who sees us won't know we're women. What if marauders come along? What if they're hiding behind the hill? No one will ever know what happened to us! We'll just be gone."

Soraya bit her lips, spots of color appearing on her pale cheeks. Her narrow nostrils pulsed. She glared at her mother with the hottest hatred. She wanted to visit the malang but dared not oppose her mother. Khadija would have to do it for her.

"Don't you think any raiders would have shown themselves by now?" she scoffed. "This malang has been up on our hill for weeks!"

"Easy for you to laugh, Khadija," Ibrahim's aunt said. "You weren't here when the raiders came."

Khadija's lips tightened. Yes, when the raiders came, she happened to be in Sorkhab, at a cousin's wedding. They never tired of telling the stories, never failed to remind her that she wasn't there, she had missed the drama and the tragedy, one more proof that she might live *in* Char Bagh but was not *of* Char Bagh. The raiders were Pushtoons, probably men who had gotten separated from some army or other and had gone into banditry for themselves, a throwback to the grim days after Emperor Ahmad Shah died and his offspring started scrabbling for his throne. The gangs spawned in that era had roamed the land for years and years.

The band of scoundrels that hit Char Bagh had come specifically for women. They needed women. They must have watched the village for days, memorizing its patterns and habits. Then one summer afternoon, when the women were puttering in their gardens around the compounds and the men were all in the fields by the river, the raiders struck. Khushdil's mother bashed one of them with her short spade and knocked him off his beast, but two of his companions ran her down, and she later died. One of the Haidari boys came running out of his compound house with a poker, but he was just a boy and they were men. He darted among their horses for a few brave minutes, but they wrestled him to the ground and hit him with a stone until he stopped moving. By then, the others had dragged seven girls onto their saddles, and they all galloped away with their haul.

The survivors of the raid went screaming to the fields. The men set off at once on mules and donkeys and on their very few horses, but they lost the trail on the stony ground beyond the Red Pass. No one ever learned where those marauders had come from or where they went, and no one ever saw them or any of those girls again.

The people of Char Bagh still grew uneasy when raiders and marauders were mentioned. Khadija knew better than to dismiss their anxiety or make light of it. If she was one of them, she would feel it too, so she made every show of feeling it. She spotted Ahmad and a couple of those do-nothing Asadullah boys playing in the courtyard, those big, cheerful fellows. "Boys!" She pushed the window open. "Come here, you. Take us up to the malang."

As soon as she had secured an escort she felt better. The other women had a point, you could never be sure who might see you if you left the village limits. On the path, one of the women began singing to keep up her courage. The others joined in, for they all knew the song. Then suddenly it was exciting to march along in the open like that, feeling a breeze through one's eye mesh, a breeze that cooled one's forehead and diluted the stuffy heat inside one's *chadari*. Some of the younger girls had never been this far from home. They found the malang sitting against one wall of the shelter the men had built for him. When he saw the women coming, he bent over his prayer beads to shield himself from their femininity but, within minutes, they had him surrounded, their *chadaris* fluttering. Now and then, the breeze lifted the hem of a veil just enough to reveal a foot or even an ankle. The malang muttered audibly, refusing to look up.

Ghulam Haidar's girl Shahnaz, who was just then ripening into marriage age, a girl whose mischievous ways had already caused her mother much disturbance, broke into the shrill teasing tone that girls took with each other as a way of flirting with any boy cousins who might be looking on: "Malang-sahib, won't you lift your head. Are you 'fraid of us? We're not going to bite you. We're not going to eat you. We might take just a little nibble of you, just a wee little taste, but it won't hurt."

The malang turned away from Shahnaz, and his muttering rose higher.

"Malang-sahib," Shahnaz teased on, "if you could have any one of us—"

"Hush!" cried her shocked sister.

"—which one would you pick?" Shahnaz finished merrily. Under her *chadari* she muffled a giggle with her hands.

Some of the younger ones joined her in giggling, but Soraya's stern mother let out a chuff and turned to glare. Cloaked though she was in her *chadari*, she let the others feel her disapproval, and the chuckling died away. The women stood silently, then, surrounding the holy man like spectators ringed around a bird fight, but there was nothing to watch, and none of them knew exactly what to do next..

"Malang-sahib," Khushdil broke out finally, "will you give me an amulet? My ankles hurt constantly!"

The malang looked up. "An amulet won't do you any good. You weigh too much and you work too little. Get up early every morning and carry water for your family. Stop eating *halwa*. After a year, your ankles will stop hurting."

The women gaped, astonished to hear the malang speaking, and at such great length—and with medical advice to boot—advice that displeased its recipient. Khushdil clapped her hands to her hips indignantly, making her *chadari* ripple. The malang went back to his prayer beads, shrinking against the wall as if cowed by these fluttering females.

"Malang-sahib, did you decide which of us you want to marry?" naughty Shahnaz sang out again. "Do you need to see our faces, the better to judge us?"

She made as if to lift her *chadari*. The women on both sides of her gasped and jostled close to pin her arms. Her sister hit her veiled head. "You filthy little devil! You're out of control!"

"I was only joking," the girl protested. "Malang-sahib knows a joke. Don't you, malang-dear? Tell them"

"Don't joke with Malang-sahib!" her sister scolded. "You never joke with a malang."

Khadija frowned. "Malang-sahib, the girl is very young, forgive her, she's suffering from a fever too, she doesn't know what she's saying, what comes out of her mouth is no different than the sounds that come out of a donkey's mouth when it is braying."

Soraya kneeled next to Khadija. "Malang-sahib," she whispered, "my husband came to see you the other day—he's our headman, you know? He loves you soooo much! We all love you. Will you stay with us forever?"

Khadija wished she had thought to say those words. She set the basket down in front of the malang. "We brought you some *halwa*, respected sir."

His head snapped up, making his long locks jiggle. "Who died?"

Even Khadija found herself chuckling. "No one, sir. It's not funeral *halwa*, just our way of saying welcome. It's still warm. We'll leave the bowl."

Just then, however, horse hooves sounded. The women clumped together with frightened little shrieks as half a dozen horsemen came over the pass. Then Khadija recognized several of her relatives from Sorkhab. The group pulled up on the pass and dismounted. Three of them came down the path toward Baba's Nose.

"Rashid!" Khadija exclaimed. "What are you doing here?"

He grinned, recognizing her voice. "Is that you, Khadija-jan? We've come to pay our respects, we heard about Malang-sahib." The young man from Sorkhab gazed directly at the women of Char Bagh, anonymous in their *chadaris*, then committed an act of flirtatious daring he never would have attempted if someone older than Ahmad and his cohorts had been escorting the women: he nodded to them! He didn't push it, though. He didn't address a remark to any of the unknown girls, nothing that extreme. His gaze settled on Khadija's cloaked form and he said, "After all, you Char Bagh folks are not the only ones who could use a malang's blessings."

Khadija nodded. "May you live long. We entrust you to God's care. We must go back to the village now. Convey our salaams to your people."

She led the women down the slope without further words. Not until they had gotten out of earshot did they begin to buzz. Sorkhab had sent a delegation to see the malang? What did it mean? Would they try to lure him to *their* village? What would they offer him? What might tempt a malang?

10

Nothing distinguished the mosque from any other building in the village except the skinny tower rising from one corner, a minaret just big enough to accommodate a ladder inside. Farmer Ghulam Haidar squeezed himself into this shaft and climbed to the top, where shutterless windows faced each of the four directions. There, he began to chant the call to prayer.

The village relied on him for this service because he had a loud voice and thanks to three reliable roosters, he was never late with his *azaan* in the morning. It was evening now, just past sunset, and he rarely chanted *azaan* for the evening prayer; most of the men performed this prayer at home; but today was special. And as soon as Ghulam Haidar's voice wafted through the valley, men began leaking out of all the compounds.

The mosque filled up quickly. The men washed their hands and feet in the antechamber, their chatter filling the whitewashed room with a ringing din. They lined up in rows behind Ghulam Haidar, who led the communal ritual efficiently. He was no mullah, but he knew several dozen verses of the Quran by heart, and the village made do.

After prayer, the men seated themselves in a circle. Woven reed mats covered the floor, which Ghulam Haidar had swept clean (for he also acted as caretaker of the mosque.) The ten or twelve leading men formed a tight central ring. The others arrayed themselves in looser rings around the core.

Malik Ibrahim launched the meeting with *"Bismillahi rahmani rahim."* In the name of God, the generous and merciful. Then he gave a short speech about his intended visit to Sorkhab, but Ghulam Dastagir broke in before his voice had even quite stopped sounding. "I'll go with you, Ibrahim. No, no, it's settled. If this thing comes to blows, you'll need a strongman."

Anyone could see that this offer was not entirely welcome to the headman, nor proffered entirely in a friendly spirit. But Ibrahim gave the older man a respectful nod. "Certainly. You must come," he agreed. "You and others. We'll form a delegation."

"A show of strength," someone shouted. "Bristling with knives, That's how we'll come."

"Perhaps not this time," the headman counseled. "This time, let us arrive as if we've come to negotiate. If they won't negotiate, may the consequences be on their heads, but let us not be the ones to start a fight. After all, we've celebrated Eid with these people. Some of us have kin there."

"*You* have kin there."

"I and others." Ridges of muscle bulged on Ibrahim's sallow cheeks. "Our forefathers shared these waters and besides, kinship aside, are we not all Muslims?"

Ghulam Dastagir slapped the clay floor, raising a billow of powder. "This attitude of yours, Headman-sir. This attitude is dangerous, it's dangerous." His breath blew swirls in the chalky dust that his slap had raised. "You and your family are men of words, we all respect your words, but sometimes, son, courtesy can look like cowardice."

"I am no coward," Ibrahim declared. Nor your son, he thought.

"And God forbid I should ever imply such a thing!" Ghulam Dastagir protested. "Out of respect for your great, great brother, God forgive him, I would never! But the men of Sorkhab! What will *they* think when you come to them wheedling softly—"

"No one spoke of wheedling—"

"—appealing to their sense of mercy like a humble servant? Forgive me, Malik-sahib, but in martial matters you must let me be your teacher. A fight is won or lost the moment the two fighters cross eyes. One bears down, the other looks away, and it's all over but the blows. And let's be blunt, boy, this will come to a fight. It's water we're talking about here. If a man is not ready to fight for water, what will he fight for? Now let's think about strategy. We'll be fifty or sixty men of fighting age, they're two or three hundred—how can we win? I'll tell you how: with ferocity, boy! We have to burn hotter! Talk, by all means, but let it be warrior's talk. From the moment we walk in, we have to make them know in their bones what it will cost them to say no to us."

"We walk in like that and there will be a fight for sure," said Ibrahim.

"From which I will not back away," Ghulam Dastagir scowled.

"Nor I," boasted his cousin.

Ibrahim struggled to keep his voice level. "Nor I, if it comes to a fight. But let me be clear, men. I intend to greet the elders of Sorkhab with respect. The first discourtesy will come from them, not from me. That is my way. Whoever objects to my way, speak now. If you want another man as your malik, this is the time."

Throughout the silent mosque, men bowed their heads in thoughtful contemplation. All avoided the youthful headman's eyes.

"We put our faith in Allah," someone muttered finally.

And then Ghulam Haidar burst out: "Ibrahim, we've chosen you, we stand behind you. When you go to Sorkhab, you speak for all of us. You alone will decide what to say and how to say it, but I beg you to remember, to consider, to never forget that a malik is like a father to his village, even a young one like you. I know a father's obligations, I have babes at home right now weeping for milk. If I can't keep my fields irrigated through the summer...those babes...oh, Hajji-sahib, we're entrusting our very *lives* to you."

Ibrahim understood. The decision would be his, but if things went wrong all the blame would be his too. "Allah is generous," he said. "Who will go with me? Ghulam Dastagir, and who else?" Glancing around the room, he quickly picked out two men he could trust to counterbalance Ghulam Dastagir.

ॐ

The next morning, after bread-and-tea, a group of five set out for Sorkhab on foot. They arrived in the early afternoon. At the headman's compound, a teenaged boy opened the gate. Ibrahim recognized Khadija's nephew. The boy bowed to them all, greeted Ibrahim by name, and led the whole group inside.

Then with a lurch of the heart, Ibrahim saw a brace of horses tied to a tree in the courtyard. Malik Mustapha had guests, important ones, it seemed: men who rode horses. Men from far away.

The boy showed them into a sitting room where four men sat drinking tea around a cast iron pot filled with glowing charcoal. Ibrahim recognized two of them at once, Mullah Yaqub and Malik Mustapha, but the other two men were strangers—and what strangers! They wore resplendent vests, their beards were precisely trimmed, and both sported expensive caps made of baby lambskin. Only city men owned such hats.

All four men got to their feet, but the two visitors rose with the languor of high rank. When Ibrahim reached out, the nearest one, a lanky man, extended his hand palm down as if expecting it to be kissed. And Ibrahim complied because you never know.

Malik Mustapha introduced his guests, but Ibrahim caught only the phrase "—from Kabul." He could scarcely follow the rest, for he was too busy bowing, kissing lordly hands and blurting out courteous, even unctuous, rhetoric—"Your excellencies… what service can we…? Oh, your graces!… welcome, welcome…"

"These great men have come on the king's business," the malik of Sorkhab warned.

"The king! Ah!" Ibrahim exclaimed. "I see! Yes! How *is* our beloved Dost Mohammed Khan? We pray for his Excellency's health, your lordships. Every day! Around here, we call him Dost Mohammed the Great—" but the ardor leaked from his voice as he felt a chill rising in front of him. How had he offended the men from Kabul?

Malik Mustapha came to his rescue. "Dost Mohammed Khan has been overthrown, God be praised. The true king has reclaimed his throne at last, Ibrahim-sahib. We can finally stop pretending to revere that worthless cuckold and reveal our true allegiance. After thirty years, his majesty Shah Shuja is back on the throne."

Thirty years. So he must have held the throne around the time Ibrahim was born. He must have been one of those many kinglets who rose and fell during the bloody years of civil war that still figured in the elders' whispered horror stories.

"Isn't it wonderful? Rejoice, Ibrahim, rejoice. The age of justice is at hand!"

"I do! We do rejoice! Oh, most heartily," Ibrahim stammered, trying to remember what he knew about this Shah Shuja. "God is great!"

"Our beloved emperor must be smiling," the portlier of the two city men agreed. "His mighty grandson is back on his throne. Every traitor will suffer now! You fortunate men have this early chance to proclaim your loyalty."

The emperor. So this new king was one of "Papa" Ahmad Shah's many grandchildren. Ibrahim thought the whole stinking brood had killed one another off long ago. This one must have been hiding somewhere like a cockroach all this while, biding his time. Ibrahim kept the fulsome praises flowing from his lips while struggling to calm his private thoughts, because he had to stay cool, he had decisions to make and they had to be cool ones. He couldn't broach the issue of the river, not now, that was clear, not in the presence of these mighty lords. In fact, he had to get himself and his men out of here before the lords started talking taxes.

"In short," Ibrahim wrapped up, "we send our prayers to his majesty. His triumph will live forever in our stories. We just stopped in to say salaam. Now, with your permission—"

But the headman of Sorkhab was already telling the great lords, "These friends of ours come from Char Bagh, your excellencies. It's a pleasant village downstream from ours."

"Char Bagh." Four Gardens. The plump lord fingered his beard. He obviously liked the sound of that name. "Is your village as lush as it sounds?"

"Oh, hardly, your Excellency. We are small and poor, a poor village only half the size of Sorkhab. Less! We're descended from soldiers, four of them, stranded here from the armies of Babur three hundred years ago—they weren't farmers, they tried to scratch a living from the soil but in vain! They nearly starved. People called their settlement Char Bagh as a sort of joke. And things have never gotten much better for us. We scarcely have one garden, much less four. And the river has been shrinking of late, our fields are drying up. We barely have two hundred souls anymore, counting babies. We can barely feed ourselves."

"Hmm." The lord continued to squeeze his beard. "Well, we shall judge of all that for ourselves. Let me repeat what I just told your friends. A new king reigns in the capital, he's taking a new look at every village. That scoundrel Dost Mohammed let the country go to seed. He gathered taxes badly. He filled his armies with his own tribesmen, cuckolds and pimps one and all—how long since this valley sent any of its sons to serve in the king's army?" He cocked an eyebrow at Ibrahim. "Just as I thought. No wonder that scoundrel failed. Well, the new reign will be different—stern but fair is our vow. Everybody owes their welfare to the king," he warned. "Everybody will give the king his due. No favoritism, no excuses. Everyone will pay. These elders of Sorkhab have agreed to donate a hundred donkey loads of wheat a year, plus fifty hides and fifteen able-bodied young men for the king's draft. This good man Malik Mustapha has told me, 'Whatever the king needs, take. He is my father, everything I possess is really his.' Such loyalty! What say you men of Char Bagh? Can you match his loyalty?"

Ghulam Dastagir asserted himself. "Your Excellency, we're thrilled to meet a representative of the King's justice. This village of Sorkhab, which you praise so highly, is doubling its fields at our expense. No wonder they offer so much. They can afford it, they plan to grab all the river water and let us just dry up and die—they don't care! In the name of our hungering people, we call on his majesty for help. Poor folk depend on the king's sword for justice, God praise his highness Shah Shuja! God accept him into the ranks of saints."

"Did I hear you correctly?" The lanky lord's words whistled through a split in his lip, probably some old war wound. "This village pledges unlimited loyalty to his majesty . This village is the king's friend. And this village is your enemy, you say? The king's friends are your enemies?"

"Not at all!" Ibrahim burst in, chuckling so hard it raised his sweat. Chuckling was always easier than laughing when he felt no mirth. "Sorkhab and Char Bagh are like brothers. My companion is just distraught, sir. Anxiety makes his tongue wander. He has sick children at home. Ignore him, Excellencies, come to our village, we beg of you, assess what we can give. Our granaries belong to the king—I too look to his majesty as my father. If he asks for my very life, show me the abyss, I will fling myself into it! We'll hasten home now to prepare for your visit. Come to us soon," he urged. "Char Bagh is not far away, just four hours by foot, less on horses. Do you have a doctor in your retinue? I dearly hope so. Great men like you always travel with scholarly doctors. We long for such a one. A plague has seized our village, you see: our children—well, it's not just the children, to be frank! Men, women, everyone—the illness isn't choosy! Black sores, your highness. Lumps that grow, then burst—we came here to consult with Sorkhab's mullah— we don't have our own, you know—we're too small, too poor—we came for amulets, but if you have a doctor—"

"Black sores?" the lord whistled.

"Black as a dog's eyeball, sir. At first it's a hard lump, but after a few days, the lump bursts, pus runs out, and after that, you have a week to live if Allah favors you. We're eager for your visit, my lord. Famous men like yourselves may lift this curse from us just by visiting. When may we expect you?"

"Alas, our host here is too powerful," the portly lord rumbled, nodding toward the headman of Sorkhab. "Escaping his hospitality will be difficult. And the king expects us back by the crescent-moon. One cannot keep a king waiting, you know. We'll visit your village next year. Did you say you were leaving now? Well, if you must, you must."

"By next year, we may all be dead," Ibrahim said mournfully

"Allah forbid. Allah is merciful. We must not keep you. If you're going, go."

"Well, with your permission…" said Ibrahim.

Malik Mustapha walked them to the gate. As they passed through the courtyard, Ibrahim took the opportunity to mutter, "We came about the water, you know. How could you lay such plans? Are you out to kill us?"

"What can we do? We're growing," Mustapha Khan wheedled. "We have children to feed! And now this plague of officials. I was planning to inform you soon."

Ibrahim looked to see what Ghulam Dastagir made of this, but the older man had stormed ahead. "If you take more water, some of us will certainly die. You will have killed them."

The malik of Sorkhab looked at the sky, the ground, at everything but Ibrahim. "The king's men have found us. What can we do? We must increase our yield. I just hope they won't find you. Let's not quarrel about the river. I'll protect Char Bagh from their curiosity. These men from Kabul are a threat to us both. Our two villages share a single beating heart." His cordial tone did nothing to hide the threat he was leveling.

"They'll find us no matter what you do," said Ibrahim.

"God provides. We must have faith," Mustapha uttered piously.

"God provides, but God places limits too, on mortal greed. One must not plant more than one can water. All must accept the limits placed by God Almighty."

"Those limits, we accept," the malik of Sorkhab came back at him coolly. "What we don't accept are the limits other men try to force upon us."

Ghulam Dastagir would have hit the man for this. "We'll talk again," Ibrahim warned. "Starve a dog, expect to feel its teeth." But his counterpart met his stare with eyes as hard as kiln-fired clay.

On the road home, Ghulam Dastagir fumed and seethed. "This time I held my tongue, but next time? By God? And you let that man walk all over our faces, Ibrahim."

"It was the wrong day to squabble with Sorkhab. We'll come back."

"Your way of coming back be fucked," Ghulam Dastagir growled. "I'll come back my way. Knife in one hand, sickle in the other. Damned water thieves!"

"Water is not our only problem anymore," Ibrahim said. "The king's men know about us now. That story about the black sores won't hold them back forever."

Ghulam Dastagir gave him an appraising look. "That was a good story," he conceded. then he looked up at the sky and clutched his cloak shut at his throat. "Let's hurry, boys. We don't want night to catch us on the road."

11

A commotion had started in the bazaars along the road that entered Kabul from the southeast. Storekeepers climbed out of their stalls and joined curbside idlers to peer at the great billows of dust in the distance. Gossip went buzzing from stall to stall until everyone knew what was raising the billows. The new king and his retinue were returning from their winter sojourn in the warm southern city of Jalalabad.

The royal procession approached at a stately pace. Not until the front of it had passed into the shadow of Maranjan Hill could shoppers in the Grand Bazaar begin to hear the noise: the baying of camels, the whinnying of horses, the grunting of mules carrying great boxes of houseware that had provided for the king's comfort in the south.

At last the front of the column moved between the bazaar stalls. First came a row of mounted warriors, carrying lances and banners. Behind them cantered more rows of warriors cradling muskets, long barrels pointed skyward but ready to be lowered and fired at a moment's notice. Behind the warriors came the creaking carriages of the king and his foreign friends, the British officials who had kept him company on his vacation. Behind them all came the wagons. The merchants leaned forward, craning for a glimpse of this long-limbed, red-nosed, silken-bearded Shah Shuja, whom the foreigners had brought with them from India. Everyone remembered his grandfather, the great man who had built the Afghan empire. No one had forgotten how great man's sons had battled for possession of the empire after his death, nor how the great man's grandsons, this Shah Shuja and his brothers and cousins, had ripped the land to shreds fighting over the bones and scraps. Everyone had rejoiced when better men drove the lot of them away. But now this one-time flash of a king was back, surrounded by exotic *farangis* who had put him on his throne.

The merchants watched the king's retinue tromp through the bazaar, stamping muddy water onto bystanders as they passed through puddles. Long after the parade had disappeared down the road, a bubble-thin layer of slip was still drying on the fruits, meats, coats, toys, bolts of cloth, and other goods on display in the intricately colorful bazaar, leaving the merchandise glazed with silt.

The royal procession rumbled along the river on a highway paved with cobblestones, turning left at last to ascend the royal highway to the fortified heights of the Bala Hissar palace complex. The king himself sat in the second carriage from the front, comfortably wedged among overstuffed silk cushions. William Hay Macnaghten, Great Britain's chief political envoy, sat across from him, gripping a silver-topped cane between his knees. A lovely Hindi woman sat cuddled next to the king, encircled by his arm, chewing pistachios and raisins, sometimes passing the pulpy mass from her mouth to his.

Macnaghten turned away from this spectacle with no attempt to hide his disgust. "Your highness," he grumbled, "your subjects would find your behavior abominable. Will you not refrain until we pass from public view? Have some dignity, sir. Your highness? Sir! Do I have your attention, sir?"

Shah Shuja snickered. He enjoyed ruffling the pompous pieties of this proper fool of an Englishman. "Mr. Macnaghten, you got to understand the East. Here, a king's subjects are his slaves. What is the point of wearing a crown if you must tremble before your meanest of subjects? If such things they see it differently in England, I pity your king."

"We have a queen."

"Yes, yes, I forgot. Well, what can you expect from a country that lets itself to be ruled by a woman, eh? Anyway, this is not England. This country is my property and thirty years away from my royal rights have left me in no mood to kiss and bow to rabble. Samira, my doll, off the cork from that bottle, would you? I feel a thirst."

Macnaghten folded his hands in his lap and sighed. He gazed at the corner of the carriage while the King of Afghanistan continued to spoon with his mistress. After a few minutes of moist smooching, the king pulled away from the woman and drew the back of his hand across his lips. "How did you like Jalalabad, Mr. Macnaghten? What a favorite city of mine. How pleasant to be back among one's own people! But excuse me, you're not among your own. Poor Macnaghten! Are you lonely among us?"

"My wife resides in Calcutta, I will see her before long," the envoy said stiffly. "As for the other Englishmen, they are bearing up. Quite a number have sent for their wives and for their, well, um—their wives and such. They may be on their way to Kabul already—" Macnaghten broke off to stare through the carriage window at a figure swinging from the ramparts of a building they were just passing. "What the devil...?"

The king looked, then shouted an order, which was echoed by other voices outside, and the whole procession came to a halt. Shuja squinted through the glass. He blinked at the dead man dangling by his neck from the rope. He sniffed. "Shall we see?" He opened the door and called out. A Pushtoon servant came riding to the carriage on his horse.

"Your highness?"

Shah Shuja questioned the man in Pushto: "What's that hanging from the building? Who is that man? Why is he hanging there?"

"I will find out, sahib."

The king sat back to wait. His mistress pulled away and smoothed her skirts. Dust drifted and danced in the hot air.

Macnaghten said, "Your highness, I will attend to this." He reached for the door handle, but the king restrained his hand.

"Don't trouble your honorable self. My man looking into it."

A knock came on the door—the Pushtoon servant again. He and the king muttered together for a few minutes and then Shah Shuja closed the door and sat back, and the carriage began to move again.

"Well?" Macnaghten glared.

The king waved his fingers. "Nothing to worry about."

"The devil! Who was he? I insist on an answer," Macnaghten hrumphed.

The king rolled his eyes. "Mr. Macnaghten, bad elements run through this city. *Badmash* we call them. How you would say it in English? Bandits! Twenty years of ruling by this Barakzai tribe has left the city *rotten* full with plotters and bandits. Until every plotter has been dealt with, there is no order. That man was working for Dost Mohammed Khan, the pretender your people have in prison—for which I do thank your queen, your governor, etcetera. Never am I ungrateful, but now I must have a free hand to clear out all the nest of mice. I understand this country. You do not."

Macnaghten frowned. "Well…" He subsided back into his seat. "I don't doubt there are a few conspirators still skulking about."

"Oh, Mr. Macnaghten, you have no idea. These people are like children. They require the stern hand. Once they understand who is master, they will be good. Until then, believe me, it is—how do you say it?—a hayfield for the Czar. These people will do any mischief for money, and the Czar spends freely, as you know."

"The Czar must never—"

"I understand. I am your servant in every matter concerning our foreign neighbors. So long as I rule, this city is closed to Russians. Closed to the Shah of Persia. Closed to everyone but your queen and her servants. This makes you happy, yes? In return, sir! You *must* permit me to deal with my home problems in my own way."

Macnaghten shrugged. "I don't give a hang about your home problems. You know our concerns."

"I do. We are in agreement. I am very glad of it." The king fell into a moody silence, staring at his lap. Suddenly something hit the window, leaving a red splash against the glass—a tomato! Shah Shuja's eyes blazed, and he pounded on the front wall of the carriage compartment, shouting at his driver in Pushto.

Macnaghten blanched. "No, no," he pleaded. "Don't stop here. Let us make the safety of the fortress walls."

"Run from my subjects? Are you joking? You Englishmen! This is some troublemaker, I can not permit him to go unpunished! Let one of these rascals get away with it, all his friends will be at it next week. Do you know nothing about kingship? You brought me here to rule, do not tie up my hands." The king's face twisted with contempt and rage.

The carriage had creaked to a halt by this time. Shah Shuja opened the door. The road was lined with city folk, many people deep, but when the king appeared, they surged back, muttering and buzzing. Shah Shuja scowled at them. Five of his guards rode up to flank the royal carriage, cantering slightly on their horses, reins in one hand, rifles in the other. All five were Indian *sipahis*. Unlike the king's own treacherous countrymen, these men could be trusted for they were paid by the British and were loyal to their salaries.

The king climbed onto the running board of his carriage. On that ledge, he stood level with his mounted guards, giving him the imposing air so necessary to royal dignity. The buzzing died away. The crowd stared, thousands of eyes trained on the king.

"Who threw this tomato at my carriage?" the king asked in Pushto.

His Pushtoon guard repeated the question in a booming tenor.

People shuffled in place and glanced around to see if anyone would come forward. Shuja surveyed the crowd. In the front row, a surly young man with a hennaed beard caught his eye. As soon as the king looked at him, he looked away. Shuja made his decision. "That one." He pointed at the man with the dyed beard.

Two guards wheeled their horses upon the youngster. He wasn't hard to catch for the crowd hemmed him in. The guards half-carried him to the carriage. When they let him go, his knees buckled. Recovering quickly, he scrambled up, but the guards had dismounted by then, and held him in place by the arms.

"Give him a beating," said the king. He climbed back into his carriage but left the door open so that he could watch.

Macnaghten said nothing. The Indian woman cowered as far away from the door as she had room to cower, her scarf lifted to her mouth. The young man looked up, bewildered now. The guards were pulling his jacket off. "Don't beat to kill," said the king. "Twenty or thirty blows should be enough. Teach him a lesson, teach them all. Herald, tell the crowd what they should be learning from today's lesson. Woe to anyone who tests the king! Announce it."

The Pushtoon nodded and broadcast his message in a ringing monotone. "Slaves of his majesty, learn from this man's fate. Mischief will not be tolerated."

The guards set to work, hitting the king's victim. After two or three minutes, the fellow went to his knees, but he kept flinging his arms up to fend off blows, then dropping them to yelp and rub at his forearms where a stick had hit, only to throw his arms back up as sticks kept crashing against his skull.. His head began to bleed. Macnaghten leaned forward. "I say," he began.

Shah Shuja waved him back. "Not now," he barked. "Really, Macnaghten! I have some experience in kinging, you know."

"Your experience lost you the throne, you miserable sot," Macnaghten snarled. "If it wasn't for us, you wouldn't be here," and he spat the addendum, "Your highness!"

A grin lit up Shah Shuja's features. A gold cap gleamed on his right bicuspid. "Well, well! You show some spirit! But I am assuring your lordship, with these people, you cannot be gentle. They will take you for weak and swarm you like dogs. They only understand strength. That was my mistake. I was too gentle with these people the last time, too good to them. They lost respect for me. This time they will not lose respect."

Macnaghten threw up his hands with a snort and rolled his eyes. "Just take care not to exhaust *my* patience, your highness. We put you on that bloody throne, we can bloody well take you off again."

"Mr. Macnaghten!" the king smiled, comfortably encircling his mistress with his free arm again. "Rage, rage, but I have spoken with his lordship. You need me. I need you also, that is the case. So why don't we just learn to get along?"

12

So this was India. Rupert Oxley stared at the scenery slipping past the glass. He saw a spired temple …He saw a banyan tree with leaves the size of fans…He saw two men washing an elephant… He had seen such sights in pictures and had always thought they would seem so much more transporting and wonderful in real life but somehow, now that he was here, it all seemed …ordinary.

The air sopped into his lungs, warm and wet and heavy as gravy. Yet the horses trotted along briskly. How they managed in this heat, Rupert could not imagine. He mopped his brow. Of course, it wasn't just the temperature making him sweat, but the tension too. The next few hours might set the course of his whole life. He cast a glance at Colonel Hollister, but the old dodger seemed lost in thought. He had said very little since Rupert arrived, just the obligatory inquiries about his family and a few formal welcoming remarks.

At last the Governor General's domicile hove into view, what Colonel Hollister had termed a bungalow, but Rupert could see at one glance that "bungalow" meant something different here in India, something altogether more grand—and why should it not? Everything seemed bigger in this land. Why, on the map that once hung in Rupert's nursery, he remembered how all of England could tuck into the bottom corner of India, right in the jungly part that was adorned with tiny pictures of tigers and monkeys—how he loved those little tigers and monkeys… that map… the nursery…

Lord Auckland was a florid gentleman whose girth made the gaps between his waistcoat buttons bulge. That afternoon, he and Lady Auckland had attracted nearly two dozen social callers, over whom Lady Auckland presided like a queen. Just moments after they arrived, an older woman with a moustache collared Oxley and would not let him wriggle free.

Seconds later he lost all desire to wriggle free because a pretty young copy of the matron, her niece perhaps, appeared at her side: Amanda Hartley, blond of hair and green of eyes, a perfume of femininity surrounding her person. Looking closely, Oxley could see a faint down on her upper lip and a squareness to her jaw that might one day harden into her aunt's masculine cast but not yet. Not now. Now she struck Rupert Oxley as perfect. He only wished he could give her his full and close attention, but his head was like a hive of bumblebees, he was so nervous about the conversation he would have to muddle through with Lord Auckland sometime this afternoon, a conversation in which he would have to seem easy and sociable, even though his whole Indian career depended on the impression he made. Listening to Amanda through this buzz of anxious thoughts, all he could do was nod and sometimes say "Yes mum" as she chattered on.

Lady Auckland was offering nothing but black tea as refreshment, but Oxley had a flask of stronger stuff hidden in his khaki jacket and was able to sneak a fortifying nip in the hall now and again. By the time the tea things were cleared away, he was surprised to find his supply drained. He felt a bit bright about the eyelids, but not incompetent. He had done well to brace himself, he thought. Once the Governor got to quizzing him, he would need all the confidence he could muster. The Old Man no doubt expected staffers to know heaps about politics. Oxley was not wholly ignorant, he could carry on about the tariff and the Reform Bill and even the damned Chartists, but those were all English topics. They must have different topics here. A sober Rupert would have succumbed to panic, but the fortified Rupert felt equal to any challenge, even though he had no idea what would be asked or what he would answer when the time came.

Finally the guests began to take their leave. He saw Amanda following her aunt toward the door. She cast a look back at Oxley. He had barely spoken to her, she barely knew him. Her attention seemed to strain toward him even as she was turning away, or was it merely his attention clinging to hers? He didn't want her to go, he might never get another chance with her. Then it was too late. She was gone. They were all gone, all the guests. He was alone with Colonel Hollister, Lord Auckland, and some other rooky his own age. Rupert's palms were sweating, but it wasn't nerves, he told himself: it was the heat.

"New to the colonies, youngsters?" Auckland beamed at both young men. "It's a great deal to take in, I know. I remember how it was for me. We all go through this period. Mr. Oxley: the colonel has been good enough to share your particulars with me. You come well recommended. Arthur, my boy, I hope you left your parents in good health. Dear friends of mine. What do you think of India so far, gentlemen? You've been with us a week now?"

"Two weeks, sir. Dreadful climate," Rupert responded, "but a fascinating country. Full of surprises."

"It does take some getting used to," said the other rooky.

"It does, it does, but you'll get used to it. We all do." Auckland strolled to the sideboard and opened the mahogany doors. "Claret?"

"A bit early for me." Colonel Hollister smoothed his moustache with his thumbs.

"I'll take half a glass, sir," Arthur said politely.

"Wine?" Oxley was surprised. Auckland had started out in the admiralty and those navy men were hard drinking chaps, he'd always heard. "Wine would suit me, sir, unless you have something stiffer."

"Perhaps some cognac then." The governor-general of India reached deeper into the cabinet and brought out a bottle from which he poured a finger's worth of amber liquid. Oxley accepted the cut-glass vessel, put his heels together and tossed it back in one gulp, just to show himself a soldier and a man. He set the glass down on the sideboard and wiped his lips. Good stuff, by God.

Suddenly, the richly appointed room swamped his attention. Flocked golden wallpaper. Polished window trimmings of beveled wood. Ivory inlays on the sideboard and on other bits of incidental furniture. If only the lads back at the Leicester School for Boys could see him now, amidst such splendor. The room was too damned small, though. This Indian climate! Oxley loosened his collar.

"I'm always interested in fresh word from England," Auckland said. "We get reports, but it's different hearing it from the horse's lips. What are they saying about Afghanistan?"

Arthur stretched his long legs. "Very little, my lord. Wait-and-see is the attitude."

Oxley was astounded. Clearly his rival had not been keeping up! "Actually," he declared, "it's quite the hot debate in Parliament these days, Afghanistan."

"I know what they say in Parliament." The Governor's eyes were bland, his voice dry. "What do people say privately?"

"Privately!" Oxley's head was swimming, although not unpleasantly. "Privately, ah well, people are saying it's a baaaad business. Terrible things happen in those mountains. Stories get around."

"Do they. And yet…" Lord Auckland took a pinch of snuff from the back of his hand, "the whole affair has gone extremely well. Does that story not get around?"

"Very well *so far*," Oxley cautioned, remembering an argument about this question in which someone defeated someone with this very point. *So far!*

"Nonsense!" Auckland insisted. "The Dost has surrendered to us, we've brought him to India, not one Afghan has peeped—it's over. We've secured the empire. And yet the old women in Parliament go on debating resolutions." The Governor-general took out a handkerchief and wiped his ruddy cheeks. "Can you explain *that* to me, Mr. Oxley?"

"Well, sir…" Something was tickling at Oxley's brain. Something they were saying about Afghanistan at the officer's club the other day. Some telling phrase hovered just outside his reach. But he couldn't hook it, so he changed tack. "Well, now, this new king."

"New!" Auckland scoffed. "He was king thirty years ago! His grandfather was emperor. Who has a better blood right to that throne than Shah Shuja?"

"But he's a bounder, isn't he?"

Auckland stared. "A bounder?"

Hollister kept shaking his head. Some sort of tic, perhaps. Oxley turned back to the Governor, but the whole room turned with him, and kept turning. He paused to let it finish whirling, wishing he could get another nip of that excellent cognac, just to steady himself. Auckland didn't seem to know what a bounder was. "A snake?" Rupert offered helpfully.

"A snake." The governor had the oddest habit of repeating a man's words. "Well, Mr. Oxley, if he's a snake, he's our snake. Without Shah Shuja, good Lord! Russia rushes in. With Shuja on the throne, we push forward. Forward, young man! Remember that! Afghanistan is a *thrilling* success."

"Well." The other rooky cleared his throat.

"Well what?" Auckland shifted his scowling gaze.

"I hope there is still work to be done. I hate to think we've missed all the fun."

Auckland's features relaxed. "Yes, boys, there's still the odd agitator or two, you soldiers will have your chances, but we make progress every day. A time will come when you'll be able to ride a carriage from Rawalpindi to Kabul as easily as you go from Leicester to London. And on that day, you fellows—"

At that moment, a snicker squirted out of Rupert. "I just remembered what they're calling this whole Afghanistan business!" Colonel Hollister now shook his head vigorously, but Rupert pushed on, because it was a splendid joke, and his lordship seemed like a good enough egg to appreciate it. "*Auckland's Folly!*"

Silence dropped over the room. Rupert glanced at Colonel Hollister. A frown was gripping the man's face like a crab. Rupert heard the words he had just spoken echoing in his mind. "Not that I—" he stammered. "Not that I would ever..."

But then Auckland burst out laughing, and seeing that it would be okay, Oxley released his own hilarity. Auckland and Oxley laughed together. The governor was a good fellow after all, this Auckland. Colonel Hollister smiled uncomfortably. The other rooky drew in his limbs and shifted his bottom on the sofa. In that moment, Rupert felt that he and the Old Man shared a companionship the other two could only envy.

But the Lord Governor's mirth vanished as water into sand. "No one tells me these things, Mr. Oxley. It's refreshing to hear from such a fearless young man." He smiled, and Rupert smiled back, relieved. "Arthur, m'boy," Lord Auckland went on, "perhaps you'd give Mr. Oxley a lift back to his quarters. I need to keep the Colonel for a bit."

&CR

Auckland dropped down across from the colonel and opened a cigar box.

The colonel shook his head. "I've acquired a taste for these native *bidis.*" Out of his pocket he drew a box covered with line drawings of swollen-breasted Hindu goddesses. From it he extracted a very thin cigar, a single leaf wrapped around a few pinches of tobacco. An acrid odor rose with its smoke. "Filthy habit," Colonel Hollister acknowledged. "I know."

Lord Auckland began stuffing his pipe. "This protégé of yours. Oxford, is it?"

"Oxley. Son of an old school chum of mine."

"Well, he won't do. I can't use him."

"He has some growing up to do, I see your point. But he'll smooth out," Colonel Hollister offered anxiously.

"I'm sure he will but that's not it. A clumsy chap like him is one thing in barracks, but on my staff? Colonel, you know it's all political work, what we do up here. One wrong word with these Pathans, with the Sikhs, with some of these Rajas—good lord: catastrophe. I need men with a feel for nuances. This boy doesn't have it, never will."

The colonel sighed. "It's just that I promised his father I would do something for him. He got himself in a pickle in England, nothing serious. Youthful high spirits. I had one or two rough moments myself early on..." The colonel bit his lips. "Rupert's grandfather got me into the regiment and that's what put me at Waterloo, and Waterloo, George,

Waterloo's what saved me. This boy can turn around, I'm sure. We were all young once. He just needs a clean slate, George, and India's the place for it."

The governor paced to the window. "Auckland's Folly."

"Tactless, I grant you, *most* tactless, but he's a decent soldier."

"If it's a clean slate he wants, why not send him to Afghanistan."

"Oh now! George—"

"Yes! Afghanistan!" Auckland insisted. "It's perfect. Let this boy get a first-hand look at the forward policy. He'll see for himself how well we're doing, and when he goes home, he'll broadcast it to others. And they'll tell others. He'll be a walking argument for the great work we're doing here. Yes, Afghanistan is the perfect post for this boy."

13

Rupert endured a deadly week in Peshawar, waiting for the convoy, a week he spent brooding about his blunder and what his father would think about his disgrace, and how his brother would smirk at the news of it. He took his meals in his room and rarely went far from his quarters. Where would he go? There was nothing to see out there in the city. Peshawar was a labyrinth of narrow, filthy streets, clamorous at all hours with the sounds of people shouting and fighting and singing, the sounds of animals baying and wild dogs barking—it was the noisiest place Rupert had ever been. No one seemed to sleep in this country. Least of all Rupert. Auckland's Folly, he kept thinking. Oh, how he wished he had never blurted out that bloody phrase!

Finally the convoy arrived, a wagon train of goods and people bound for Kabul. Rupert was to join the small detachment of John Company escorting them into the mountain kingdom. After his idle week, he was good and ready.

The convoy creaked out at dawn the next day. It would have to make its way through treacherous, snow-choked passes to reach the rude frontier outpost, he was told, and along the way it might have to fend off hostile natives, but it could be sure of a warm welcome in Kabul because of the wagonloads of goods it was bringing in, civilized amenities such as smoked hams, cognac and cigars, chandeliers—even a harpsichord. More important, it was bringing women: its passengers included over a dozen English ladies and twice that many Indian women, wives and consorts and maidservants. The cargo was loaded onto camels and donkeys and packed into wagons hauled by mules. The women rode at the end of the train, in wagons that were covered and had seats inside and springs above the wheels to cushion the ride.

Nothing could cushion the ride entirely, however. The road over the Khyber Pass was achingly narrow and terribly bumpy, and it had many false summits. Again and again the convoy would top a rise and start down, only to find its path tilting upward again. The work was beyond taxing. Rupert and the others had to ride up and down the line, keeping the carts away from the edge and guiding them around the hairpin turns. Any misstep might prove fatal. Once, pausing at the edge of the dusty path, Rupert looked down a long, steep slope of rocks and dirt and saw the tops of trees, hundreds of feet below. He shuddered at the thought of going over! Even if a man survived the fall, God only knew what the natives would do to him.

At that moment, he heard a melodious voice. "Mr. Oxley?" He turned and peered. A young woman with blond sausage curls was waving to him from the nearest wagon—good God, it was Amanda Hartley, the pretty one from Lord Auckland's bungalow!

He blushed and tipped his hat to her but felt too shy to stammer out more than a brief greeting. It struck him that she might have heard of his drunken blunder that day, might have laughed about it with her friends. A humiliating thought! Well, he had no time for ladies anyway, he huffed to himself. He had work to do, important work, keeping the wagons bumping over the rutted road. If not for him the train might not make it over the Khyber, much less to Kabul. Besides, he had to watch the hills for danger. He was a soldier, and this convoy might come under attack at any moment. Perhaps he would distinguish himself, fighting the natives. Perhaps he would save Amanda's life. Then she'd see! And the news would filter back to his family…Rupert, hero of the day! The smirk would drop off Robert's handsome face. His father would bluster and grump but pride would shine through his bluster. Perhaps a posting to Afghanistan was not the worst of fates. A man might prove himself …

The next rise proved to be the real summit. From that point on, the train steadily descended, but the urgency of the work hardly diminished, for every hand was now needed to keep the wagons from rolling too fast and crashing into the mules. Probably, they should have unhooked the animals from the front and yoked them to the back to restrain rather than push, but there was no place to make the switch, and so the convoy kept going, all the men heaving and sweating and grunting and shouting, until it had descended out of the mountains and was rolling over relatively level terrain. Now they were truly in the land of the Afghans. And now at last the guides called a halt for a much-needed rest. The wagons pulled up within strolling distance of a clump of shade trees, the only greenery to be seen in this dismal landscape. Nothing else met the eye in any direction except scrubby gray brush, dotted by an occasional purple blossom. A warm wind had started to blow. Despite the seeming desolation, a crowd quickly gathered: boys at first, then bearded, swarthy men. They kept their distance, but the wind carried the sound of their guttural voices to the wagons. They all wore turbans, the tails of which were wrapped over their mouths and noses, leaving only their eyes showing. Many had eyes rimmed with kohl too, which in London would have made them look effeminate, but here only rendered them the more sinister.

The women had climbed down from the wagons and were sitting on makeshift stools beside the road, refreshing themselves with fruit and water but the stares made them nervous, as how could they not. Rupert heard some of them murmuring anxiously. He longed to reassure them but didn't know what to say. He felt all too ill at ease himself.

In the end it was Captain Scott to the rescue, Scott who had been probably in and out of Afghanistan a dozen times. "They're just villagers," he assured the ladies. "They're curious, is all. Just ignore them and they'll leave you alone."

But privately he told Oxley, "Keep an eye on the buggers."

"Are we in danger then?" Rupert asked, thrilled to the marrows by the prospect of seeing his first action.

Scott shook his head. "No, no, they won't test us, we have our rifles, but people do make their living by thieving in these parts, so don't let any of them sneak close and grab something. We'll be fine as long as we make it to the fort by nightfall."

Unfortunately, a lame mule slowed them down, and dusk found them nowhere near any fort. They would have to sleep in tents that night, on the open plains. Scott had the men collect dry brush and build bonfires around the circle of wagons, then selected men to stand guard in shifts. Rupert's turn came sometime after midnight. Two other pickets shared his shift, but they spread out. Alone in the dark, Rupert roamed the edge of the encampment, peering into the desert for intruders, but it was perfectly still out there, still and lonesome.

At dawn, he studied the tents clustered together at the center of the camp. Amanda was sleeping in one of those. He wondered which one, and what she might be dreaming. He wondered if he would be able to sleep when his shift ended. He wished he had spoken a few more words to her when he had the chance. She seemed amenable, now that he thought back to her smiling face and wide blue eyes. Or were they green?

The next day, they reached the fort, an imposing edifice surrounded by thick cob walls. Its gates, made of heavy timbers, took two men to swing open. Once shut, they were secured with an iron bolt as long as a man's arm. Within the walls, four buildings surrounded a large yard. Indoors, native servants lit oil lamps and bustled about making the travelers comfortable. Soon, those same servants brought forth a dinner prepared by the fort's native cooks, and it was surprisingly delicious, unless the rigors of the journey had given Rupert such a hunger that anything would have tasted good; but if so, the whole company was affected, for when he looked around he saw them all, even the ladies, falling upon the grilled meats and baked rice and stewed vegetable with the same ravenous appetite.

After dinner some of the officers got up a card game. Others surrounded them to watch and a certain gaiety began to warm the room. Rupert, however, found himself a more distant seat on a platform against the wall. As it happened—he didn't plan it—Amanda Hartley was sitting up there too. They gazed down from their high perch, over the heads and shoulders of the other observers, to the card table, where coins glittered in the light of oil lamps and candles. But the light seeped only a little beyond the circle of players. Sitting outside the bubble, Rupert and Amanda shared a convivial togetherness in the near-dark. At least,

Rupert felt convivial and thought Amanda shared his mood, but he couldn't be sure without looking at her, and in this dim light looking would not be enough: he would have to stare. And of course he couldn't stare, it would be beastly rude; but he wanted to, if only to refresh his memory of her face; because, when he tried to recall her from that first day, what he remembered was not so much her features as his own feelings, gazing at her features. And perhaps it was only the warmth of whiskey in his belly that he was remembering. Lost in his thoughts, even though his thoughts were all of her, he didn't notice that she had started speaking to him. He woke to the sound of her voice only as it stopped.

"I beg your pardon? What was that?"

"I was asking, do you play cards yourself, captain?"

"I am not a captain, ma'am, only a lieutenant," he confessed. "I squandered too much loot, playing cards back in Calcutta in the barracks while I was waiting for orders. I think I learned my lesson for a week or two."

"Ah. Poor Mr. Oxley." She clucked her sympathy. "It must have been such an anxious time. Were you pleased to learn you had been posted to Afghanistan?"

"Pleased?" He didn't understand.

"Well, for a soldier," she declared. "What a privileged assignment this must be. A place where the empire is really at stake each and every day! Surely they send only the bravest and best? I suppose your family must be very proud of you."

Her eyes were on the card game, but her words left a soft roaring in his ears. He could not bring himself to check her face for a mocking smile. A tinkle of laughter rose from the card players, about what, he could not tell. Whitby suddenly raked in a heap of coins.

"No," Rupert sighed finally. "I don't imagine my family is proud." His spectacles were slipping down his nose on a lubricant of sweat. He nudged them back into place. "For me this posting to Afghanistan isn't an honor, it's more of a punishment, you might say. Seems I made quite an ass of myself that day at Lord Auckland's. You hadn't heard?"

"Um…Auckland's Folly…?" she ventured.

His cheeks blazed with shame. "Yes. I see. It *has* gone about. I thought it might, it's too good a story, I suppose. Oxley's Folly!"

"Aren't you being a little too hard on yourself, captain? You told the Old Man to his face what the whole world is saying to his back. Is that so bad? I don't think that's so bad. Someone had to do it. It took courage, they say. There is honor in it."

"Is that what they say."

"Some do."

Honor. He let it pass. She was trying to comfort him, that alone was touching, he should simply let it warm him. "Thank you." He wouldn't tell her his courage had come out of a bottle. Why bring that up? He wanted to change the subject quickly now, before she changed her mind about his courage. "Tell me though—if I may ask. What brings you to such a wild country, ma'am? Afghanistan is no place for a woman."

"Are there no native women in Afghanistan?" she said with a light laugh.

"An English woman, I meant."

"Of course." She set merriment aside, then, and gave him a sober answer. "I am joining my husband in Kabul. We are newly wed."

The news hit him like a blow, but he bit back his first response. His second response was no better, so he bit that one back too. In the end, he offered no response at all. For a few long moments they watched the card game in silence, a sudden bristle of discomfort between them. Then the coincidence of her last name struck him, and he saw a way to revive the conversation. "Hartley," he mused. "I knew a Major James Hartley in Derbyshire, fearsome taskmaster! By Jove, you're not married to his son, by any chance: are you?"

"Not to his son," she answered quietly. "Major James Hartley is my husband."

"Oh, by Jove! What I meant—I was speaking only about—" His stammer weakened. "I didn't know him, really. I was a raw recruit then— he was an older fellow…" Rupert's voice ran down utterly. He had put his foot in it again. He tried to picture the Hartley he had known. Ruddy face. Big white whiskers—good heavens: how could such a lovely, smooth-skinned girl be that man's wife? A voice was already whispering in his head. "…old man… young, pretty wife…" He squelched it. Only a fool makes the same mistake twice. But of course he couldn't keep a fleeting image of Lady Lydia out of his mind. And Lord Ashton. A longing wafted through him, faint as perfume.

"You're very silent suddenly, Mr. Oxley."

"I'm sorry. My thoughts wandered…something quite unrelated. I'm sorry."

She unfolded her hands from her lap. "I feel smothered in here. Don't you find it too warm? I wonder if it's safe to go outdoors."

"Captain Scott!" Rupert raised his voice. "Can Mrs. Hartley walk in the yard? Is it safe?"

"Of course, old chap, we're on English soil here in the fort. Do escort her, though, it's beastly dark out there."

Amanda was already on her feet and walking toward the door. Oxley followed at a decorous distance. It *was* dark out in the yard. The crescent moon had sunk below the fortress walls. The stars were numerous and so luminous they seemed to bulge from the sky, but they were only stars. By their combined glow, Rupert could only barely make out his feet. As Amanda strolled beside him, her arm repeatedly brushed against his, but she seemed to mean nothing by the closeness. When she spoke, it was in a casual, friendly voice. "I am not to be pitied, you know."

"Good heavens, certainly not. I would never presume—"

"Ah but you would presume, Captain. You did. I could hear it in your voice when I spoke of my husband. I don't mean to be harsh, you're not the first, I get that reaction often, and I've grown accustomed to it. I only wanted *you* to know that I am very happy to be joining James, even in this wild country. I feel fortunate in my match. I feel contented with my lot. "

"I will remember that. I hope I have given no offense."

"I know you meant none. I forgive you. I only wish to be understood."

"Thank you. Yes, I understand. I wish you and the Major every happiness."

"I say this only because I think you and I could be friends, Captain Oxley. Rupert. We could be very *good* friends, so long as we understand each other. Very good friends."

"I hope so, Mrs. Hartley. I wish for it devoutly."

He understood the words she spoke, but not their meaning, entirely. He understood that she gripped his arm as she spoke those final words, and that even after she let go, his arm remembered her grip. She probably didn't notice touching him, but for Rupert, the impression of her slender fingers lingered on his skin long after they went indoors.

ℰℭ

For the next three days, the convoy moved steadily north through the mountains, but on the fourth day, it slowed to a crawl, for it entered the most alarming stretch of the journey, a crack of a canyon where the road thinned down to the narrowest possible thread. Keeping wagons and animals moving safely exhausted the men and reduced the ladies' nerves to twitters. Nightfall brought them to a town dominated by a hilltop fortress of mud, but this could not be their refuge, alas, for it belonged to a local chieftain of dubious loyalty. The convoy had to put up at a caravanserai on the outskirts of the town.

Late that evening, as they were dining on bread and kebabs, a hubbub sounded outside. Suddenly, a group of Afghan men burst through the door. A few of the women shrieked. Mrs. Hartley thrillingly sought Oxley's hand under the table. Captain Scott jumped to his feet.

Mohan Lal, their Hindu interpreter, stepped forward to engage the men. After a few minutes of heated conversation, he turned to Scott. "These chiefs are unhappy, Captain. Your man in Kabul forgot to pay them their subsidies. They are wanting money to let you pass."

Scott muttered an oath.

"Are they bandits?" Rupert sidled up.

"No, Lieutenant, local tribesmen. We've been paying a queen's ransom for safe passage, but Parliament won't tolerate the expense anymore. The subsidies have been cut."

"Do you mean we haven't paid the toll?" Amanda moved into place behind Oxley, her breathy voice issuing from a halo of hushed blond fear.

"Toll! More like extortion!" Scott kept a smile trained on the chieftains, but they only glowered at him. The lamplight seemed to magnify their black beards, their looming size. Scott came to a decision. "Tell 'em the money's coming with the next convoy, Lal. Persuade them I'm too junior to bother with, they'll catch bigger fish if they let us through and set a trap for the next one. You might hint that the governor himself will be in that one."

Lal began talking to the Afghan chieftains.

"I say, Captain, it's not true, is it?" Rupert grinned, delighted with the ruse. "About the Governor?"

"Stow the smirk, you fool They can read your face. No, it isn't true, but it'll hold 'em till we're gone."

"And after that?" Amanda queried.

"Yes," said Rupert. "when we come back, won't they take revenge?"

"By that time we'll have all these passes cleared," said Scott. "But Oxley: when you get in to see Macnaghten, tell him about this dustup. He has too rosy a view sometimes."

One of the Afghans cocked his head as if to listen. "*Engrayzee*," he growled, "next time you see what Macnaghten he can do!"

"Good Lord," the captain blinked. "You speak English?"

"Tell Macnaghten this *khawk* our *khawk*—this!" The Afghan stamped the floor with the butt of his long barreled rifle. Suddenly he seized Amanda's wrist and yanked her close. "Gold or woman. If you no gold, how much this woman?"

Oxley never later remembered having moved, but he must have moved, for suddenly he found himself pressed against the tribesman with his pistol pushing into the man's throat.

Instantly, the man's companions clapped their rifles to their shoulders. No one moved, no one spoke. Later, Rupert remembered the men's bristly beards and Amanda's frightened face floating inches from his eyes, her breath warming the knuckles of his trigger finger.

"Let her go," he croaked. "Let her go. I'll send you to hell, you bastards!"

The Afghan flung Amanda away. No guns went off, no shots rang out. The whole tableau simply reconfigured. Everybody was safe.

"Everywhere king you?" the Afghan spat. "King you no here." He gestured to his men and they all stalked out of the room, insolently exposing their backs on the way out.

That night, when lots were drawn for sentry duty, Oxley got first shift. The women were assigned to rooms within the caravanserai building, but the soldiers had to bunk in the courtyard in their tents. After some commotion of dispersal and preparation, the travelers subsided into slumber.

Rupert roamed the grounds in solitude, catching only occasional glimpses of his fellow sentries. He found himself wandering into the building where the women were sleeping. Well, he had a duty to watch over them too, didn't he? He thought one door along the corridor stood ajar and—worrying that some intruder had violated these quarters—he crept closer. Just doing his duty. He saw a dark figure standing in the doorway! His heart beat hard. From the faint scent in the air he knew he was looking at a woman but could not make out her features, not even from two feet away. Then he felt her fingers exploring his face. Heard the rustle of her garments and the susurrus of her breath, achingly close.

"Amanda?"

Lips touched his cheeks, grazed their way over his skin, even brushed for a moment over his lips...but she stepped out of his attempted embrace. "Mr. Oxley, you were *heroic* today."

He reached for her again but she was gone. The door shut. Only the memory lingered, of her lips on his, the light, moist touch of them. Oxley took out his kerchief to clean his fogged spectacles.

14

The journey from Peshawar to Kabul took nine days in this season, for even though spring had greened the plains somewhat, winter still hung on in the passes. The sky above was mostly blue, but the Kabul River and all its multitude of tributaries ran through sheets of frozen waterfalls, and the wagons kept slipping on the ice. Every time the camels sank into the snow, they bayed and bayed until their wallahs wrapped pillow-like coverings around their foot pads and beat them into moving on.

At last, the huts and hovels of the city hove into view. In Calcutta, Rupert had heard Kabul called "the city of a thousand gardens," but what he spied in the distance now was a miserable warren of mud heaps no different than Peshawar.

His opinion did not improve as they moved forward. The road lapsed into a city lane that passed between two rows of merchants stalls. Armies of feet had ground the snow into the soil to form a muddy slip. The natives stared at the convoy and Rupert saw murder in every eye. Then they rounded into a public square and his pulse went ragged. There, in plain sight, swinging from gibbets, were five dead men naked below the waist, with desecrated groins. He wanted to shield the ladies from the sight but it was too late.

They turned off the main road toward a set of looming mountains. At the base of these, a long wall stretched across a field. A gate in the middle swung open, and Rupert glimpsed the first of those "thousand gardens": the British headquarters in Kabul.

It was a small city within the city, the whole of it surrounded by that wall. A middle-aged sergeant named Hudson took charge of Rupert. He hailed from Leicestershire, not far from the Oxley estate. "Right this way, your worship," said the burly Midlander. "I'll show you to your rooms, sir. This way, your lordship."

"Stow the 'lordship' talk," Rupert blushed. "What's your Christian name, Hudson?"

"Edward, sir. Good of you to ask."

"Well, Edward, I must report to Mr. Macnaghten before I do anything else. Where will I find him at this hour?"

"Beggin' your pardon, sir, but you smell like old fishwrap, sir. You'd best have a hot bath before you go in to the guv'nor."

Rupert had to laugh. "A hot bath! Can you supply such a thing?"

"We're not so savage as all that here, sir. I'll have the girl prepare it."

"Girl?"

"Yes, sir, we engages a native girl to take care of the needs in this here bunkhouse. Whatever comes up, you mought say." Edward winked at him. "Have a sit in your room and let the girl pull off your boots."

Rupert enjoyed a long soak in a bath prepared by a girl he could barely see for her swaddlings. Then he was drawn into having tea with several officers from the garrison, good fellows about his own age. After tea, he turned down an invitation to an evening performance of *The Repentant Schoolmaster, a Comedy in Two Acts*, by Cantonments' own amateur theatrical society. Time enough for entertainments, he thought, after he had properly impressed his superiors.

Sir William Hay Macnaghten, the Queen's envoy to the court of Kabul, was a man of medium height, but he looked shorter, due to his barrel-chest. Rupert could have sworn someone had stuffed a pillow under his shirt. His cheeks and cherry nose shone with a ruddy glow. His waxy forehead extended up as two high domes. His thinning hair was brushed back and tamped down with oil. He was sitting behind a large table, playing with his watch fob. "Ah, Lieutenant Oxley," he said when Rupert knocked. "Come in, young man. Welcome to our rude camp. I trust your journey went well? Good, good. What will you have? I can offer a passable Madeira." He gestured at a bottle sparkling on the table next to his elbow.

"Fine, sir…or if you have some whiskey?" Rupert glanced about, calculating where to sit—on the divan across the room? On one of several large armchairs arranged around an oriental carpet? On the straight-backed chair across the table from the envoy?

Macnaghten jingled a bell and a servant came gliding in but to Rupert his servility smacked of insolence. "Sahib?"

"Whiskey for the gentleman." The servant did not immediately leave. Macnaghten repeated the command slowly, separating the syllables as if talking to a simpleton, and finishing with a native word. "F'meedi?"

The servant nodded and departed. Rupert handed over Lord Auckland's dispatch and took a seat. "M'lord Governor asked me to deliver these papers to you."

Macnaghten glanced through the contents of the envelope until the servant came back with a glass of whiskey, which Oxley sipped slowly while he waited for Macnaghten. Finally the envoy set the letters aside. "Fresh news from England is always welcome," he sighed. "One comes to miss even the fog. But perhaps you've not been away long enough to know what I mean."

"It's more that I'm green enough to know exactly what you mean, sir. I'm still getting used to things," said Rupert.

"We'll keep you distracted," Macnaghten assured him. "I only hope you won't find it tedious here. You young men come east looking for adventure, but it's all administrative work now. Frankly, this whole enterprise has been more of a job than a war—and yet Parliament remains squeamish, I understand."

"The talk in London has been alarmist." Oxley picked his words carefully. "If Lord Auckland mentioned that I—well, if he drew the inference that I—well, if he said that I said 'folly,' what I meant by 'folly'—"

But Macnaghten wasn't listening. "I send reports, they don't believe me," he interrupted. "What will it take to convey the message, Mr. Oxley? How can we get our countrymen to appreciate the magnitude of our success in Afghanistan?"

Rupert cleared his throat. "It's all in how you put it, I suppose. But sir," he ventured, "on the road from Peshawar…"

Macnaghten's pin-prick eyes gleamed. "Road from Peshawar? What about it?"

"Something happened, Captain Scott said to let you know."

Rupert reported their encounter with the Ghilzai chieftains, keeping his own heroism down to a modest mention. He could see Macnaghten relaxing as he spoke..

"Is that all?" the envoy smiled. "The Ghilzai like to bark, but they have no bite. I regret I ever started them on subsidies. It was never really necessary. You should have seen their fortress in Ghazni, my God, Jerusalem never looked so stout! When Keane blasted through those walls, every hill village heard the shots. They know what they're up against now, Mr. Oxley. After Ghazni, I don't think you'll see anyone in this country putting British arms to the test again, least of all these Hindu Kush hillsmen."

Rupert sipped at his whiskey again and ran a fingertip across moist lips. "Yet, when we entered the city…" Should he mention the men hanging from the gibbet? He lifted the now-empty glass to his lips to buy a moment of consideration.

"Speak," Macnaghten demanded uneasily.

"We saw some men hanging from gallows. It gave the ladies a start."

"Did it."

"Yes. They were wondering if a good bit of hanging goes on here. What makes it strictly necessary, so to speak. The ladies were wondering."

"The city is quite secure, Mr. Oxley. Tell them so. Scattered incidents, yes. The pretender had a sizable clan, some of them still lurk about, it's true. Incidents can happen. On top of which, Ivan isn't quite ready to concede defeat. Still, there are five fewer scoundrels this week than last, eh? Once we've rooted out the last of the ringleaders, we'll have no further trouble. Every city has its Cheapside, Lieutenant, but if you take sensible precautions, you'll find Kabul no more dangerous than London."

15

The day that Rupert Oxley arrived in Kabul, the village of Char Bagh was in something of an uproar. The men had come back from Sorkhab and the story of their trip had aroused much consternation. Women were on the move among the compounds, seeking each other out for information, gravitating gradually to a few central households where they clustered to confer. Ibrahim had called the men to the mosque for another meeting to discuss, not just Sorkhab's water grab, but this new king and his supposed tax collectors...For all the restless anxiety, however, no one suspected the day would end in tragedy.

The distraction of the grown-ups made this a happy day, however, for two small boys, Ahmad and Karim,. It meant that no one was paying attention to them. No one was scolding them for being naughty or loading them up with chores. The boys were free to do what they wanted. And so they decided to climb the steep slope west of the village that day, to a place no one else knew about, a secret cave just deep enough for two, from the mouth of which, sitting cozily side by side, the boys could take in a tremendous view. From up there, they could see that their little valley was not the whole world but just one of many valleys extending like folds of drapery from a single enormous peak. From there, the river looked like a skinny little ribbon. They could see where it entered the valley, thundering out of a narrow gorge that exhaled the mist of many unseen waterfalls. They could see how it snaked among the fields and past the tiny toys that were their own compounds.

Downstream, they could see where their valley tightened again into a narrow crack, into which the river disappeared.

Looking west, over the lip of the bowl that contained their village, they could make out another valley, much vaster and much lower. Cliffs cut them off from that country, but on a clear day, the boys could see a road down there, pounded into the earth by generations of caravans. On that road, sometimes, they could even see bands of nomads, several hundred strong, traveling along with camels and sheep beyond number, with mules and dogs and horses...

Ahmad loved the cave because the sight of the road, and the caravans, helped him to dream his dreams of traveling. Sometimes, he spent whole afternoons telling Karim about the distant cities he would visit someday, grand and glorious places such as Kabul, mysterious places like the City of Eyeballs, which figured so heavily in his mother's nighttime tales.

Karim listened patiently, never scoffing. If such stories made his friend happy, they made him happy. He, however, liked the cave for a different reason: up here a fellow could talk with a buddy about secret things not meant for adult ears. Today, he wanted to tell Ahmad about a fantastic spot he had discovered among the rocks, just above the river. You had to crawl through brush to get to it and if you lay flat on your belly, no one on the river bank could see you, but you could see—"Hey!" He nudged Ahmad. This was the good part—you could see anyone who happened to be at that spot by the river, and that spot—Karim poked his friend. again "Listen." *It was the spot where the women washed clothes.*

"Hey! Are you listening to me?" Karim nudged his friend a third time, trying to get him to appreciate the implications. There where the women washed clothes they sometimes washed *themselves* too. They rolled up their sleeves—they took off their pantaloons ... lifted their skirts—"Ahmad! Are you listening to me, boy?"

But Ahmad was not listening. "What's that?" His shallow breath rasped in and out. He pointed to the road.

Karim shaded his eyes and stared. Two rows of men in red coats were marching side by side on that distant road. "I don't know," he said finally. "Men."

"What men? Why the red coats?" Ahmad jumped to his feet and dusted off his knee-length shirt. "Come on, Karim-jan. Let's get a closer look. Coming?"

"Coming where? Ahmad, it's a two-day journey to The Road!"

"Let's climb the other side. We'll see them from the cliffs. It'll be closer. They'll be right down there."

Karim frowned. "We'd have to cross the river."

Ahmad shivered in the stiff breeze and looked up at the darkening sky. All morning, light and darkness had been wrestling each other. Clouds kept gathering to gray and then breaking into fleecy blobs again. If it rained when they were on the other side of the river, they might be in trouble. "We'll cross where it's narrow," he said. "If those men are marauders, you should warn your father. You know you should. Your father would want you to. You're not scared, are you, Karim?"

"Scared!" Karim jumped to his feet. "I'd better lead, little guy."

On the way down the slope, Karim found a couple of round stones just big enough to nestle in his palm. He slipped them into his pantaloon pockets where they swung pleasantly, like an extra set of balls, heavier than his own. How fine it would be to have balls that heavy, he thought. Did the weight of a man's balls matter when it came to Doing It? Of course, you didn't do it with your balls exactly; he'd watched couples rutting whenever he could, hidden away in certain places that only he knew about, but the people he managed to spy through chinks and cracks did their work under blankets, so you couldn't see the details. But animals had given him a more precise picture. He heard a crack of thunder, but it was far away.

Donkeys, by God, now there were some beasts with good equipment—when the time came. But before, or later, if you looked between their legs—nothing. The sun went behind a cloud and it made the wind feel colder, wetter. Karim slapped himself for warmth. Maybe a man grew like that, too, when the time came. He tried to picture himself with a rod the size of an aroused donkey's. How difficult would it be to steer such an instrument? How big was the hole, he wondered? Was it obvious where to stick it in? He wanted to quiz Ahmad on this, get his opinions, but Ahmad had hurried on ahead.

Karim ran to catch up. After all his big talk, he couldn't let the little guy go first. But Ahmad had pulled up short by the river bank, looking dismayed. The boys had waded across the river at this very spot many times in late summer, but the water was lower at that season. The swollen spring current they saw now could easily sweep them away, and if it hurled them into Needle Gorge, they'd be gone: no one got out of that gorge alive.

"We have to turn back," said Karim, secretly relieved.

"I knew *you'd* say that."

"Are you calling *me* a coward? Look at this river, you damned fool!"

"We could still get across," Ahmad insisted. "Look. See that branch sticking out? If you dropped from the end of it, onto that boulder? Then if you went jump, jump, jump—from that stone to that stone? The last bit is shallow. We could wade."

Karim studied the route, his long arms wrapped around his chest to keep himself from shivering. He didn't want Ahmad to mistake his cold for fear. "Jumping down is easy," he said, "How do we jump back?"

Ahmad moved to the edge of the river bank and examined the other shore. He could barely see it over the immense stones jammed into the current. The water crashed around the smooth boulders, splashing up billows of white and feeding a continuous spray of fine mist into the air. "We don't have to come back here," he shouted over the roar. "We won't be in a hurry later, we could follow the river back to the village. I've waded across a hundred times up there. Haven't you?"

"In summer," said Karim. "But all right. I'll go first."

He climbed the tree and scooted to the end of the branch that stuck out over the river, then slid off until he was hanging by his hands alone. He couldn't look down to see how far he would have to drop or if the surface was wet. He should have removed his sandals. It would be easier to land on a wet rock with bare feet, but he couldn't chin back up to the branch now. He had no choice but to let go. He dropped through the air, feeling spray wetting his cheek, hearing Ahmad shouting something over the roar. His feet struck the rocky surface and he crumpled to keep them from sliding out—hey, it worked!

On the river bank, Ahmad was jumping up and down in excitement.

"Take off your shoes," shouted Karim. "It's easier if you're barefoot."

"…need them on the other side…" Ahmad's voice came to him faintly.

"Throw them to me, and I'll throw them to the other bank!" But Ahmad only looked puzzled. The wind was against Karim, his voice did not carry. "Look!" He pulled off his own slippers and threw each one hard, sailing it to the far bank. Ahmad understood. He was barefoot already, a shoe in each hand. He nodded to Karim to get ready and then flung one shoe. It came end over end, but Karim caught it, turned, and sailed it onto the opposite bank. He turned, nodded, and Ahmad's second shoe made its two-step journey to the other bank.

Now Ahmad was climbing the tree. To make room for him, Karim went ahead and leapt down to the second boulder, which was easy. From there he jumped to an even lower rock and then to another, and then onto a flat stone. Now he was standing close to the current. He stuck a toe into the swirling gurgle of it—ouch! Freezing cold, by God!

Fortunately, the other bank was not far. Karim could wade the rest of the way, just as Ahmad had said, and if he moved fast, he would get to dry land before his feet froze. There was nothing to gain by waiting. He rolled up his pantaloons and stepped into the current.

Instantly, the water buffeted his thighs with such shocking force it made him reel. Karim recovered his balance just in time. Then he had to lean against the current to remain upright. He started moving with crablike caution, searching the river bottom with his toes for places where the stones were neither too jagged nor too slippery.

The cold crunched into him like a dog biting through meat and bone. He could not hurry, however, or he might stumble, and then the current would shoot him into Needle Gorge. Why had he agreed to this? Why rush to see a bunch of strangers in red coats? What did it matter who they were? He cursed Ahmad and his damned curiosity! The stones in Karim's pockets—his spare testicles—felt heavier now. He stepped forward, and his toe jammed painfully between two rocks. He was tripping. Fear spouted inside him. But even as he pitched forward, he saw that one good leap would get him close enough to the river bank to grab the bushes growing there. He leapt forward, reaching—weeds came into his clutch, and he hung on. The current dragged at his feet, but he pulled himself painfully toward shore until he had his footing again.

He turned to tell Ahmad not to try it, this was too dangerous, but Ahmad had just dropped onto that first boulder, from which point there was no going back. A lump filled Karim's throat. If only he could light a fire. He sat halfway up the bank, shivering in the river's frigid breath. Rubbing his shins and feet didn't help much: his hands were wet.

Ahmad made it to the third boulder. Two more to go and he could start wading. Karim rubbed his skin furiously, trying to get his blood moving again. The men in red must have reached the foot of the cliffs by now and would soon pass out of sight. Crossing this accursed river had been for nothing.

Ahmad negotiated the next jump perfectly, his skinny little body swaying for a moment when he landed. He had a lithe little frame, Karim was thinking. A good-looking boy. He pictured stroking Ahmad's lean legs.

Now, Ahmad was letting himself down into the water. He had not rolled his pantaloons quite high enough. The water licked and lapped at the fabric, and he shouted a little cry of merriment mixed with alarm. "Wai! Fuck this river in the asshole! It's pure ice!"

"Hurry," Karim yelped. "The longer you wait, the colder you get."

He should look for something to hold out to Ahmad, he thought, something his friend could grab when he came close enough. He found a dead tree branch with leaves still clinging to its finger-like ends. He dislodged it, and turned to the river just in time to see Ahmad lose his balance right where Karim had slipped. Down he went. He actually disappeared under the water. Disappeared! Then his ball of a head bobbed back up, but the current instantly carried him off.

It would have ended right there, if Karim had lost his head, but he didn't lose his head, he didn't even hesitate. He thrust that branch out with lightning bolt speed. Ahmad's flailing arms got tangled in it and he clutched. His body whipped around, his head knocking hard against a rock barely sticking out of the water. His sudden weight nearly pulled Karim into the water. The older boy braced and held on, pleading to dear

God for help, straining against the river current, staring into his friend's eyes. Then, his desperation won out and he dragged Ahmad closer and closer until the lad could grab handfuls of the same shrubbery that had saved Karim. Crying and coughing water, he crawled onto the muddy shore.

Karim fell to his knees and began massaging his friend's icy limbs with his own frigid hands. Ahmad's clothes were soaked right to his chin. Even his hair was wet. Even his eyebrows were dripping. His eyes had a bulging stare to them. His skull showed a bulge too, where his head had hit the rock. Karim's chest fluttered. He had to get Ahmad warm somehow, the boy was going stiff before his very eyes. He pulled at Ahmad's hands. "Come on, *jan-im*. Get up, let's go. Can you walk?"

Ahmad shook droplets out of his hair. "Did we miss the men?"

"Yes, buddy. They're gone. Too late. We have to head home. You're cold."

"We should gather some pine nuts!" Ahmad chattered. "Nana wanted us to gather some pine nuts today."

"We'll get them tomorrow. We have to get you warm."

"I can walk," Ahmad insisted, though his face looked blue.

Karim put his arm around Ahmad and helped him uphill to where the sun was still shining. They walked upstream in silence, both of them knowing they would have to get back in the water eventually to cross the river and neither of them wanting to talk or think about it.

Then Ahmad began to lope. "That's good," Karim applauded. "Run, my boy. I bet I can beat you to that tree. Want to race? Whoever wins gives the other a head rub."

He himself broke into a gallop and for a moment exulted in the freedom of his young limbs, but he beat Ahmad to the tree too easily, and when he looked back, he saw his friend moving slowly, looking sick. "Dearest!" he wailed, rushing back. "What is it? What's wrong?"

"I'm cold," Ahmad grunted. His whole body was trembling. And then, God be praised, Karim spotted a man with a donkey in the distance. He jumped up and down, waving his arms. "*Allahu Akbar!*" was all he could think to say, shrieking the words like an *azaan*.

"Allaaaaaaaaahu Akbar!" The donkey stopped and the man craned his head.

"Help!" Karim shouted. The man started toward them, and Karim recognized the disreputable barber's even more disreputable brother; but this was no time to be choosy. He gladly let the man load Ahmad onto his donkey and shambled along behind them on foot until they reached the water's edge, where he climbed on too. The donkey carried all three riders across the river. They arrived in Char Bagh just as the sun was setting.

Ahmad's mother was standing in the doorway of her compound, waiting for her son. When she saw him slumped on the back end of a donkey, she let out a cry and rushed to grab him, just as he was slipping off. She helped him totter into his compound. "What's the matter with you?" Then she turned on Abdul Karim. "What did you do to him?"

"Nothing," Karim said guiltily. "He fell in the river. He's the one who wanted to cross. I didn't do it. I didn't do nothing. It wasn't my fault."

But Karim already knew he was going to get a whipping for this one, and in truth he wanted a whipping, because this *was* his fault, somehow. He didn't know how, but he knew he would be told. Before or after his whipping, he would be told exactly how he was to blame for this.

16

Soraya brought her son indoors and marched him to the room behind the kitchen. A flue carrying hot smoke from the bread oven to the chimney passed directly under this floor. She changed her son into his only other clothes, the festival outfit she kept in her special chest with her jewels and finery. At least they were clean and dry. She piled a blanket on top of him and lay down to give him the heat of her body. Soraya never knew a living human being could feel so shockingly cold. All night she pressed against him, but she couldn't seem to get him warm. By the following afternoon, his forehead felt hot to the touch, and yet he kept shivering. Another day passed and he stopped eating. She was dimly aware of Ibrahim flittering about, uselessly asking how the boy was. Soraya told him to go away and he went away, flustered and helpless. When she looked at Ahmad again, his eyes had a glazed look. In her mind, she saw a group of men lowering Ahmad into his grave. The image was so vivid, she let out a cry, but no one came, because she had told them all to go away.

After dark, Khadija peeped in. "Soraya-jan? How is he?"

"He's sleeping," Soraya snapped. She held this against Khadija. She didn't know how Khadija could be held to blame, but she didn't want to hear excuses. She blamed Karim as well, because the boys were together when this awful thing happened. She knew almost nothing about the accident because Ahmad had said nothing yet, but Karim was older, he should have known better. His father was probably giving him a beating right now, breaking stout, solid sticks on his legs, his arms, his buttocks—good. He deserved it. Let him yelp. Nothing he suffered could equal what she was suffering, lying next to her son, waiting for him to come out of his fearful lethargy.

Khadija came all the way into the room. "I brought some broth and tea. Do you think we should wake him and get him to eat something?"

"Wake him! When he's finally getting some sleep?"

Khadija shrank back in deference. "You know best."

Soraya looked up. She beamed hatred at her sister-in-law. Khadija had always wanted Ahmad to die so that neither of them would have a son and they'd be even and she could move in on Ibrahim. Yes, yes, Soraya saw it all! Unable to bear a child herself, Khadija resented her for giving Ibrahim his heir. With her own husband dead and gone, she must be brimming with spite, this barren widow. Her ill wishes had probably caught Satan's eye and brought on this catastrophe. Who could tell what damage a hating heart might do?

"Take those things away," Soraya seethed, but her voice broke before she got the last words out, and she started to cry. This was so awful. She wanted help, she wanted comfort, the comfort that only Khadija could give her, and now she'd gone and forfeited all right to her sister-in-law's love. Oh that she could take back that bolt of wordless hatred she had fired.

Khadija settled next to her. "Dinner is ready Why don't you go eat? I'll watch him for a few minutes."

"I can't," Soraya moaned. "I can't leave him. I have to stay beside him."

"Stay then," Khadija murmured, squeezing the frail woman's bony shoulder, "but you need to eat. Why don't you have this broth I brought for Ahmad-jan? I'll get some bread for you too, and I'll keep the rest of the broth on the coals so it will be hot when he wakes up, okay, Soraya-jan? You eat now. Keep up your strength. Ahmad will be well, *inshallah*. He will be up and singing songs tomorrow, may God grant it. We put our faith in Allah."

"You're so good to me," Soraya sighed, her voice laced with shame. "I don't deserve your kindness, Khadija-jan. Leave the broth, I'll have a little."

But Ahmad did not improve the next day. His bright, black eyes turned dull and acquired a film. His forehead went from warm to hot, and when he coughed, his lips ended up flecked with blood. The itinerant barber happened to be in town, and he prescribed a tea made of sour clover. Now at last, Soraya agreed to leave her son's side. She veiled herself in her *chadari* for safety, even though the barber would be with her. Together, they went past the outermost fields of the village and up the northern slopes to gather the herb. Picking and climbing, picking and climbing, they came within sight of the malang. The barber called to him. "Salaam aleikum, Malang-sahib."

"Waleikum a'salaam," the other replied from his perch. "How are you two?"

"May you live long, Malang-sahib, the world flows by. Allah is great."

The malang nodded and watched without comment as they worked. Under the vagabond's gaze, the barber straightened up self-consciously. "This woman's little boy has fallen ill, sahib. He fell in the river and now he has a fever. He got knocked about a little too. His head... I'm thinking she should make him some clover tea. Do you agree?"

The malang nodded.

"Do you know about herbs and such, Malang-sahib? What is your advice?" The malang bobbed his head slowly. "Give the boy plenty of hot broth," he said. "Boil a lamb bone rich with marrow. Wipe his brow with a cool cloth when he sweats. Keep him covered with a light cloth. Say your prayers at all the appointed times, do not miss a one and say some extra ones besides. God knows what is best. Trust in His mercy. He makes the wheat to grow and the leaves to fall. He makes the seasons turn. Every year he buries the world in winter, every year he makes spring rise up again. We are all mortal. Nothing lasts but Allah. Yield to his will and await his mercy."

The barber and Soraya made their way back to the village thoughtfully and silently. The boy sipped the sour clover tea listlessly, but his forehead remained hot to the touch. The lamb broth seemed to give him a few hours of peace and he fell asleep, the rattle in his breath diminishing.

Then sweat began to bead up on his forehead again. He tossed under the light cloth Soraya threw over him in obedience to the Malang's instructions. The sweat turned cold and the boy began to shiver. He clutched her hands and buried his face in her lap. "Mama?" he whimpered, "I'm so cold. Mama?" His words came out through clattering teeth. The night was dark but warm, oh so warm How could he feel cold? It was almost summer now. Next door, the oven blazed away: Soraya had ordered that it stay lit. Even the air coming through the open window felt like the oven's hot breath to Soraya. The malang had said only a light cloth, only a light cloth, but her darling boy was shivering. She must obey his body's needs. She fetched out a heavy cotton-padded blanket and gently spread it over him. The next day he lay still, but when darkness fell, his fever rose again. Soraya lost track of the hours and the days. People came in and out of the room like figures in a dream, offering advice, murmuring consolation. Soraya hugged the boy to herself and whispered all the Quran she knew, and blew her healing breath onto his body, the breath that always made him and other children feel better when they had a scratch or a bee sting, but her breath had no healing power now. This was not a scratch. This was not a bee sting. In the late hours of that moonless night, when the misty Trail of Straw glowed across a sky powdered with stars, her boy released his soul to heaven. Oh, it wasn't fair! Her beautiful, beloved boy! His young body so full of promise. His head so full of dreams. Her boy who shone among all the boys, his father's pride, a future leader among the men of the village, the carrier of the family name. Gone. Gone, gone, gone, he was gone, and he took the very life force from Soraya's body when he left. A sob came out of her, and another, and another. Then she gave herself over to howling, and the sleepers rose from their huddled clumps in this room and that room and the other room—they all came rushing to the mother to gape at the source of her misery and to comfort her with hugging arms and to stroke soothing fingers over her cloth-covered hair, but it seemed to her that nothing could ever soothe the anguish blazing in her heart. She cried herself dry as night bled into morning and went on crying until the sun lit up the pale features of her dead son.

17

The men took Ahmad's little body to the grave, while the women gathered in Soraya's compound to mourn. Every woman in the village came. They filled the houses and hallways, the pounded-dirt verandas and the yard. They wailed so loudly that donkeys began to bray throughout the village and dogs to howl in sympathy.

The men gathered in the mosque for pre-burial ceremonies. His dear little body was placed on the dais at the front of the room, covered with a green cloth on which inscriptions from the Quran had been intricately embroidered in gold thread by women who didn't know how to read but merely transcribed shapes from a page with such scrupulous care that not a single diacritical dot was out of place. Under the cloth his body seemed impossibly small. Another whole body could have fit on that dais with him. In death, he seemed no bigger than a cat.

Ibrahim stood in the front row. The men lined up on either side of him and when the line stretched from wall to wall of that rude mosque, they began to form a second line behind the first, and a third line behind the second one and still people kept crowding in until there were seven rows in all and half of an eighth row; but no one wanted to be part of an incomplete row so the men jostled to get into the next row forward, and each row shuffled apart to accommodate more men, until at last they formed just seven tightly-compacted rows of men standing with shoulders touching.

Mullah Yaqub began the funeral prayer, lifting his thumbs to his earlobes and mournfully chanting out "Allahu Akbar!" His voice twanged out the Arabic syllables. All seven rows of men moved as one, bending at the waist and supporting themselves with their hands on their knees, letting the sacred sounds sweep over them. Ibrahim spoke the syllables quietly under his breath in unison with the mullah, craving some comfort from the divine syllables, some relief from pain, but his throat kept trembling. He remembered this sensation from his childhood; it meant tears were coming up. Oh, if ever there was a time for tears, this was it, but not during prayer. He should hold them back at least until the procession to the graveyard. The men stood up, and he felt his own body straightening as if connected to the others. They all went down to their knees, prostrating themselves before the observant gaze of God, and Ibrahim tried to feel Allah's compassion but could not. This merciful God had just snatched away his only son. This God had ended all his hopes. His son dead, his wife a wreck dissolving into madness—she would never bear another child. He could feel it already. Something was wrong with Soraya. He had always known it. Her sensibilities were too delicate for this world. The loss of her son was going to unhinge her. She would let go of all worldly duties and sink into a morass of lamentation. He had heard of such things. In his father's generation, it happened to a woman of Haidar's clan. Allahu Akbar. God is great. Oh, God is great.

Stand up, he whispered to himself. The time had come. The four men appointed to the task lifted the wooden slab that bore his son's body. The others parted to let them through and then formed a tattered line that followed them out the door and down the steps of the mosque and into the gray light. The sky was filled with clouds. The valley had a deathly stillness to it. The men marched solemnly up to the graveyard. They could hear the lamentations of the women from Ibrahim's compound, piercing the morning air, mingling with the squawking of crows circling above the marsh on the other side of the river.

The men made their way over a rise in the path and down a short incline to the graveyard. Ibrahim was breathing hard. The short climb had stolen his breath, but only because his chest was so tight, he could scarcely breathe to begin with. They passed his brother's headstone, and then his father's. Crocuses had sprung up on his father's grave, he noticed. The hole in which his son would be buried had already been dug. The men set the burial slab on the mound of soil and formed up at either end, then seized the ropes and lifted the board up, one of them unnecessarily saying, "Y'allah," as if to muster the men's energy—unnecessary because the board was so light, the dead boy being so very small. Why did this innocent boy have to give up his soul at such an age? Ibrahim remembered all the times the boy had pestered him with questions about his travels to Mecca, what he had seen in all those distant cities …He had given him short answers, turned him out of the room, told him to go pester his mother. He thought of the one time he had broken a stick on his son's outstretched palm to punish him for losing a bucket into the well. Biting his lips, he wished he could have his boy back just long enough to tell him he had punished him out of love, that he loved him even as he beat him, that he took pride in him for growing up so curious…

The boy was lowered into the Earth's heart. The men separated into two masses, just to make room for Ibrahim. The time had come for each one to drop three fistfuls of dirt onto the boy's shroud. And with the first fistful to utter the Arab syllables that meant, "from dust you have given us human form," and with the second to say, "unto dust you will resolve us again," and with the third to say, "and out of dust again, yours is the power to resurrect us." And when Ibrahim had finished he muttered quietly to himself, "Forgive him oh Lord of the universe."

He moved to the other side of the grave and his cousin took his place. Now men were picking up fistfuls of dirt on all side of the grave and flinging them into the hole in showers of gray-brown soil.

And then Ibrahim sensed a hubbub among the men on the other side of the grave. He peered past the men and saw a solitary figure making its way down the mountain slope—the malang was coming.

Wrapped in his tattered cloak, gazing straight ahead and never at his feet, the malang picked his way steadily among rocks, down a pathless slope, approaching the cemetery from above. With stately grace, he moved directly to the open grave, and those who stood between him and the pit moved aside spontaneously to clear the way. At the edge of the grave, the malang stopped and drew himself up to his full height. He tossed his head back, closed his eyes, and began to recite Quran. His melodic voice rolled across the valley, sounding more like a chorus than a single voice, sounding like a whole plangent chorus. The crows stopped cawing and the keening of the women stopped.

The malang sang for long minutes and whatever had been rustling and stirring when he started, faded into silence. The men around the grave began to sway in time to the malang's incantatory voice. Then abruptly he stopped chanting and crouched beside the grave. He took a fistful of moist soil and dropped it in. He looked up at the men, spoke the ritual Arabic lines, but then went on to say in Farsi, in their own familiar tongue, "Tell us, where have all the great kings gone, with all their knights and courtiers? Gone into the belly of the Earth to mingle with the meanest of their subjects and the greatest of their ancestors!" He clutched another fistful of dirt and sprinkled it into the grave. Again he chanted in Arabic and then switched to Farsi. "Tell me! Why are the mothers weeping? They are weeping because their children have died and because the children who survive will also die and because all will die and mingle with this soil which is our heart and home."

He tossed a final fistful of dirt into the grave. Then he stood up and raised his arms in supplication, facing west toward Mecca. "Oh, Allah, my darling compassionate God! Oh, my beloved! Cherish this brother, this son, this treasure of his parents' hearts. Accept him into your grace and splendor. Accept our prayers and deeds on his behalf, our loving remembrances. We honor him and through him we honor You. We love him and through him we love You. We surrender to your will, Almighty God. In your boundless generosity You know best for all of us. We say farewell to our beloved Ahmad-jan, but we will see him in the river flowing past our homes, and we will see him in the wheat lifting its green face out of the soil by the millions this spring, and we will see him in our hearts as we see You in our hearts, Allah, when we see the air and the earth and the sky. We will see him as we see You in all things and in our own hearts, forever may we sing Your praises."

Ibrahim had closed his eyes and given himself over to such weeping during this recitation that now when the malang's voice stopped he could not remember where he was. He opened his eyes, aware of a strange snuffling sound all around him. Opened his eyes to find himself among the hundred and thirty men and boys of the village, all weeping uncontrollably.

But that was not what startled him and lifted his heart into some other realm. No, what astonished him was the fact that the sun was shining. When he closed his eyes the day had been impenetrably gray. Now, sunshine was gleaming off every leaf and rock.

Then a wind began to blow. Above him, fleecy, gray, bulbous, chunky, edible-looking clouds floated across a blue surface, chased by this sudden inexplicable wind. And with the sun still shining over much of the valley, with the sun still gleaming on the distant compounds from which the wails of the women once again rose to bird-like pitch, rain began to fall on the graveyard. As far as the men could tell, it was falling nowhere in the world except on that graveyard. The men turned about in place, holding their hands out in wonder, tasting rain on their lips, the big heavy sweet-flavored drops of water, and they looked at one another, and they looked in wonder at the malang—but he was no longer among them. High up above them on the slope, they could see him pursuing his solitary way back toward his chosen perch, on top of the hut the village of Char Bagh had built for him, against the gray wall of Baba's Nose.

18

The mourning died away finally. The communal readings of the Quran ended. The last sheep was slaughtered and roasted in a pit oven and the meat sliced off and served with rice from vats as big as horses, to all the people of the village, and the poorest ate till their stomachs groaned. For three days, no one went hungry and for three days everyone wailed. The women gave their condolences to Soraya and the men to Ibrahim, and those who could not get close to either parent consoled Khadija or old step-uncle Agha Lala or the cousins next door, or any close relative they could find.

The malang's appearance at the gravesite had left all of Char Bagh drenched in awe. Along with stories about Ahmad and his cheerful nine years of mischief, those who witnessed the event recounted what they had seen and felt. Those who heard their stories passed them on with embellishments. The legend of the malang's appearance at Ahmad's grave permeated upstream to Sorkhab and beyond. Womenfolk wove it in with other stories commonly told and retold, stories for example about the famous funeral of Ibrahim's father, where certain disturbances in the weather had also been observed—although nothing like this time!—and tales from the *Shahnama*, the Book of Kings.

"He raised his hands, and the sun turned dim," people said. "When he began to sing, the rain started falling. It watered the grave like a river. The malang has power, they say, power over wind and water and sun."

When such stories were told, people gazed up toward the gray prominence of Baba's Nose, searching among the featureless shrubs and rocks for that solitary figure. He was most often seen on the roof of his hut, just sitting there cross-legged, a speck in the hazy blue distance.

Finally, the stories gave way to everyday life. Work had to be done, chores had to be picked up again. Bread had to be made, the fields urgently needed plowing. Ibrahim took his buffalo out and dragged his iron-tipped plow across one of his wheat fields but he could not keep going. By mid-afternoon, his body felt bruised, though he knew it was really his spirit that hurt. Plowing felt pointless, now that he had no son. For whom was he growing these crops? If he were to plant a row of almond trees now, as he had been thinking of doing, who would harvest those nuts? Someone else's son, after he was dead. Asad, his foolish cousin, had six sons, each stupider than the next, all as healthy as bulls, and likely to multiply. In two generations, Ibrahim would be forgotten, while the progeny of Asad or Ghulam Dastagir filled the village.

Ibrahim unstrapped his buffalos, loaded his plow, and drove his animals back to his compound. Khadija took charge of them at the gate and led them to the stables, while he headed upstairs without a word to seek the comfort of poetry. In the grim aftermath of his son's demise, he needed strong poetry. He sat staring at the page, but his eyes refused to take in the words. His son's face kept interposing, and then his mind was drawn back into his dreams and memories, back to his own boyhood and his father's hopes for him and his brother. The great man had only two sons, although he himself had been one of eight boys. The surviving uncles all had sons, but in his father's line the male seed had run thin. His brother had spawned no children at all, and out of Ibrahim's loins had issued only Ahmad and the three girls.

Well, God was merciful, and he was still young. He remembered his fruitless search for gray hair in his beard and the memory brought a sad grin to his lips. Being a young man with a younger wife had a good side to it after all: he could spawn more children. God was merciful, God would not let Ibrahim grow old and die without an heir. God would grant him another son.

The door creaked. He looked up to see his wife's tear-stained face and grief-swollen eyes. She came without a word, slouching like a beaten dog, her shoulders humped with defeat. Whatever his own grief, Ibrahim felt keenly how much more his wife was suffering. The day after Ahmad's death, some of the clan worried that she might do herself an injury. She tore her hair so violently, she thrashed her body against the unyielding floor, she flung herself against the walls. No one had seen her this way except when the eerie invisible *djinns* took possession of her body. She broke pottery, she screamed, she reeled next to the oven, and her sister-in-law Khadija had to grab her wrist to keep her from falling into the pit and roasting alive.

Now, she was subdued. Along with the wet, bleak distance in her eyes, Ibrahim saw something else, a clench to her that stretched her lips even thinner. Maybe this was a good sign. His wife looked wounded but alive at least, more alive than she had been at any time since Ahmad died.

She settled next to her husband on the mattress pad and rocked in place. He left her alone and tried to read his book. She wanted his company, he supposed, yet he felt no desire to share his thoughts or to give her any warmth. He wished she would go away. Worse, he detected in himself a desire that Khadija be in her place. Khadija to whom he could blurt, "W'Allah, the hurting won't stop." If he said this to Khadija, she would say something like "Hajji-sahib, we feel your sorrow, but we all need your strength now. You have other children. You are father to us all."

Soraya was too weak herself to prop his emotions. If he tried to lean on her, he might crush her. He glanced her way and found her gray-green eyes on him.

"Hajji?" Strange that she should use his honorific.

"Soraya-jan," he murmured. "How do you fare?"

"Hajji, I want to say something."

"Speak, my dear. What do you want? Anything you desire shall be yours."

"I don't want to make you angry," she whimpered.

"How could you make me angry? Heart of my heart, what do you need? Tell me. I am not just malik of the village, you know. I am your husband too. I know what Allah requires of me, Soraya. I want to end your suffering. If only I could! I feel it too, you know. My wife, my dear wife, my heart is not made of stone. I miss our son too!"

She began to cry, and the tears began flowing from him as well. He bowed his head and bit his lips, and felt his shoulders shaking, and he held himself as still as possible, trying to contain his grief. His wife made no attempt to restrain hers. She let them pour, and as she wept, she crept ever closer to him, until she was huddled directly against him like a baby animal against its mother's pelt, and he thought, this would do, this was permissible, no shame in this, she was his wife and he, her husband; let her look to him for what shelter and affection he could provide—no shame in this at all. Hesitantly he put his arm around her body. His own tears had dried, and he merely held his wife until her sobs died away. Finally she recovered herself enough to say, "I want to talk about that day."

"Yes, my dear, talk, of course. But you know, God has taken his dear soul from us. Perhaps it's time we move our thoughts to other days…days to come. We still have those."

"I mean the day we buried him."

"Oh," he said. "That day? What about it?"

"When the malang came down to the village? They tell so many stories. They say the skies opened up. They say the malang waved his arms and the rain started falling. They say Ahmad was seen—he was *seen*, people say. Rising out of the soil, and then…"

"And then?" Ibrahim felt breathless. "What do they say?"

"They say he was sitting on the malang's shoulders with an angel holding each of his arms. Is it true? Is it *true?* You were there."

Ibrahim thought about her question. "I don't know," he said finally. "My eyes were shut at the time, but that's not the important thing, Soraya-jan. Something happened that day, that's the important thing. That part is true. God was certainly there."

"You felt something." She seized on this eagerly. "Yes! That's what I mean! That's what they're saying. The malang blessed our boy and in death, Ahmad was chosen. He will lift this village, isn't it so? People will come to his grave to pray. Don't you think?"

"Yes they will, my little one." Ibrahim told her sweetly, sadly.

"Hajji-sahib. Ibrahim-jan. Oh, my husband." She clutched his arm entreatingly.

"What?" Her sudden intensity alarmed him. Never far from madness, this woman. He was always watching for the signs. Now, her eyes had the glisten that he feared.

"The malang must not leave Char Bagh. See to it! See that he never does—make sure of it . You have the power—make *sure* of it. You're the malik. What is your duty if not to keep the malang in Char Bagh?"

"What more can I do, sugar cube? He's already chosen us. What are you saying?"

"He sits above our village, yes. But Sorkhab wants him! They want him, and they have ways to draw him away. They will build a mosque for him. Yes! That's what they'll do. They're big, they have money. They sell flax seed oil to the nomads."

"The malang can't be drawn away with money. Are you joking with me?"

"Don't laugh," she cried out. "It's not a laughing matter. They will steal our malang. You mustn't let them. You mustn't let anyone take our malang. You can't!"

Spittle shone on her lips. Her hair had come undone, and she was thrashing her head wildly back and forth as she spoke, beginning that side-to-side flinging motion of hers. In another moment, she would be hurling herself against the walls, trying to break her own bones. She had broken her own bones this way before. The malik made a grab at her arm, but he couldn't catch it.

"Do you think I'm crazy?" she shrieked. "Do you think I'm the one who needs care? You're the crazy one, if you don't bind this man of God to our village."

"How?" he yelled back, shaking her.

Her body went limp. Her madness had fled from her as quickly as a wild cat bolts from a house. "You know how," she said. "You just don't want to say it. But I'll say it. I will say it out loud. The malang needs a wife. Give him a wife."

"You want *me* to give him—?"

"Who else? Yes! You! Give him a wife."

Suddenly he knew what she was asking. He stared into her eyes, and she stared right back. No calculation showed in her gaze, no madness, just determination: a determination to hold her position and let no one budge her from it.

"Give him your sister-in-law," she said.

She knew his secret. She knew what he felt for Khadija. Here she stood, on the edge of madness, her delicate sanity a knife at his throat. He must acquiesce or see her fling herself into darkness. And at that same despairing moment, he knew something else: Soraya was right. Marrying Khadija would tie the malang to the village irrevocably. But did the malang want a wife? Would he marry Khadija? And if he did, how could Ibrahim let her go?

"I'll talk to her," he said to Soraya, his voice dull. "I'll see what she says."

"See what she says? Who cares what she says? Don't ask her, tell her! She's your dependent. What choice does she have in this? You're the lord of this household, you own her!"

"I will talk to her," Ibrahim repeated firmly. "If she consents, we'll see. I will not act without her consent, Soraya. I owe my brother that much."

"Your brother! This has nothing to do with your brother," she cried out. "You're the one—"

He clapped his hand over her mouth, muffling her next words so fiercely he felt her teeth against his palm. "I will not hear slander in this house," he growled.

Her eyes stared at him, white and fearful but unblinking. He let her go, and she wiped her lips. "All right," she said. "Talk to her in your own way, then. You know best."

19

Khadija spiked her long-handled fork into the heap of dried alfalfa and lifted as much as she could into the stall for the household's two cows to grind on. A shadow cut off the light from the doorway, and she heard Ibrahim murmur, "Khadija-jan."

She looked over her shoulder and felt his eyes sliding down her body. His gaze was like a hand. She set her pitchfork down, pushed the pail away, and turned to him. His grief was still so fresh. It thrilled her that he kept coming to her in this state. He had not even bothered to wipe the wet away from his eyes this time before seeking her out in this stable.

"Ibrahim-jan," she responded tenderly.

"What are you doing?"

He knew what she was doing. She did the same chores every day. Animals needed to be fed, even if the malik had lost his only heir. The cows didn't know about such things. They lowed and munched and gave milk, but only if someone tended them.

"Just, the work, my dear. Grieve till you're done. Grieve. Your own Khadija will keep the household going in this time of your sorrow."

He bowed his head. "You are the pillar of this compound, Khadija-jan. Listen, I want to talk to you about something. The welfare of the village is at stake. Come to me, upstairs when you are finished with your work. It's a serious matter and we must be of one mind about it, you and I."

Her heart dropped. He was planning to take a second wife. A second wife was a serious matter. She disrupted the balance of a household, set off a power struggle, and forced a rearrangement of the household hierarchy, and yet he might feel he had to look for one at this point to maximize his chances of producing an heir. And so it wasn't going to be her. He couldn't possibly marry a barren woman after burying his only son. Oh God, he was going to ask her for advice. He was going to ask her who he should go after. He might even ask her to go courting for him, do the *talabgari*. What could she possibly tell him? How could she pretend to advise him when her own heart would be breaking?

She wiped her hands on her skirts, conscious of her palms pressing against her thighs, conscious of his eyes traveling down to watch that pressure. Then his gaze lifted quickly to her face. At that moment, she knew she would never be his concubine. His sense of honor was too wounded and too strict. He had his uneasy relationship with God, which no one knew about and which only she, of all his kin and fellow villagers, could understand. On top of that, he doubted his own worth. The best man she had ever known doubted his own worth. That, more than anything, was what endeared him to her. That, more than anything made her long to be his wife. She alone, of all the women in the valley, could make him shine in his own eyes. No other woman could give him what he needed. If only he would risk everything and take what only she could give him.

She nodded. "Go upstairs," she said. "I will come to you before *namaz.*"

೮೦೦೪

He was leaning against his brocaded pillow, one hand on his knee, looking contemplative, and unbearably sad, but he brightened at the sight of her. "Ah, there you are, Khadija-jan. Come sit with me. Soraya is downstairs, keeping the others busy with dinner and chores. No one will disturb us. We must talk openly, dear sister-in-law."

"Yes, Hajji-sahib. About what?"

"You have been to see the malang, Soraya tells me. You led a group of women up there one day?"

Her heart pitt-a-patted against her ribs. "Was that wrong, Malik-sahib?"

"Not at all. But you know what the malang means to the village and... to me."

"He's important to us all."

Ibrahim nodded. "It isn't just what he said that day, Khadija-jan. I regard him as my sheikh, you know. I regard him as my father, my brother, my friend, and my guide. Someday all the world will see him as I do."

"I see," she murmured, disquieted by his passion.

"Why do you suppose I tell you this?"

"I am only a woman, Hajji-sahib. Explain it to me. I don't know."

"Let me ask another question. The day you women went up to see the malang, who else came there?"

Khadija frowned. "Some men from Sorkhab. Why do you ask? Oh, not at my invitation, Hajji! Is that what you think? It wasn't me! I scolded them, I warned them, I cursed them. Is this why you wanted to see me? You think I am conspiring with Sorkhab? I would never—"

"No," he assured her. "I have never doubted your allegiance. To me."

He gazed directly into her eyes and with that gaze he melted her very bones. Her body was desire, yearning toward his arms. "To you," she whispered. "Yes, Ibrahim-jan. Everything I do, I do to make your life sweeter. My allegiance is to you."

He cleared his throat awkwardly, pulling back. "And I am the malik of Char Bagh. Everything I can do to protect this village, I must do. We are of one mind on this. Yes?"

"Yes," she agreed, puzzled.

He leaned forward. "Khadija-jan, what did you think of the malang? Did you like him?"

She smiled. "Yes, of course. He tugs on every heart. Why do you ask?"

"As a man, I mean. Could you serve him as you would serve me? Can you—"

"What?" Her pulse suddenly went ragged. "What do you mean?" Suspicion opened up inside her like an infected sore. "Is this Soraya's idea?"

"It doesn't matter what Soraya wants. It's just you and me now, Khadija. It is I who am asking you. Tell me what you think about our dear malang. I must know."

She half rose on her haunches, despair writhing in her heart. How had she failed to foresee this diabolical move by Soraya? "Malik-sahib, what are you asking of me?"

"If he marries from among us, he will never leave us," said Ibrahim. "I am asking you to serve this village as you would serve Allah, Khadija. It lies in your power to ensure that Char Bagh enjoys this holy man's favor and protection to the end of his days. I am asking you to bind him to our village, so he will never move to Sorkhab or—God forbid—leave this valley of ours altogether."

"And so?" she uttered aggressively. "To put it plainly?" she said fiercely. "When all is spoken and done with? What are you asking? *Put it in plain words!* You are asking me to …what? Say it! Say it!" she hissed.

"Khadija-jan." The malik took a breath and closed his eyes. When he opened them again, he looked away slightly. "I want your blessing to offer malang-sahib a wife from our village. And I am asking you to be that wife."

In the awful silence that followed these words, in the awful stillness that pressed against the walls of the room like the air inside a balloon, Khadija found suddenly that even here, so deep in the compound, she could hear the frogs croaking by the river.

Despite her fiercest intentions, tears swelled in her eyes and her head swayed from side to side, her rebellious body's lamentation for herself and for all the helpless widows in this world, doomed to do what they must. "I was your brother's wife," she whispered. "Your brother whom you cherished and revered. I was the malik's wife," she pleaded, "presiding over this whole compound, east and west."

"I know, my dearest sister-in-law—"

"All the women looked up to me! I was somebody. And now you say I must—"

"I plead with you," he broke in. "I never said 'you must.' I entreat you. I have spoken to no one else yet, and I will speak to no one unless you say yes! Khadija, appreciate how I am respecting you."

"And after your brother died and you rose to occupy his place," she pursued relentlessly, "you looked to *me* for counsel and comfort, came to *me* when you needed someone to hear your woes and weigh your thoughts. You have a woman of your own, but you came to me. I know you, Ibrahim, you opened your heart to me, I know you, and you know me. I have felt your eyes upon me. Never deny it. Between us, there have been…"

"Khadija-jan," he cautioned.

"Feelings," she said. "Between us there have been—"

"Khadija!" His voice cracked out.

It slapped her out of her trance. How could she have forgotten herself enough to say such words to him? She had come so close to saying she had hoped to be his wife. Or worse. That she would be his concubine, if it was the only way. She wanted to say those words to him. Must they remain unspoken forever? All her soul longed to say it. Your concubine. *Ibrahim jan-i-qund-i-gulim.* My-dear-my-sweet-my-flower. Take me!

She clenched her jaw to keep the hurt from showing, and when she spoke, her lips did not tremble. Silence would have been safest, but she had to speak, she had more to say, and he needed to hear it. "Now you would send me to the hills to live with this malang and keep him as my husband. I am to live with him in a hut no bigger than an outhouse. I am to wear rags and wake up sleeping on dirt and see the village children come to taunt me. *He's* a malang, *he* can live that way! But me—"

He reared his hand as if to slap, his eyes sternly full of might. "Stop it, stop whimpering, woman. Don't you even understand what I'm offering? Wallowing in dust? He's no wallower-in-dust, our malang. He's a scholar, a poet, a mystic master—a sheikh! *My* sheikh! The only man I will ever meet who truly *knows*! Mud hut, you say? Curse you, Khadija, listen! I'm going to offer him half of my land. Half of everything I own! Now do you see? By Quran, with God's grace, I'll find a way to rescue all of my brother's land from debt and you'll bring *that* to your marriage too! Your husband will be the first man of the village, above me even, above Ghulam Dastagir and Ghulam Haidar and the rest. And I will rally them to build a compound bigger than this one for Malang-sahib. If Sorkhab can add buildings, so can we. Your husband will rival any man in the valley, your status will be unquestioned, *that's* what I offer you. Do not ask what I'm giving up in asking you to do this, Khadija. I would give up Samarqand and Bokhara for just—but we can't talk of that. Only tell me you're willing. I must hear it from your own lips. I will not put this proposal to the malang unless you tell me you'll go to him gladly, contented and full of joy. Will you do this? Look at me. No, don't drop your head like that, look at me! Will you do this?"

She raised wounded eyes to his, and her heart broke as she released her grip on all the life she had imagined for herself, let it slip away like a stream into a river. Her mind reeled with anxious dread and then she embraced the dark unknown of all the universe and said to her brother-in-law: "Yes, Ibrahim. My darling. If he wants me, tell him I will be his willing wife, and I will be contented with him and full of joy, because you command it. I will do it for you."

20

The malang stood outside his hut awaiting the men of Char Bagh. Ibrahim led his group forward, arms extended. "Sheikh-sahib, we come to express our gratitude."

"For what?" the mystic asked idly.

Ibrahim glanced at the others, but saw no guidance there. "You have elevated our village," he declared. "We cherish you, friend of God. End your wandering, settle among us, we beg of you. We embrace you as our own. Accept from us a gift of land."

The mystic turned about and looked in each direction. He held his hands up in the attitude of prayer and stood silent for a time. Then he faced the villagers. "Excellent! I have been sitting on borrowed soil, now you give me the soil I sit upon. Thank you!" He began bowing to the elders.

"Oh no! Not *this* soil," Ibrahim blurted in dismay. "What kind of gift would that be? We want you to accept fertile land down below, in the bend of the river, close to our irrigation works. From my own inheritance, from this good man Ghulam Dastagir's acres, from others. We've prepared several plots close together, easy to work. Beets and carrots, fine red onions, even sweet peas are growing there now, and there is pasture too, for growing clover. You will have animals."

The malang brushed a blue butterfly away from his beard. "I accept your offer of land, but only if I can choose the land," he said, "and I choose this land, up here. I want as much of it as..." The malang gazed about, then opened his arms as if to encompass the entire world: "as I can encircle with my turban."

A thunderstruck silence greeted this announcement. Ghulam Dastagir grinned in admiration. "Malang-sahib, your wisdom inspires us all. Truly, the deepest riches are not of this world. Never fear for your bread-and-tea, Hajji-sahib. You will not know hunger so long as I draw breath, I swear!"

"Oh, Sheikh-sahib, no!" Ibrahim cried out despairingly. The wreckage of his plans for Khadija smoked in his mind. The thought of her living up here, buffeted by wind and rain and snow—intolerable! But what could he do? Ibrahim's ardor for his sheikh wrestled with his longing to lavish luxury upon his brother's widow. "Take this land, if you want, but take fertile land down by the river, too. What's the harm?"

"Now, now!" Ghulam Dastagir scolded. "Malang-sahib knows best. His reasons are too deep for simple souls such as you and me to fathom, Malik-sahib."

Ibrahim ignored his fellow villager. That bastard was glad of any excuse to renege on his promise to contribute land to the cause. "We are your own people now," he implored. "We are your brothers and sisters, your children! As much land as you can encircle with your turban—? That's out of the question."

But the mystic shook his head stubbornly. "I want no more land than my turban can encircle. Come back in seven days with picks and shovels and I will show which land I mean."

The men went back to the village, puzzled. Picks and shovels? The week crawled by. On the seventh morning, Ibrahim collected his cousins and joined the long procession up to Baba's Nose. The malang stood on the slope wearing nothing but a skull cap on his head, which left his long locks to stir in the breeze. Once the men had assembled, he gestured sweepingly north and south. "This is the land I want."

"This land can be had by anyone who claims it," Ibrahim grumbled. "We want to honor you with a gift, and this is no gift, this worthless hillside. This is nothing."

The malang ignored the village headman and addressed the entire group. "I see you have brought your tools. Good! I will get my turban."

He ducked into his hut and popped out carrying a ball of silken thread as big as a cow's head. "This is my turban." He had unraveled the cloth into separate threads and tied them together painstakingly to make a single long string: the ball he held up now.

The gaping villagers watched him tie one end of his string to a bush above his hut. Commanding them to follow behind and keep the thread from getting tangled, he rambled down the hill, along the hill, and finally up the hill again, trailing string. His meandering path eventually brought him back to his hut. Remarkably, the thread ran out just as he arrived at his original position. He tied the two ends together and stepped back, beaming.

The thread that used to be his turban now encircled a roughly rectangular patch of land that included the entire boulder known as Baba's Nose. Malik Ibrahim frowned. His sheikh had gone to much trouble to claim a precise amount of worthless rain-fed mountainside. Ibrahim was reminded again of Mullah Nasruddin. The famous fool lay buried in a fortified mausoleum he had built for himself, a citadel with a door of walnut planks, padlocks of stoutest iron, and walls of stone—but only three of them. The fourth wall was missing. Anyone could walk into the tomb by going around to the back. Some said the tomb expressed a profound message, some that the Mullah was mad, and some that he simply forgot about the fourth wall. Others said that his tomb, like his whole career, was just a good-humored but meaningless joke.

Now, here was their own malang, matching Mullah Nasruddin's zaniest antics.

"You men promised to help me dig," the malang reminded them all. "I warn you, the work will not be done in a day. Will you help every day until the work is done?"

The men shifted in place. What "work"? They hesitated to make an open-ended commitment to an unknown task, but Malik Ibrahim jumped into the silence. "Of course, Sheikh, whatever you need. We intended to build you a house all along. We can finish digging trenches for the foundation today, if God wills. Where should we start?"

"Up there." The malang pointed to the cliffs above Baba's Nose.

"There, Malang-sahib? Are you sure?" Ibrahim gulped. Building a compound on that steep slope would be difficult.

But the malang was already climbing. At the base of the cliffs, he began to dig. A terrace would have to be carved into the hillside before any sort of house could be built, but the malang seemed uninterested in any terrace. He gathered the men close together and urged them all to dig in the same spot, shoulder to shoulder. Watching from below, Ibrahim could see that they were digging more of a hole than a trench or terrace, a horizontal hole thrusting directly into the hill. And then he knew, and his heart withered. The malang wanted a cave. He was having the men dig him a cave. Khadija would have to live in a cave if she married this man! Ibrahim climbed frantically up next to the malang, who was urging the men on with cries of: "Don't lose heart. Once you tunnel past the rocks, it's all soil, boys. Into the mountain we go! Dig, dig, dig!"

"Into the mountain, Hajji-sahib? How far?" Ibrahim cried out.

"As far as necessary. Not one hair further. Pick up a shovel, Headman."

In the blaze of that commanding eye, Ibrahim could not object, not in front of all the men. He fell to laboring like the others. After three hours, the others went down to the village to perform their prayers and eat lunch, and Ibrahim knew none would return that day. How many would come back the following morning? Meanwhile, the malang was still digging. A man could already walk several paces into the tunnel but he seemed to want an even deeper cave. He swung his pick like a lunatic, pausing every once in a while to grunt at Ibrahim, "Fill that bucket. Move that dirt out." Finally, even the malang dropped his tool. He wiped his brow, dusted his hands against his pants, and moved to the mouth of the cave, where he hunkered down.

"Sit next to me," he urged Ibrahim. "Did you bring a pen?"

"No, sir. Why would I bring a pen?"

"Always bring a pen when you come to me. Paper and ink as well."

"For what reason, Sheikh-sahib?"

The malang squinted at him slyly. "Because I might start singing."

Ibrahim pushed his turban back to scratch his scalp.

"Yes," the malang confided, "Sometimes I just start spouting song and I would like to know what I sing at times like that. The next time I start, be ready with a pen. Write down every word. Do this for me, and in return, I will let you tell me about your deepest difficulties."

"You can solve my deepest difficulties, sheikh-sahib?"

"Who said anything about 'solve'? I said I would listen. Solve—that's different. Tell me, Malik Ibrahim, when you feel confused, weak, helpless and small, who do you go to?"

Ibrahim stared.

"Who do you show yourself to in your weakness?" the malang insisted. "Who do you trust that much? Whoever it is, that man is your friend. Tell me his name."

Ibrahim bit his lips, unable to utter a syllable. The only one he could name was a woman, but how could a man's best friend be a woman? "I am friend to every man in the village," he muttered evasively, "but I am the malik. I must show only strength."

"Then all you have are allies and followers. You have no friends," the malang declared emphatically, "except me. In the eyes of God, Ibrahim, you are an ant. Less than an ant. A mote of dust on the foot of an ant. A speck. So am I. So is any being that can utter the word 'I.' So is your village and this valley and those mountains and the entire world— specks, all specks. Insignificant. Today, one man is a king, another a slave. How we shout about it! In a hundred years both men will be dust. What does it matter which is which today? You're a king or a slave for a flash, like a spark that floats up from a fire and then turns to ash! Dust. You'll be dust for endless centuries. Which are you truly, then? The form you take for fifty or sixty years? Or the one you take forever?"

"I won't be dust forever," Ibrahim protested in alarm. "I am a soul! I will be restored on the Day of Judgment, God be praised, for God is one and Mohammad peace-be-upon-him-and-his-descendants is his messenger!"

The malang tossed his head back and laughed. "That will help you on the Day of Judgment, but what good does it do you now? Now you're alive and drowning."

Ibrahim prickled with bewilderment. "What are you trying to tell me?"

"I am *telling*, not trying! All right, I will tell you again. Bring a pen and paper up here next time and record what I sing. That's what I'm telling

you. In return, I will listen to your deepest troubles. In fact, I will pay in
advance. Talk to me, Malik-sahib. You're not at peace. What is wrong?"

*I have come to ask you to marry the woman I have wanted every moment of every
day since I saw her at my brother's wedding eleven years ago.*

The words rang in his mind, spoken in his own voice, though he had
never said them out loud or thought them before. He swallowed hard.
What could he tell the malang? A man does not go through such turmoil
as this over a woman. He had a wife, and he could have another, it just
couldn't be Khadija. Why should that trouble him? What good would it
even do to marry her? Khadija was barren. She wasn't even young. He
could find a young new wife, even more beautiful than Soraya, some girl
from Sorkhab…He sat with his head bowed, ashamed to realize that his
throat was tightening, his eyes glistening. The malang sat grasping his
knees with his big hands, gazing out across the valley and breathing in
the flower-scented air with manly enjoyment.

"You're right. I'm weak." Ibrahim admitted at last. That's what it
came to finally: his deepest fear. Here it was, spoken out loud finally. The
confession relieved the pressure behind his eyelids. "I am not big
enough to lead this village. People have lifted me to this height because
my brother had stature. They look up to me because my father was great.
One day they will realize that I am not my father or my brother. I have
the heart of a boy and the strength of a mouse, and people will find me
out someday and I live in dread of that day, Malang-jan. Now some of
the men are pressing me to start a fight with Sorkhab. They're eager to
fight, and they want me to start it. But we have kin over there! If blood
gets spilled, it will be on my head. Today they want to shed blood but
someday they will regret it, and then they will say who started that fight,
and they will look at me, and they will say it was *you*."

"Start a fight over what?"

"Sorkhab is planning to take more water from the river. If I let them,
our fields will shrivel and our children will starve, and that will be my
fault. I don't know what to do, Malang-jan. They are putting the whole
decision in my hands and they will certainly blame me if things go
wrong—as they will."

Abruptly the malang began to sing. He let go of his knees and leaned back to let his chest expand. His voice sounded like two voices singing in harmony.

> *This creature with a thousand heads*
> *grows a thousand more when you're not looking,*
> *grows a hundred thousand heads*
> *for each one harvested.*
> *When I ask my hundred-thousand-headed friend*
> *Where are you from? Who sent you here?*
> *My Friend replies with tongues of grass*
> *I descended from the sky.*
> *I erupted from your heart.*
> *Grieving dreamers by the river*
> *know what flows to heaven through these seas.*
> *The love that brims from every wound*
> *is me, and every wound a kiss,*
> *and every kiss a memory of that first intoxication,*
> *just you and me and me and you,*
> *the night the great dome was colored blue.*

Ibrahim lost all sense of the world as he listened, felt himself drowning in a stream of sound. When the singing stopped, he had no idea what the malang had just sung, but he was thrilled.

"Did you write it down?" the malang demanded breathlessly. "What did I say?"

"I didn't have a pen," Ibrahim confessed humbly.

"Next time, scratch in the soil with a stick," the malang commanded. "If it's dark, if you have neither stick nor soil, open a vein, Malik! Use your blood to write on stones if you must. Now, go home and recite *namaz*. Be with your family. In the morning, bring the men back, let's complete the work."

"Sheikh-sahib," Ibrahim choked out. The time had come to speak about Khadija. "I have one question."

"The answer is yes," the malang cut in.

"But the question—"

"Last week," the Malang interrupted again, "when I told you what land I wanted, you argued with me. Your friend said I had reasons, but you doubted me. Ibrahim!"

"My friend was so quick to give in to you because he didn't want to give up any land. Ghulam Dastagir accepted your decision out of greed," Ibrahim said.

"You know *his* reasons. Good. Have you plumbed your own reasons?" Then suddenly the mystic added, "I came to this village to meet one person."

"One person—?" Was the Sheikh about to anoint him as his acolyte?

"It wasn't Ghulam Dastagir," said the malang, "It wasn't Ghulam Haidar. It was none of those fellows. If they benefit from my presence, those men, Allah be praised. But I came here because my Beloved whispered in my ear and guided my footsteps. I confided as much to your blessed boy when I arrived."

"Well, he did report—but I thought you meant—"

"What exactly did he say? Think back."

Ibrahim bit his lip. "That you were on your way to meet your bride."

The malang nodded solemnly. "My bride is here."

"Oh," said Ibrahim. So this had all been foreseen. Grief lapped inside him but there was no turning back. By relinquishing her forever he would exalt them both. *Grieving dreamers by the river know what flows to heaven through these seas.*

"My brother who was malik before my time—"

"Our Prophet tells us to care for widows. You have done your part, Ibrahim. Now it's time to lay down your burden and let me take over." The malang set a hand as heavy as a haunch of lamb on Ibrahim's shoulder. Ibrahim looked into the malang's large gray eyes and saw himself reflected in those mirrors.

"I should go," he murmured. "Tomorrow, I will bring you a new turban."

That night, he told his wife quietly, "I proposed the marriage. Malang sahib agreed. Tell Khadija. We'll plan how to announce the news."

Khadija served dinner that night without meeting his eyes. He couldn't tell if Soraya had talked to her yet. Men from other compounds were visiting—kinfolk all, but still, with outsiders about, the women were staying in the shadows. He longed to sit with Khadija and explore how she felt about the news and what it would mean. He wanted to reassure her, in case she had heard about the cave: he would build her a compound, even if the malang didn't want one. He would muster all his cousins. He would work on it with his own hands. It didn't matter if the rest of the village joined in or not. He would never let Khadija live in a cave. He wanted her to know this, but how could he tell her anything if they could not sit side by side and talk? And in that crowded compound, they could do no such thing. How would it look if he pulled her aside for a private conversation when visitors were about? What scandal it would raise!

ॐ

The malang's hut was empty. He was already up in the hole the men had dug the day before. He waved and boomed a greeting. His unkempt hair looked moist, and his hands were covered with soil. Had he been working all night? The men didn't know. They climbed up to his level and stood there, shuffling sheepishly. The malang gazed over their ranks like a king inspecting his troops. "*Alhamd-ul-illah,*" he said finally. "You have all pledged to help me, but today you must take turns because I extended our tunnel during the night and it's so tight in there that only two men can work at one time. You and you—" He pointed to Ibrahim and Ghulam Dastagir. "Go first."

Frowning but obedient, these two men followed the malang through the mouth of the cave single file. Inside, the malang had enlarged the tunnel into a room just big enough for the three of them to stand side by side. "Start at the very back," the malang instructed. "The tools are there." He retired to the mouth of the hole, and his body partly blocked out the light, so that the men had to feel their way into the tunnel blindly.

When they reached the back, they found it surprisingly muddy. At that moment, a notion began to dawn on Ibrahim, but he said nothing.

"Dig," the malang barked out. "I've worked all night, it's your turn now, Allah be praised. Don't bother with the sides, just keep tunneling in. Go deeper into the mountain, boys, deeper. Deeper! Deeper into the heart of the mountain!"

Ibrahim's shoulder pressed up against Dastagir's. They could not swing their picks in a space this tight for fearing of hitting each other, but the soil was soft enough to dig out with hand trowels. The men said nothing to each other but didn't have to. The cave smelled of water. They both knew now. They knew the malang had chosen them to witness and complete a miracle. They plunged their tools into the soft soil as easily as plunging spoons into lard. They were scooping the mud out with bare fingers now. After a time it was no longer mud, but muddy water. Soon after that, the back of the cave was oozing moisture so abundantly, they were standing in a growing pool. The malang moved out of the doorway and in the shaft of light that shone through the opening, the men could see a trickle of clean, siltless water bubbling out of the hole into which they were still reaching mud-smeared arms.

There would be no battle with Sorkhab, after all, no need for it. Char Bagh had a *kahrez* of its own, a spring that would pour abundantly out of the mountain, water enough for all their wants, water they could collect in deep wells all year long and distribute throughout the village as needed—a fountain from the "worthless mountainside" the village of Char Bagh had just bestowed upon their dear malang.

Khadija would have a dowry, after all, and her dowry would be life itself: this wet abundance.

21

In mid-July, Kabul welcomed another large convoy from India. It brought several dozen more wives and a surprising number of unmarried women—sisters, maids, second-cousins and the like. By this time, Rupert had found his stride here in the frontier. In the early morning, he often climbed the hills near Cantonments and took in the view. Sometimes, of an afternoon, he roamed the Grand Bazaar, thrilling to the sense of storybook adventure all around him. But if he didn't want to brave the public streets, he never had to. The British garrisons, compounds, and cantonments formed a complete world in themselves. There was plenty of work to be done in there, and the work was fulfilling enough in its way; but there was also polo to be played in the afternoons, dinner with pals, cards after dinner, and sometimes—if he was lucky—invitations to social evenings hosted by one of the officers' wives. Had it not been for the loneliness that never left him, Rupert might almost have described life in Kabul as…fun.

The new convoy set off a particular flurry of tea parties and dinners. One day, Colonel Johnson's wife stopped Rupert in the yard and told him she was going to stage an actual ball at her husband's mansion east of cantonments one week hence. "Only quality invited," she confided. "No bumbling sergeants stepping on their partners' toes! Will you come, Lieutenant?"

Rupert bowed, delighted to know that he was considered quality—and rightly so: he could certainly be trusted in a cotillion.

"Amanda Hartley will be there," Mrs. Johnson added. "Do you know her?" Then, (strangely enough) she went on to say, "Her husband has just been dispatched to Kandahar. He's got papers to deliver to General Nott."

Rupert studied Mrs. Johnson for a moment, trying to puzzle out what she was up to. A journey to Kandahar and back could not be done in less than ten days; on the night of the ball, therefore, Amanda would be, as barracks lingo had it, a "field widow." Now why did Mrs. Johnson feel compelled to tell him this? Or was she merely passing along a message from…Amanda?

All that afternoon, Rupert banged about the barracks as restlessly as a lovesick hound. Sergeant Hudson twinkled knowingly, mistaking Rupert's agitation for the ordinary symptoms of a man with unspent needs. From the first week, he had been urging Oxley to relieve the pressure he must feel with the native girl who drew his bath; now, he pressed that option upon him again. "You pays into the collection, sir: you mought's well sample the goods."

Rupert had to admit he had noticed the little trollop. She crept into his room with such a coquettish show of hesitance every other day, and she always took her time filling his bath and laying out his towels and his soap. She liked to play the flirt, pulling her scarf over her mouth, hiding all but her eyes, and pausing at the door to squeak out little sounds in her own tongue—God only knew what she was saying! On this day, tentatively, he asked her to stay. She didn't speak English, but she seemed to understand and she lingered bashfully, looking at the floor while he undressed. He climbed awkwardly into his bath and asked her to rub his back with soap and afterwards to dry him. She obeyed willingly enough. He didn't know how to ask for more, but she guessed what he wanted and lay down of her own accord and remained unnervingly still as he mounted her. Afterward, just as he had been warned, she kept repeating *"Baksheesh. Baksheesh."* Hudson had assured him that the man who brought her to Cantonments each day was well paid from the collection the oafish sergeant took up around the barracks, but "baksheesh" was money the girl kept for herself, so Rupert paid the poor creature willingly.

Pretty though she was, he felt disgusted with himself after the act, perhaps for mixing his oils with those of another race, although none of the other men seemed much troubled about this. Then again, Rupert suffered twinges of self-loathing even after bedding English trollops. Yet what could a man do? In his younger days, Rupert had succumbed to onanism, not knowing that it could drive a man blind. The day he learned about the terrible risk the filthy practice posed, he also realized that his eyesight had indeed been growing weaker! He vowed to reform, but the animal urge overwhelmed him again and again, despite the danger. At last, some older companions escorted him to his first bawdy house and Rupert was saved, but it was a stopgap medical measure at best. He longed to establish a real romantic connection with a woman closer to his own social standing. He thought he had found such a one in Lady Lydia Ashton, but romancing her was what led to all his troubles, even though it was she who invited his advances. Romancing her was the reason he now found himself in Afghanistan. He no longer dwelt on his hopeless longing for Lydia, no longer thought of her at all, but the longings themselves remained: he had transferred them to Amanda now, who was just as hopeless as an object of desire, but much closer.

The Friday set for the ball arrived at last. That evening Oxley rode with several of his fellow officers to the Johnsons' compound, which lay beyond the neighborhood of the Qizilbash tribesmen, outside the city proper, in an area marked by wheat fields and apricot orchards. The fields were interlaced with trickles of water, which the autumn rains would transform into rushing brooks, but autumn was months away, and the land was pleasantly dry that night. A slight breeze blowing down from the slopes bore a warm chaff of weed-scented pollen. The men led their horses into the yard and gave them to servants to stable. They themselves proceeded into the commodious house and made their way over blood-red Turcoman carpets, through rooms furnished with varnished cherry wood furniture hauled up from India in wagons (nothing so fine was made locally), arriving at last in a stone-tiled "ballroom" lit by a chandelier whose hundred candles shed a warm unflickering light through twice that many glittering bits of cut crystal.

Men stood near the food-laden tables at the end of the room, sipping their chota pegs and nibbling shelled pomegranate seeds from heaping bowls. They conversed in loud voices for the benefit of any ladies within earshot, about military matters, native customs, hunting—anything to make themselves appear seasoned and settled and fearless. The old sweats carried it off, but most of the rookies only managed to sound conceited. Rupert held his tongue, hoping silence would give him an air of strength. He tried to keep his belly sucked in, for it did tend to bulge slightly over his belt. There was nothing he could do about the bulge of his brown eyes behind his round spectacles, but he hoped his strong chin and thick corn-colored hair would counteract any impression of inadequacy his weak eyes might give.

The ladies sat on chairs arrayed along the walls, clad in gorgeous gowns and frozen into postures that must have been arduous to maintain. Some looked like they were sitting for portraits. Those who had been in Kabul for some time conversed easily amongst themselves, but the new ones held their poses, and though they did not turn their heads, any gentlemen passing by could feel their attention turning, as a needle turns to follow a magnet, and any gentleman approaching them could feel the growing tension of their expectation. Clearly, the Fishing Fleet had arrived in Kabul.

Oxley should have risen to the excitement himself. Was this not precisely what he had been hoping for? English women of his own station, unattached and available? Not for marriage, of course, but fellows in the barracks said a man could find prospects among the widows. Even as he approached the row of females, however, he caught sight of Amanda, and all of his enthusiasm for the Fishing Fleet vanished. Amanda's husband was in Kandahar—he had not forgotten, but the knowledge rushed through him now with tidal force. And she was gazing right back at him! Dressed in a gown of green silk, she looked lighter than summer itself. None of the others could compare. He tasted again the memory of her lips brushing over his in the gorge that wonderful night. Surely that gesture had meant something beyond the moment. What had she said to him, there in the darkness? *You were heroic, sir!*

His shadow fell across her knees and she looked up. "Mr. Oxley! What a pleasure to see you. You have made yourself scarce lately. Tell me, are those heartless commanding officers of yours working you to the very bone, then?"

"Oh, it is awful! You have no idea," he laughed. "What refreshment may I fetch you, m'lady?"

"Your company is refreshment enough," she smiled. "Tell me: what news from home? Any letters recently?"

"Not recently." The confession gave him a twinge of genuine sorrow. "They've forgotten all about me back there, I'm afraid. This is my entire world now." He opened his arms to include the room, by implication all of Cantonments, all of Kabul.

"Oh, I'm sure they haven't forgotten you at all," she assured him. "I'm sure they are still telling stories about your heroism in the gorge that night. And I'm sure they'll be singing about you the moment another opportunity for heroism arises. You know what faith I have in you." She bathed him with a smile so luminous it made him blush. It was then that he realized he was entirely and helplessly in love with Amanda Hartley, a most distressing fact. And she loved him too, he could see it in her eyes, hear it in her words. Such a useless fact. Distressing even, because there was nothing to be done about it. Ah, the two of them: Tristan and Isolde, or whatever the devil their names were—he never remember which was the woman and which the man. Doomed to a lifetime of unsated yearning. Unless…into his head sprang an image of himself consoling Amanda after the sad news of her husband's demise on the dangerous road from Kandahar…

"Do you know Lieutenant Oxley?" Amanda was speaking to her neighbor, a proper memsahib, all shoulders and meaty bosom. "He escorted us from Peshawar. You should have seen him how he stood up these most forbidding tribesmen who burst in upon us, waving rifles—oh! Without his protection, we would all have been massacred, right there. I'm sure you've heard the story."

The matron beamed at him, and Oxley bowed. "Doing my duty," he murmured.

"Do you hear him? Modesty is his best quality. I hope you will ask me to dance once the ball begins." He detected a hint of a smile tugging at Amanda's lips, a deliciously furtive message. "I hear Mrs. Johnson has rounded up something of an orchestra." He strained for the meaning behind her words. Was dancing the least of what they would do together on this night? Was that her secret message?

He bowed gravely. "It will be my pleasure, Madame." He dared to emphasize, ever so faintly, the word *pleasure*.

He could not risk staying near her after that. His heart was too close to bursting. He went to join the crowd around Lord William Elphinstone, high commander of the British forces in Kabul since late April. Macnaghten outranked him, being Her Majesty's Envoy, but Elphinstone led the military corps. He had arrived just several weeks ago to replace the doughty Willoughby Cotton but had proved even doughtier than the man he replaced. Tonight he was languishing in an armchair, as was typical for him. He rarely stood up, even to drink, for he suffered from both gout and pleurisy. He paid no attention to Oxley's arrival. He was in the middle of telling some story, which the officers ringed about him took in politely, some tedious yarn about his exploits during the Peninsular Wars thirty years ago.

"And my horse foundered on the last leg—had to shoot the beast. Then I walked, gentlemen, walked the last half mile on foot, yes. Ahem. Bullet in my thigh and all—arrived all covered in mud but arrived, by God. Wellington could scarce believe his eyes. William, he kept saying. William? I remember it clear as yesterday. Is it you, he kept saying. Is it you? 'Course, I was younger then, we all were, but *that*, gentlemen, was a war. Nothing at stake since those days. Still, we soldier on." He sighed and lifted his large head to see what reaction his story had drawn from the officers. He had a cataract in one eye and floaters in both, so he had to move his head about to assemble a picture of the whole scene. Some of the officers clapped politely and said "Bravo, sir."

"Well might you say so, lads, but now it is your turn. You lads must do your duty too. Do your duty. England still needs good men, though the Age of Greatness may have passed. With luck, you too may find your Bonaparte. Your Bonaparte. Can't have a Wellington without a Bonaparte, you know. And Afghanistan is good seasoning. Tough it out here and by the time you get home, there will be man-sized work awaiting you on some more glorious field, I assure you. I assure you."

The officers clapped politely again, but Oxley could see that they found Elphinstone only slightly more inspiring than a bucket of steaming horse manure.

At last, the musicians began to play. Most were officers in the military bands that had come to Kabul with the Army of the Indus from the start, but some were regular soldiers who happened to play a fiddle and a few were Wily Oriental Gentlemen, as the boys called the more upstart Hindus—wogs, for short—some of whom knew how to play a proper dance tune on a Christian instrument. The music wobbled a bit at first, but the gentlemen had imbibed enough gin and the ladies had waited long enough for the dancing to begin that no one minded the deficiencies, and after a few numbers, the musicians found their footing, and the ball turned really lively, for all its primitive accoutrements.

True to his word, Oxley went looking for Amanda, but she was already on the floor with a partner. Jealousy tied his belly into knots, but what could he do? He took another small gin with tonic and a slice of lime to calm himself, but his gut remained clenched.

The dance ended, but Amanda and her partner stayed on the floor as if ready to dance again. Oh, this would not do at all. Offers had been made! Oxley made his way onto the floor and put his case graciously, he thought, with an air of easy wit. "M'lady promised me a dance and now I must collect."

"All in good time, Oxley," said the other officer with rude heat. "Wait your turn. Mrs. Hartley has promised the next number to me. Find yourself another partner, my good man. There are enough to go around for once."

Oxley reluctantly selected a partner from among the Fishing Fleet, a youngish thing who looked pretty from a distance; but as he led her to the floor, he saw a pimple on her cheek. Her hair was pulled back so tightly that it seemed to shine like varnished wood, and it lifted the skin of her forehead unattractively. He had a sudden intimation that this was a mature woman who had stretched a mask of youth over her face by devices known only to her sex. He danced with her soberly, his attention and sometimes his gaze fixed on Amanda Hartley, elsewhere on the floor.

When the music stopped, he escorted his partner back to her seat with brusque impatience. Amanda was a popular partner and he had to move quickly if he wanted her. He did manage to slide in just ahead of some self-satisfied fellow with pretty lips and a small moustache curled at the tips, whom Oxley had glimpsed about cantonments but whose name he didn't know. Amanda accepted his hand graciously and allowed herself to be led out to the floor again. "You flatter me, Mr. Oxley, but you must not show yourself quite so eager," she murmured on the way. "It will raise remarks."

They began moving through their set. The orchestra was sawing out a reel, which gave little opportunity for conversation. The dancers separated into lines. The men clapped hands, beckoned to their partners, stamped four times and jump-stepped—and then, accursedly, Rupert found himself dancing with the next woman down the line. So it went, as the dancers traded partners through the formation. When he had Amanda back, he said, "I can't help how I present myself, Amanda. I can't express how lonesome I have been all these months. I long for your conversation. I miss—"

"Now, now, Mr. Oxley." Her voice turned tight and prim.

They turned about and went back into the reel.

He could not let her go, though, when the dance ended. He held her by the waist. He had thought she wanted his company as much as he wanted hers. Why was she pulling away? "I believe this next one will be a waltz. I really must keep you on the floor, Amanda. I insist."

She acquiesced, her face smiling, and the gleam of her teeth struck him like the sun coming up at dawn. "I'm on fire," he whispered as he led her across the set to their places.

"Good heavens, Rupert. Please!" she scolded.

She had called him Rupert! This was looking promising! The dance began, and he concentrated on moving through the figures. He was a good dancer when he put his mind to it, and women liked that. He and Amanda swung their corners and returned into a right hand star. Then he had her in his arms again. "Oh, Amanda. Don't hold me at arm's length, there is so much in my heart. You have shown me such warmth. I know James is in Kandahar. You have no idea of my feelings. Every time I set eyes on you, I wonder what destiny brought us together so late in life, why could we not have grown up together as children and been promised to one another by our parents and been married as soon as we reached the age! Oh, Amanda, I—"

"Hush! Hsst!" She leaned away from him, the blazing candles bathing her face in glow. "What on Earth are you saying? It's impossible! We can only be friends. I thought we understood each other. Please. And you make it difficult even to be friends."

"Amanda. That night—"

But she turned out of his embrace and released his hand. He had missed a step. They were supposed to do a back-to-back, but they were out of time with the music now, and with the other dancers. Her eyes flashed impatiently at his mistake. She reached for his hand to pull him around so they could mesh with the dance again, but he was too far askew from it now, and his mind was in such turmoil: he could not sort out dancing from romancing. At that moment, he knew nothing but sorrow and the raging ball of misery burning in his belly. "You can't treat me this way. I will not stand for it," he growled at her. "What do you take me for? You must—"

"I must? I must? Mr. Oxley, you forget yourself."

"Oh no, I remember myself quite well. It is you who have forgotten, Amanda! It is you—" He had stopped all pretense of dancing now. He tried to seize her by the waist, but she wrenched away and her arm came swinging up in a blur of motion—which he caught. He caught her wrist before her hand could slap resoundingly across his cheeks. They stood for a moment, frozen in that tableau of scandal and woe. Their voices had risen just above the pitch of the music and their dissonance with the dance had drawn attention from the nearest couples. Eyes had turned their way. High spots of color burned on Amanda's cheeks. Her eyes blazed with furious dismay. Oxley's heart fell to his shoes. He let her go, his courage and his anger and indeed all his manly essence wilting, as he suddenly knew himself disgraced and humiliated in the eyes of this whole company. Before long, his father and brother would both know of his shame this night. He could picture them opening the report of his humiliation—surely someone would write to them, surely the story would travel all the way to Leicester. Oh, he could hear their laughter now!

One or two seconds passed, seconds that felt endless. Then he grasped control of his senses again. Amanda stepped away from him, into the requisite figure, hands on her waist, doing her turn. Oxley did his corresponding turn and they came together pas de bouree, well executed and performed the traveling waltz steps together and then the dance was over.

She did not offer her arm to let him walk her back to her place. She only nodded her head curtly and said, "Mr. Oxley," and retreated. He too turned at once, trying to pretend nothing had happened. No one was staring at him, not obviously at least, but he could feel the attention of the whole room burning on the spot between his shoulder blades, as if public calumny were a torch.

22

At that moment, someone touched his elbow. He glanced to his right and saw the pretty-mouthed gentleman he had beaten out to secure Amanda as a dancing partner. "Rupert Oxley," said the man. He spoke as if testing out the sound of the words.

"Yes. I'm Oxley. You have the advantage of me, sir," Oxley retorted curtly.

"You don't know me? Odd that I should know you and you know nothing of me. Is Kabul really so large?"

"Who the devil are you then?"

"My name is Burnes," said the man. "Alexander Burnes."

The Alexander of the East! How could he have failed to guess? Burnes was second only to Macnaghten on the political side, here in Kabul, and according to every rumor, he would soon be supplanting Macnaghten as Her Majesty's Envoy to the court of Shah Shuja. Oxley blushed furiously. He had made his second gaffe of the evening, and this time his very career might be at stake. "Mr. Burnes! I beg your pardon! Of course I know *of* you. All England knows *of* you. Why, the papers could talk of nothing else when you returned from your journeys to the heart of Asia. Sekandar Burnes, that's what they called you! We schoolboys—I was just a schoolboy then—I assure you, sir: every one of us dreamed of shaking hands with you someday. Sadly—I say, your face—that is, we've never—"

"We've never formally met," Burnes agreed dryly. "The press of business. Also, I do not haunt Cantonments, I prefer to live in the city, among the people of this land. But I have heard about you, Mr. Oxley. I have been following your career with interest."

"You have?"

"I keep an eye on promising subalterns. One day we ancients must hand over the reins, we must leave the empire in good hands. Eh?" Burnes spoke with a twinkle in his eye. He looked to be in his early thirties, scarcely more than ten years senior to Rupert Oxley, but if it pleased the great man to play Father Zeus, so be it.

"I hope the reports have not been too discreditable," Oxley stammered.

"Well, the notes you've added tonight do not entirely exalt you."

Rupert straightened his knees, fighting down the shame. "I lost my head. I've been distraught. . ."

Burnes squeezed his shoulder and said in a kindly voice, "I understand what you are feeling, Mr. Oxley. I assure you, I know what it is to be spurned, but I have rescued friendships out of it, and so must you. Why don't you come away with me? A ball is no proper place for men like us. We shine in other settings. I will be pleased to instruct you on some alternatives to...." He leaned closer and dropped his voice to a whisper. "Romancing the wives of other English officers."

Oxley glanced about in dismay but saw that he and Burnes were actually quite private where they stood, just two men quietly conversing in the corner shadows of a crowded room. "I will gladly go wherever you lead me, Mr. Burnes."

"You may call me Alexander," said the other, his pouty little lips smiling. "Or better still, Sekandar. I have grown accustomed to the name."

They bid their hostess farewell and took their leave of Lord Elphinstone, who hrumphed and accused them jovially of abandoning their posts in the middle of a battle. "Won't do, you know. Won't do. Wellington would take the cats to you men."

They retrieved their horses from the stables and rode into the cooling crispness of a Kabul summer night. No moon showed. They rode by starlight alone. Oxley felt some trepidation, riding through the city at this hour, but Burnes displayed a careless ease and once or twice even called out in one of the native tongues to some cloaked figure.

At last they arrived at Burnes's compound, south of the Kabul River. It was tucked against the foot of the mountain spur upon which Bala Hissar, the royal fortress, loomed. Burnes called out, and servants opened his compound gates. The men relinquished their horses, and Oxley followed Burnes indoors. The house was furnished luxuriously in an Oriental style, with marble floors, thick carpets, and mounds of silken pillows. The few items of furniture were shelves that contained musty bottles of fine liqueur and ancient brandy, glasses as thin as soap bubbles, and hookahs. Everything about this domicile invited one to recline and indulge. Suddenly, it occurred to Rupert that Mr. Burnes might be an invert. That warm greeting, those fingers touching his shoulder, his hips, his face, the confidential tone he had taken with Rupert —and why on Earth should a man in Burnes' position have been following the career of an undistinguished subaltern? Rupert loosened his collar, wiped sweat from his neck and wondered how he might make his escape without shutting his career in a coffin.

"Yes, do make yourself comfortable. By all means." Burnes picked up a small hammer and tapped a bronze plate suspended from a decorative wooden stand. A gong sounded. A native servant appeared almost instantly. He must have been lurking just behind the door, awaiting his master's summons. He and Burnes conversed rapidly in a language Rupert didn't understand. Then the servant departed, and Burnes turned back to his guest. "Now Mr. Oxley, we have merely to wait."

"Hmm. Wait…for what exactly?" Oxley cast a nervous glance about the room.

"You shall see. You'll be pleased, I think. Be seated," said Burnes. "I have a small matter to attend to. I will rejoin you instantly."

Reluctantly, Oxley let himself sink into the nearest pile of cushions. Languishing on the floor like any Roman, alone in this sumptuous room, made him feel entirely degenerate. After a few minutes, Burnes reappeared. He had doffed the pigeon colored gabardine slacks and the checkered waistcoat of an English gentleman in favor of a flowing shirt and baggy pantaloons.

"You've gone native," Oxley gasped.

"I recommend it. These outfits are astonishingly comfortable,

Oxley." Burnes splashed brandy carelessly into a glass and handed it to Rupert, then flung himself upon the cushions next to the younger man. "I wear nothing else at home. You should try a turban too. While we're waiting, let me ask you: what is your impression of the Afghan countryside?"

"Outside the city, you mean? I have scarcely been off station," Oxley admitted. "I have seen the country south of here, but nothing more. As to scenery—if that's what you mean—well, I find it stark but rather ... stirring."

"I wasn't thinking of scenery. Incidentally, she doesn't love him, you know, and he abuses her, but she's dutiful. That's a good quality in the end. You should be glad of it." Burnes held his gaze for a moment and then said, "What would you think of going north? After tonight's fiasco, I imagine you'll want to make your face scarce for a bit."

Oxley colored. "Was it that bad?"

Burnes shrugged. "I've seen worse, but in your place I would look for opportunities to remove myself for a time. Her heart will soften in your absence. It's not punishment I'm suggesting, it's opportunity."

"What exactly are you suggesting?"

"I'll have to clear it with your commanding officer, of course." Burnes stared at the ceiling, composing his thoughts. "Mr. Oxley," he said finally, "the British Mission in Kabul as been very successful so far. I'm sure I don't have to tell you."

"Oh, I agree, sir. When I spoke with Lord Auckland—"

"Precisely. Now that you're here, you see for yourself. You have eyes."

"We seem very well established."

"Well planted. Yes. The Afghan has accepted us, Ivan is stymied. In a year or two, we shall be straddling the Oxus, and with that we will have secured all that we need. We are only here to protect the empire, Oxley. Never forget that. With the Oxus at our backs, the Czar will finally understand the futility of his designs on India."

Oxley was thrilled. If only his brother could see him now, sipping brandy and discussing deep matters with none other than Sekandar of the Steppes! But where was this leading? "I see what you mean," he agreed, wrinkling his brow to suggest thoughtful consideration. "You have such a clear way of putting it, sir."

"Of course, incidents have occurred," Burnes went on. He leaned to his right and stretched to reach a bottle, not the brandy he had given Oxley but a smaller bottle of something from a lower shelf, a liqueur, it seemed.

"Yes, I know," said Oxley. Even now he could picture vividly the five men he'd seen hanging from gallows on his way into the city.

"But nothing worse than we expected," Burnes went on. "When the Dost fled north, the Amir of Bokhara was supposed to clap him in prison. We had it arranged, you see, money changed hands, but we were deceived. Those two were thick as thieves, in fact: they're cousins, you know, plotting together. They sent agents down to Kabul to stir up trouble. We caught them, I'm happy to say, we arrested every one of them but I told Macnaghten we'd get nowhere until we cut off the head. Well, last November the Dost finally came south and engaged us at Pandit Pass. He cut us to pieces, frankly, but his victory was just what we needed. The Dost only wanted to redeem his honor, you see: show himself a man. Once he'd bloodied a British force, he turned himself in and that's all we wanted from him in the first place. We secured with defeat what we never gained with victory. Well, that seemed an end of it. The source of all conspiracies, caged—and we have him now in Ludhiana, eating tamely from our hands. He's in the self-same palace where we had Shuja tucked away. Not a peep of trouble."

Rupert didn't know enough to make an intelligent reply to this. A silence stretched out awkwardly. "Excellent," he said finally.

"Excellent, yes, except—you said it yourself: incidents continue. Last April, a band of hoodlums attacked the Shah himself. The king barely made it back to his palace, leaving five or six of his guards hacked to pieces on the street. We traced it all back to five *badmashes* and hung them in a public square."

"*We* did that?"

"Not we personally," Burnes said with some impatience "The Shah took care of it. The point is, we caught the plotters. But since then—" He cleared his throat, then began to reel off a list. "There's been that trouble with the Ghilzais. The attack on the convoy from Jalalabad. Two Tommies beaten in the bazaar and delivered to cantonments in burlap bags, naked." Burnes voice took on a sonorous tone as he continued to list "incidents." He stopped in mid-sentence and fixed Oxley with his blue-eyed gaze. "What do you make of it?"

"Clearly, there are still some troublemakers about…" Oxley hazarded.

"At least! Or perhaps we've not *really* cut off the head. Or the monster has grown another head. Oh, make no mistake: our situation is fundamentally sound, I assure you, but conspirators still operate from the countryside. Saboteurs receive their orders out there somewhere, then they filter into the city and stir up trouble. The only question is, does some controlling hand keep the Afghan agitated? I think so, but who is it? Who's behind it all? Is it one of the Dost's sons? His pup Akbar has showed up in the north, you know, but it can't be him alone, he's too young. Is Ivan at it again? That's my greatest fear. I've talked it over with Macnaghten, and he agrees, we must trace all this plotting to its root. We'll never be rid of trouble till we've put the real ringleaders behind bars. I don't mind telling you I have a stake in this myself. As soon as the situation is stable, Macnaghten will return to England, and I will take charge here as her majesty's envoy and *then* we'll see some progress! I understand these people, Oxley. I've lived among them, I speak their language, I know how they think. There is much to be said for the Afghan. These are a brave people, Oxley, a fine fierce people, properly handled. It's absolutely essential that Mr. Macnaghten depart and I take charge. Do you see?"

"Of course—when you put it that way." Rupert furled his brow. He had an intimation, now, of where Burnes was going, but he wanted to hear it said.

"All this conspiring originates up north somewhere," Burnes insisted. "Akbar is there, but he can't be the spider at the center of the web. Too young! I need some agents up there, watching and listening. In particular, there is a little village called Char Bagh. That's where I want you. The tax collectors went to that area a while back. They got within one town of the place and ran into a few of their elders by chance. Until then, no one even knew the town existed. I ask you: what better place to headquarter a conspiracy? The headman gave the tax collectors some cock-and-bull about a plague in their village—just to keep the king's men away, it seems. As soon as I heard, I started wondering: what's their game? That's what I want you to find out, Mr. Oxley. What's their game? Who's playing the hand? I want you to station yourself near that village and mark who comes and goes."

"Why me?"

"What I need in Char Bagh is a man who won't recoil. Mrs. Hartley told me how you acquitted yourself on the road from Peshawar. Now that's the sort of chap I want on the spot. Officially you'll be there to…I don't know. We'll think up some pretext."

"Do you … know Mrs. Hartley quite well, then?"

"She's been a good friend to me." Burnes cast him a glance laden with irony. "Do not jump to any conclusions. I will give you one bit of advice, my friend. It bears repeating. Leave the English women alone, especially the married ones. In Kabul, there are other amusements to be had."

"I'm sure I don't know what you mean," Oxley declared stiffly, shrinking from Burnes's affectionate pat. He wasn't sure he wanted to know.

"I mean—" Burnes stopped talking and cocked his head. "Ah, I think our wait is over. Stand up, Captain Oxley."

"It's, um, lieutenant."

"Stand up, Lieutenant Oxley. We have guests to greet."

Voices could be heard on the other side of the door. A cautious tap sounded, and then a gloved hand opened the door. Two women stepped inside. Both were covered from head to foot in the veil that most Afghan women wore on the street. They were giggling inside their bags. Then they lifted the veils away, and Oxley saw two strikingly beautiful young women: Afghan girls, he supposed from their dusky complexion and their almond-shaped eyes, but clad in fashionable dresses such as any well-bred Englishwoman might wear, although rather shorter: their legs were naked.

"Mestar Boornus. Friend tonight?" said one.

Burnes looked at Oxley. "And they even speak English of a sort."

"Do you mean—?"

"Oh, this was arranged some time ago. I meant to have both myself, but since you're here—well, greed is a sin. Have one, Oxley, either one.

Take your pick."

The girls giggled again, clustering closer together.

"But—but who are they?"

"Does it matter? Later, I'll teach you how to make arrangements of this sort on your own. Tonight, I ask you simply to indulge. I want you to appreciate that an Englishman can do very well in this country. If you help me, I will see to it that you have a most satisfactory posting here, Rupert. May I call you Rupert?"

"Um, yes—um... Alex?"

"I prefer Sekandar," the older man corrected him.

"Oh! Sekandaaarrrr!" the women laughed, flocking to either side of Burnes and stroking his arms.

"As for the cost—do not even think of it. Tonight is my treat," Burnes said.

23

The morning of her wedding, the women of the household bathed Khadija, dressed her in finery, and brushed her hair. The widow sat quietly, thinking about that day last spring when Ibrahim had come home covered in mud and shining with sweat to tell the household there would be no fight with Sorkhab after all. "Sheikh-sahib has found water for us." And then he went on to make the stunning announcement: "Sheikh-sahib has consented to marry our own Khadija-jan."

All that day, wherever she went in the crowded compound, Khadija felt wonder-struck and disquieted eyes upon her until at last she sought refuge in the stables. Ibrahim found her there in the early evening hours. Distance already hung between them, but he approached her for a chaste and ordinary embrace, such as any two related people might perform upon meeting or leaving one another—only they were not meeting or leaving one another, so it was not at all chaste. He kissed one side of her neck, and she his other; they switched sides and kissed again, switched and kissed a third time, the normal greeting ritual. Then they should have let go, but instead his hands settled on her hips and he went in for an impermissible, a stepping-dangerously, a break-all-the-rules, an inconceivably erotic *fourth kiss,* and she let her grip on him tighten, her face sinking into the warmth between his neck and collarbone. Oh, reckless desire! People were conversing just outside the door, people were milling in the courtyard, people were teeming outside the compound walls; people were whispering all over the village, people who must never see them like this!

She drew back and stepped away, and he let her go, although his excited breath still came and went like a brushfire. She pulled her scarf across her mouth, and her whirlpool eyes sucked at him. What must she look like, she thought, all disheveled with desire—and yet she could not deny herself one final murmured complaint. "How am I to let you go?"

He dropped his gaze. "You will see me every day. Sheikh-sahib is like a father to me."

"Oh. So you will be my *stepson* now." She tossed her head.

He permitted himself a faint grin. "I will be in his house every day He is my sheikh." Ibrahim turned to the window, then, and she began to push some hay into her cow's feeding bin. This had been their entire parting from each other.

Now at last her marriage day had come. By noon, she was just as beautiful and womanly as her helpers could make her. That afternoon, Ibrahim and his male relatives formed a team to escort the veiled Khadija up to the malang's new house. Several boys scurried alongside, pelting her with flower petals, just for fun. Had she been a virgin, they would have carried her on a throne, but a public wedding for a widow would have been unseemly.

At least a real road ran up to Baba's Nose now, for the villagers went up there often these days to say their prayers or just to lounge about, and the constant traffic had worn the path wide and smooth The malang's compound had four structures within its walls. The front building was a single large room for visitors and opened directly onto the world outside. In the great man's private quarters, another building containing kitchens and washrooms formed a side wall. Across from it was the outhouse. A fourth building abutting the back wall of the compound contained three rooms for the women folk.

All that afternoon and into the night, Khadija and the malang sat in the large public room, side by side on a dais, while Ibrahim and his close relatives feasted and the women beat tambourines and everyone sang and made merry. Khadija wore a veil that covered everything but her eyes.

After the platters had been polished clean, Soraya and a laughing collection of veiled women tossed a large green blanket over the newly-married couple. It was Soraya's idea to give the couple a simulacrum of the climactic moment of a real wedding ritual, the one that would have been performed if she were a virgin. Under that sudden tent, Khadija breathed her new husband's exhalations. The laughter, clamor, and music continued to sound around them, muffled by the intervening fabric. A woman's hand thrust under the cloth, holding a long-handled mirror. Khadija heard a stifled giggling and the sound of someone slapping someone, attended by harsh admonitions to take this seriously. The mirror came to rest directly between Khadija and the malang. With fluttering heart, Khadija undressed her face for him, pulling the headscarf down from her nose, pulling it down from her mouth, down from her chin, stripping her features naked for him, letting the malang see whom he had married. And this was her moment, too, to get her first frank look at him. But when she gazed into the mirror, she saw only her own face. Then the malang's big hand tilted the mirror, and his face appeared in the glass: large, broad. He was old, she realized with a start, older even than her first husband. And yet the delighted curiosity in his large brown eyes made him look childish too. A cool sensation permeated her flesh, and then she veiled her face as the blanket was lifted away and the merriment swirled again around them.

Eventually the family drifted out of the compound. Even after the last of them were gone, Khadija heard drums still beating in the village below, heard the reedy wail of shepherds' flutes. Even though there was no official wedding ceremony, the village was celebrating the malang's marriage to one of their own, but that was revelry in some other world. Khadija was here in her own house, alone with her strange new husband.

She sat in her green finery, waiting. Her cheeks wore the painted blush her helpers had applied with the precious morsel of rouge she had gotten as part of her dowry eleven years ago when she married for the first time, rouge that she had kept (and assiduously kept moist) in her chest of personal belongings all these years, always hoping to use it in a private celebration with her husband the day she got pregnant—for which reason it was still available now.

The malang stood up and pointed wordlessly and Khadija understood that she was to precede him. She stepped into the sweetness of a Char Bagh summer night and started across the courtyard. Half a moon was just sinking out of sight, but the sky hung over them, pregnant with starlight. Her silent husband followed her to their private building. Although no one would intrude back here, Khadija closed the shutters and drew the bolts. Now, the only light in the room came from the two lamps they had carried in with them, clay pots filled with precious cottonseed oil, each containing a wick and shedding a halo no larger than an armload of light. But they shed no smoke either, and very little odor, Allah be praised.

Khadija could make out a cleanly swept floor covered with a mat woven of saw grass. In the corner she saw bedding heaped upon a mattress rolled into a tube. She unrolled it and pulled it to the edge of the room furthest from the windows. It was closer to dawn than to midnight now, as dark as the cycle of day and night would get. The moon had drowned. At any moment, roosters might begin to crow.

The malang was only a shadow to her. She felt rather than saw him move from the other side of the room, saw rather than felt his hand upon her face, so light was his touch, so very light. He said nothing to her, not a word. She held still for the tip of his finger running along her cheekbone, over her eyebrows, and down the other side of her face.

"Strong bones," he commented.

Strong bones. Was it good to have strong bones? Was this to be the extent of their marriage? Did a malang, perhaps, not even want…?

"Don't be afraid." His voice was a rumble. He stroked her lips, which parted slightly to allow her breath in and out. She didn't know what she felt, only that her heart was pounding and her head swimming, but when his fingers came to rest on her cheekbones, and then touched her lips, and then grazed down to her hair and lifted the long locks from her shoulders as a boy lifts water in wonder and lets it slip and splash between his spread fingers, she knew that what she felt was fear indeed.

But she shook her head, not wishing to displease him.

He went on investigating her body, touching her shoulders and her arms; he seemed like such a little boy now that fear seeped out of her and something acutely maternal took its place. Suddenly, she imagined a child at her breast, felt a vivid yearning to bear and to nourish life. He took her hand. Hers was not a small hand, nor particularly soft, a hand weathered by years of labor, by all the scrubbing and cleaning and scouring and cooking and sifting and sewing she had done, a hand that disheartened the woman in her, a hand she wanted to hide. But in his hand, hers felt small and delicate. Against his tree-bark skin, hers felt luxuriously smooth. He pressed her hand against her own breast and she felt the thumping of the bird within her ribcage.

"Good heart!" he declared. He had both her hands now. He set them against her cheeks, enclosing them with his own, encasing her whole head with those gigantic hands. "Good head," he hummed with childish glee.

His hands slipped down to her back. Encircled by his arms, she must stand closer. The front of his voluminously clothed body pressed against the front of hers. "You have carried weight," he marveled, "so much weight upon these shoulders..." Then he went into a sort of recitation, his voice like the wings of flies on a sleepy day. "Thinking ahead to winter all summer was your work. Thinking about what to store... What to dry and what to smoke and what to lay away... How much to cook each day. What to serve at funerals. At weddings. At wet seasons and dry. Generations coming and going ... You, all the while, measuring and holding back as needed, staving off the greed, ignoring slander. Lay your burdens down, Khadija. Lay all your burdens down. Living with me will not be difficult."

At that moment, he seemed not at all boyish. How could she have made that mistake? He was as big as a bear, and she that three or four year old child, sitting on her father's lap, as safe as any bear cub. His arms around her tightened and she became aware of her breasts and her thighs. His eyes, in the almond-colored light of two oil lamps, beamed down at her with astonished delight, bathing her until she grew more beautiful than she ever imagined she could be. Her first husband never really looked at her, he took her only under the covers, tearing at her clothes with blind fingers in furious haste. He was never in the mood until the mood had him in a violent hurry. She knew his body only as ambush and desperation. Now, standing fully clothed before the clothed malang, her body glowed with pleasing shame. The malang was not ashamed nor in a hurry. She stopped imagining what was to come and leaned into his mountain of a body—fell through, as it seemed, into a vast geography of her own undiscovered self. This wasn't after all like being with a man. His arms became the sky, the mountains, the embodiment of everything ancient—and yet his delighted, wholly human curiosity kept flowing over her and she heard him laugh at one point. Her body awoke into pleasure, she awoke into every part of herself that was body: she was her fingers, her breasts, her neck, that place that curved in just below her hairline, she was a country with mountains and valleys of her own, and fields full of grass and flowers murmuring with love, an entire world where nothing mattered because *here* she had a friend.

Then love softened into light and light transformed into the material daylight of the wonderful country she had entered, which thickened into darkness, and she was herself again, standing in the attitude of *namaz*, hands folded across her belly, hearing syllables of Quran in her mind, in a feminine voice but not one she recognized as her own. Somewhere nearby her husband was quietly chanting. She didn't know if he had taken her. She felt more as if *she* had entered *him*, as a bird enters a glade. But he must have taken her, else why would she be naked? She looked down and realized it wasn't her clothes she was missing, but her body. She wasn't wearing her body. No wonder she felt so naked. But she was only imagining herself standing up in *namaz*. She was in bed, actually, under bulky covers. Not naked but fully clothed. Alone. Nothing had happened. Everything had happened. The malang's chanting voice was only in her head. Her husband's body—she knew without even looking—was outside, on the roof.

SOCR

After the marriage, Ibrahim settled into his discipleship. Others might study at the malang's feet and aspire to learn from the great man, but a true sheikh makes one of his students heir to his vocation, and Ibrahim was this chosen one. Everybody knew it, and everybody now acknowledged what Ibrahim had known all along: the malang of Char Bagh was a learned Sufi sheikh, a mystic of the highest order. Ibrahim visited him every day and never stopped marveling at how this man without a stick of possessions could recite whole books from memory and explicate the meaning of any line Ibrahim recited, even though his explanations were often more cryptic than the original—and just as fruitful to explore.

What Ibrahim appreciated most was not any specific wisdom his master imparted but those moments when the malang burst out singing. Ibrahim kept all his writing supplies at the malang's house and traded a bundle of treated goatskins to Mullah Yaqub for that man's entire supply of paper. Mullah Yaqub could always get more paper, he had family connections in Baghlan. Ibrahim could have gotten his own paper through those channels, but it would have taken time, and he didn't want to risk waiting. He wanted to be sure he had all the paper he might need, close at hand.

He could congratulate himself on his foresight one night in the month of Saratan when the malang burst into a fountain of free-flowing song. Ibrahim had spent the evening at his house, keeping his eyes, mind, and heart off Khadija, who hovered about the room cleaning up, listening in, and serving food and tea—Ibrahim could mingle with her freely, for Malang-sahib treated him as a member of his private family.

On that particular evening, he and his sheikh had eaten dinner and performed *namaz* and were drinking a final pot of tea when suddenly the malang began to breathe raggedly, and his eyes rolled back in their sockets. Incoherent melodic sounds began to issue from his lips and throat. Khadija quickly brought the box of writing supplies over. Ibrahim snatched a sheet of paper, smoothed it out, and dipped his pen in the ink bottle that Khadija had hastily set before him. By then, the malang's moans had resolved into words, so Ibrahim began to write. He missed the first few lines, but after that he blazed away. Khadija kept his supplies in order, organized the pages as he filled them, handed him fresh sheets as needed, kept a reed pen sharpened against the moment when his own broke or wore out, and generally relieved Ibrahim of every duty except taking dictation.

The malang sang all that night and all the next day and on into the following night. Dawn came again but nothing staunched his flow. Ibrahim kept writing in blind haste. Khadija fed him morsels of bread dipped in soup to relieve him of distraction. He scarcely noticed her loving fingers sliding between his lips as she fed him. Over the course of those exhausting, exhilarating, astonishing days, he wrote down over 10,000 couplets, a sizable book, taken directly from the mouth of his ecstatic sheikh. By the end of that first night, Ibrahim himself was in a kind of trance. The master's voice filled his ears, filled his soul. The universe of all things he could touch or see, the walls around him, the mud, the reed, the table, the pen, the shadowy motions of Khadija nearby, all—all!—were transformed into richly swelling music.

When the malang stopped singing at last, Ibrahim let the pen drop from his hand, his head slumped, and he fell asleep where he sat. When he awoke it was evening. His last memory was of daylight, so he guessed that he and the malang had both been asleep for half a day. But Khadija corrected him. He and the *sheikh* had slept through one whole day-and-night cycle *plus* half a day.

During the marathon, Soraya sent messengers to find out what had happened to her husband, and Khadija sent them back with a warning not to let anyone else come up to the malang's house. She told the boys the malang and Ibrahim were engaged in a spiritual ceremony that must not be interrupted or disrupted. At that news, Soraya wrapped her scarf around her head and came trudging up the hill to see for herself, but what she saw so bedazzled her that she began to weep, cuddled in a corner of the room, and then she simply watched and dozed, woke and listened, dozed and woke and watched.

Despite Khadija's warnings, some of the men came drifting up, because the rumor got out, and curiosity seekers would not be denied. They gathered at the windows because Khadija and Soraya would not let them into the house. From outside, they could not make out the words of the malang's song. They could merely catch the flavor of his melody and gawk in awe at the sight of the malang singing and Ibrahim writing. When the singing stopped, the listeners staggered away from the windows like men who had been drinking wine, murmuring to one another about what they had seen. The stories spread and soon Sorkhab, too, was buzzing about the event. Mullah Yaqub came to Char Bagh to read Ibrahim's manuscript. Ibrahim would not let him take the pages away with him. By then he was busy making a legible copy of the couplets he had scribbled, but he would not give this to the mullah either. It was too precious. Finally, having no other recourse, the mullah seated himself next to Ibrahim and began to make his own copy from the one Ibrahim was transcribing. He took this manuscript back to Sorkhab, where it was copied by others, including visitors from larger towns along the road from Charikar to Puli Khumri. Years later, handwritten versions of the malang's masterpiece duplicated by anonymous scribes during that summer and later could be found for sale in bazaars as far away as Kabul and Rawalpindi. But these unauthorized copies contained many errors.

As stories about the malang spread, strangers began drifting to Char Bagh to touch his garments, beg for his breath on their injuries, and seek amulets from him. To keep them from the village, Ibrahim oversaw the construction of a rude hostel half a *k'roh* distant from the village, just over the pass. It was one large room. What did pilgrims need, after all? Just a place to sleep until their visit was over.

But eventually, some visitors began showing up with womenfolk, who were just as intent on getting amulets to meet *their* peculiarly female difficulties—infertility, the illness of a child, the hope of a husband, the productivity of their animals, sometimes even the downfall of a rival. It might have seemed odd, the malang's own wife being barren, but outsiders knew nothing of that, of course; and the villagers of Char Bagh made no comment about it, a miracle in itself, since no other matter related to sex, marriage, childbirth, fidelity and infidelity, health, madness, crime, jealousy, or any other human interaction had ever in living memory escaped the rumor mill. The malang's intimate affairs were the first topic ever to elude evisceration by gossip.

Toward the end of summer, the malang said he would see no pilgrims over the winter, because he did not want people trying the snowbound passes merely to see him. Gently, he began to discourage the pilgrims who did show up. He told them he would be open to visitors again next spring, if God willed it. The pilgrims kept coming, but the word spread and gradually choked off the flow.

24

"Strangers coming! Get the women out of sight! Hide, hide! Strangers coming!" Karim ran down the mountainside yelling and puffing. Hard on his heels came his new best friend Farid. Women working in the fields looked where the boys were pointing, up toward the notch of Red Pass, but since they saw nobody, they went on with their business. The crone, who was sunning herself outside Ibrahim's compound, began to ridicule the boys. Then Ghulam Dastagir came out to see what the noise was about. Hearing Karim's cry of Strangers! Strangers! he shouted at the women to get indoors fast and advanced upon his son. "What's all this? What is it, boy? Are you lying? You'd better not be lying …"

"Strangers!" his son hollered. "Coming on horses, Papa! Three of them!"

Ghulam Dastagir frowned and walked across the village to alert the malik. Minutes later, he and Ibrahim rode out on donkeys. At the foot of the path to Red Pass, they did indeed see three men on horses, coming down toward the village. One looked normal; he was wearing a long shirt and a proper turban—but the other two! Who were they, what were these strange red coats? Ibrahim glanced at Ghulam Dastagir, then kicked his donkey forward. The strangers reined up. One of the men-in-red barked something, but it wasn't Pushto or Farsi or Baluchi or Arabic or any other tongue Ibrahim had heard.

What was the proper greeting for such men? Nothing in the rules of etiquette seemed to fit. Was their headgear meant to offend? To insult? One wore nothing at all—he was riding about the countryside with his hair completely exposed. The other—it was almost worse!—wore a pot-shaped hat with a shelf attached to the front and a feather poking up from the top. Both creatures had pink skins and chins shaved obscenely bare. Their pants were so lasciviously tight that the shape of their legs showed. Indeed their garments seemed designed for just such a display: Their heavy red jackets were shorter in front than in back, and they had tucked their shirts into their waistbands as if on purpose to make their crotches glaringly visible to anyone looking. In back, their jackets divided into two tail-like segments just above mid-buttock. Ibrahim instinctively brushed his own knee-length shirt down over the capacious pantaloons protecting his privacy. The men were sitting on horses at this moment, but Ibrahim had to wonder: what did they do about their buttocks when they were performing prayer? How did they cover their hindquarters during their prostrations? Or did they simply bend down and—God-forbid-it!—wag their butts for all to see?

"Salaam aleikum, sahibs," Ibrahim called out soberly. "Welcome to Char Bagh. How can we serve you? Are you lost?"

The third member of the party pushed ahead of his red-coated companions. His grin revealed a gold bicuspid. "W'aleikum a'salaam, villagers," he said and went on in fluent Pushto. "Good health. What a beautiful valley you have here!"

"We can manage in Pushto," said Ibrahim in that language, "if that's what you speak. Are you fellows Pushtoon?"

"If Farsi is your tongue, let us by all means speak Farsi, Farmer-sir," the man said in elegant court Farsi. "Is this the world-celebrated village of Char Bagh?"

"Well…it *is* Char Bagh," Ibrahim allowed. "Have you some business with us? Where are you fellows from?"

"Gardez, my friend, many days south of here. Do you know my country?"

"We're not well-traveled," Ibrahim apologized and then went on to lie politely, "but we have heard your country celebrated in stories. Men speak well of you. Your visit honors us. What of these others? Are they also from Gardez?"

The Pushtoon turned to his companions and conversed with them for a few minutes in that strange language. The red-coats grinned the whole time as if Ibrahim's question had been a joke. The translator turned back. "No. These men hail from a tribe called the Engrayzee. This man is Oxley—Officer Oxley. That one is Hudson."

"Okusley," Ibrahim tried out the unfamiliar sound. "Hadasan."

"English!" one of the redcoats shouted, standing up in his stirrups. "Englishmen!"

"Ingriz," Ghulam Dastagir repeated. "Engriz-mein."

"Engrayzee," the Pushtoon corrected him. "It's the biggest tribe in the world—enormous. They come from a country much further than Gardez. From the west, my friends." He pointed toward the setting sun.

"Closer to Mecca then?" Ibrahim hesitated, not wishing to boast, but then went ahead and stated the important fact about himself. "I have been to Mecca. I went with my father as a boy."

The Pushtoon nodded respectfully. "Hajji-sahib," he acknowledged. Then: "From that direction, yes, but their land lies far beyond Mecca."

"Beyond Mecca!" Ghulam Dastagir exclaimed. "What do they want here?"

"They want to lodge here until the snows come."

"Here?" gulped Ibrahim. "With us? By all means. A thousand times. The honor is too great. Really, much too great. You see, we cannot offer such important travelers the luxuries they rightly expect. We can give them nothing but bread to eat and straw to sleep on. This is a poor village, sir. Entirely at their service, such as it is, but all we have to share with them is our misery. Sorkhab is the place for them. Up the river."

"No, they've seen Sorkhab. This is the place they want. They don't ask to lodge in your village. If I gave that impression, I beg your pardon. They only mean they would like to set up lodgings near your village."

"Why here, particularly?" Ibrahim glanced at Ghulam Dastagir, and was not surprised to see him frowning. Over his shoulder, he could see Ghulam Haidar and two of his cousins approaching. The boy Karim was with them. Word had spread. Soon, many more villagers would be coming to investigate the excitement. They were all in a nervous state already. Every week, something new—the pace was almost unbearable. Pilgrims, okay, but men with red coats and strange headgear from a land beyond Mecca? When would it end? Ibrahim didn't want his women to glimpse these men with their tight pants and open jackets and naked chins and exposed heads. He certainly didn't want such men setting their hungry eyes upon his women!

"These men are doctors," the Pushtoon explained smoothly. "They are studying illness. We hear that illness has come to your village. These men would like to examine your patients and suggest cures. They have great learning, these men, great learning."

"They are very kind," Ibrahim replied. He turned to his friend. "Do you see Allah's compassion, Dastagir-jan? The Almighty has sent us doctors." Then he addressed the strangers again. "But the illness has already done its work here. Some of our people have died, God forgive them. The rest have recovered. There is nothing here for doctors to treat anymore. Allah bless you for your compassion! Before you move on, have some bread and tea, whatever poor hospitality we can scrape up, an onion perhaps—"

"Well, but these men," the Pushtoon cut in. "—these doctors would like to explore your hills a bit. They believe rare medicinal plants grow here, plants with the power to cure terrible illness. If they find such plants, they will show them to you and explain their uses. This is their real mission."

"Ah," said Ghulam Dastagir. "They wish to gather precious plants from our hills and take them away to Kabul to sell. Is that it? What about our wheat crop? Our fruit trees? Would they not like to raid those as well?"

The Pushtoon kept his composure, but his fingers tightened on his reins. "Hajji-sahib," he said to Ibrahim, "Where is your headman? It's him these doctors would like to speak with."

"You're speaking with him now," Ghulam Dastagir spat out. "The man you're talking to, that's our malik. What would you have him know? Speak, stranger. Don't be nervous. Malik Ibrahim won't hurt you."

"My friend." The Pushtoon turned to Ghulam Dastagir soothingly. "You all seem angry. Why are you so angry? Don't be angry with me, I am only a translator. These Engrayzee pay me to help them. And let me confide in you, they have more money than you have seen in your dreams. What's more, they mean no harm. In some ways, they're like children! They don't even ask to set foot in your village. They noticed an empty building on the other side of the ridge and that's where they'd like to lodge for a time. They have their own supplies. Mules will follow along with their goods. They will pay you, of course, and let me tell you, as one Muslim to another, I've squeezed endless cash out of these men and you could too. Take my advice: do not let this opportunity slip past you."

"Pay us how much?" said Ghulam Dastagir.

But Ibrahim inserted himself quickly, "That building you saw is for guests of the village." He did not wish to mention the malang before these strangers.

The Pushtoon was undaunted. "Guests of the village. Why, that's just how they hope to be considered: as respectful guests. Surely, you would not deny travelers the use of a ready-made shelter that stands empty?"

"How much will they pay?" Ghulam Dastagir repeated.

"How much are you asking?" said the interpreter.

"We must have five rupias a day, not one rupia less. Do you hear me?"

The interpreter paused to talk this over with the red-coats. While they were conversing among themselves, Ibrahim contended quietly with Ghulam Dastagir: "This matter touches the whole village, brother. We can't agree to anything till I call a jirgah."

"Call a jirgah, fine! Who will say no? Maybe we can milk enough out of these strangers to build a water mill. If they stay on the other side of the ridge, what's the harm? Our own mill, Malik-sahib! Think of it!"

"And where will pilgrims stay?"

"Malang-sahib is discouraging pilgrims from visiting him until spring, isn't he?"

The interpreter finished consulting with his patrons. "They accept your terms—"

"They haven't heard our terms," Ibrahim cut him off brusquely. "I alone have the authority to set terms. If you take over our guest house, we'll have to build other lodgings for our usual guests. Our men are busy with fields to tend. This will inconvenience us. We cannot accept less than twenty rupias a day for that building. I'm sorry, but those are the terms."

The Pushtoon was grinning again. "They knew you would say that, Malik-sahib. They could tell they were dealing with a man of the world. Well, you can't blame them for trying to get the best price—that's the way of the world too—but there's no putting one over on a man like you. Twenty a day then. Agreed." He reached down to shake Ibrahim's hand. Ghulam Dastagir was gaping at the village's good fortune, but Ibrahim felt uneasy. The man had agreed too quickly; he must have set his price too low. They would have paid twice what he was asking. Now they were congratulating themselves on outmaneuvering a pair of village bumpkins. Yet how could he now reject terms he himself had set?

25

Karim crawled down among the boulders with all the noiseless craft of a master warrior, then inched forward on his belly until he could peep over the edge, right down into the compound the Engrayzees had claimed as their own. It didn't look like it had a month ago. These strangers had spent lavishly, hiring the villagers of Char Bagh to improve the one-time guest house—fortifying the walls, installing a gate, adding a second story to the building. No one asked what they wanted with such a fort. People were just glad of the chance to suck so much coin out of those bottomless Engrayzee pockets.

Karim, however, had kept a close watch on the men. No one had asked him to, but he knew his duty. The village would thank him someday. If these Outsider bastards were up to some mischief, he'd be the first to know. Karim almost hoped the Outsiders *would* try something, so he could tell his father.

His belly was itching. He wriggled a bit to scratch it against the rough surface of the rock. Then he froze. One of the Engrayzees had come out of the building. He stood in the courtyard, fingering his bare chin. He was the one with the strange tool attached to his face, the tool with stems that curled around his ears and a frame that perched on his nose and held two tiny windows in front of his eyes. Ahmad's mother sometimes told a story about The Bald Boy who had a magical tool that allowed him to see through walls. The device she described looked very much like this one the Engrayzee had. Or maybe his device allowed him to see the future.

Or what was behind his own head. All these devices had appeared in Soraya's stories.

But Karim had to chuckle. For all his magic, the man had no idea he was being watched. If Karim had a gun, he could pick the bastard off right now, one shot. From this distance, he couldn't miss. No one would even know how it happened. They would come out and find the man lying dead in the dust as if by magic. Ha! Unless the other two were in the building. They might come running out at the sound of gunfire and spot Karim up here on the rock. But he would have three guns, all of them loaded and lined up next to him. Bam, the first one went down. In his mind, he snatched up the second gun, smooth as the river over sand. The other two were running out now. They were looking up—bang! The Pushtoon went down. Then it was just Karim against the last remaining Engrayzee, man against man. The Engrayzee had a pistol. He aimed. He shot. He missed! Ha! It was all over now and he knew it. His face gleamed fear. Karim had the third gun in his hands. He was sighting down the barrel. The man was on his knees, pleading for mercy—

Karim woke suddenly out of his reverie. The courtyard below was empty. What happened to the Engrayzee? Did he go back into the house? Karim turned and stretched, only to experience a second jolt: the Engrayzee was standing right behind him, with a bag in his hand, casting his shadow over the boy's legs. The sneaking bastard *kafir* dog!

Karim shrank back. The Outsider advanced on him, holding out his hand as if in appeal. He said something in gibberish, all the while smiling. Karim studied the man's hand. He recognized the posture now, the gesture. It was like holding out a piece of meat to coax a wild dog closer. Only, what this man was holding out was a coin. "Bak-sheesh?" he said, in the very voice you use to soothe and attract a dog. "Bak-sheesh?" he crooned.

Bak-sheesh—what was that supposed to mean? Was that the man's kafir-bastard-gibberish for "take-the-money?" Money for what? Karim had done the man no service. Maybe he wanted something. Maybe this was payment in advance. Well, why not take the money? Everyone else in the village was getting rich. Why not Karim?

The boy reached out and took the coin. He had never held money in his hands before, and it felt wonderful, that hard, round shape in his palm. It flooded his mind instantly with images of good things he might buy. A knife with a folding blade. He could carry it in his pocket. If anyone gave him trouble—snap! The blade was open. Not so brave now, are you? Slice! Thrust! Ho ho!

The man crouched down to Karim, his knees spread apart. Karim found himself staring at the obscene view between the Outsider's thighs. He could actually see a bulging bumpy place where the man's cock and balls were tucked. He remembered telling Farid on that first day how these men dressed: "They're fitted out with big ones, like donkeys," and Farid responding, "They'll catch you behind the village one day and ram those clubs up your ass, they will," and Karim taunting back, "Oh, no— it's you they'll be ramming. They try that with me, I'll split their heads open like melons, just you watch." Now, in the man's shadow, he felt how small he really was, and how big the man. A shiver of nervous dread ran through him. But the man sat back and the unnerving view disappeared. He took a sheet of paper out of his bag, stared at it, and said, "Solem."

Karim guessed what he was trying to say and replied helpfully, "Salaam aleikum, sahib."

"Solem. Ah – lay - kum. Suh-heeb," the man repeated. He touched his own chest. "Roo Prt," he uttered. "Okk... slee. Yoo?" He touched Karim's chest. "Yoo?"

"Rooh pawrt," said Karim. Probably the man's name. "I am Abdul Karim," he told the man. He clapped both hands to his chest and added, "Abdul Karim, son-of-Ghulam-Dastagir, son-of-Abdul Bari, son-of-Mohammed-Tahir, son-of-Abdul-Haq, son-of-Qudrut-Shah, known as The Lion of the Valley." It was best to tell the man his entire lineage—let him know he was not dealing with some nobody.

The Outsider tossed his head back and let out a roaring laugh. He said something in his own tongue, shook his head, and opened his bag. Out of it, he drew what appeared to be the penis of some animal, thick as a donkey-dong and about as long as Karim's forearm, with a wrinkled, leathery-looking brown skin. The man offered it to him. What was Karim supposed to do with a dried animal dick? Karim shook his head emphatically.

"Salami," said the Outsider. Then, to Karim's horror and disgust, he took out a knife—just the kind Karim coveted—and cut the penis in two. Next he cut the shorter piece into a dozen round slices *one of which he began to consume!* The cross section of the meat was pink with flakes of white in it. (So that's what a dick looked like inside!) "Salami," the man insisted, munching away, still offering one coin-shaped piece to Karim.

"Salaam aleikum, salaam, but no," Karim retorted, his gorge rising.

But then they kept sitting on that rock, side by side, clumsily exchanging half-understood words. Their shadows shrank against their bodies and began to grow again in the other direction. Warming up under the hot mid-day sun, Karim began to feel somewhat at ease with the Outsider, and he wondered at the feeling. How was it possible to feel comfortable with a man who would eat an animal cock? And yet his mind easily quelled the image. Instead, he wondered what he might do to get another coin out of the Engrayzee. Maybe offer to carry something for him, or…his mind quailed at the dangerous thought: offer him one of the family's sheep? No: a missing sheep would be noticed and the loss would quickly be traced back to Karim. He would take a hell of a beating.

Then the Outsider himself answered Karim's question. He leaned over until his head was close to Karim's. "Keyrim," he murmured in a tone of hushed conspiracy.

Karim snickered. The mispronunciation of his name meant "my erect cock." The word put a picture in Karim's head, of the man without his pants, his cock erect. His throat thickened with tension. Maybe *this* was how he could get another coin out of the man. Give him just a glimpse. Like he'd given Farid for free. What harm could it do? But he would insist on seeing the man's cock in return. The same deal he'd made Farid. Fair is fair. At last he'd know if these Outsiders had donkey-sized dongs, like some of the women were speculating.

"Keyrim. Duktaar?" said the man. "Char Bag." He waved in the direction of the village. That's how he pronounced the name. Char Bag. *"Duktaar?"*

Duktaar? What was that? The man said the word as if one should know it. Karim stared at him, trying to plumb his meaning.

The Engrayzee carved out a flowing shape in the air with his hands. "*Duktaar*," he repeated. Then, with a pebble, he scratched out a shape on the rock. It looked like a man with thick hips and a waist as thin as a wasp's. Next, the man paged through his notebook again, with fumbling fingers, and found something he wanted. "Zun," he said, staring at the page. Oh: woman. He made the flowing shape in the air again.

Karim got it now. Not duktar but *dukh*taar—girl. "*Zun!*" he exclaimed.

"*Zun!*" The man had produced another coin from somewhere. He held it up between his thumb and forefinger. "*Baksheesh.*" He touched his eyes and made a gesture of peering. He wanted to look. His coin glistened in the sunlight. "*Zun. Baksheesh.* You. Keyrim. Char Bag."

Karim wanted to hit the man. The filthy God-blasted dog didn't know who he was talking to: the secret guardian of the village's honor! The protector of the women. Karim wanted to kill the dog. Because he did know of a place he could show the man. Why, he would split the donkey-cunt's head open like a big fat watermelon. All he needed was a fist-sized rock. One good swing—but if they got to fighting the man would not be the one to die. The cold truth hit Karim and chilled him: this man would not die, he would kill. Suddenly, Karim felt the terrible impotence of being young. He was a breath away from his own death. He had never felt so frightened. Because he did know of a place he could take this donkey-fucking bastard. Frightened but aroused as well, a terrible, potent brew. And there was something else in there, even more toxic and uncontrollable. Desire of another sort. Those coins. The Engrayzee was holding three of them in his palm now. All the things Karim could have with four coins! Sell the man a glimpse. That place above the river, above the spot where the women did laundry, and sometimes washed themselves, believing themselves unseen. No one else knew about that spot. Karim had discovered it a year ago and had never told a single soul except Ahmad, who hadn't really listened and who was dead now. Karim had only dared to go there a few times himself. Forbidden skin. And now to let this stranger, this *Outsider*—!

"*Baksheesh*," said the man, jingling a fistful of coins and smiling in a friendly fashion as if they were talking about some game, not the ruination of Karim's honor, the destruction of his soul, the worst of all possible betrayals. It would not be like giving the man a sheep. This would be incalculably worse. But it would be different in another way too. No one would ever have to know. He'd been to that spot and sneaked away and no one knew about *him*.

His fingers found a rock just behind him. His fingers closed around that rock. He eyed the man's waist, where a gun was holstered to his belt. Karim realized his cock was hard. Transgression was arousing! He shook his head, to let the man know that the answer was no, it was no, a thousand times no, but somehow his shake ended up as a nod. He heard a hoarse voice that could not possibly have been his own voice croaking out softly, "Give me the money. I will show you a place."

26

Shahnaz stuffed the soiled tablecloth into the basket with the other laundry. "All right, all right," she trilled over her shoulder. "You don't have to nag."

"Did you give the cows their hay?" said her mother.

"I can't do everything," Shahnaz screamed. "What do you want me to do, wash the laundry or feed the cows? Why can't Ghiyas feed the animals?"

"He has his own chores!" her mother scolded. "When I was your age, I'd have the laundry done and the animals fed by this time of day, and I'd have said my prayers and swept the yard too, you lazy wench. All right, go! I'll tell Ghiyas to take care of the cows. Go do the laundry—but don't go alone. Take Rahila and Mahboobah along. You're always going to the river by yourself. It's wrong! And ask next door before you go. See if your aunt has anything to wash. I better not see you back till the clothes are dry. *Wai*, a mother's hardships with such girls. We'll have to give you to a stranger! No one who knows you will ever marry a lazy, bad-tempered wretch like you!"

"Ha," Shahnaz snorted under her breath. Her stupid mother thought men wanted girls for their skill at washing clothes. Shahnaz, with her budding body, knew what men wanted. If the elders would only get out of the way, she could have a husband any time. The elders were always fussing about could a girl sew, did she have a sweet temper. As if anyone cared about things like that except the prospective mother-in-laws. But then, the elders only knew the mother-in-laws. The girls were beneath their notice except to order about. The mothers used to be girls themselves but they wanted to deny it or maybe they had forgotten. And the elders set their own standards for the groom too. How much land did he have? How many animals? An iron-tipped plow or just a wooden one? What was his status in the village? All the traits they considered desirable added up to some smelly, doddering old wreck. If only she could be like the girls in the stories, romanced by a warrior passing through. Shahnaz could picture it now! She would be doing laundry by the river, he'd notice her from the rocks above, where he'd tethered his horse and lain down to rest. He would gaze in fascination as she, quite unaware that she was being watched, slipped her dress off her pure milky shoulders…

Come to think of it, what did she need Mahboobah and Rahila for? Her mother fussed too much. Nervous wreck of a wasted little woman whose time had come and gone! Very soon now, one way or another, Shahnaz would be queening it over a household of her own. Her husband would be absolutely in her thrall, fascinated by her beauty, dumbstruck by her saucy wit, helpless in the grips of her charms, ready to give her anything she desired—yes, anything: embroidered blouses purchased dearly from merchants in Baghlan. Mascara, bought from the nomads. Kohl to rim her lovely eyes. Jewelry. Money for tattoos in secret places. Oh, once she had a husband, she would be expert in the arts of love…once she had a husband to practice on. Rahila and Mahboobah assured her of it: they knew!

With her basket of laundry on her head, sometimes balanced on its own, sometimes held in place by fingertips touching lightly, Shahnaz made her way down the narrow path to the river. Her calves brushed against the tall weeds lining the snake-like path to the river. Snakes were fascinating creatures. She saw one frequently in the vegetable garden, a green whip-like fellow with a lighter green stripe down his back. She wondered if it was true what Auntie Bilquis said about a man's equipment being very like a snake. Surely it could not be as long as that—or could it? Donkeys and horses certainly had equipment that grew as long as a snake when they were in the mating mood. Maybe if a girl stayed attentive, she would sometimes see a man's equipment poking out from below the cuffs of his trousers. Perhaps that was why Prophet

Mohammed commanded (as she had heard tell) that men wear their pants no shorter than ankle length. Of course, she had seen men in the river with their pants rolled up high, yet nothing showing, but they were not in the mating mood then. At a time like that, their "thingies" would be curled up inside them, same as a donkey's.

Shahnaz came to the edge of the grassy weeds. The path widened here and descended a small hill to the river bank, which was a mixture of gravel and sand. The air smelled wet. She enjoyed the sound of the water here, the ever-changing conversation the river was having with itself: gurgle gurgle, never quitting. What if she possesed a magical head scarf that would turn the language of the river into Farsi? She imagining putting on such a scarf and suddenly hearing words instead of gurgle-gurgle. What would the river be chattering?

Maybe, "Salaam aleikum, Shahnaz-jan, welcome back, you make me so happy, you are the most beautiful creature in the valley—no, in the entire world—no, the most beautiful woman the world has *ever* known... it's good to be alone with you, take off your clothes, Shahnaz-jan, let us be one..."

Shahnaz hummed as she let the imagined conversation with the river run through her mind. She set the basket down and pulled out the soiled tablecloth. What an ugly stain! Mawmaw's vomit. Uqh! Why did the old man have to gobble his food so quickly? As if he was competing with everyone else for his dinner. Now Shahnaz was stuck with the results of his horrid greed. She let the cloth float out into the current, holding on to just the tiniest corner till the water had pulled away the chunks of solid vomit. What a shame that the loveliest woman in the world should be saddled with the chore of cleaning up Mawmaw's vomit. She pulled the cloth back and held it to her nose. Well, it didn't smell anymore. She wrung it out, spread it over the rocks, and began rubbing at the stains with a flat stone.

When she was done, she rinsed her hands and glanced around. How nice to be alone! She was hardly ever alone. Why did she relish solitude so much? Perhaps there was something wrong with her. And yet, in Nana's stories, Tahmina was alone just like this, washing clothes by a river when the handsome Rustum spied her, just as Tahmina had loosened her blouse and slipped the material off her shoulders... Shahnaz tested how Tahmina might have felt at the moment. She unbuttoned one button of her blouse and tugged the material to one side to expose her shoulder. No harm in this. She was alone.

Then she heard the man.

She pulled the blouse shut, not that it was ever really open. He could not have seen much except her face. Oh no, her face! She clutched the wet tablecloth to the front of her face, glancing about wildly, trying to spot him. (Uqh! A faint whiff of Mawmaw's vomit still infused the cloth.)

The noise came again. It wasn't a word, just a sound. She looked up to see where it had come from and saw—*w'Allah*, one of those Engrayzees everybody was talking about. It had to be. But they were only supposed to roam the mountains up around Red Pass. They had agreed not to come down to the village, people said. She stared at him, stupefied. He was coming down. What could she do? Should she run? She ought to run! But her whole body felt as stiff as bone, so she just stood, while the man picked his way down to the river bank, wearing a wide ingratiating grin. Well, what was the point of running now, the damage had been done, he'd seen her face, there wasn't much left to hide.

Anyway, he wasn't really a man, exactly—was he? Were the Engrayzees men like other men? Or was this more like being seen by a stallion or a bull? As far as she knew, the Quran never said there was any shame in being seen by a male as such; only by a human male. A monkey, for example, would be permissible. Perhaps this Engrayzee was more like a big, hairless, clothes-wearing monkey than an actual man. And he did seem harmless. He was making little clucking noises, as one might to coax a reluctant child closer—which made Shahnaz laugh. *She* was no child! She felt sudden pride in her swelling, ripening body, her woman's body. He was holding something out for her to look at. She squinted and saw that it was a bottle.

She flinched from it: could he be trying to tempt her with wine? She had no way to know, she had never seen or tasted wine. She decided to let him edge closer just so she could get a better look. When he came within an arm's length, he took a sip from his bottle and wiped his lips, then offered it to her, uttering a sound like "Gud."

She took the bottle then, and sniffed at the mouth. It smelled a little like pomegranate juice. There was no rule against pomegranate juice. She put the bottle to her lips and let a small swallow enter her mouth.

It was not like the pomegranate juice they had here in Char Bagh, it stung the back of her throat when she swallowed, but it tasted rather good. It wasn't wine, though. Wine would be sweet, she assumed. This wasn't sweet.

She looked back at the man and laughed. What should she be ashamed of? With the tablecloth held to her face, she was mostly covered up. Only her feet, her hands, and her eyes were naked to his gaze. Not that her mother would agree that she was covered up. Not that any woman in the village would forgive her for staying here. Every single one of them would consider it scandalous, those frightened rabbits, but Shahnaz was made of different stuff. She had a curiosity about the world that none of the others felt. None of them could ever understand her longing to step outside the lines laid down for her, her hunger to see, to breathe. This was not so wrong—taking a drink from the Engrayzee's bottle. It was merely pomegranate juice, and quite tasty. Even if he was a man, he probably wasn't looking when she pulled her blouse to one side. Her face, okay: that he'd seen, but if he was like a monkey, he'd probably forgotten it already.

She glanced at him again, never intending to let the look signal flirtation, but something took hold of her—a desire to see if the look she had practiced so many times in private on her girl-cousins would work on a living male, even if it wasn't exactly a human male but a sort of large, hairless, clothes-wearing monkey-male. She cocked one shoulder, bowed her head, and looked up at him with just her eyes.

To her astonishment, when she looked, he was holding up a coin. It looked like a gold coin. Gold! She remembered what everybody was saying: the Engrayzees were rich. Many people in the village were getting rich, doing things for the Engrayzees. If he would give her a coin, just for one coquettish look, what harm would it do to throw him a look? Who would even have to know? She would stop at that. She reached for his bottle and he let her have it.

"Baksheesh," he said invitingly, waving the coin back and forth.

৪০৫

Shahnaz pushed open the compound door. Lights burned in the second-story veranda of the compound, shining through panes of thin, greased lambskin stretched over tiny window frames. Had anyone opened those shutters, they could have looked upon the courtyard and seen her creeping in, but no one looked, no one saw. Disheveled and confused, Shahnaz stumbled into the stable and pushed her way amongst the animals to curl up on the warm straw. Shame flowed through her veins like sewage. She could barely stretch, her body just wanted to coil into a ball. A hot discomfort burned between her legs at the heart of her womanhood. She dared not guess at the cause. It was not pain, but it disturbed her more than any pain she knew of. It blanked her thoughts and spread from her feminine center to her belly, up into her chest, and out to all her extremities.

Her life was ruined.

Her fingers were digging into her palms. She forced herself to unclench them and realized she held a fistful of metal disks. She remembered what she had been thinking earlier, that these coins—if they *were* coins—would turn into mascara and eyelid blackener and perhaps a pair of silver earrings the next time the nomads came by to trade. As if she could purchase such things, she realized now. As if she could just walk out to the nomads and offer them money in exchange for goods. Everyone would ask where she got the money, and what would she say? What had she been thinking?

And then the Engrayzees would laugh and say she came to them willingly. And she did, she remembered. She made a choice. Dread bubbled in her throat, and she wanted to throw up, but couldn't. Her stomach was dry, her mouth arid. That drink they kept giving her must have done something. It wasn't pomegranate juice after all. She scarcely dared to let herself admit she must have let wine into her body. And by doing so had forfeited God's mercy. Oh, Allah, what what *had* she been *thinking?* How could she have let herself do it? What had she been thinking?

The stable door opened. A pad of footsteps. The rustle of straw. Her mother's face between the legs of two cows. On her hands and knees, peering in at her daughter, hidden in the stable. "Shahnaz? What are you doing? Where have you been? Everybody's been looking for you!"

"I was here," stammered Shahnaz.

"No you weren't!" her mother growled. "Your father saw you come in! You were outside. What happened to the laundry? Where did you go all day?"

Shahnaz shook her head. Her lips moved but no sounds came out. Children bunched up in the doorway and in the courtyard outside, watching and listening fearfully. Shahnaz's hair poked out from under her head scarf, a scarf now pitifully filthy and torn.

Her father came out of the house and into the yard. "She won't answer," said her mother. "I think she's ill."

"Come on," said her father. "Come, my child. Let's go to the malang. He will know what to do. Come on."

They didn't have to wake the malang. He was already awake, standing outside the gate of the house the village had built for him, statuesque in his posture, a faint figure bathed in the scant light shed by countless brilliant stars and one thin crescent moon.

"Malang-sahib," Shahnaz's father began.

The malang raised a finger to silence the distraught man. "I know," he said. "Leave her with me. Later, send your wife to take her home. The girl will need much care tonight."

After the girl's father had left, the malang led her indoors. She followed him with a beating heart but a certain peace flowing through her limbs. She could let go now: the malang was in charge, and he would know what to do. The only man who could intercede with Allah on her behalf was now in charge.

He sat her down on pillows in his private room, facing his own customary spot. Then he got down on folded knees and sniffed at her mouth. "Open," he said. She opened her mouth wonderingly, and he sniffed again. Then he sat back in his spot, and picked up his prayer beads, shaking his head ruefully.

"You went to them."

She clenched up timorously, her fists tightening. She shook her head.

"It's no use lying, " the malang murmured. "What's done is done forever. When, child?"

"Before. Before sunset. They said just to eat something. It was only—others have done it, Hajji-sahib! I was hungry! I was thirsty—I didn't know what it was. I didn't know…wai Allah! Suddenly it was night, and they were taking me…taking me somewhere? I didn't want to, they forced me." She began to cry.

The malang sighed. "My wife will give you some milk-tea and then you must go home." He left the room, left Shahnaz crying, put on his slippers, tossed a cloak over his shoulders, and picked up his stick, a branch from a walnut tree, stripped of bark and worn smooth by weather. The thick end had been whittled to thin its girth. The top consisted of a gnarled knob the size of a small fist, which the malang's hand engulfed entirely.

He picked his way down to the village. Where the road widened into a sort of square, he stood with his open hands held out in supplication, gazing skyward and murmuring. Then he closed his hands and ran them over his face as if to wash himself in prayer. Men came out of all the compounds and watched from a distance.

The malang wrapped his cloak around his shoulders and headed up the path toward the Red Pass. At the compound inhabited by the Engrayzees, he beat his stick upon the door. An Afghan guard opened up and the malang pushed past him, ignoring the guard's protestations.

27

Rupert Oxley came out of his first-story quarters, pulling on his jacket and adjusting his spectacles. "What's all the commotion? Eh? What's going on out there?" He peered about with a queasy grin. He had fretted about this possibility all night. Not that he could blame himself, that much he had settled in his mind. It was Hudson who took things over the edge, and even Hudson could not be held to account. The wench offered herself so willingly, up to a point. So willingly! And yet— again—the whole episode left Rupert feeling slimy with remorse.

Now he stood buttoning his fly and hoping the man in the courtyard wasn't her husband, or father, or some blasted thing. He could not make out the fellow's features, but the darkness seemed to magnify his size. In fact—good lord. He loomed like a horse! Rupert moved hesitantly into the yard. Perhaps he could set matters right with a few words of explanation. The girl's willingness—that was the point to stress. Her almost frightening willingness. He might offer a bit of advice, too: rein her in, he might say. Oh, where was the damned translator when he was needed! "See here, old man—"

But the beggar pushed past Rupert with the wordless force of a boulder dislodged from a mountain slope and moving on a course set by gravity itself. Rupert remembered some story about a mad old hermit who lived in the hills. He caught a flash of molten eyes. The intruder swept upstairs to the second story and flung open the middle door of three. How did he know that Hudson lay in there, asleep? The madman strode right to Hudson's bedside and without a word of warning brought his staff down—thwack!—on the poor man's belly. Hudson let out a scream. Jerked out of slumbers, he balled up and clapped his arms over his head to defend against he knew not what.

The hermit raised his staff again. Rupert had to do something. He rushed to the old man from behind, wrapped his arms around him— "Hoy! Here now!" —and tightened his grip to squeeze the fight out of the lunatic, his mind fluttering with punishments he would order once the brute had been subdued—beating! imprisonment! Attacking an English officer in his sleep, good God!— hanging, perhaps! An example must—

But the hermit broke his grip and flung him away like a discarded jacket. Rupert slammed against the wall and dropped to the floor. How—? He watched Hudson scuttle on all fours toward the open door, trailing bedclothes. Rupert jumped up to grab the hermit's cloak and keep him from giving chase. "Get my pistols!" he roared to Hudson.

At that sound, however, the hermit turned and came at Rupert, swinging his stick. He held it by the thin end. The other end was knobby and looked like a mace. Rupert made a grab but the knob hit his palm with such force it left his bones tingling, and then he couldn't close his fingers! The hermit yanked the stick back and reared it for another blow. Rupert had no choice but to dive under the man's raised arm and roll out to the corridor, where he got entangled with Hudson. In that moment, the hermit jostled past them. Now he towered between the Englishmen and their weapons, which were in a room at the end of the hall. There was no getting past the man: he seemed to fill the corridor, floor to ceiling, wall to wall. He was shaking his great head but the tangled tuft of beard sprouting from every part of his face barely seemed to move.

Rupert could not gather his thoughts for he had to watch that club, had to dodge it, retreat from it—and thus he fell back toward the stairs, with Hudson by his side. Then, in one mad rush, the old man drove them down to the yard. There, he set to beating them in earnest. Wherever Rupert scrambled, whichever way he jumped, that eerie madman was somehow there ahead of him. Was this a dream? Along the wall, Afghan servants stood watching idly. Rupert did not yell to them for help. What help could he expect from them? Tears of indignation blinded him. The stick cracked upon his forearm and broke the bone. He knew for he felt and heard the snap! Panic unleashed in him a gibber of mad thoughts. He would die in this courtyard, thousands of miles from home, unknown, unmourned. Dogs would tear up his mortal remains and leave the scraps of him to rot upon unholy soil! It was all one single conviction, all one single emotion. Torn apart by dogs. He mustn't let them—must preserve his life. Torn! No shame in escape—his feet scrabbling against dirt—the stick missed, the madman turned on Hudson—Rupert saw his chance to shoot through the compound door—no shame in this. On the other side, a dozen or more of the savages stood on the loft of the hill, enjoying the sight of English officers getting drubbed. Yes, though all of them had taken his money greedily enough!

Rupert tore past them all, toward the open hills, the only direction that felt safe. Blind instinct told him to put distance between himself and the madman, just gain a few seconds of respite. Two or three seconds was all he needed and he would rally. Then he would go back and rescue Hudson. Ah, but Hudson had already saved himself. Here he was, coming fast! Hudson caught up, fell into stride next to Rupert, and the two men raced along the ridge of hills, huffing and gasping, heading toward the upper valley, where a small contingent of soldiers awaited them in a makeshift fort near Sorkhab. Hudson's head was streaming blood. A scalp wound, Rupert hoped. For if the man's skull was broken, he was done for—unbearable thought. Better not to think, just run. But at last, instinct gave way to exhaustion and Rupert's feet slowed down. Hudson pulled up too. Silence surrounded them. They had outrun the madman. They were alone in these wild hills.

Only then did Rupert feel a tingling. Looking down, he realized he was not wearing shoes, just his heavy regimental socks. Hudson didn't have even that much: he was barefoot. Now, with panic fading, disturbed thoughts began to squiggle in Rupert's brain. What had he done? He and Hudson, two of her majesty's crack troops, had just let one elderly native lunatic rout them with a stick! A stick! How would they ever explain this?

Hudson seemed to read his thoughts. "I wouldn't say elderly, sir. He broke your arm. He broke my head. I counted thirty of 'em. How many did you make it?"

Rupert frowned. Thirty? Yes, he might have seen that many along the hilltop. They were merely watching, but dogs turn into a pack so soon as they smell blood. Thinking back, he could almost hear the snarls. His hair prickled over his narrow escape. "Thirty or forty," he agreed. "There was nothing we could do against so many."

"And their leader—the horror! We're lucky to come out alive."

Rupert nodded, and they stood for a moment, letting their agreement congeal. Hudson rubbed his hands for warmth, lifting his bare feet up from the ground, first one, then the other, for although the day had been warm, the night had turned very chilly.

"Aye, but look here, " Rupert burst out, "you can't get to the garrison barefoot. It must be miles yet. You'll need shoes, Sergeant. We must go back We'll need shoes for you, and horses. We'll get sticks along the way. And rocks perhaps. We'll fight him."

Hudson made no comment. They clutched themselves and shivered. The minutes tiptoed by and a formless dread rose inside them both, some black feeling rooted in nightmare. "Thirty or forty," Rupert repeated.

"Or a hundred by now, maybe more," said Hudson. "And they've got our firearms. What good'll sticks and rocks do? I could bind my feet with handkerchiefs, sir. I have one, if you have another. We could push on to the fort."

"Yes. Yes, that might best." Rupert fumbled his handkerchief out of his coat pocket. Hudson pulled one from his sleeve. They wrapped his feet in these dressings well enough to let him pick his way over the stony ground.

By the time, they reached the fort, a hint of dawn stained the sky. The servants must have been asleep, for they took a damnable long time responding to fists pounding on the gate. Hudson stumbled as they entered, and Rupert had to pull him upright and support him, even though he himself felt three-quarters dead. Rupert's socks had worn through, but his frosted feet felt no pain, perhaps because of a greater pain masking it: that of his broken arm, which had swollen up alarmingly. But Sergeant Hudson was in worse shape. "Rum," croaked Oxley.

Rum was brought, cold rum at first, but with assurances of hot rum on the way. Hudson said nothing. A nasty bump showed under his blood-caked hair.

The fort had no surgeon, but an old quartermaster named Sheehan had some art in these matters from his days in the Peninsular wars. He washed and dressed both men's wounds and prepared tubs of warm water in which they could soak their swollen feet, feet which he then rubbed tenderly with grease and clad in warm, dry woolens.

Other soldiers gathered around to find out what had happened; they muttered angrily when they heard about the bearded madman and his surprise attack on Her Majesty's soldiers. "What set 'em off?" Sheehan quizzed.

"Who can tell with such people?" Rupert retorted dully.

"Some offense to their religion," Sheehan speculated. "They're mighty techy that way. Fanatical, you know. You mought have stepped on their sacred cow. No telling what'll offend the gods they worship. Their Allah, now, that's a vengeful one, and they got others, too— strange gods, bloodthirsty gods with animal shapes as'll make you tremble. I seen 'em in Calcutta, sir, some of them temples? Horrible goblins, like, each one with that many John-Thomases as you wouldn't believe! A hundred pricks to a creature, and that's what they prays to. I seen 'em in Calcutta. And here in these mountains, it's bound to be all the worse. Well, you'll have to take some men back there and teach them a lesson, sir."

"Best do nothing till we hear from Kabul," Hudson grunted, his mouth clenched against the pain.

"Tomorrer," Sheehan agreed. "After you've 'ad a bit of rest, the both of yer. We'll put you on 'orses and send you to Baghlan where they got a real surgeon, and all the comforts. Can you ride, d'ye think?"

"We'll have to see," said Rupert.

"Best you go soon, if it's Kabul gives the orders. Better not to let a thing like this fester and steep, it only encourages the natives. The guv'nor'll want to know about that man. If he took a stick to you, what else mought he be cooking up? A blooming ringleader, he is. A black-hearted troublemaker, sir!"

"I shouldn't wonder," Rupert agreed with mechanical melancholy.

"It's out here they cook up all their plots," Sheehan confided, fussing about them like an old woman, stirring the mulled rum and pulling blankets over the men's legs. "Oh, they have thousands'n schemes, sir! They like nothing better than to cut English throats. They meet in hidden places like your Char Bag and none the wiser—meet and stir their horrid brew."

"Could be, could be," Rupert agreed. Then he sat up. Something flared in his memory—the isolated compound he had seen clinging to the slopes above Char Bagh, and the line of people he had seen trudging up to it almost every day. The first time he spotted it, he wondered why that dwelling stood separate from all the others. Now suddenly he understood. "Hudson," he croaked. "That building on the hill, above the village! Do you know which one I mean?"

"Aye, sir, the one as gets visitors every day."

"Exactly. That's where the hellhound lives! That's his lair, Hudson. And who is he? Why does *he* get such a stream of visitors? Why, in fact, our place was built to lodge his visitors, they implied as much that first day—remember?"

"Now that you mention it, aye. And mighty uneasy they were 'bout letting us have it. They implied as he was a hermit, sir, but what sort of hermit gets a stream of visitors, like you say? And his house—a mite grand for a hermit, I should say."

"He's no damned hermit," Rupert declared. "That place is his fort."

"He's their bleeding captain, he is," the garrulous Sheehan asserted. "They come to 'im for orders. Won't you 'ave a bit more rum, sir? It'll warm you."

"People come from miles 'round," Rupert crowed. "Miles, the boy said!" He took the glass from Sheehan. "We've caught a big one, Hudson. It was right under our noses. I had my suspicions from the start. He must have felt it. That must be what set him off."

"Right you are," Hudson affirmed stoutly. "You had your eyes on 'im, sir, oh 'e knew the jig was up. He figgered if he killt us both, his secret'd be safe."

"That village would be the place to plan something!" The excitement inflating Oxley made him forget his woes. With rum burning in his belly, his extremities were warming up at last. "Cut off at top and bottom by gorges! The only way in or out is through that one narrow pass—why, you could pass within a mile of it and never know the place existed. We'll ride tomorrow, Hudson—three or four days should get us to Charikar. Major Pottinger is there, he'll know what to do. By God, I could earn my captain's stripes out of this. I wonder what Lord Auckland will say!"

"And your father," Hudson offered.

"Oh, exactly. 'Rupert saves the empire.' If only I could be a fly on that wall! By God, it's worth a lump on the head to roust a plot like this one, eh, Hudson? You'll get full credit, Sergeant. The way you battled the man and his whole troop—a tiger, you were. You'll get promotion out of this—Lieutenant! I'll see to it!"

28

A fog of melancholy permeated Char Bagh. At first, no one outside Ghulam Haidar's compound knew exactly what had set the malang off, but rumors circulated: it had something to do with a woman of Haidar's clan. Once the villagers got hold of that much information, they compared notes and traced the trouble back to willful Shahnaz, that outrageous rebel, always skirting the edge of decency. Some of the women recollected how she had teased the malang the time a group of them went up there, how she had told him she was available... They remembered how the malang had turned away from her lascivious teasing. Now, she'd brought catastrophe upon the village. The first night she returned to her father's compound, outsiders in the nearby alleys could hear her shrieks and guess at the punishment taking place behind those walls.

Within Ghulam Haidar's compound, the traumatized women retreated to the darkest corners, pressing their headscarves against their mouths to contain their shock and cringing from the beating underway, instinctively separating themselves as best they could from the fallen girl. Ghulam Haidar administered the beating in the tight small space behind the outhouse, hidden from the inner courtyard by sunflower bushes. His eldest son kept him supplied with branches cut from the willow tree in the center of the courtyard. Once in a while, as he brought the branch down across her back, her arms, her neck, or whatever part of her anatomy presented itself, he let out a curse or screamed out an imprecation—"May God strike you dead, you filthy dog!"—but mostly he just brought his whip hand up and down, up and down, following her as she tried to crawl away, and toward the end, weeping as he beat her. At first, she spat at him, screaming, "I hate you! I wish you'd die! You're not my father!" Outrage and betrayal made her voice crack and shrill. But toward the end, more wounded than enraged, she just sobbed, "I didn't do it...it wasn't my fault..." The father exhausted ten or twelve branches on his daughter but dropped the last one and turned, biting at his lips, pushing his sons out of his way like a blind man pushing through a thicket, making his way alone, defeated, and humiliated up the steps and into his house.

The women then came out of their hiding places and crept toward the corner of the compound where Shahnaz still lay on the ground, moaning inarticulately, curled into a fetal position, rocking slightly. Sensing the presence of the women in the gap between the sunflowers, she lifted her head and sought out her mother. She felt the depth of her transgression now, in her toxic shame, yet she struggled to her knees and dragged herself toward that only possible source of comfort, reaching out in penitential entreaty. Her mother stood hesitating for a moment, but when her daughter came close enough, she slapped the outstretched hand, then grabbed it and dragged the debased girl to her feet. She pulled her savagely toward the stable and pushed her through the open door, so that she fell onto the straw between the cows, onto the straw and the steaming heaps of cow dung. "That's your place!" her mother spat at her. "That's where you belong—among the animals, on top of their shit, you slut! How could you do this to me? Your poor father! Who will marry your sisters now? How will your brothers walk in the village with their heads high? You will never sit among us again—be certain of that. This is your place, this is where you spend your life now, you worthless clod of dirt!"

She dragged the stable door to close it. Shahnaz's older sister grabbed at their mother's sleeve and remonstrated with her—"Let her out. Soften your heart, it's not so bad. Just for tonight, comfort her tonight—just till her bleeding stops—" but the devastated mother snatched her arm away and put her shoulder to the door to swing it shut, howling her misery.

Meanwhile, those who walked close enough to Ghulam Dastagir's compound at the other end of the village would have heard blows sounding behind those walls too. The great wrestler had driven his son Karim to the wall and was hitting him with his open hands, slapping the boy across the head, and when those mighty blows sent the boy to his knees, kicking him on the backside, launching him forward to pitch face-first onto the dust. "Get up!" Ghulam Dastagir snarled. "Get up and be a man."

Ghulam Dastagir's wife yelled at him from the steps. "What are you beating *him* for? How is this *his* fault? Leave him alone, God curse you! Wai wai!"

"Keep out of this, woman," Dastagir shouted without turning his head. "This bastard-son of yours should have kept an eye on those accursed *farangis*. How many times have I told you, boy? How many times have I told you, eh? When outsiders are about, keep your eyes open and come to me the moment you see mischief. A tragedy like this does not jump out of a hole. You should have known."

He started beating again.

Karim took the punishment without his usual cries of wounded innocence. He didn't even try to protect his head. The spectators wondered at the boy. They knew Ghulam Dastagir was beating his son simply because he had no one else to beat. Tormented by the events of that night, he was venting his need to punish. No one moved to intervene. It would toughen the boy, and a father had a right to deal with his own son as he thought best. Those who were old enough remembered the beatings Ghulam Dastagir took from his own mighty father, and look how the beaten boy grew into a man that no one in the valley dared to cross. Someday, Karim too would strike fear into the hearts of his enemies, but there were some who pitied what he must go through to become that man. There were some who pitied him tonight, as they stood at a safe distance and watched his father go after him. Many of them knew that Ghulam Dastagir would vent whatever was left of his fury on his wife, later on, and after that, if he was still raging, who could tell?

At last, the patriarch turned away from his son and pushed his turban back to wipe the sweat from his shining forehead. He barked out a demand for water. Karim had gotten to his feet as soon as his father turned away. He sat huddled against a wall, blinking back tears, pretending to wipe his nose so that with the same gesture he could surreptitiously wipe his eyes and thus hide the fact that he was crying.

All that week the people of Char Bagh shuffled about their business with lowered heads. The men whispered amongst themselves over tea, too shocked for vigorous conversation. The women tended their animals and puttered in their vegetable gardens. They cooked and cleaned as always, but in eerie silence.

Many went to the malang's compound each day at sunset and prayed just outside the walls, but the malang did not come out to greet them or speak to them, and no one except Malik Ibrahim dared to knock and go inside. Ibrahim reported only that the malang was preoccupied with his prayer beads at this time.

In the evenings, many of the men instinctively gathered in the mosque to perform *namaz* communally, as if it were Friday. Karim tagged along with his father, and Ghulam Dastagir let him. His rage had waned. Once, as they entered the mosque, he was even seen with his arm around the boy's shoulder. In the wake of the latest beating, strangely enough, he had developed a tenderness for his youngest boy. Karim scarcely noticed. His troubled eyes made him look even more wounded than Shahnaz's father. He was taking this shameful episode very hard, showing a fine concern for the reputation of the village, but when anyone tried to pat the boy, he shook the gesture off.

Just as life was getting back to normal, the Engrayzees returned, and they came in numbers this time, twenty-strong, all wearing red coats, except for the original one, the man with the yellow hair and the eye-equipment, who was now dressed in blue.

Karim saw them from the barley field and let out a cry. Ghulam Dastagir ran to the malik's house to report. By the time a string of villagers started up toward Baba's Nose, the Engrayzees had reached the

malang's compound. Several had dismounted and were banging sword
butts against his door. Ibrahim broke into a run, but he couldn't move
fast enough running uphill. The Engrayzee had already pushed into the
compound and now they came out again, three of them shoving the
malang along, a fourth one scurrying along behind, trying to bind his
hands with rope. Khadija came after them. She snatched at that last
Engrayzee and tried to drag him down with her weight, but he knocked
the woman to her knees. Ibrahim's every breath was a blast of fire.
"Stop," he panted, "Stop, bastards!"

The Engrayzees saw the crowd coming. Five of them dropped to
their knees and lifted their rifles. Five more moved into place behind the
kneeling men to form a second line of gunmen. From the redcoats came
a cry of "Halt!" The villagers had no idea what halt meant, but they
understood pointed rifles. They pulled up and stood there, clenching and
unclenching their fists, swearing at themselves for coming up empty-
handed, cursing at the red-coats, screaming out the dire things they
would do to foreigners *next time*—break heads, cut throats—the whole
time watching in impotent rage as one of the soldiers flung the malang
over his horse like a bag of wheat.

The villagers moved forward cautiously, each side watching the other
in grim silence—the villagers watching for an opportunity to charge, the
Englishmen for the moment when they must fire. The mounted soldiers
cantered backward, keeping their rifles trained on the villagers while
those who had dismounted got back on their horses. They certainly knew
how to handle horses, these Engrayzees. Then they strung into a column
and, one by one, starting from the rear, they turned and galloped away.
As the last man wheeled, Ghulam Dastagir lunged and grabbed onto the
horse's tail. The soldier swung his rifle butt back. Ghulam Dastagir
dodged it and got the rifle stock in his clutch, but the horse burst into a
full gallop now, and it dragged Ghulam Dastagir off his feet. The
Englishman spurred the horse and wrested his rifle out of the Afghan's
grasp. Ghulam Dastagir dropped to the ground. He scrambled up at
once, but the foreigner turned in his saddle to fire a shot, and Ghulam
Dastagir went down.

The big man's friends rushed to him with cries of rage and pity, but
Ghulam Dastagir had merely twisted his ankle. He sat up chagrined,

rubbing the joint.

Ibrahim, meanwhile, had rushed to the malang's compound. Khadija sat on the covered porch, her scarf askew, her mouth grim, her face wet, her eyes blazing. She fell into his embrace and they stood for a moment, body to body, lost to any consciousness of what eyes might be watching them, united in shock and sorrow. When she pulled away at last, he turned guiltily to see if the door stood open, but no, thank God, he had pushed it shut as he entered.

"Oh, Ibrahim-jan! Oh, Hajji-sahib!" Khadija shook her head and brushed her face as if to clear away hair, even though no hair hung there. She rubbed fretfully at her cheeks. "They took him away. And you *let* them!"

"They had guns."

"You let them! You *let* them—"

"How could we stop them,? They had guns, Khadija! The next time—"

"What next time? He's gone! Go after them!"

"They're on horseback."

"Don't we have horses? They took our malang!" she screamed. "What's wrong with you cowards? Catch them before the pass, fling their bodies into the gorge! Kill them all, get our malang back!"

"Hush, Khadija, I'll take care of this." He put his arms around her shoulders, still trying to comfort her. "You shouldn't be alone at a time like this. I'll send Soraya up. I must go to the mosque now to confer with the men—"

She brushed him aside and strode to the gate. She flung it open, and stood before the men of Char Bagh, bare faced. The wind rushing down the slope made her skirts billow in front of her, made her headscarf stream toward the crowd. Strands of her hair, shaken loose, fluttered wildly.

"Don't a single one of you dare to tell me I should not stand here in the open in front of men," she yelled. "Don't you *dare* tell me I should be ashamed. What men? I see no men here, only rabbits! I see only mice! I see ants! *You* should be ashamed to be seen by *me*. You, who stood and watched infidels fling our man of God on a horse like a carcass. What stopped you? They had *guuuuns*, your headman says! *Guns?* Bastards! You valued your shameful skins above our precious malang? You traded his blood for your own, the malang who found water for us! Have you no shame? You let infidels come and dishonor a woman of this village right under your noses. I wondered at it before, but I wonder no more. Who can wonder at such things in a village without honor? Oh, if only I were a man—"

"Khadija." Ibrahim pulled his sister-in-law into the privacy of her own yard, spun her around by the shoulders and glared into her face. "You've said enough. Get into the house and wait for Soraya. Don't come out again today!"

Her jaw jutted, her eyes churned with ferocious demand, but finally she said, "Go on, then, but you better save the sheikh. You call yourself malik of Char Bagh, prove you're big enough, Ibrahim. God gives you this chance."

29

Most of the men were already at the mosque. Ibrahim plunged in and took his place at the center with Ghulam Dastagir and the other elders, painfully aware that he was the only one in that circle without a single white hair. Stragglers would keep arriving, lesser men, younger ones, boys too, but the *jirgah* could not wait.

"Malik-sahib," someone blared, "you'd better control your sister-in-law. The day I tolerate such talk from a woman—"

"You'll do *what* that day, you ass-fucked dog? What will you do on that day?" Ghulam Dastagir jumped to his feet, craning at the speaker. "*Now* you've found your courage? Now? The woman was right. Why, I'll pound your God damned face if you—"

Ibrahim yanked the big man back down. "Calm yourself." He cleared his throat. "Companions." He cleared his throat again. Emotion blocked his breath. "Terrible things have happened to us."

Uproar broke loose. Terrible things indeed! Everybody wanted to list them. Everybody spoke at once. Each man had to have his say, even if no one was listening. When the clamor died down at last, Ibrahim continued.

"Often you hear me call for caution but, my brothers, not this time! This time, Ghulam Dastagir has it right. Only blood can wash us clean of shame. As Muslims, we yield to God, but our first concern…"

The men leaned closer instinctually.

"—must be to rescue Sheikh-sahib. I don't know where they took him, but no matter where they're going, they'll have to pass through

Baghlan first." Ibrahim rubbed his feverish hands together to keep his mind calm. "So that's the first thing to do, I'll go to Baghlan and make inquiries. If I hurry, I might even catch them there."

Ghulam Haidar raised a timid hand. The poor fellow spoke hesitantly, for his daughter's catastrophic transgression had broken him. His head always drooped now, and his eyes bore a permanent stamp of humiliation, but he forced himself to squeeze out his ominous thought. "Malik-sahib, even if you catch up with them, what can you do, one man against a pack of twenty, thirty—and you heard their Pushtoon that first day. It's the biggest tribe in the world. Kill these ones, their kinfolk will come after us."

Ibrahim fingered his beard. "You're right. You're right. In the end, I see no choice—I'll have to go to Kabul and petition the king himself."

"The king!"

Several young men snickered at the audacious thought.

"Will the *king* consent to see you?" Ghulam Haidar was only posing the obvious question. "No disrespect," he added. "Your blood is equal to any man's blood but … the *king*?"

"I can knock on his gate. The poet Sa'di once described a king who—"

"We don't have kings like that anymore," Ghulam Dastagir interrupted. "You saw the color of this king at Sorkhab. Now you plan to pound on this bastard's very gates?"

"I'll do anything to save our Sheikh. Companions, I am telling you right now, I will bring him back safe or leave my dead body on the field!"

A storm of voices rose and faded. "Well," said Ghulam Dastagir into the silence. "If you can be so bold, Hajji-sahib, so can I. What's a king, after all? Just another mortal. In a hundred years, we'll all be dust. I'll go along, Ibrahim. You'll need a strong sword arm. Everyone knows the love I bore your brother. I'll back you as I backed him. You'll get through to the king if I have to wade through blood to clear your path!" The *jirgah* cheered.

After the meeting dispersed, Ghulam Haidar made the rounds of the village, collecting money. Nearly every man had taken money from the Engrayzees. Every one of them was glad to contribute those filthy coins to a clean cause: a purse for Ibrahim and Ghulam Dastagir to fund their epic journey.

Karim, meanwhile, followed his father and Ibrahim to the central crossroads and crowded in between them like a little man entitled to a share in men's discussion.

"What are you doing, you knave?" Ghulam Dastagir glared at his boy. "How dare you push your elders about?"

"I want to go with you!" Karim flinched from the expected slap but held his ground. "Take me along, Papa. I want to help."

Ghulam Dastagir lowered his hand with unaccustomed gentleness. "You're too young, boy. This is man's work." But he couldn't help fluffing his son's hair with awkward pride.

"I have my sling, Papa. Let me come," Karim insisted. "I won't eat much.."

Ghulam Dastagir looked at the headman, but Ibrahim shrugged. This was not his decision. Karim gazed up at his father with anxious longing. "All right," his father conceded. "Run home and tell your mother to pack enough bread for both of us. Get the stallion ready, and a donkey too. We'll need a pack animal. You can ride on the bags."

Karim let out a chirp and raced off toward his clan's compound. The boy's excitement sent a twinge through Ibrahim. Ahmad would have begged to come along on such a journey too. Ibrahim remembered his own voyage to Mecca with his father when he was younger than Karim. His unrequited longing for God had begun in the closeness he enjoyed with his father during that journey. Ghulam Dastagir did not appreciate how fortunate he was to have a son with whom to share a journey like this. Ibrahim longed to unburden his heart, and he didn't even know what was in his heart, but whatever it was, he couldn't tell Ghulam Dastagir. His gaze drifted up to the compound on Baba's Nose. It struck him that he ought to say goodbye to Khadija before he departed.

30

It took two days to reach Baghlan, for their way lay through steep gorges, often on mere goat tracks, with the donkeys setting the pace. Once they reached the city, Karim rubbed his eyes in disbelief and even the men gawked a bit, especially in the bazaar—not that stores astonished them, they had seen stores before: one of Mullah Yaqub's nephews kept a store in Sorkhab, stocked with everything from snuff to skull caps, but the bazaar in Baghlan had literally dozens of merchants' stalls, and each one bristled with literally hundreds of items: unthinkable abundance!

But the malang was no longer in Baghlan. Several idlers had seen a company of red-coated soldiers ride into town with a trussed-up prisoner slung over a horse, but others had seen the whole troop ride out again the next day, on the road to Kabul; so the travelers kept going.

The next leg of the journey took four full days. Toward the end, they kept arriving at substantial towns, but each time they asked if this was Kabul, people greeted them with hoots of scornful laughter and pointed further south. Each new settlement seemed bigger than the last, and they saw ever more numerous cultivated fields, until finally one town scarcely gave way to wilderness before another one appeared in the distance.

Late on the fourth day, with the sun sinking below the mountains, Ghulam Dastagir suggested they find shelter for the night, but Ibrahim insisted they perform their sunset prayers and push on, because Kabul simply *had* to be the next clump of houses up the road.

And it *was* a road now, a broad track of pounded earth topped with gravel, wide enough to accommodate a dozen men walking abreast, ascending toward a distant notch between two hills. They started up, and daylight drained out of the air as they climbed. Upon reaching the crest, they paused for breath—and at that moment caught their first glimpse of the other side. The men gasped. Karim let out a cry of wonder. The entire valley below them twinkled with lights! For one vertiginous moment Ibrahim felt as if the sky had been inverted and he was looking down into a bowl of stars.

Three or four mountain ridges thrust into the light-spattered bowl and the valley meandered out of sight among them. Even in that gloaming, the travelers could make out walls and houses filling up every scoop and groove and crack, every hole and hollow of the valley, each compound abutting directly on another and another and still another, with no fields or farms between them, and indeed no fields or farms to be seen anywhere below, making it difficult to imagine what people in this city ate and where they got their food. Even from so high above, the villagers could see dozens of streets dividing the sprawling fabric of human habitation into patches and could see thinner, darker lines too, alleyways that sliced the various patches into smaller sections. A river bisected the entire valley, and it too meandered out of sight east and west among the hills. Across the river, on a promontory just touched by the last of the light they saw a gigantic fortress.

"There's your king, I suppose." Ghulam Dastagir gave a jerk of his head.

Ibrahim nodded. He was trying to imagine knocking at the gates of that castle.

"Father?" Karim pointed to a structure on their side of the river, a compound so enormous, all of Char Bagh could have fit inside it easily. "What's that?"

All three stared silently for a moment. Whoever owned that compound must stand nearly eye-to-eye with the king himself. "That, my son, is where the Engrayzee live," Ghulam Dastagir declared softly.

Somehow, Ibrahim knew he was right. Another long moment passed in silence. Then Ibrahim said, "Well, are you ready to go down there?"

Ghulam Dastagir wore a mask of indifference, but it was only a mask. Karim shuffled in place, stroking his donkey's broad grey side and glancing uneasily at his father's hesitation.

Finally Ghulam Dastagir said, "I'm ready."

ॐ

Later, thinking back, Ibrahim tried to connect the events of those first few days into a story he could tell people back home, but his memories of them were just a jumble of random fragments, shards of a shattered pot: vivid images jumped to mind readily enough but they felt as meaningless as dreams: the three of them sleeping in the street, for example, huddled against one another, clutching the horses' reins. How many nights did they pass that way? Three? Two? Seven? Once, Ibrahim woke out of a restless dream, convinced that someone was trying to steal the donkey, and found himself staring into a shock of darkness through which, disturbingly enough, city men were hurrying purposefully, even at that hour, as if midnight were the same as midday here. God only knew what purpose men could have at *any* time in a place like this, where no one even had fields to tend.

He remembered day-lit moments too: trying to strike up conversation with strangers who shrank away from them as if from men with smallpox. One of them said, "Get away from me, you beggar!" Who was begging? Worse yet, another time, someone pressed a coin into Ibrahim's hand: "Here, you poor vagabond. Be in Allah's care." By the time Ibrahim realized what was happening, his humiliating "benefactor" had disappeared.

As for directions to the palace, people only laughed when they asked. One day, Ghulam Dastagir popped the question to a young boy and within minutes a ragged band of urchins collected around him, hooting ridicule: "Bumpkin's come to see the king. Oh yeah! Step right up to the palace, gentlemen! King's been expecting you clodhoppers!" How could Ghulam Dastagir deal with a bunch of jeering boys? What good was his muscular ferocity against children? When he tried to slap at them, they scattered like minnows, still hooting. And when Ghulam Dastagir looked up, people were staring at him with contempt: a grown man trying to hit kids. Even much later that day, Ibrahim noticed how his companion carried his head tucked down between shoulders hunched in shame. Karim felt his father's disgrace, and he sullenly threw rocks at feral dogs.

Everywhere they went in that maze of a city, they found themselves flanked by high compound walls. They lost their bearings, lost track of which way the big compound lay, lost sight of the king's fortress. Quite by accident, they stumbled across the river one day, only to scare up a flock of women washing clothes along the banks. "What are you gawking at, oafs?" the women yelled. The travelers scuttled away before the women's relatives could come after them with sticks and knives. How did so many clans and tribes manage to live squeezed together like this, especially if they let their women wash clothes outdoors, in plain view?

Then one day, as they rested by a bridge, Ghulam Dastagir said the dreaded words. "Ibrahim, my boy, we should never have come. This was a mistake. You'll never get in to see the king, and even if you do, he'll never take your side."

"We can't be sure of that," Ibrahim objected. "Our cause is just."

"Our cause. Who gives a damn about our cause, except you and me? As for justice? In this world, everyone sides with his own kind, Malik-sahib, the great with the great, the small with the small. We are the small."

Ibrahim felt betrayed. Hard enough to keep a grip on his own resolve! How could he prop up his companion's confidence too? "Don't talk like that, Ghulam Dastagir. We must stay strong."

"My father *is* strong," Karim blurted. "He's always strong. He's the strongest man of all."

"My boy's right. If I'm not strong, there is not a strong man left on Earth." Ghulam Dastagir spat out snuff and wiped his gray beard. "But what good is strength in a place like this? What we need is good judgment. It's what we needed from the start."

"Are you questioning my judgment? " Ibrahim demanded resentfully. "I never asked you to come along, you know. You made your own decision."

"Yes, I share the blame," said Ghulam Dastagir, "but so what? Only a fool never reconsiders a decision."

"Only a fool," Karim parroted.

His father reproved him with a glare, but turned back to Ibrahim. "I share the blame, but I'm man enough to ask what we were thinking. What were we thinking, Ibrahim? For God's sake, leaving our homes behind, our women unprotected, our fields untended—we lost our heads. Marauders might be hitting Char Bagh even as we speak. And here we stand, seven day's journey from home and kin."

Ibrahim wished he could shut out these poisonous but indisputable words. The thought of going home, cloaked in failure, after all his big talk—the thought of facing Khadija—even Soraya would look at him with diminished respect—and the village....? He could not live with such humiliation. "You and Karim go home. Tell the others I would not give up."

"Nonsense. I can't leave you here. Who would look after you, youngster?"

Ibrahim's jaw clenched, and then it burst out of him. "Let that be the last time you call me 'youngster'!"

"Why?" grinned Ghulam Dastagir. "It's the simple truth."

"It's disrespectful," said Ibrahim. "I am the malik of Char Bagh."

The big man knew he had his malik on the run now. "Don't be so touchy, Malik-sahib!" he said savagely. "Good heavens, if you can't take a little ribbing, what will you do on the field of battle? I never meant to offend you. Why, the respect I bore your brother, may his memory be green—"

"My brother," Ibrahim interrupted sharply, "was a great man, Allah forgive him, but he's gone now. So's my father. I'm malik now, and I'm telling you, respect me, respect what I am, or tell me that you don't and we can have it out right now. Then we'll see who's strong and who's weak!"

Karim let out a soft whimper, looking anxiously from one man to the other.

"Since you bring it up," his father said, "let's stop pretending. Do you really want to hear the truth? The only reason the village accepted you as malik—"

"Accepted? They didn't 'accept' me, they acclaimed me!"

"Acclaimed your bloodline, you puppy, not you."

"Since you bring it up, Ghulam Dastagir, let us be *completely* honest. You always thought the men should have chosen you. When they chose me instead, it embarrassed you. It made you angry. That's why you call me youngster every chance you get."

"I'm not angry, just disappointed. The village went mad that day, by God—choosing a whelp like you over a seasoned elder like me. I'm just concerned about the village, that's all, concerned for all of us, you hear? They call you 'malik-sahib,' but I'm the one who really has the village in his care. I came along to look after you and keep you out of trouble. I can't shirk my duty just because the village went mad one day."

"The village knew exactly what it was doing that day. You don't have the qualities to be malik, and everybody knew it. *That's* the real truth, and I'm glad I said it finally."

"I—?" Ghulam Dastagir sputtered. "I don't have...? I don't...? Why, I could break your head open like a melon!"

"Yes, breaking heads is all you know. All you can think about, you fool! That's why no one chose you. There's more to being malik than breaking heads."

"Let's just see about that!" Ghulam Dastagir started toward Ibrahim. Karim grabbed at his father's skirts, but his father slapped him to the ground and wrapped a corded arm around Ibrahim's neck.

Karim jumped right back up, and grabbed his father's leg. "Look, Papa! Look! That man on the bridge is staring at us. Look at him, Uncle! He's staring at us!"

The men stopped wrestling and both looked toward the bridge. Both were panting, both still ruffled. On the bridge, a short, round man with cherubic cheeks and substantial biceps lolled against a stone balustrade. "What the hell are you staring at?" Ghulam Dastagir cried out.

"You three." The man gathered himself up and started forward. "Friendly gaze, brother. Just a friendly gaze. You're newcomers, aren't you? I can tell. City's got you topsy-turvy, eh? I know how it feels, I was new here myself once. I'm Abdul Haq the woodseller. Abdul Hak of

Wardak, they call me. I sell wood when I have wood to sell. My first day in Kabul, by Quran, I fainted dead away. That's what the city did to me at first."

A sudden hope warmed Ibrahim. "But you live here now? You know your way around? Could you help a traveler, brother?"

"I'm a Muslim. Of course I'll help. What do you need?"

Ghulam Dastagir flashed his headman a warning: why should this man be so friendly? He must be up to some big-city trick. But Ibrahim ignored the look. "A good night's sleep, a little shelter, some bread and tea—that's all we want. We can pay. And also, directions to the palace. We're here to see the king."

For once, this announcement sparked no ridicule. "What do you want from him?"

"Justice," said Ibrahim, and he told his story. This was the first time anyone had let him tell it start to finish. He kept it as short as he could, but his voice betrayed him finally, with its tremble.

When he was done, the short man nodded. "Forget about the king. I know a mosque that lets travelers sleep in the back. Come along, you fellows, I'll take you there. This malang of yours ... they call him the Malang of Char Bagh, I suppose. You're from Char Bagh, I think. Isn't that what you said?"

"Yes. Have you heard of our malang?" Ibrahim exclaimed.

"Almost," said the other. "Very nearly. I came *this* close to hearing about him the other day. My friend Hakim Shamsuddin the hat merchant has heard of him. He's an expert on geography, is my friend. He knows every place, and everyone who lives in every place—everyone important, that is. My father knew his father, we're *this* close, so anyone he's heard of, I've almost heard of. You've heard of Hakim-sahib, surely?"

"Oh, surely, surely," Ghulam Dastagir and Ibrahim stammered politely.

"Healer, hat merchant, scholar—what a man! Do you suffer from snakebite? Hakim-sahib's the man to see for *that!* One chuff of his celebrated breath and you'll thank God for the serpent that sent you to this doctor because Hakim-sahib doesn't just restore a man, he *improves* a man. Forget about the mosque, in fact, why don't you fellows stroll with me to the Grand Bazaar? I'll introduce you to Hakim-sahib. He takes an interest in malangs and such. No man alive outdoes him in hospitality. He'll get you out of the rain. Oh, he'll see to that, he will!"

Ibrahim and Ghulam Dastagir exchanged a glance. The unfinished business they had broken open hovered between them, but this prospect of shelter pushed it to a back shelf. They fell in beside Abdul Haq, who chattered on as he led them through a network of streets, past occasional mounted men, a great many pedestrians, a team of donkeys dragging logs, a string of six camels, each one connected to the next by a rope.

The Grand Bazaar turned out to be a row of store fronts stretching out of sight along a broad avenue. Crowds milled about in front of the various stores, bickering and bargaining, or merely socializing. Ibrahim tried to keep his face still and his eyes hard so as not to seem the village bumpkin, but the profusion of merchandise robbed him of speech. Gorgeous carpets draped over clothes lines, the better to display colors and patterns! Saddles and stirrups and cavalry regalia! Cups and teapots of every conceivable design! Cutlery, swords, bolts of cloth—spices, powders and potions—hassocks and pillows—furniture of wood or silver or beaten brass, all with filigree designs etched or carved into them—houseware made of iron and leather and ivory, cunningly worked together, the eye could not tell how—hookahs adorned with beadwork—shirts, embroidered and unembroidered…Mascara. Kohl. Henna—flesh paint of every description. Beads and bangles, wristlets and adornments galore … Everything the nomads had presented on trade parlays plus a thousand items more!

Dark gaps broke the row of storefronts at intervals, looking like missing teeth in a grin. These were alleys thrusting straight back from the avenue. Glimmers of light revealed these too to be lined with stores. The Grand Bazaar of Kabul was deep, then—no telling how deep.

Suddenly a hubbub of curses and laughter sounded down the block. Ibrahim saw four horsemen coming. And although he had never seen the men before, he recognized the clothes, the red coats they wore, the tight black trousers, the white straps criss-crossing their chests over golden buttons. Each had a sword swinging at his hip. Ibrahim sensed Ghulam Dastagir tensing up next to him.

Afghans were shouting insulting jests at the Engrayzees in Farsi and Pushto.

"Who farted! Oh—foreigners! Should have known!"

"Bring your mother down here, mister. We'll fuck her, she wants it."

Each insult sparked bursts of laughter among the Afghans. The Engrayzees were conversing casually amongst themselves, but they smiled at the Afghans occasionally, waving as if acknowledging applause.

"Hey, infidel! Want a donkey-dick? Throw me some *baksheesh*, I'll lend you my donkey."

"*Baksheesh?*" beamed one of the foreigners. He stood out of his saddle, grinning, dug a few coins out of his pocket and flung them to the crowd. "*Baksheesh,*" he announced. The resultant burst of laughter elicited a bow from him. Two little boys rushed to gather the coins like chickens pecking up corn.

As the foreigners rode away, Ghulam Dastagir clutched Abdul Haq's arm. "Who were those men! Where did they come from?"

"Foreign parts," the other shrugged. "Come along, now, let's get you to Hakim-sahib," and he marched into the bazaar. Night had fallen, but every store had charcoal burning in a brazier, and most had lanterns too. The first alley was open to the sky, but there was no moon to see yet, only stars. Then they entered a covered lane, and the stars disappeared. Soon Abdul Haq turned right, then left, then right again. The villagers lost all sense of direction, moving like moles through that complicated network of fire lit tunnels crowded with shadows.

At last they arrived at the store of the healer and hat merchant. (He was also a scholar, Abdul Haq reminded them.) Hakim Shamsuddin was a solemn fellow with a great, large belly, bushy eyebrows, drooping cheeks, and melancholy eyes. He greeted the travelers gravely and poured some tea for them out of a gigantic tin samovar. A boy popped out of a back room with bowls of pine nuts, raisins, and hard candies. The travelers nibbled at the snacks and sipped tea, while Abdul Haq poured out his distorted version of the Char Bagh story: an army of Engrayzees had appeared one day without warning, had poured over the hills in numbers greater than any invasion of ants—

"Not entirely without warning—" Ibrahim corrected him politely.

"Two of them were living next to our village for a month and more—collecting herbs, they said. And we let them. And when they came for the sheikh, they were only twenty-strong, give or take a few, but they came with guns. They took us by surprise."

"By surprise. Exactly," Abdul Haq agreed. "By surprise. Twenty men stomping in on elephants. Every elephant hauling twenty cannons. The ground trembled. Suddenly, they were everywhere! Hakim-sahib, the whole village fought like tigers, but it was no use. These two survived. They've come to Kabul for vengeance."

"Well, for justice. That's why we want to see the king."

"This sheikh of yours..." The healer leaned back against a hard cushion, resting his hands on his belly as if on a small table. "There is talk these days of a man up north somewhere—the Malang of Char Bagh, people call him. He wrote a book called *Turbulence of Love*...Is he, by any chance, the one you mean?"

Ibrahim stared. How could a shopkeeper in Kabul know about the sheikh? His book? Ghulam Dastagir, however, took the question in stride. "That's our sheikh. Malang of Char Bagh. Exactly. That's our village! In fact, Sheikh-sahib dictated his great book to this man right here before your eyes. This malik of ours!" he boasted. "He can read, he can write—he's been to Hajj, even."

"Only as a boy," Ibrahim blushed, "with my father."

But a new mood suffused the room and would not allow his modesty. "The great man's scribe." The healer sounded awed. "You are the great man's scribe..." He stroked his beard for a moment, sunk in thought, and then raised his hand for silence and declaimed: "*Fill the ruby goblet...Let the wine be stirred... The music is forever there. The lyre makes it heard... Air is emptiness to us ...Not so to the bird.*" He stopped and looked at Ibrahim. "Did your sheikh write those words?"

"It sounds right. I don't know every line by heart, but yes: it sounds like his. Oh, do you know him, then?" Ibrahim leaned forward eagerly.

"Hakim-sahib knows everyone," Abdul Haq crowed.

"Is he in Kabul?"

"I don't know where he is," the healer intoned. "The book is known to us, not the man. People have been talking about him, though. Copies of his book have been turning up all summer. I have a few pages myself. But this is the first I've heard of Engrayzees abducting him. It's shocking! It's shameful!"

"Could the king order a search?" Ibrahim pressed. "Could he make the Engrayzee confess what they've done with our saint?"

The healer rolled his eyes and put a pinch of snuff under his tongue. "You're a long way from home. Does news never reach your village?"

"What news? What do you mean?"

"The king can't tell these Engrayzees what to do. It's they who rule him. They're the ones who brought him here two years ago. They came with cannons and women and wagonloads of goods, they drove out our own Dost Mohammed Khan, and they put this vicious fool on his throne. This is a better king for you, they said."

"Better—? By what right!" ?" Ghulam Dastagir spluttered, "Who are they to say which king is best for us? Why do they even care who sits on our throne?"

Hakim Shamsuddin permitted himself a pained smile. "It's always about land and gold and women, my brother. Always. Such is the way of the world."

"Could I petition their own king?" Ibrahim asked. "Does he know what his kin are doing here to us? Are they at least Muslims, these people?"

"You must be joking!" Abdul Haq exclaimed. "They worship idols!"

"So they're Hindus?"

"Not Hindus exactly. Pagans, though. They worship one idol mainly … a naked man nailed to a stick. They carry statues of him around their necks They have his picture hanging in their mosques. And there in their mosques, they guzzle wine, people say. They feed on pig meat."

"Pig meat!" The village men recoiled from this repellant information. "Have you seen this with your own eyes?"

"A friend of mine sells them wood. I've seen it with *his* eyes."

"Do they drink pig's blood?" Karim squealed, rubbing his lips as if to rid himself of a foul smear, but also titillated by the scandalous news. "Do they eat pig shit? What do pigs look like?"

"About the offal, I can't tell you, but if they eat the flesh, why not the offal? Every part of a pig is equally filthy. Still, I wouldn't swear to it. I only know they ride about the city like khans and dandle this king like a plaything of theirs."

"But what of the real king? What have they done with Dost Mohammed Khan?"

The hat merchant shifted position, cleared his throat, changed the subject. "Are you fellows hungry? Let me get you some bread and cheese. Is the tea still hot?"

"Thank you, bless your house. About the true king, though—where is he now?" Ibrahim persisted. "Is he dead? Did they kill him?"

"Worse than dead," Shamsuddin burst out, snorting as if relieved to say it finally. "He's living in Hindustan, on Engrayzee charity, like a servant. They stuffed his mouth with gold and he yielded like a worm— after he beat them in battle too! Imagine! What the Engrayzee can't shoot, they buy, that's their way, but this king of ours! He dishonored us. He should have died in battle."

"It's not true," Abdul Haq pleaded, wringing his hands in miserable agitation. "His Majesty would never sell himself. He has a plan, Hakim-sahib. You know how I respect your every word, but you're wrong about the Great King. His Majesty has a plan. When the time comes—you just wait. His forces will rise up everywhere! You'll see. His son is here— young Akbar, mighty Akbar, seeing to it for him. There's a plan! There is!" But the woodseller himself sounded depressed and unconvinced by his words.

The hat merchant turned sad and baggy eyes on Ibrahim. "We live in shame," he sighed, "but Allah knows best. You men, though: please! Consider my humble shop your home and refuge as long as you are in Kabul, as long as it takes you to accomplish what you've come to do. I would be honored to host the scribe of the great malang of Char Bagh."

31

Ever since Rupert Oxley returned from Char Bagh, his status in the community seemed to have changed. One day his new orderly brought him a cream-colored envelope containing an invitation to dine with Colonel and Lady Baldwin. The Baldwins! He thought it must be some mistake, for the colonel and his lady kept an exclusive guest list, but no: there was his name on the envelope, and there it was again above a chatty paragraph penned by Harriet Baldwin, begging his attendance on Thursday evening at a dinner for a few dear friends.

Of course he had met the woman; everyone eventually met everyone in Kabul, but he never dreamed she would include him in any group she described as her "few dear friends." Puzzled and dazzled, he brushed his best coat that Thursday and set off. No sooner had he shed his outerwear at the Baldwins and greeted the brittle little Colonel Baldwin, then he saw the Envoy himself, Sir William Hay Macnaghten, standing by a window, deep in conversation with Colonel Oliver and with Rupert's mentor, the wonderful Alexander Burnes. Elevated company indeed!

Near them stood three younger men whom Rupert knew from cards: Captain Whitman, Captain Havelock, and the Envoy's own nephew Lieutenant Connolly. He glanced around, pretending to feel at ease in this high atmosphere. There stood Lady Florentia Sale, wife of the eminent General Robert Sale, who had gone south recently to clear the passes of Ghilzai tribesmen. Harriet Baldwin came toward Rupert with her skinny arms outstretched, her small, round head bobbing like a sparrow's. And then, just as she clasped his hand, he spotted Amanda

Hartley framed in the far doorway and his heart went thump.

But he tilted his head as if in merest greeting, an iron exercise in self-control. She smiled back, showing no hint of last summer's disapproval. Had the wonderful Mr. Burnes interceded for him? *Thank you, Alexander Burnes!* Rupert willed himself to turn his back on Amanda and join the conversation of the men, glowingly aware of the cast on his arm, the badge of his great deed in Char Bagh.

Drinks were served in a long drawing room that looked out upon a pretty yard blanketed with moonlit snow. On impulse, Rupert refused whiskey. It struck him suddenly that his conduct mattered. People saw something in him now, something worth admiring, and he must keep them seeing it. When questions were put to him, he answered with thoughtful restraint, suggesting that he knew more than he could say.

When dinner was announced, Amanda came gliding alongside him as if by happenstance and asked if he would take the seat next to hers. Asked very casually but with a hiss of shy breath that gave her invitation a furtive flavor of romance. He thought the sudden thunder in his chest might startle the company, but no one noticed their exchange, the others being too engrossed in the conversation they carried with them from the drawing room: was Afghanistan growing less or more hospitable to the British? This was the question of the day and it raised a lively chatter at the table.

"What do you think, Mr. Oxley?" Amanda lowered her voice to make theirs a private conversation. "You have seen so much of the country now."

"I defer to my elders," he replied with grave good humor. "If Mr. Macnaghten says the situation improves, it must be so. And what is your opinion, Amanda?"

She moistened her lips. He ignored the faint shadow of down above her mouth. "I feel insecure," she faltered, "but then, just now, I am what you young men like to call ... a field widow."

"Yes, I heard." Amanda's husband Major James Hartley was away with General Burnett on a diplomatic mission to the chiefs of Kohistan, up north. "Are you all alone, then, in your big house?"

"I stay with Florentia mostly. We field widows must stick together.

And when I am home I have my servants, so I'm not entirely alone."

Florentia overheard this. "What comfort are native servants?" she demanded in a loud harsh voice. Rupert saw two spots of color on her cheekbones and thought she might have taken too much wine until he noticed how the skin above her lips was worn red from blowing her nose too much: the poor woman must have been crying. "It's those very servants make me anxious," she complained. "I catch them whispering sometimes! Heaven only knows what they're plotting."

"You mustn't fret," Harriet Baldwin counseled her. "We all feel a little frayed right now because of poor Sergeant Flannigan."

Tommy Flannigan had been stabbed in the face on a road near the palace. Rupert didn't know the man very well but had seen him with his heavily bandaged head. The knife chipped his cheekbone, it was said.

"That was banditry, pure and simple. It was not political," the Lord Envoy declared. "The villain wanted a purse, and he didn't care whom he struck, Englishman or Afghan. Overall, civility is gaining ground, I assure you. Take heart."

"You have such a sunny disposition, Sir William." From other lips, those same words might have registered as praise, but the tremble in Lady Sale's voice colored any intended flattery with reproach. "I wonder what it would take to convince you there is *ever* any cause for alarm."

The envoy made no immediate answer. Florentia was clearly in a state, and he, it seemed, would not risk breaking her fragile calm, but his silence plainly struck her as condescension, for she raised her voice again. "You tell us all is well, but every day brings a fresh incident, Sir William." She sniffed as she spoke the word 'incident.'

The envoy cut his boiled lamb carefully into portions, then spoke with studied composure. "Every incident disturbs our emotions, that's understood, Florentia. But if we let emotions rule us, we take alarm unduly. We think the sky is falling, we think the abyss yawns! The facts are not so cruel if you look at them coldly, as I must do. Every day, another village pledges allegiance to the king. Every day, his majesty's army grows in discipline. Day by day, tax collection improves. Everywhere I look, I see progress. I say, by Christmas—"

"Oh! You promised us Christmas last year!"

"And last year, at this time, Lady Sale, we *did* pass a watershed. We took the Dost into custody. Ever since then, everything has—"

"Yes. Tell us how wonderful 'everything' has been *since* then!"

Several of the guests cleared their throats. Embarrassment clouded the air. Lady Baldwin's hands fluttered in helpless dismay. Lady Sale was spoiling the gaiety, but who could restrain her? Who could criticize? The woman was distraught. No telling what a woman in her state might say. Everyone shrank from her in spirit, hoping not to be the one who triggered her explosion.

"Since then," Macnaghten said with grim self-assurance, "there has been some increase in violence, but this was entirely to be expected. Entirely!" He gazed sternly about the table. Rupert held up under those cold eyes, but wondered why they seemed to linger on him particularly. Macnaghten took off his spectacles and cleaned the lenses with his handkerchief. "Every time we apprehend another ringleader, the remaining rogues grow more desperate." He spoke in the patient, level voice of a schoolmaster. "They shoot their bolts because they must. They know their time grows short. If the beast thrashes, Madame, it's because we have it by the throat."

He put his spectacles back on and adjusted them on his nose, then returned to his meal. The rest of the company followed suit, glad of the distraction. Lady Sale seemed to know she had said too much and ate in chastened silence.

Then Captain Whitman set down his fork, "Sir William is right. You are quite right, sir. The native warms to us, I can attest to it. Just the other evening, we were riding through the grand bazaar—Well, Havelock was there. Tell them, Havelock."

The bony captain waved a bony hand. "You tell."

"Well, the mood was cheerful, I can tell you that much," Whitman said. "The people in the streets waved to us, called out greetings. There was friendly banter. It moves me, I must say, when English officers draw such smiles from the natives! And of course there was the usual call for *baksheesh.* I always dispense the coin lavishly when I am in the bazaar."

"What sort of banter," Burnes inquired. "What exactly did they say?"

"Oh, that I can't tell you," Whitman shrugged. "I lack the language.

But the mood was unmistakable."

"Shame on you," Burnes said without courtesy. "Take some trouble with the language, young man." His severity took the whole company aback, and Burnes tried to soften his scolding. "We are living in a land not our own," he continued. "We should show a decent regard and learn the local tongue. It would not be asking too much. If we wish to civilize this country, we should at the very least conduct ourselves as civilized guests!"

"Guests!" Colonel Oliver exclaimed in amazement. "I hardly see myself as a guest here, Burnes. You show the native too much deference."

"Oh dear," Lady Baldwin lamented. "We're all on edge tonight. Perhaps the stars are misaligned, or the moon. Can the moon be misaligned? Let us take our pudding in the drawing room. I hope you won't think it too informal to retire as one single party, ladies and gentlemen together—we live in a wild country, after all!"

She led a procession back to the drawing room, where scented candles now added perfume and color to the lamplight. Gecko lizards could be seen, clinging to the screens over the windows. Servants brought out individual bowls of rice pudding with warm milk and cinnamon. There was cognac too, but Rupert made do with green tea.

"Well," said Oliver, "If we are making headway quelling these troublemakers—and I think we are—we have young Oxley to thank, in part. I dare say, he's brought in one of the worst of them. Congratulations, Mr. Oxley. I mean that fellow from Charikar, of course—what a bad sort! Charikar, was it not?"

"Char Bagh, actually. A tiny village further north. Quite a bit further, sir—closer to Baghlan, actually." The praise brought color to Rupert's cheeks and confusion to his heart. He felt the eyes of the whole room upon him. He dared to look directly at Amanda and found her looking right back at him, her green eyes sweet with admiration. He saw opportunity there. He quelled his hopes. Dignity, he thought. Leave the married Englishwomen alone, Burnes had said, and he must comply, for he was a man of parts now. His conduct reflected on others—on his mentor Mr. Burnes, for example. And yet, how he yearned to sneak his fingers onto Amanda's lap, where her own small white hand nestled.

To his dismay, Lady Baldwin said, "Can't we take up a more cheerful topic?"

Rupert could think of no topic more cheerful than his own glory, but he could not be the one to keep himself on stage. Someone else must do it. And then Havelock blurted the worst possible thing: "I hear that fellow is a sort of holy man to the Afghans."

"Where do you get that?" Rupert demanded. Surely, he had captured a dangerous rebel mastermind, not some ha'penny holy man!

"It's servant's buzz." Captain Havelock replied.

"And how do you come to hear servant's buzz?" Macnaghten inquired.

Havelock's modest head sank between his shoulders. "I have a little Farsi, and I do make a point of chatting with the cleaning people. They take our reputation into the country, you know, so I try to imprint a good impression."

Indignation swelled in Rupert's jealous heart. He knew who the blackguard meant by "cleaning people" and how he did his "imprinting." Shameless hussies! Rupert could afford his lofty scorn, for he had broken himself of those beastly habits. Not once since Char Bagh had he so much as touched any of the barracks whores. A man who hopes to command others must first command himself. "Supposing he is a holy man, what of it?"

"Exactly," Oliver chimed in. "What of it? Many a fakir has a knife hidden beneath his cloak!"

"In fact," said Macnaghten, "the czar seeks out just such holy beggars as his agents. Why not? They roam the landscape freely. What better couriers in a country like this? I'll hear of no exemptions for holy men. If this one has nothing to hide, let him say so. His silence speaks volumes."

"Very possibly," said Burnes, "And yet I should like to know more about this man. If he's really a mystic—well...I take an interest in that sort of thing."

Rupert flinched. If his mentor abandoned him, all the pleasure he had taken from Colonel Oliver's praise and the Envoy's endorsement turned to ash. Burnes mattered more than all the others put together. Guilty doubts about his own achievement began to squiggle in his heart. He was relieved to hear Harriet Baldwin intervene.

"Amanda dear, we must distract the men from politics. Will you play something?"

Mrs. Hartley nodded, demure dimples appearing above her broad chin. She gathered her skirts and made her way to a battered harpsichord in the corner, for no pianos had been carried over the Hindu Kush yet, but Amanda's somewhat stubby fingers drew a serviceable sonata out of this humbler instrument.

Suddenly a frantic banging sounded at the outer gate. Amanda stopped playing and cocked her head. The gate was distant and the sound faint, but a raw tension surfaced so instantly, it must have been simmering down there all along.

A servant came in with a folded note. Lady Baldwin reached for it, but the servant took it to Amanda Hartley.

"What is it?" Lady Sale inquired anxiously. No one attended to her. All eyes were fixed on Amanda, who had risen for the note and now, having read its contents, fumbled for a chair. Oxley, alive to every fluctuation in this woman's state, sprang to catch her and lower her to a sofa.

"What is it, dear?" The affectionate word escaped him unintended, but nobody marked it, for all sympathies strained so strongly toward Amanda that Oxley's tenderness only gave voice to a unanimous solicitude in the room.

"It's James," she stammered. "My God, it's James this time!"

Macnaghten retrieved the note and read it with darkening eyes. "Madame! My deepest, deepest condolences!"

Oxley snatched and scanned the note. *His life given for the cause he served...cowardly attack on the road from Kohistan...Major Hartley and two others felled...bodies brought back for burial...Fine gentleman... unlikely to see his likes again....* The civility of General Burnett's language did nothing to alleviate the brutality of his report: Amanda's husband was dead.

He met her stricken gaze. While the others fussed about her person, he poured her a glass of sherry at the sideboard. She took the glass, her lips forming noiseless words of gratitude. He bowed, and with their two heads close, he murmured, "Your servant, dearest Amanda—forever."

Even later, he could not fault himself for his utterance. It was no attempt to thrust himself into the sudden vacancy in her life. He spoke from affection and unmitigated concern. He could never fault himself for his passion.

Nor did she, for she said out loud. "Rupert, you are kind." Then she struggled to her feet. "I must go home and see to this."

"Home! In this state?" Lady Sale protested. "After all our talk? I won't allow it. You will stay here tonight. Mrs. Baldwin has beds enough, I'm sure. I will stay with you."

"Let's not lose our heads," Macnaghten broke in huffily. "The city streets are secure. We'll escort Mrs. Hartley home. The men who did this thing will be hunted down, but let's not forget this mischief happened in the hills. Here in Kabul, all is well. You shall see."

But Amanda shocked them all by shrieking at the envoy: "All is well? All is well?" Her shriek shattered all pretense of normalcy. Suddenly, Rupert saw the whole company as savage animals incongruously clad in frocks and topcoats—and not as wolves and lions, but as rabbits and antelopes and mice—as prey. "Because the Governor must have it so?" Amanda screamed. "All is well? Will you never stop saying that? Progress, progress, every day? My God! No one tells the truth anymore! Not here."

"Amanda—"

"I should hold my tongue? No, I *will* not hold my tongue. I won't be still. No! Sergeant Finnegan stabbed in the face—all is well! Dr. Farley's servant killed—all is well! My husband...*all is well!* ALL IS WELL!"

Harriet Baldwin took her arm. "Now, now," she whispered. Amanda shook her off, but Colonel Baldwin himself restrained her. "Dry your tears, dear. You need to rest," said Harriet. "Come lie down. Don't fret, this house is well-protected. Lady Sales will stay with you tonight. Whatever needs doing can wait till morning."

And so the ladies clustered together, and so the Baldwin household rallied to comfort Amanda, but the dinner party was ruined and the guests had to find their own way out.

32

On their fifth day with the hat merchant, the men of Char Bagh suffered a setback: little Karim went missing. No one noticed at first, because no one kept track of the boy. He did what he wanted dawn to dusk. Once or twice Ghulam Dastagir asked if anyone had seen him and someone said oh, he's around, he'll turn up.

But night fell, the healer sent out for kebabs, and still Karim's hungry little face had not popped up. Ghulam Dastagir took a stroll down the lane, casually asking strangers if they'd seen his rascal. Some said yes, but none could remember when or where, although one storekeeper claimed he had spotted the lad playing knucklebones with a bunch of bad seeds and another vaguely recollected seeing him wrestling some bulky city boy down by the well, but was that yesterday or today? He couldn't recall.

The kebabs arrived, wrapped in hot bread and smelling of coriander and smoke. Ghulam Dastagir returned to the shop. As usual, some half dozen men had come by to eat with the generous healer. Most were there to meet his guests, for they took an interest in the Sufi path and they had read *Turbulence of Love* and felt the spiritual longing it provoked; now they hungered to meet the poet's scribe, hoping to feel the master's glow second-hand. Gathered around a dinner cloth, they plucked at morsels of meat, elicited tales about the great mystic, clucked about his abduction, cursed the Engrayzee, and shared reports of other rumored abductions: girls lured into the foreigners' compound, never to be seen again— frightful. Frightful. One name came up again and again: Boornus. Al-Iskandar Boornus —the worst of them all, people said: a sort of

Engrayzee vizier. A frightful glutton for virgins. Had a taste for little boys too, so people said.

Ghulam Dastagir went outside to scan the lane again. When he came back, he met Ibrahim's gaze but shook his head and reclaimed his spot in the circle. The dinner guests were now discussing how an ordinary man could get into the palace. The old king used to host a grievance day, they said: anyone could come to court and present a petition; but this new bastard? Not a chance!

"He's afraid someone will run a sword through him!"

"He doesn't show his face much."

"The Engrayzee won't let him. There's something wrong with his face."

"Yes, I've heard. It's not a human face. He has the snout of a wolf."

"Teeth out to here!"

"Allah preserve us!"

After the visitors departed, Ghulam Dastagir slapped the wall. "That damn fool of a boy!" he raged. "Where could he have gone to?"

The healer tried to sooth him. "He's made new friends. He went home with one of them and found a better dinner, that's all. It got late, his friend's people kept him for the night. I would do the same, wouldn't you? Your son will come home tomorrow morning, *inshallah*. Who would harm a boy? Allah will guard Karim-jan, never fear."

Like he guarded my poor Ahmad? Ibrahim thought when he heard these words. And then he felt sickened by the bitterness that surged up inside him. Was he blaming God now? If so, he was truly lost!

The healer had a house somewhere in the city and went home to it every night, leaving his shop to his guests. Tonight, he mouthed the usual courtesies as he made his usual preparations for departure: he wanted the men of Char Bagh to consider this store as their own. He was honored to give them a home and a headquarters. He should be thanking them, actually: their presence kept away the brutish thieves who infested this bazaar at night—

The stricken look on Ghulam Dastagir's face warned him of his error. He backtracked hastily. Lately the thuggery had dropped considerably—why, the bazaar was practically as safe as a caravanserai these days. He saw himself out, stammering these kindly lies. The men bolted the doors behind him.

Seven candles were still burning, a profligate indulgence, but Ibrahim snuffed six of them. they sat for a while with their knees drawn up, lost in private thoughts. Ghulam Dastagir broke the silence finally. "Where have you drifted, philosopher?"

"Nowhere. Just into idle thoughts, my friend."

"What thoughts? Share them, Malik-sahib? The night gets so lonesome."

"I was wishing I could be a better Muslim," Ibrahim confessed.

"Quit worrying," snapped his traveling companion. "Whatever you've done, God will forgive you. You're a good enough Muslim."

"Good enough isn't...good enough," Ibrahim sighed.

Ghulam Dastagir poked a straw into the melted wax pooled around the candle wick. "Yes," he murmured. "We all know how you feel about that. Maybe that's why the men choose you as malik. You're so earnest about all this. Why don't you go easy on yourself, though, Hajji? You say your prayers, you keep the fast. After you die, you'll go to heaven. You're assured of it more than most. More than me."

"There's more to being a Muslim than praying and fasting."

"No, there isn't. That's all there is, Ibrahim. Everyone falls short sometimes, but we do the best we can, you more than most. And yet you gloom about, complaining that you're not good enough, you're not good enough. If that's what you think of yourself, what must you think of the rest of us? We sense your attitude, Malik-sahib." He was picking an argument to keep his mind off Karim.

"I'm not judging anyone," said Ibrahim. "But I see your point." What he saw, however, was how pointless it was to explain himself to this lunk. Only the malang understood. The loneliness seethed in his breast.

Ghulam Dastagir would not let the quarrel go. "I'll tell you what your problem is, Hajji. You want to go to heaven before you die. That's not our lot as slaves of God. Allah commands us to live. He'll decide when to take us. If we rescue the malang, good. If we fail, we submit to His will and go on living, it's the only way. Go on living and doing the best we can. There's no shortcut to heaven." This wasn't about the malang. He was ruminating about Karim, of course, and how he'd cope if he had lost the boy. Easy for him to talk: his loss was purely hypothetical at this point. Karim would almost surely come back in the morning. Ahmad was dead forever.

Ghulam Dastagir clambered to his feet and rolled out his prayer mat. Ibrahim joined him and they began their ritual, standing side by side. Since this was the last namaz of the night, they recited the words silently. Nothing disturbed the perfect stillness except the rustle of clothing as the men moved from one position to another.

Ibrahim's anxiety about Karim and his sorrow for Ahmad ebbed to the background like a constant stomach ache. In the stillness, he sensed a voice in his mind, a nuance of sensation so faint he couldn't tell if it was real or imagined. Sometimes, when he was a little boy playing in the fields at dusk, his family called him home from a rooftop. At first, his ear could not discriminate between the distant human voice and the rumble of the river, the hum of the wind through the leaves—and yet something always made him stop and cock his head, because a voice imparts a flavor unlike any other to the noise of nature: the flavor of meaning. And when he did finally separate a voice from all the other rustle and bustle, what came into focus was never just sound but always words: *Ibrahiiiiim*...the voice called. *Come home...*

And now, amidst the syllables automatically sounding in his deepest mind, he sensed that same faint flavor of meaning, a sensibility not his own, calling to him like a voice from some distant rooftop: *Ibrahim ... Come hoooome* ... Surely this was God. Surely he was sensing the call of Allah amongst the thickets of Quranic syllables. The Loving One! The Beloved! His attention went chasing after that hint of divinity, chasing and searching, but God was too quick for him, as always, eluded him as always. Slowly the syllables turned into mere sound again, he drifted back down to the disappointment of another shallow night laced with human trouble—

And then small fists started beating on the door and Karim's voice came piping through the crack. "Papa? Let me in. Hey, it's cold out here!"

Ghulam Dastagir slid the bolt back, snatched the door open, and grabbed his son by the ear. "Son of an accursed father! Bastard son of a Goddamned accursed father!" he yelled, dragging the boy over the sill.

Karim clung to his father's forearm, trying to lift himself up to relieve the pulling on his ear. "What'd I do? Let me go! *Wakh!*"

"I'll *wakh* you!" Ghulam Dastagir roared. "Where the hell have you been? Your uncle here was worried sick!"

"I went spying like you said to do. I found out about the palace!"

Ghulam Dastagir paused, Karim's ear still clamped between his fingers. "You what?"

"Forgive him," Ibrahim pleaded, "just this once," tugged at the raging father's sleeve. "What was that you just said, boy? You learned what?"

"I was doing what Papa told me!" the boy hollered, smarting at the injustice. "Go find out stuff, he said, so I did! And now he's hurting me. It isn't fair!"

His father let him go. "Grown men don't know a damn thing about the palace. What could you know? Don't lie to us, Karim!"

"Some of the fellows told me. It was Sakhi. You know the one. He follows women around the bazaar. I went with him today, Papa. You should have seen this one woman—oh, what an ankle! Sakhi was funny! 'Pretty-lady-dear, show me your foot! Show me your pretty ankle.' We were laughing so hard—"

"Never mind about pretty-lady and her ankles," growled his father. Nothing on this trip had been more unsettling than the women. They were everywhere in the city and there was no telling whose women they were—covered from head to foot, to be sure, but a man knew what was moving under those pleated garments. "Shut up about the women! Tell us about the palace—if you have anything to tell."

"I've got plenty," Karim boasted. "Sakhi's father goes up there with his donkey twice a week to haul away palace shit. He sells it to farmers for night soil."

"So? So he hauls shit from the palace. So what?"

"He's been inside, Pa. He's seen stuff."

"And he's decided to tell you? Oh, sonny-boy, spare me the headache!"

"No. He told his wife. And Sakhi was listening and he told me."

Ghulam Dastagir sat back frowning, because this sounded credible. "Well?" he demanded. "What did he say about the palace? Go on now."

Bathed in his father's interest, Karim swelled into pomposity. "It's very grand up there. They call it Bala Hissar—"

"Everyone knows that!" his father scoffed.

"—and there's only one road goes up to the palace and there's five guard stations along the way and the guards are mostly Hindus and a few Pushtoons—none of our kind."

"Just as I thought!" Ibrahim erupted. "None of our kind!"

"But lots of people go up anyway," Karim went on. "To deliver stuff. Coal and stuff. Pistachios and stuff. Potatoes. Meat and stuff—lots of stuff."

Ibrahim dismissed all this. "We can't get in that way. The tradesmen must be known to the guards. No one knows us."

"No, and besides, we have nothing to sell," Ghulam Dastagir noted. "My boy, what you've learned weighs less than a fart."

"No, uh uh!" Karim contested hotly. "There's another way to get inside—*that's* what I found out!" He broke off and peered around the shop, sniffing like a hound.

"Well?" his father prodded.

"What's the other way?" Ibrahim coaxed.

"I'm hungry. I smell kebabs."

"The kebabs are gone. You can have some bread. But first—get to the point."

"I'm thirsty, too," said the boy.

"You can get some water later. What's this other way?"

"You pulled my ear." The boy reproached his father. "I did good and you *hurt* me for it, Papa."

Awkward silence filled the room. Then Ghulam Dastagir gruffed out, "I thought the Engrayzee had stolen you, son. They steal children. If you think I'm a hard man, you should have grown up in *my* father's house. And the world is ten times tougher than your grandfather and me put together. Don't you know why I'm hard on you? I'll say this only once, so listen closely. You're my heir! You're precious to me! I don't want the world to eat you alive, I want you to kick it in the teeth if it tries. And if something happens to you, I'll burn the fucking world down in revenge. You hear me? Now, your Uncle Ibrahim has been good to you, and look how you've repaid him—worrying him half to death. You've been clever, though. Clever and brave. You've done the family proud. Now tell us what you found out, or I'll beat you so hard you squeal. How do we get into the palace?"

The boy went on snuffling for a moment, but his father's words mollified him. "Tell the guards you know about a plot against the king. As soon as you say that, they take you up to the palace."

Ibrahim snapped his fingers. "Why didn't we think of that?"

"Well, Hajji—possibly because we don't *know* of any plots?" Ghulam Dastagir shrugged. .

"That doesn't matter. The thing is to get inside. Tell somebody our story. Once they know what's been done to us, up there in the palace, they'll set the business right, I'm sure. I'll go tomorrow and by night— *inshallah*—we'll have the Malang back."

∞∞

The next morning, Ibrahim passed three times under the Quran held high by his friends and made his way out of the bazaar. The month of Aqrab was nearly over, and the sky was overcast. The grimy remnants of recent snow remained piled up against the cob walls flanking the road. Ibrahim had left his horse behind today: he couldn't risk losing it, so he started up the royal road on foot.

At the first checkpoint, he saw five guards. They had a tea service set out on a small roadside table. They scrambled to their feet with clackety-clack alacrity to bar his way. One guard barked something, but Ibrahim missed what he said or didn't know the language, so he kept on walking.

The guard switched to Farsi. "Where do you think you're going?" He lowered his rifle until the knife tip pointed toward Ibrahim's belly.

The headman forced a smile. "I've come to see the king."

"You think any beggar gets to see the king?"

"I am no beggar, I'm the malik of Char Bagh."

"Char Bagh?" the young man hooted. "What's that, some dusty little village in some shitty little nowhere?" He winked at his fellows.

218

"I've come for justice. Is that such a joke? The great kings of olden times meted out justice. People say this king is their equal. Are you saying he's not?"

The young man scowled and poked his bayonet against Ibrahim's shirt. "Are you being insolent, peasant?"

"No, he's being witty." An older man in brown livery nudged the first guard aside. "What's your business with his majesty?"

"A gang of ruffians assaulted an honest man in my district. They tied him up and hauled him away—"

"And you want the king to set him free? Are your own arms broken? Go get your comrade back, who's stopping you! Are there no men in your village?"

"It's not like that. You see, sir, these ruffians have been plotting against our king. I've come to report the plot. So that justice might be done. To the plotters."

"A plot, huh? Well, we'll send a messenger up and see if the big-shots want to hear from you. What's your friend's name?"

"He's a great sheikh, revered in our parts."

"Sheikh-Meikh, what's his name? And what parts?"

"Sir, we are situated by a river called Sorkhab. Our village is Char Bagh. Our valley is Tarana Dara. We are located in the Khwadja Mohammed Mountains, two days journey east of Baghlan. Baghlan is four *serais* by donkey from—"

"I know where Baghlan is! Why didn't you say so in the first place?" He nodded to the younger soldier. "Run up to the guard house and see if they want to speak to a man about plots in the Baghlan district. Tell them a fellow from Char Bagh has uncovered a bad business there, connected to some sheikh."

The youngster grumbled at having to climb the hill, but he went. The older guard told Ibrahim to sit down and join the guards for tea. It was all very sociable, until the young guard came skidding back down. "Villager," he panted. "Did you say 'malang of Char Bagh?' Is that who you came about?"

"I did!" Ibrahim felt thrilled to the bone. "Do they know about him even up here?"

The younger guard whispered to the old veteran who suddenly

turned grim. "Show me your hands," he ordered Ibrahim. "Both hands together, mister, out in front of you. Let me see your fingernails…"

Ibrahim stretched out his hands, bewildered. The guard flicked a rope around them and, with a few quick motions, bound his wrists together. "What are you doing?" Ibrahim yelped.

"Orders," said the other. "We're to bring you up to Bala Hissar."

"You don't have to drag me with a rope, brother. Up there is where I want to go."

"You must be tied. It's orders. Go with the boy."

"I'm not a boy," the younger guard pouted, but he yanked the rope attached to Ibrahim's wrists. "Come on. I don't have all day."

"Nor I," Ibrahim grumbled, although this was not strictly true.

They marched up to the fortress and no one stopped at them at the next four stations. At the base of the mighty walls, Ibrahim felt like a bug. The gate alone loomed taller than two men standing one atop the other.

The guard called out and the gate swung a few feet open. The guard prodded him through, but did not himself follow. On the other side stood two new guards wearing Afghan clothes under heavy blue overcoats. It was starting to snow a little now. Icy flakes came dancing down. Ibrahim gawked at the world within the fortress walls. He was standing at the edge of a courtyard of flat gray stones edged with fallow flower beds. Beyond them stood rows of willow trees, and beyond the willow trees, walkways, and more bushes and more trees, and in the spaces between all the ornamental plants, Ibrahim caught glimpses of a beautiful building surfaced with blue and gold tile.

But the guards had no intention of taking him to that building. They prodded him along the base of the perimeter wall. He went where they pushed because escape was impossible and besides, his whole mission had been to get inside this fortress, so why should he resist? And why should he be frightened? No one had beaten or wounded him, no one had even insulted him much yet. He was tied up, but he might be untied once he made his business clear. He just had to talk to someone higher than a guard. So he marched compliantly into a smaller courtyard. Stone steps led to a narrow doorway in a stone building. The guards poked him through. The antechamber inside had one thin window facing the courtyard, but it didn't let in much light on a day like this. The guards pressed Ibrahim down onto a stone bench and then fastened him quickly to a chain anchored in the wall. At that, Ibrahim tried to jerk his hand out of the cuff and looked about wildly. One of the guards said, "Calm down, they just want to ask you some questions. Answer truthfully and you may well see your family again today."

"Who's 'they'?"

"Shut up and trust Allah."

The guards departed, leaving Ibrahim alone, but only for a moment. A door in the corner soon opened and out came four new guards. They released Ibrahim from his chains and said, "You're wanted downstairs."

"Downstairs?" Ibrahim could not keep a quaver out of his voice, for these new guards had torches with flames dancing from the tops. They led him out of the room that faced daylight, down a narrow staircase, into a darkness lit only by torches. At that moment, Ibrahim felt a loss of control, a sudden unwillingness to be taken down into these depths, a fear that he would be left in blackest night, surrounded by stone, unable to know whether he was above ground or below. He stifled the urge to make a sound, fearful that any sound he made would shame him. He stifled the urge to ask questions, fearful that his panting breath would betray his inner cowardice.

They came to the bottom of the steps. About a half-dozen men were milling about at the other end of a long corridor. Ibrahim could not make out who they were at this distance. Prodded by guards, however, he moved toward them. Along the way, he realized that the corridor was lined with doors. Each one had a window cut out of it, but each window had iron bars across it. These rooms were cages. He saw faces behind the bars. Was he going to be caged here too? Surely not! What had he done except to make polite inquiries? That was no crime. Surely, once he had a chance to explain...

The guards' torches lit up faces in those little cells: luridly, fleetingly. None of the prisoners cried out or said anything distinct. Some of them may have been murmuring or muttering, but Ibrahim wasn't sure. The rustle of his own clothes, the rasping of his own breath, and the tramping of the guards' feet drowned out all peripheral sounds.

The end of the corridor enlarged into an actual room filled with the men Ibrahim had seen from a distance. Most were Afghans, but one was an Engrayzee wearing his arm in a cast. Ibrahim recognized the man with the little window attached to his face. He stared at Okusley with revulsion and dismay.

Okusley spoke in Engrayzee to one of the Afghans, who spoke to Ibrahim coldly in Farsi, "Mr. Oxley asks a favor of you."

"A favor?"

"He has a man from your village here. He wants you to make the man talk."

"What man? Is Malang-sahib *here*?" Ibrahim cried out. "What do you mean—make him talk?"

"He hasn't said a word since he was brought to this place. All they want is the name of his contact. But don't try that 'Malang-sahib' shit on me. I can't be fooled, and I won't pass on your trickery. We know what he really is. Just get the bastard to tell what he knows and you'll be released. Agreed?"

"Take me to him," Ibrahim shuddered. He could not help blurting out, "You're an Afghan, you pimp! Why do you serve these infidels?"

The translator ripped a backhanded slap across Ibrahim's face, knocking his head sideways and jarring his jawbone. Two guards instantly grabbed Ibrahim's arms to keep him from striking back.

"Where do you think you are?" the translator snarled. "In your father's cozy little house? You're less than a worm here! We can plant your dead remains in a hole and no one will know what happened to you or even ask. Understand? Do you dare to question what *I* am doing here? Do you care to insult me again?"

Ibrahim kept his feelings clutched inside him, kept his eyes studiously dead. He saw shame behind the churn of anger in the translator's red-rimmed eyes.

"Oh! Now this one won't talk!" the translator sneered.

"Take me to Malang-sahib," Ibrahim rasped out.

So they took him back into a dark corridor. Halfway down the length of this tunnel, they opened a door, which led down some steps into another corridor. A few paces into this tunnel, they stopped. The Afghan leading the way drew a clanking ring of keys out of a pocket in the draperies of his long shirt and opened a padlock. He pulled the door open, and they all entered, a guard gripping Ibrahim's right arm.

The malang was sitting in the furthest corner, looking blankly toward the middle of the room. His lips were moving, and in moments of silence, Ibrahim could hear him saying: *la illaha il-allahu wah Muhammadu' rasul-illah.* Over and over. *No God but God and Mohammed his messenger. No God but God and Muhammad his messenger.* His clothes were in tatters, his hair disheveled, and when the torchlight fell on his face, Ibrahim saw that this dear sheikh, his mentor, his teacher, his intercessor with God was disfigured by cuts and discolored with bruises, his right eye swollen almost shut by a purple bump.

At that, Ibrahim exploded. In one leap, he buffeted Okusley to the ground. A hand clutched at him, but he flung it off. Someone smashed a club into his ribs, but he was falling backward, which mitigated the blow. He grabbed somebody's head in a wrestling hold he had practiced as a boy, never with much success, but lost his balance. No success now either. Dragged down into a scrambling heap, he tussled right to the feet of the malang and back toward the middle of the room, while men kept trying to grab parts of him.

They were too many for him finally. The man he was holding by the neck got free, the others pinned his limbs. The two men not fully occupied in keeping Ibrahim restrained fell on him with their fists. He never stopped fighting. He broke free and scrambled to the corner but was too exhausted to stand and lay where he fell. The others got to their feet, panting. Someone kicked the door shut. Okusley shouted an order and all the men closed in on Ibrahim.

The translator leaned over him. "They were going to let you go, cretin! Now they can't. You've doomed yourself. They'll come back every day until you give them what they want. Make your friend talk or cough it up yourself—the Russian agent's name. What is it? Who is he? What's his disguise, who are his contacts in Kabul? You think you can hold it back? The Engrayzees are a bit squeamish, but *we* have no such qualms. We'll pull your fingers off one by one until you scream for mercy. If the fingers don't do it, we will start on your toes. Then your feet will go, your arms. Have you not heard about Dost Mohammed's brother? Cut to pieces alive in public—his eyes open, watching his testicles suffer the knife? Do you think we're joking? This is not entertainment. Oh, we are serious men here, very serious men, and we will get to the bottom of these riots and murders. Believe me, we will hunt down every plotter in his lair. Whoever you are, we'll find out your name, wherever you are, we'll drag you into the light, we'll kill every last one of you!" He showed his teeth and turned away.

The Engrayzee said something, and the translator turned back. "He says we took you for a simple villager, but trying to kill an Engrayzee changes everything. Now we know there is more to you than meets the eye. It's a good thing we executed the prisoner in the next cell this morning, it's created a vacancy just for you. Spend the night next to your malang and let's see how you feel about talking in the morning."

Ibrahim could not postpone or escape his imprisonment, but he wouldn't make their work easy. He kicked and struggled and tried to bite as they encircled him. Even so, it took only a few minutes. The malang ignored the commotion and went on with his meditative repetition of the Muslim's fundamental testament: *No God but God and Muhammad is his messenger, No God but God and Muhammad is his messenger,* as the guards dragged Ibrahim into the neighboring cell and flung him against a corner. While he lay in a heap, the others hurried out and threw the bolt. Ibrahim recovered his senses just in time to rush across the cell and throw his weight against the door but only bruised his shoulder bone, for the door opened in, not out; and by the time he started pulling, it was bolted. Ibrahim gave up then and just stood, listening to the footsteps diminishing into the distance.

33

As the sounds dwindled, so did the light from the guard's torches. Shadows jiggled and jumped on the irregular stone surfaces of the walls growing ever fainter until a distant door slammed shut, at which moment all the shadows merged into undiluted darkness. Ibrahim listened for voices, but if this block contained any other prisoners the uproar had stunned them all to silence. Then his eyes adjusted, and he realized that the darkness was not undiluted after all. A faint light was seeping through two horizontal slits in one wall, near the ceiling, slits just broad enough to slide his hand into. The bulk of this cell might be subterranean, but those slits were above ground. Otherwise, where would that light be coming from? And at least some air was entering the stone room. If he could peer through those slits, he might be able to see what lay outside this prison. But the slits were situated a little higher than Ibrahim could reach on tiptoe.

He felt his way around the room, looking for something to stand on, but the room was completely featureless except for a hole in one corner and the smell told him not to stick his hand in there.

He returned to the slits, jumped, and got his fingertips lodged in the opening, then tried to pull himself up, but his fingers slid off the wet stone. He jumped again and managed to thrust four fingers of each hand deep enough into one slit to hang his weight from them. He pulled his bruised body up, letting his feet drag against the stone, up and up—but just before his eyes came level with the slit, the top of his head bumped against the ceiling. An instant later his fingers slipped out and he crashed to the floor again.

He lay panting and aching: what good would it even do to look through the slits? He couldn't escape that way. He couldn't get any useful information from the view. Still, there was nothing else to do in that empty cell, no other goal to set, nothing else to try, so he went back to work. This time, when he pulled himself up, he tilted his head sideways and got one gratifying glimpse through the slender aperture. The wall was thick and the slit was deeper than he could reach through with his arm, but at least it gave him a bug's eye view of the yard outside: gravel and dirt a few fingers above ground level. His cell was mostly below the earth, as he had feared, but not entirely.

He had now achieved the only thing there was to achieve in that cell. He had nothing else to look forward to unless his jailers planned to bring him food. His cell door looked like a solid block of wood, unpunctured by any window or porthole, but feeling along its surface, he found a shutter so snug in its frame the crack was barely palpable. It did not budge to his push. It must be bolted on the outside. No doubt, the jailers communicated with prisoners through this shutter. They could push food through the hole without opening the door.

Ibrahim put his ear to the crack, tapped the wood, and spoke loudly. "Sheikh-sahib. Are you awake? It's Ibrahim. I'm in the next cell."

A voice answered, and though it was muffled by wood and stone and distance, Ibrahim could make out the words clearly. "Salaam aleikum, Ibrahim-jan-i-shireen."

Peace be upon you, Ibrahim dear-and-sweet! The words flowed over him like warm honey! "Thanks be to Allah , you sound strong. Sheikh-sahib, I'm ashamed."

"You have no cause for shame."

"I betrayed you. I am so ashamed—"

"You could never have stopped them from taking me away, but you've come for me now, dear one, reckless of your own safety."

"That's not it, Sheikh-sahib. Not all of it. I have to tell you—"

"About your new friend. Tell me about your new friend."

Ibrahim was forced to pause. "Do you mean the hat merchant? Shamsuddin is a good man. He's been very good to us."

"Before the seven rosebushes give up their petals your new friend will open the door for you."

"What? Rosebushes? Open what door, Malang-sahib? What friend?"

"Then at last your yearning will end and you will see water."

Ibrahim's heart was jumping. "Water?" His father's cryptic last words had been: *Now at last I will see water.* He had raised himself slightly, uttered those words, and then died. "What do you mean by water, Sheikh-sahib?"

"The water that turns into wine when Love does the pouring. You have yielded to our Friend, Ibrahim. You have yielded at last. You belong to God now. Do you see?"

Ibrahim knew what answer he *should* give. He knew he *ought to* feel his impotent captivity now transforming into something luminous, submission to a power mightier than his jailers. "Yes," he said hopefully, "I do in a way. I think I see." Oh, he knew what to feel, if only he *could...* "Perhaps I see."

"Tell me what you see." The malang's quiet voice carried as if in a well. Ibrahim did not even need to press his ear to the wood. Perhaps his ears were adjusting to the silence, as his eyes had adjusted to the darkness. "What can you see, Ibrahim-jan?"

"From here, you mean?"

"From where you are," the malang whispered. "What can you see?"

"Not a thing."

"Nothing at all? Are you quite sure?"

"There isn't much light, but in any case there isn't much to see."

"Where is the light coming from?"

"From two thin slits in the wall. Why are you asking, Malang-sahib?"

"I am teaching you to see." Suddenly his voice boomed out, sending a shudder right to Ibrahim's bones. "Prisoners!" he trumpeted. "What do you see?"

At once a tumultuous chorus of voices broke out! Where were all these people? Where? "We see walls, malang-sahib! We see stone!" the prisoners shouted.

Malang-sahib! So they knew him. Elation spouted in Ibrahim. This cell block wasn't empty. People surrounded him, all of them prisoners to be sure, but people! "We see stone," they all babbled. "We see walls! Stones and walls, malang sahib."

"And you, Hajji Ibrahim?" The malang's voice came through the wall like light passing through water. "Do you really mean to tell me you see ... *nothing*?"

"No! I didn't understand your question," Ibrahim cried out. "I see what the others see. Walls and stones." Then he realized, "And I see the light coming through those two thin windows. . And earlier....through those windows I saw a yard. I saw gravel."

"What else?"

"Nothing, just dust particles floating in the light. I see them now. And drops of moisture. I see my own breath. I see...an insect flying— but what of it, Sheikh-sahib? What should this mean to me? What are you teaching me? I don't understand!"

The malang made no answer. The entire prison had fallen silent. Ibrahim bent his head to the door and pressed his ear to the wood. The noiselessness made him think about the grave. Suddenly he doubted the voices he had heard a moment ago. Where did all that shouting come from? It must have been coming from his own mind. It was all inside his head. He and the malang were alone in here. Now that doubt had taken root in him, it swelled. Was anyone else here? Even the malang? The silence from next door felt deeper than a mere absence of noise, deeper and more frightening. It came to him that he had dreamed it all: the malang, the journey to Kabul. Perhaps even Char Bagh and Khadija, perhaps his son Ahmad, his precious daughters, Soraya, his entire life— perhaps none of it existed. Perhaps this was his life: alone in a black cell. This was where he had always been and would always be.

He shook away the creeping horror. "Malang-jan? Are you there?" His voice sounded lonely and small. "Speak to me! I'm so frightened! Are you there?"

"I am here. I will always be as close as your jugular."

Ibrahim took a deep breath and let it out in a long sigh. "What can you see from your cell? Can you see the courtyard?"

"I don't see the courtyard," the malang declared.

"What do you see, then?" Perhaps there was something better to be seen from the neighboring cell. "Do you see flowers? I passed a garden on the way in. Do you see the garden? Or horses perhaps! Do you see horses?"

"I don't see gardens. I don't see flowers. I don't see horses."

"Only walls then? Stone walls? Is that all you see?"

"I don't see stone," said the malang. "I don't see walls."

A thrill came creeping up inside Ibrahim. "What *do* you see, Malang-sahib?"

"I see God. I see only God." The malang's voice dissolved the darkness. "Everywhere I look, I see only God."

Then he began to sing, and the melody that issued from his throat had an eerie beauty unlike anything Ibrahim had ever heard. The moment the song began, he knew the malang was singing his masterpiece and that he must write it down—but he had no pen, no ink, no paper—and he could not see anything. It was either too dark or too blindingly bright, he didn't know which. The malang was singing his masterpiece, and he could not write it down. He uttered a frantic cry that obscured a few words of the song. He remembered then what the malang had said to him on the hillside in Char Bagh that day, when he first told Ibrahim to write down everything he sang. *If it's dark and there is neither stick nor soil but only stones, do not scruple to open a vein and write my song with blood.* The malang had foreseen this moment and given precise instructions to cover it. Ibrahim felt in his pockets for a knife, but of course they would never have let him keep a knife. Minutes of the malang's precious song had already leaked into oblivion. How could Ibrahim open a vein? He searched the floor with blind fingertips, looking for anything sharp but found only a straw, too weak to break his skin. So he lifted his arm to his mouth and bit through the flesh. He tasted salt and felt a warm liquid flowing over his skin. He had ink.

The malang had already sung so many verses, and even the echoes of those words had died away, but he was still singing, there was still song to record. Ibrahim dipped the straw into his blood and began to scratch words out on stones, unable to see what he was writing, weeping as he wrote, not from pain or sorrow, but from some other nameless emotion. His head swam. Consciousness was draining out of him. Showers of dusty starlight erupted around his head, blinding him to his own fingers, and still the malang's song ran through his heart and out of his fingertips onto the stones of that prison cell. He saw a whole river of light somewhere up ahead, the light he had craved to bathe in all his life. He reached for it, but it receded. He reached again, but it receded further.

The light turned dark and he was falling. He woke up lying on the floor, knowing only that time had passed and his head was pounding and he had failed to break through. He had failed again.

Voices sounded in the corridor outside his prison cell.

34

How could he even see his cell door? He glanced around and saw dusty light streaming through those two high slits. The sun must be on that side, hanging close to the horizon; but was it sunset or sunrise? Was it the same day or the next?

The bolt scraped in its cylinder. Ibrahim struggled to sit up. His lips tasted of salty mud. On the wall next to the door, he saw the words he had scratched out with his blood, but they were just reddish-brown smears. He dragged himself to the wall and found that he had made no intelligible marks except in one place, where his imagination could connect the broken smears and allow him to guess at what the words must have been: *only God.*

Then his cell door opened, and a prison guard stepped inside, holding a torch. "Come on."

"Where?"

The guard shrugged. "The higher-ups want to see you." Two more guards waited in the corridor. They marched Ibrahim upstairs to that original interrogation room. Dozens of candles filled the room with steady yellow light: an aroma of warm wax permeated the underlying whiff of dank stone.

An Engrayzee in a dark blue coat sat behind a table, a pen in one hand, a notebook before him, a stone inkwell at his elbow. He was writing in his notebook, but when Ibrahim entered, he looked up. This was a handsome man radiating animal vigor, radiating a maturity that has forgotten childhood and knows nothing yet of old age. His brown hair curled slightly. Above his shaved chin and short pretty mouth perched a moustache with curled tips. His eyelashes were long, and they too curled at the ends.

A nod from this Engrayzee sent the guards fading back to the entrance, where they stood in stolid silence. The Engrayzee leaned out of his seat to extend a hand, a courtesy that surprised Ibrahim. He didn't want to shake this foreigner's hand, but he pressed his palm to his chest politely. "Sekandar Boornus," said the Engrayzee in fluent Farsi. "What is your name, sir?"

Iskandar Boornus—the name jolted Ibrahim: here was the devil himself! But Ibrahim's temperament would not let him answer courtesy with discourtesy. "I am Hajji Malik Ibrahim of Char Bagh," he answered softly.

The Engrayzee pointed to a bench. "Please be seated, Hajji-sahib. I'm sorry I can't offer you a more comfortable seat." He clapped his small hands and the sound rang out like gunshot. "Tea for our guest!" He turned back to Ibrahim: "You had a difficult night, they tell me. I apologize for the misunderstanding. I thought you and I might sort things out."

"Sort what things out?" Ibrahim mastered the urge to armor himself in visible resentment, hoping to convey a menacing self-control by speaking softly. "I came to this place to make inquiries, that's all. Polite inquiries about a man kidnapped from our village. I came here without sword or gun or anger in my heart. Tell me, Mr. Boornus—in your country—how do you speak with a man who asks respectful questions and asks politely? Do you tie his hands behind his back? Is it your custom to beat him the way that your men—"

"My men?"

"Men in your pay, I presume. These Afghans, these Hindus—these vermin who dragged me into your prison—how long have I been in this place? Can you at least tell me that? I don't know what my traveling companions are thinking. Are they searching for me, did they go home? Or did they come looking for me here? Were *they* flung—"

"Please." The Engrayzee lifted his hand. "You have met with some injustice, certainly, but not at my hands. The men who arrested you work for his royal highness Shah Shuja—the king of your country. He has responsibilities to his subjects. Disorder threatens everyone, and there have been crimes, you know—attacks, murders. His Highness is under pressure to find the criminals and bring them to justice. If he fails in this duty, many innocent people will be hurt. Security comes first, I'm sure we all agree. That said, I believe you're innocent. That's what I want to explore. Yesterday, some officials acted hastily. Unnecessary actions were taken, necessary questions went unasked. Let us start over, you and I, and let us speak frankly. If you tell me what I need to know, I may be able to persuade the king's officials to release you. You say a man was kidnapped from your village, a malang of some sort. Tell me about him. What is his actual name?"

"Men call him Malang-i-Mussafir."

"God-Intoxicated Wanderer. Yes, I know. But does he have an ordinary name like other men? Mahmood? Asghar? Anything like that?"

"We respect him too much to address him by name. I call him Sheikh-sahib. He is my teacher and master. You will never understand."

"Sheikh, you say. You consider him a Sufi, then?"

"What I *consider* him is beside the point. He *is* what he *is*, Engrayzee: the vessel of Allah's grace, the channel of His compassionate light. You who worship idols and do not seek union with the One cannot possibly understand."

"Don't be so sure," said Boornus. He considered Ibrahim thoughtfully. "How long have you known the sheikh? Was he born in your village?"

"No," said Ibrahim. "He came to us last spring."

"Where was he before that?"

Ibrahim colored under his black beard. Where had the malang come from? He didn't know. It embarrassed him not to know, his embarrassment irritated him, and the irritation made him resent this Engrayzee all the more. "It doesn't matter where he came from, only where he's taking me."

"I see," Boornus opened his notebook, dipped his pen, and scribbled something. Ibrahim craned to look at the words but didn't recognize this type of lettering. Apparently, letters that worked well enough for both Arabic and Farsi weren't good enough for Engrayzee. "To sum up," said Boornus. "You don't know where he came from, who his people are, or what name his parents gave him. Could he have come from the north?"

"Why not? North, south, east, or west!"

"North of the Amu River, perhaps?"

"Of course, anywhere, I said. What's your question? Nothing is beyond the sheikh."

"He's had a great many visitors, I hear?"

"His fame has spread, yes. Everybody longs for his blessings except you who put him in chains, tear his flesh, bruise his eyes, but someday, sahib, even you—yes, even you will brag to your grandchildren that you saw him. 'I was *this* close, you'll say, *this* close to the Malang of Char Bagh,' you will tell them. 'I heard his song,' you will say. Years from now you'll realize that you heard it and valued it at nothing, and then you will curse yourself and wish that you could live your life again."

Boornus nodded solemnly, made some notes, and took up his interrogation again. "What can you tell me about his visitors? What manner of men were they? Did any of them come from the north?"

Again this obsessive interest in the north. "From everywhere!" Ibrahim retorted impatiently. "Don't you understand a thing? The sheikh has devotees everywhere!"

"But *including* the north? Be specific. Did Russians ever visit him?"

Now it was Ibrahim's turn to study his interrogator through narrowed eyes. Clearly the man had some enemy in the north, and he seemed to think Malang-sahib was in league with him. "What is a Russian?" he asked. "Some type of Uzbek?"

"No, a Russian would be a white man like me."

Ibrahim sliced him with a cynical laugh. "No one like you came to see Malang-sahib! Only Muslims! No Engrayzee."

"Actually, Russians are not Engrayzee. Some may have swarthy skin like yours. How would you know if a particular pilgrim was a Muslim? If he dressed like an Afghan, would you know that he was really a Russian?"

"I wouldn't know a Russian, no matter how he dressed. I've never heard of this tribe. A man can't know every tribe, there are so many. Everyone came is all I know: big and little, pale and dark. Malang-sahib never asked if someone was Sunni or Shi'a. Even you could have visited him, Engrayzee, if you had come. Our malang is not your enemy, Mister

Boornus. Our malang is a friend of God's, and so he is the friend of every man."

"Did anyone spend time with him alone?"

Ibrahim saw where this was going, and he suspected the correct answer was not the true one. "No," he said unflinchingly. "I am Malang-sahib's scribe and he insists that I stay by his side all the time so that I can write down what he says if he starts singing."

Boornus cocked his head, a slight smile playing on his lips. "Give me an example of this singing—just the words, if you wish."

Ibrahim cast back for a memorized couplet or two and recited the first lines that came to mind. *"The music is already there. It needs the lyre only to be heard. Air is the merest emptiness to you ...not so to the bird."*

Boornus nodded. Ibrahim saw something in his eyes that might have been appreciation, and his heart filled with hope. The foreigner bent over his notes again. Then he said, "Well, I think I can recommend your release, and I'm sorry for the inconvenience." He scribbled something on a page of his notebook, tore it out, and handed it to Ibrahim. "Give this to the guards at the outer gates."

"Wait! Do you mean—?" Was this an order for the malang's release? If so, then the beating, the strange night, his throbbing arm—all were worth it!

Before Boornus could answer, some half-dozen other Engrayzees came trooping into the interrogation room, clamoring about something. Boornus quickly ushered Ibrahim past them. His voice dropping to a conspiratorial whisper, he said, "Go without a fuss just now, but come to my house in Shor Bazaar a week from next Thursday, about mid-morning. Anyone can direct you. Just ask where Sekander Burnes lives. I may be able to help your malang. Will you remember my name? Sekandar Burnes. Al-Iskandar, some may say. Boornus. A week from Thursday: we'll talk further."

Dizzy with joy, Ibrahim let the guards take him to the outer gate. There he submitted the sheet of paper from Boornus. The captain studied it and said, "Wait here." After a moment in the guard house, he came back and said, "Open your hand." He poured a handful of coins onto Ibrahim's palm. "Compensation for your troubles, villager."

Compensation for his troubles? Ibrahim stared at the money.

Compensation for leaving the malang behind? For failing Khadija, for returning to the Grand Bazaar humiliated and beaten? He flung the coins away and wiped his palms against his shirt, turning to protest, but two burly guards already had him by the arms and another had a lance poked against the small of his back. The men hurried him down the broad road and gave him a rude push, toward the city.

35

The season's first snow had fallen on Char Bagh, and still no word had come from the men. It was just a light sprinkle, this first snow, like ash that a broom might have swept from the sky, but it kept falling until a blanket of flakes had built up, and then the temperature plunged and the blanket froze so hard, children could walk on it. Khadija woke up on the second cold morning thinking about Soraya.

She had visited the old compound a few times after the men left, but once the leaves fell and autumn put a snap in the air, she had too much to do getting her own compound ready for winter. Making charcoal, for example. Stacking dried dung where it would stay dry, for she would need the fuel after her wood and charcoal ran out. Burying onions and potatoes in the storeroom so they wouldn't freeze. Boiling buckets of fat and straining it so she would have clear oil for lamplight in the dark days ahead. Pounding dried mulberries and walnuts into a paste to make the sweet fruit-leather that would stretch her stores of barley and turnips. Oh, there was so much to do.

One of Soraya's nieces moved in with her to help out. Asad's boys came up every day or two to bring her wood and freshly-ground flour and other small necessities, but Khadija recruited two of her own nephews from Sorkhab to come live in her compound as well. She needed males around to do the rough work, the digging and pounding and climbing, and they had to be close relatives so the village tongues wouldn't wag.

If nothing else, she needed the distraction of their company during those desolate days. Anxiety would not release its clutch on her, the anxious memory of that last day with Ibrahim. She tired easily and took unwholesome naps in the late mornings when she should have been working. She napped and dreamed about Ibrahim and the malang, and in her dreams she was lying between them, Ibrahim in front and the malang in back, although neither one seemed to notice she was even there. They talked through her, to each other, earnestly on and on, about God and death, about time and the world. She jumped out of these troubling dreams in a sweat, more tired than when she fell asleep. Loneliness became indistinguishable from grief, and in time, grief from illness, particularly when she was cooking, for it was then, somehow, that memories of happier times twisted her up with a particular intensity.

One day, Asad's three eldest sons came up with a load of dried juniper stalks for making charcoal. After they had delivered their load, she served them tea with a bit of sweet bread for their troubles and then, as she went about her chores, she overheard them chattering about the excellent lunch they would soon be wolfing down at Malik Ibrahim's house. "No, no, boys, you're staying here for lunch" she informed them. "I need you to repair my chicken coop this afternoon."

"Awww! Auntieee…" the boys whined. "You only have bread and turnips!"

"Rude louts! What do you expect to get down there at Soraya's?"

"Goat stew!" the youngest boy readily piped. His voice had not fully changed, but even he was half a head taller than Khadija. He washed his hands reluctantly over a large pan with water that his brother poured from a pewter vase, but he really didn't want to stay here and miss the lunch down there.

"Goat stew!" Khadija exclaimed. "What makes you think they'll have goat stew?"

"They slaughtered the goat with the broken horn," the boy reported casually. "It wasn't giving milk anymore. Auntie said if it won't give milk, let's have its meat."

This didn't sound like Soraya. "Why did it stop giving milk? Our best milk goat!"

"Guess *djinns* got to it. They said to bring back onions, 'cuz you have good'uns."

"What's wrong with their own?"

"Buncha' them froze the day it got cold."

"They weren't buried?" Khadija frowned. How could Soraya have been so careless? "Are the potatoes okay, at least?"

"Potatoes!" The boys snickered at the idea that important male persons like themselves should give a damn about potatoes. One poked the other and said, "Did you forget to bury the potatoes, *girlie?*"

"It's your job! You're the girl!"

"Wait'll I cram a potato up your butt, we'll see who's the girl."

"You filthy-mouthed ghouls!" barked Khadija. "How dare you?"

"But Auntiee! He called me a girl—"

Suddenly brother number one socked brother number two hard enough to bang him against the wall. Those two boys fell to wrestling all over Khadija's floor. The third one dove into the pile, shrieking and laughing. Khadija dumped a pan of cold wastewater over them to stop the fighting. The boys sat up, spluttering indignantly. "Why'd'you do *that!?*"

"Why do you think? Rolling all over my house breaking things. Cretins! You're all staying here for lunch, for dinner, and for the night. Forget about goat stew. You buckle down because you're not going anywhere. You've got work to do right here!"

Later, over turnip soup and bread, Khadija asked the sullen boys about Soraya. "How is she managing with that big household to run now? Is her mother helping?"

"Sure, yop. Her ma and heaps of others."

"What 'heaps' of others?" Khadija squinted at the boys.

"All them as feels sorry for her. My mama goes there every day."

"Does she." People called the mother of these boys Bibi Girang: Lady Heavyweight. Nailed to the floor by her own immensity, she rarely visited her own yard, much less other compounds. What could tempt her next door? Khadija could think of only one attraction. "Does Soraya feed her 'helpers' well?"

"Oh! Mighty good feeding over there, yop!" one of the louts assured her. He tore a hunk from the flat loaf. "Auntie Khushdil's one damn good cook, she is."

"Khushdil has moved in there?"

"Sure. She's needed. Agha Lala kicks up such a ruckus these days. He's always yelling how he wants to walk to Baghlan. People have to hold him down. It takes two or three, believe me! Once? He got out of the house? They called on us for help, hee hee! He was out the door with his bundle and walking stick. We had to drag him back, and how he fought—oh! You'd never believe an old geezer like him would put up such a fight."

"He's a biter," the youngest boy noted.

"Only two teeth but he bites like a parrot," the middle brother declared, shaking his head in admiration at the biting power of the senile old man.

"Have they at least made mulberry paste for the winter?"

The boys laughed at that question. "Who knows? We never go in the storeroom over there anymore. Mama says *djinns* might get us."

"*Djinns!* Why do you keep talking about *djinns?*"

"'Cuz there's lots of 'em now. They've come looking for Auntie Soraya. She's taken bad these days. Howling and eating mud and such. It's creepy."

"She's eating mud again?" This news truly disturbed Khadija. Here she was in her fort, proud as any princess, wanting the whole village to know she needed no help, and all along, she was never the one in danger. It was always Soraya who couldn't cope. Even though she lived in a compound crawling with people, she was more alone than Khadija had ever been. And now that Khushdil had moved in, Soraya might find herself reduced to servant status in her own compound. Khadija had to go down there and defend her.

The next morning, she put on her heavy woolen socks, her sandals, her cloak, and her body veil, and followed Asad's boys down to the village. She banged into the compound that used to be her own. The moment she got inside, she could feel the beehive fullness of it. At least twenty women were lolling and lounging in the various rooms, none of them working, all of them lazing about, munching snacks, drinking tea, chatting. Khadija noticed at once that the mattresses looked flat. No one had unpacked them and re-fluffed the cotton, a standard preparation for winter. The onion bin outside the storeroom was still full of onions. Some had frozen, then thawed, and were now showing hints of rot. The rest could be saved if they were buried at once but it had to be at once, for the ground itself would soon freeze too hard to crack with any spade.

She found Khushdil with Soraya's mother in the kitchen. Soraya was sitting in there too, at the end of the bench, her arms clutched around her thin body, hugging herself for warmth and rocking in place. The other two women were swishing rice around in cold water, their sleeves rolled up to their elbows, rinsing the starch off so the rice would cook up into nice, plump separate grains imbued with flavorful spiced oil.

Khadija greeted the women affably, received their cheerful responses, and accepted their invitation to sit down and join the storytelling. She listened to ten or fifteen minutes of physical and social complaints, the usual prolog to any conversation among the women. It was not news nor even gossip so much as ritual. But then, as the conversation settled to earth, she could no longer hold her tongue.

Keeping her voice sweet, she addressed Soraya. "Why are we cooking rice today, my dear? For the noon meal, no less! We must have something great to celebrate! Has news come from the men? I'm breathless to know."

"No. It's because—it's just—you know. It's hard to explain." Soraya's teeth chattered. The question agitated her. She shook her fingers as if shaking off water. "You tell, Khushdil. You're good at explaining."

"Khushdil? Was this your decision?" Khadija turned icy eyes on the pudgy intruder.

"Who are you to ask?" Khushdil retorted. "Don't you live up in the crags now, with your famous husband? I'm here to help poor, dear Soraya-jan. Whatever she wants, it's her household. Anyway, why not rice? Ibrahim is a rich man, God be praised. You kept it from us all these years, you scrimping hoarder! We never knew!"

"Winter has just started," Khadija shot back. "That's why the storerooms are overflowing. We still have months to get through. Soraya-jan, what if the men come home and there is no rice to celebrate their homecoming?"

"And when will that be?" Khushdil scoffed. "The snows have started."

"Oh, I don't know," Soraya fretted. "It's not what I want—" she groaned.

"Look! Look how you've upset her," Soraya's mother scolded. "You troublemaker! You walk in and right away you're giving orders? This is not your house anymore! You're not even clan, not even blood! Have you lost all shame, living with that malang?"

"Are you disrespecting Malang-sahib?" Khadija demanded.

Another sharp groan cut her off. At the end of the bench, Soraya was rocking harder than ever, twisting her head from side to side. at the end of the bench. "There!" She pointing to the corner with a stabbing gesture. "See it?" Her eyes had gone wide with fear. Then her irises rolled up until half of each orb disappeared under her eyelids.

Shock pulled Khadija to her feet. Even as she approached Soraya, she felt prickles rising all over her body. Soraya was still pointing at the corner, and Khadija knew it would be empty there, but she looked.

"Don't you *see* it?" Soraya cried out "Right there! A great big one!"

The corner was dark and the darkness might itself be a shape. Khushdil had withdrawn from Soraya, shrinking into her own fat. She too was staring at the corner in horror. "What is it?" The words came gritting out between clenched teeth.

"*Djinns*, you dummy! She sees *djinns*," whispered Soraya's mother. "W'allah, they're right here in the room with us! Get back from her, Khushdil. Get back before one of them slips into you."

Saliva was bubbling from Soraya's slack lips, her slack mouth. Her eyes had gone almost completely white. The minimal crescents still to be seen had moved close to her nose. She was no longer seeing anything. She began to twitch.

Khushdil scrambled out the door, and Soraya's mother inched along the perimeter of the room to follow her. They were planning to abandon Soraya "She's your daughter!" Khadija raged, but the old woman gave her a distracted glance and bolted.

Khadija didn't have Soraya's ability to see *djinns*, but she could sense them. She knew that at least one *djinn* was in the room, knew it from the clamminess of her palms and the dread that kept rising. She could even tell roughly where it was. The *djinn* was reeling toward her. Then it veered decisively toward Soraya, intending to take possession of the easier body. But another of the creatures was already inside Soraya—it was plain from the involuntary jerking violence of her body, the vacancy in her eyes, the way her head flopped around, like a rag ball attached to her body by a mere string of neck.

Khadija forced herself to Soraya's side. Almost weeping with horror, she put her arms around that slender body. Soraya felt as cold as a corpse under her dress, and just as rigid. That's what *djinns* did when they took possession of you. They were creatures made of smokeless fire, yet they turned a body cold and stiff. It would be awful to abandon Soraya. She was still inside that body somewhere, frightened to death and lost to the world, but still alive in there. Khadija clutched the girl closer. Where they pressed together, Khadija could barely feel her own skin, as if they were two *other* people pressed together. This was so risky! At any moment, the *djinn* might seep through where they were touching, might enter Khadija. What's more, that second *djinn* was still creeping about nearby. In the old days *djinns* infested the village like roaches. The eldest elders knew this from stories their own grandparents had told them, but no living person had witnessed a possession like this one. No living person. The *djinns* had more or less forgotten about Char Bagh for generations, but they must have noticed it again when the malang came to town—as a place they must never visit; then when he was dragged away, the news must have spread among the *djinns*, and so they had come creeping in from all directions: and of course they headed straight for Soraya, the one person in the village with that rare, unhappy ability to *see* them.

At that moment, Soraya's body went soft again under Khadija's fingers. Khadija pressed her cheeks to the girl's face and found it warm and wet. Soraya's eyes were open and streaming tears. She kept biting her delicate lips and picking at herself as if plucking ants off her skin. "Khadi—Khadija?" she stammered. "Khadija-jan?"

"I'm with you. Are they gone?"

"They were here," Soraya whimpered. "Did you see them?" The words blew out of her in gusty gulps.

"Yes," Khadija lied. Surely Soraya wanted to hear this lie. Nobody wants to be the only one of anything. "I saw them too."

"Thank God," Soraya burst out gratefully. "We both saw them."

"Two of them," Khadija offered.

"Oh, yes! So you *did* see them!" Soraya clapped her hands. "A big one and a little one. Say *namaz* with me, Khadija-jan, they might come back. One of them was right inside me! You *can't* know how it feels."

"It must be awful," Khadija shuddered. "*Awful!*"

"They're slithery and cold. You can feel their nasty little fingers scraping at you from inside. Cold horrid little fingers!"

"*Bismillah,*" Khadija murmured. In God's name! "Stand up now. Can you walk? Let's purify ourselves for *namaz.*"

"Wasn't my mama here?"

"She had to leave."

"What about Khushdil?"

"They both—"

"Did they see the *djinns?* Were they frightened away by them?"

"They left just before," Khadija lied again. Soraya could not want to hear that her mother had abandoned her. "Come along, let's do our ablutions and say *namaz.*"

The women made their way to the windowless chamber where people washed their hands, feet, and faces before prayers. It was next to the kitchen, and smoke from the oven ran under it before venting out the chimney on the other side. In the morning, therefore, when bread was baking, the oven warmed the ablution-room, but at this time of day the room was terribly cold, which was good: the cold would slap Soraya back to her senses.

Khadija sat on the bench, awaiting her turn with the clay water jug. The spent water ran through a drain in the middle of the floor to a ditch below, which carried it to the fields. Suddenly, her gorge rose, and she pitched onto her hands and knees over the drain to hunch and spew.

When she struggled back onto the bench, shaken, she saw Soraya staring at her in wide-eyed, frightened sympathy. "Are you sick?"

"A little. Nothing bad."

"How long? How bad?"

"Not long. Nothing much, Allah willing. My dear malang is gone, and I worry about him, you know."

"We all do."

"I eat clotted cream. That's my downfall! My goat keeps producing and its milk is so rich. I have to skim the cream and then I can't waste it, can I? It's all I seem to crave. I know it's bad for me, but that's what ails me, bad diet and anxiety, that's all."

"No, it isn't," Soraya declared flatly. "You're ill, I can see it. You have to move back in with us, Khadija-jan. I can't get along without you. Just until the men come back. Please? They will come back, won't they?"

Khadija rinsed the taste of vomit from her mouth. "So you haven't heard a word from them either? Nothing?"

"Not a word. No one has. If I lose Ibrahim—"

"Allah forbid. Allah is compassionate!"

"After losing Ahmad—"

"God forbid you should lose him. He'll come back, may God will it."

"And he'll bring the malang back?"

"We trust in Allah, dear. All right, if you wish, I will move back here for a while. It's better for me too, until the men return. I'm all alone up there."

"If you go back up, I'll go with you, I swear. I can't stay here with my mother and *them.*"

"Never say that out loud," Khadija warned. "Don't even think it. Don't let any of *them* see that you want to run. You're the mistress here. Force them to know it."

"I need your help," Soraya pleaded.

"I'll move back, my dearest, but I can only do so much to help. You see, my very help makes you weak. It's better that you stand up to them on your own. That will make you stronger. Otherwise they'll swarm in like locusts and ravage your husband's stores. They're at it already, eating through his wealth, all the while pretending they're here to keep you company. You must defend this garrison, no one else can do it. Tell them they can stay, but it's bread and turnips from now on, except when there is reason to feast. The malik's household will be run prudently. Tell them, and hold fast."

That night, Soraya found Khushdil alone and confronted her. "You've kept me company through dark hours, Khushdil-jan, you're a good cook, but the rice-eating days are over. Since you're not here to feast, it won't trouble you to learn that from now on we'll have bread and turnips except on special days."

Khushdil's lips twisted into a sneer. "This is Khadija talking."

Soraya blushed. "No," she lied, and blushed harder, knowing she was lying. "I must—I must protect my husband's stores."

"I'm amazed you listen to that woman. I'm amazed you even let her into your house—it *is* yours, you know. She has her own house. If she moves back in with us, she'll soon be bossing all of us around, just wait and see."

"Well," Soraya ventured, "*you* have a house of your own too."

Khushdil rocked back on her cushion of a butt and stared. "Yes," she sniffed. "I do, of course, and if you want me gone, just say so. If you want me gone, I won't even pause to put on my shoes. I'll walk barefoot into the snow. Is that what you want?"

"It's not what I said," Soraya stammered. "I want everyone to stay. I need all the comfort I can get, I who have lost my son, and now I've lost my husband—"

"Oh, you'll get your husband back, God willing. That's why I wonder how you can welcome *that woman* into your house."

"Khadija? Why do you say *that woman*? What do you mean by that?"

"You're such an innocent—oh, we cherish you for it, believe me. Stay just as you are, you fragile flower. Stay innocent as long as possible!"

"Innocent about what? What are you talking about?"

"I don't want to spread gossip. I abhor gossip, as you know."

"What gossip?" Soraya pleaded.

"Well, since you pull it out of me—but it rips me in two to have to tell you. Your husband visited the widow before he left. I don't blame Ibrahim-jan. Men are weak. It's up to us women to avoid offering temptation. That's what God commands. I try my best, God knows, and so do you. But we're not all of us so careful."

"What are you saying, Khushdil? Say it or I'll scratch your eyes out!"

"Oh!" the fat woman lamented. "Oh, I hate to tittle and gossip—but it's not gossip if it's true, is it? Would it be right to hide a thing like this from his wife? I'm torn! Well, if you insist on knowing, he was seen, Soraya-jan. My boy followed him. You thought he went straight to Ghulam Dastagir's house the day they left, but no: he veered up to Baba's Nose on the way. He was alone with her from sundown until dusk, long enough to say twenty *rakats* of namaz, but I don't think they were saying namaz all that time! Do you?"

Soraya glared at Khushdil, then jumped at her, slashing at her face with her fingernails, an attack so sudden and violent it overwhelmed the bigger woman. Their screams drew the whole household. Men dragged Soraya off her cousin. She came away clutching handfuls of blood-speckled hair.

"She's horrid!" shrieked Soraya. But then she wouldn't say what Khushdil had done or said. She just shook her head and whined, "She said nasty things! Nasty!"

Khushdil sucked on her bleeding lower lip and did not contradict Soraya's accusation. Everyone went away muttering that the mistress might still have a few *djinns* inside her. Everyone kept their distance from Soraya that evening.

The next morning, Soraya found Khadija sitting in a patch of sunlight, looking pale. She had just come from the washroom where she must have thrown up again. She gave Soraya a wan smile and said, "Let me rest for a minute." Soraya turned away from her one-time sister-in-law, blinking back jealous tears. She recognized Khadija's symptoms all too well, now that Khushdil had pointed her in the right direction. She had suffered all those same symptoms herself—four times: once with Ahmad, and again with each of her girls. Outside, the djinns standing in the deepening snow began to knock on the walls, and Soraya could hear them whispering, "Come out, Soraya…come out…"

36

The appointed Thursday having come at last, Ibrahim and Ghulam Dastagir were on their way to see the mysterious Sekandar Boornus. He lived across the Kabul River from the Grand Bazaar, in that dense urban neighborhood called Shor Bazaar. The road to the man's compound began near the river, and it was a tree-lined avenue at first, with sidewalks running along the base of the walls that flanked it. The roadbed itself was paved with stones, making it accessible to the horse-drawn tongas that abounded in Kabul. But the trees vanished, and the sidewalks thinned out, and the road itself grew ever narrower as it snaked deeper into Shor Bazaar, until it accommodated only foot traffic.

Karim had begged to come along on this venture, and his father had given in to his pleadings, warning only, "Don't get underfoot." Now the boy trotted gladly between the men, grinning but smoldering. He wanted so much to please his father, the sad little fellow; but some other passion boiled in him as well, Ibrahim thought: some vengeful hatred, as if he bore the Engrayzee a special grudge. But what special hurt could he have suffered? Ibrahim had wondered about this before: did he have carnal feeling for the ruined girl, Shahnaz? Was that even possible for a boy so young?

The pedestrian traffic kept thickening. Many people were striding along with an air of grim purpose, Ibrahim noticed. He began to sense something nasty mixed into the excitement and it made him uneasy. All these people with blazing eyes—where were they going? At one point,

Karim spied a boy his own age and tried to slip away, but his father grabbed his neck.

"Stick close! Something's happening here, and I don't like it! Stick close." Oh, so Ghulam Dastagir sensed it too.

"I was only going to ask that boy what's happening, papa. He might know."

"Forget that boy! Stick close, I said! Malik-sahib," the big man growled at Ibrahim, "where is this scoundrel's house? How much longer must we walk?"

"Not much, I'm sure." Ibrahim looked about for anything matching descriptions of Boornus's compound, but the crowd blocked his view. The crowd, in fact, was plugging up the street now, because it had stopped flowing. People were just milling about in place. The plug kept tightening as more idlers accumulated. What was drawing so many to this spot?

Ghulam Dastagir elbowed through the crush of bodies, looking for a spectacle. The core attraction turned out to be an open compound door through which everybody was trying to squeeze. Well, if others wanted to get through that bottleneck, so did he. Ghulam Dastagir bulled through the opening, pulling Ibrahim and Karim along in his wake.

Inside, the villagers found a large yard partitioned into geometric shapes by walkways and flower beds interspersed with statues of men and women, some of them nude. An elegant house spanned the entire yard. From its front door jutted a veranda paved in green and black tiles. At the edge of this porch, high above the crowd like a speaker at a podium stood Al-Sekandar Boornus. He wore a *farangi*-style shirt and trousers, but his head was swathed in a bulbous blue turban. His round face looked very pink, and his little moustache looked very waxed.

"Stop this nonsense!" he was shouting in Farsi. "Stop right now, you men! What are you doing in my yard? If you have grievances, take them to your government. I can't help you. Disperse, I say, or there will be trouble."

"Good God!" Ibrahim clapped his hands to his cheeks. "It's him!"

"It's who?" Ghulam Dastagir squinted up.

"Al-Iskandar Boornus. It's him."

"I thought he said to come alone." Ghulam Dastagir glowered

around at the crowd. No one in the crowd looked back at him. All of them were fixated on Burnes. Ibrahim was peering up there too. A Hindu soldier stood just behind the Engrayzee, and another one slouched at the back of the veranda. A shadow moving inside the open doorway might have been a third soldier.

Ibrahim nudged a beak-nosed man. "What's everybody doing here?"

The man shrugged and tore his gaze away from Burnes reluctantly. "I don't know. The door was open, it looked like a bit of excitement, so I came inside."

"Me too," said a towering Uzbek. "Miss a chance to see how these Engrayzee live? Not on your life! And it's worse than I thought—look at these idols!" He gaped at a plaster statue of a woman cupping her breasts to keep them from spilling out of the sheet she was wearing. "It shouldn't be allowed." He licked his lips.

Karim hammered at his father's thighs. "I can't see! Lift me up, Papa."

"Nothing to see!" his father barked. "Just a man."

"Oh, that's not just a man," the Uzbek assured him. "That's Al-Sekandar Boornus!"

"What does he mean by 'grievances'?" Ibrahim asked of no one in particular.

"It's early," Burnes shouted. A conciliatory burr was audible in his voice now. "I will meet with your leaders this afternoon. Pick just a few, I can't meet with hundreds. Pick ten or twelve and we'll talk like reasonable men. The rest of you, go home. Honorable folks do not force their way into other men's private homes. This is not how Afghans behave. You know it's not. You are a people famous for your honor."

"You of all people, braying about honor!" someone sneered.

"*Thief* of honor," another called out, and this struck a chord. "*Thief* of honor!" came scattered cries.

"What grievances?" Ibrahim repeated.

"Papa, is this the Engrayzee?" Karim demanded querulously. "Why won't you let me get on your shoulders? I want to see him too."

"Be quiet! This is men's work. Malik-sahib, stick close, I'll get us to the front row."

"He lures them with gold and then despoils them," someone muttered.

"Gold?" piped Karim, his eyes bugging out. His high voice carried in the breeze.

"What gold?" said a man with a henna-reddened beard. "Did someone say gold?"

The jostling crowd pushed Karim against his father's leg, making the boy gasp for breath. Seeing his son's distress, Ghulam Dastagir shoved back aggressively, indiscriminately. "You're crushing my boy, you oafs!"

"Hey," barked one of the men he'd shoved. "We all have scores to settle with the bastard up there. Wait your turn, mister."

"What scores?" Ibrahim demanded. "What's he done?"

"He plunders virtue, brother," someone finally answered him. "Plucks our women out of the streets, one by one. His servants grab them by the wagonload at night. He showers them with gold, and you know how women are, they can't resist gold. This is a crowd of husbands and fathers. If you haven't lost some honor to this bastard, get out of the way, because other men have. Not me, mind you, I keep my women locked up tight, but these others—"

"What's all this about gold?" the red-beard called out again

The word was crackling from dozens of lips now. "Gold, did he say?"

Someone let out a cry and pointed to a second story window where a young woman stood, holding a curtain bunched to one side and looking down with big, frightened eyes. A general shout went up, and she let the curtain drop.

"Why—the infidel's got someone's daughter up there right now," Red-beard screamed, punching his way forward. The men he pushed shoved back. Scuffles rippled through the crowd. The three *sipahis* moved to the veranda's edge and pointed their rifles down to cow the crowd into silence. Burnes's shouting voice emerged again. "You're angry about nothing! Lies, you men! Listen to me, go now, you get ten *rupias*. Yes! Ten for any man who leaves my compound now. Ten *rupias* just for leaving—easy money."

Ghulam Dastagir made it into the front row. Ibrahim squeezed in next to him and waved to attract the Englishman's attention. Behind him the crowd was snarling.

Burnes pointed at Ibrahim without any apparent recognition. "You, my good man, thirty *rupias* if you walk out of my compound right *now*! My servants will pay you on the street. Go, now—go, go, good fellow, go!"

"I don't want your money," Ibrahim cried.

"He doesn't want your money," the crowd roared.

"Don't you know me?" Ibrahim pleaded..

"Don't you know him?" someone echoed, and then like second echoes shouts rang out from many spots: "And me?" "And me?" "Don't you know me?"

Burnes backed away from the edge. "Gold," he gasped. "I'll give you gold—to leave—my men will shoot you. I keep my promises—Sekandar Burnes—a man of my word—you know me—you'll die—I swear!"

"A man of his word!" Derision rippled through the yard.

"…women up there right now…"

"…gold in the house…"

"Bastard thinks he can buy our women with his gold," roared Ghulam Dastagir.

"Stuff your gold up your butt, you donkey!" Startled by the shrill voice, Ibrahim looked down just in time to see Karim fitting a walnut-sized rock into a sling. He had brought a sling? Oh, no! Before Ibrahim could utter a word, the boy whipped the rock around his head and let fly. The rock zinged past Burnes's ear and into the house, where something broke with a glassy crash.

Burnes flinched and flung up his arm. The rock had already missed him, but gunfire nonetheless burst from three rifle barrels: "No!" screamed Burnes.

Too late: the guns had fired, the crowd had ignited. Pressure swelled against Ibrahim's back. The roar rose. Implacably, ferociously, the whole mass began to surge toward the veranda. Ibrahim leaned back against it but the crowd broke around him like river water around a rock. Squeezed breathless by human flesh, Ibrahim glanced around for Ghulam Dastagir. His friend was looking down. How odd. And then—not odd at all for he was gazing down at Karim, who was lying on the ground for some reason, his face covered with blood for some reason. And people were stepping on the motionless boy, driven forward by the blind passion of the masses behind them. Ghulam Dastagir erupted. With flailing fists, he cleared a space big enough to lean down into. He swept up his son. Karim made no sound. The crowd would have drowned him out in any case, but there was nothing to drown. Karim was dead.

And Ibrahim felt nothing about it, no hurt, no heartache. Not yet. The noise blended into a single roar like the falls downriver from Char Bagh. He and Ghulam Dastagir met eyes over Karim's oozing head. Red rage was glistering in the big man's eyes. Someone would pay for this. Someone would pay. Ghulam Dastagir nodded toward the verandah, a gesture, a request. Sudden random eddies of crowd pressure pushed the men together till the soft corpse was squeezed between them. Tears were welling out of Ghulam Dastagir's eyes.

Then, he relinquished the weight and was gone, gone to change both their destinies, leaving Karim in the headman's arms. Ibrahim staggered to the wall. The verandah above him crashed with battle, no telling who was fighting whom. Another gunshot sounded and a man in Engrayzee livery came hurling off the verandah, hit the yard with a thump, sprang up, and raced for the gates.

But never made it. Cut down from behind. Martial music in the street. Ibrahim could not go to see who was coming. He had to stay with Karim. His mind felt the weight of this heavy death now. The boy in his arms was as dead as Ahmad. But Ghulam Dastagir had other sons. Ibrahim had none, and would never have another. This young face, a hole where a nose should have been! He would have to be buried in Kabul now: how dreadful. But every place is close to God, Malang-sahib would have said. Every place. Why could he never ever *feel* it?

The house clattered like a box with a rat trapped inside it. Windows broke on the second story, bits of wood came flying through the gaps. Windows broke on the ground floor. Wood and glass came flying out. People burst out the doorway. The mob had flushed two frightened animals. No, on second glance, they were women wrapped in blankets, running for their lives. Afghan women. Somebody's daughters, sisters, wives perhaps.

"Sluts," the crowd screamed. "What have you done with the gold?"

They flashed past Ibrahim like figures in a dream. He couldn't help them, his feet would not lift, he had to stay with Karim. Any moment now, the crowd would catch those women and tear off their blankets. Ibrahim saw a man banging at an alabaster statue of a naked woman and breaking off her arm.

"Sluts and whores!" bawled rabid voices. "Where's the gold?"

A dust devil of scuffling men rolled to the compound gates where a sudden intrusion of king's-soldiers broke it back into individuals who scattered in their flight from the soldiers' swords. But from the courtyard came a rain of stones. The women disappeared into the street, as soldiers clashed with rioters. The soldiers had guns, but the mob had stones. The man with the alabaster arm was wielding it as a club. The soldiers fell back from the fury of this mob.

Another blare of noise pulled Ibrahim's gaze back to the house. A handful of Afghans were dragging out something heavy. In the middle of the verandah, they pulled the weight upright and the rioting stopped dead and the noise gave way to stunned silence as the whole courtyard turned to look: Ghulam Dastagir and three others were holding up the corpse of Alexander Burnes, the man who had promised to save the malang. His face was disfigured almost beyond recognition, his garments ripped in a dozen places, and every rip oozed blood. Ghulam Dastagir clutched the corpse with one hand. His other held the knife he usually used to slice melons. The blade was two fingers long and today it was basted with blood. Ibrahim felt lost.

When Ghulam Dastagir let go, the Englishman's body dropped like a sack, even though three other men were holding it too. The strongman of Char Bagh came lurching down the steps toward Ibrahim and took his son back. He set the small body gently on the ground and leaned over the boy to smooth the blood-caked face with tender fingers. His shoulders heaved, his tears flowed without noise. Some of the men who had dragged the corpse out with him formed a respectful circle, honoring his lamentation. Years seemed to pass, but when Ghulam Dastagir finally sat back on his haunches, the sun was still a few ticks short of noon: mere heartbeats had passed, not even hours. Ghulam Dastagir's knife rested next to him, forgotten. One of the men said, "Commander?"

Ghulam Dastagir looked up with red-rimmed eyes . "I'm not the commander. He's the commander." He nodded toward Ibrahim. "That's Malik Ibrahim of Char Bagh."

"Khan-sahib." The man bowed to Ibrahim. "You have served Afghanistan today."

"I've done nothing," Ibrahim retorted. "Ghulam Dastagir has sacrificed his son."

"Allah forgives the boy and accepts him directly into heaven. You have fathered a martyr, Khan-sahib. You and your commander are precious to us."

Ghulam Dastagir merely sighed.

On the far side of the yard, two men with gold thread glinting in their vests and rifles resting against their hips studied Ibrahim. "We've attracted attention," said the headman. "Rich men, and they're coming for us. We'd better go." He spotted a gate to his right. "Sir," he said to a man fawning over Ghulam Dastagir. "Can you help us get the martyr's body back to the Grand Bazaar? I think those king's-soldiers are coming for us—"

"Oh! That father-blasted bastard of a king, may he choke!" the man spluttered. "Get up, friend." He poked Ghulam Dastagir. "We have horses, we'll take your boy wherever you say. Everybody! Come help carry the martyr!"

He spread his cloak on the ground, and a dozen hands rolled Karim onto it. Ibrahim kicked the little gate open and scouted the alley. The others were already prodding Ghulam Dastagir to his feet. "We're leaving now?" the big man mumbled thickly. .

"Hurry!" Ibrahim held the gate for the men carrying Karim's corpse. He pushed his friend through and stepped through himself. One of the well-dressed warriors shouted something, but Ibrahim did not look back. His spine ached where a bullet would crash through if a marksman fired now, but he pulled the gate shut and broke into a run. Behind him the gate crashed open again, but Ibrahim was already rounding the corner. He vaulted onto a horse that someone was holding for him. Then he was galloping through unfamiliar streets, surrounded by strangers who— strangely enough—revered him and Ghulam Dastagir.

37

That night, a professional barber prepared Karim's body for burial, washing it in the courtyard of Hakim Shamsuddin's tiny house just east of the Grand Bazaar. Neighbors who had learned about the boy's martyrdom came over with sweet rice porridge cooked in oil. He was buried the next day in the same graveyard as Hakim Shamsuddin's parents. Ghulam Dastagir moaned throughout the ceremony tormented by the thought of burying his boy in strange soil far from home. But taking the little body back to Char Bagh was out of the question, now that the snows had begun. Even in the best of seasons, it would have taken too long: the dead must be buried as soon as their souls have flown to God. The whole group from the Grand Bazaar attended the burial, and so did Ghulam Dastagir's growing coterie of new admirers.

The following Friday, a mullah led a funeral service for Karim at the Blue Mosque. Ghulam Dastagir's coterie acted as bodyguards, escorting him and his headman to the house of God. A harsh drizzle that was mixed with particles of ice kept the streets deserted, but inside the mosque, they found hundreds of well-wishers, from prosperous merchants and feudal khans to men dressed in rags. The mullah's sonorous chanting made the windows of the blue edifice ring. Afterwards, people came crowding around Ghulam Dastagir, eager to touch the garments of the martyred boy's father.

Suddenly, Ghulam Dastagir's volunteer bodyguards rushed in to warn that a troop of grim-faced men had just tethered their horses outside and were coming into the mosque. Ibrahim pulled

Ghulam Dastagir out a rear exit. Later, people recounted how the cavaliers had fanned through the crowded mosque, gazing and peering. Clearly, they had not come to pray but to prey. After that, on their friends' advice, the two village men stayed indoors. They didn't care to find out who was hunting them.

Friends and admirers kept them well-supplied with food and news, and the news was never good. Travel in the city kept growing more dangerous. Every day skirmishes broke out between Afghans and Engrayzees. Most of the battles ended inconclusively, which left the aggression they aroused unsated and so, in the wake of every skirmish, bands of men roamed the streets, venting their violence on Afghans of other ethnic groups, looting stores, or simply beating and robbing ordinary folks. Order was breaking down.

One morning, a pair of travelers from Charikar happened by. They said people were rising up in Charikar, and even in Jabul Seraj. There as well, what started as violence against the Engrayzee often ended up as fighting between Afghans. No one could leave their shops unattended. Bandits even broke into people's homes sometimes. Who could tell what was happening further north, closer to Char Bagh?

That afternoon, Ibrahim watched Ghulam Dastagir pacing in the cramped alley behind the hat store. "You feel caged in here," he guessed.

"I'm in pain, Hajji. I swear I don't know how people live in cities. No land, no chance to set your feet on real soil. I can't gather my thoughts. Can you?"

"Cities are not for men like us."

"What if he opens his eyes?" the big man burst out. "Under the soil! What if he wasn't dead when we buried him? I can't remember if I *really* checked."

"Hush. Karim is safe with God now, Ghulam Dastagir."

"I never taught him what to say to the angel!"

"His mother taught him. And I heard Soraya instructing him. Don't worry."

"You must think me very weak." Ghulam Dastagir looked up with uneasy shame. "I can snap a brick in two barehanded, but I can't stop dreaming that I buried my son alive. What's wrong with me?"

"I was like that with Ahmad. It's proper to feel pain. It's proper to grieve."

"But I never did, Ibrahim-jan. *I haven't wept for him.* You must think me very heartless. My little fellow..."

"You wept when he died, Ghulam Dastagir. I saw."

"I never wept enough. Never enough. What are we doing here, Hajji-sahib? Why are we still in this city? I ask the question, and I can't seem to find the answer."

Ibrahim nodded solemnly and addressed the trouble he heard beneath Ghulam Dastagir's questions. "We've been gone a long time without any news from home."

"I wanted to ask those fellows from Charikar, but what would they know? Back in Char Bagh, no one even knows Karim is dead. No one is mourning for him. How lonesome he must be in the dark. And we hide here in the Grand Bazaar like rabbits in holes. What good are we doing?"

"You have sacrificed enough," said Ibrahim. "You're right, you've probably done all you can, you should head home. If you leave at once, you might still get through the passes. But I can't, you see. I *can't* go home without Malang-sahib. It's just not possible. If I can't rescue him, I have to die trying. That's my obligation, it has nothing to do with you. Your obligations are to your boy, may his memory be green, to his mother, to your other children, your kin. If you ever felt bound by any promise to me, I release you. Know that. Return to Char Bagh, take news of me to my family, you will be doing me a great service. Start for home, I beg of you, Ghulam Dastagir. Start for home."

The big man wrung his hands. "How can I go back alone? What would people say? I came along to protect you, youngster."

Still that condescension. Ibrahim bit his lips. After all they'd been through Ghulam Dastagir still saw himself as the seasoned elder guiding a green boy. He would not give Ibrahim the respect that was due to a malik. "Well," Ibrahim murmured, "we'll talk about this tonight. Right now, danger or no danger, I must go out and get some air."

Ibrahim wrapped the end of his turban around his chin and left the bazaar. He walked up toward Behmaru, a hill north of the river, because people said that from the top of that hill, you could look right down into the Engrayzee fort. The last time he had gone up there, he had seen no one in the streets except boys playing marbles. Today, however, the maze was crowded with men holding torches, waving daggers, dancing, and yelling—all sorts of men: slant-eyed Hazaras, beak-nosed Pushtoons, flat-nosed Uzbeks, handsome Tajiks like Ibrahim himself. The feverish feeling of these crowds began to make Ibrahim uneasy.

"What are we celebrating?" he asked a passing stranger with a blood-caked beard. .

"We took the heights of Behmaru." the man grinned. "What a battle! You should have seen me, oh how I fought! This one *farangi* came at me—"

"You were brave," Ibrahim muttered, feeling suddenly lightheaded. "You were strong." What had happened in the city during these days they had spent in hiding? Ibrahim hurried on up the hill, past men with bloody turbans and wounded faces who were all giggling like children. Closer to the top, he saw fires in the streets. Men were feeding looted furniture into the flames, baking plundered half-plucked chickens on sticks. Men were singing and firing guns into the air. Strangers kept hugging Ibrahim joyfully, weeping, "My brother! My brother!"

His pulse pounded. There was no point in going to the very top. He should go down and tell his friends the Afghans had seized Behmaru. This was big news, wonderful news. Why did he feel so anxious? Was it the sight of blood and celebration mixed together? He picked his way down the hill, his head a jangle of confused thoughts and intense feelings. Suddenly a muscular Pushtoon stepped into his path. The man wore a rich cloak and a vest embroidered with golden threads, a vest that glinted even in the gray light of this blood-splattered afternoon.

38

"Salaam aleikum, Ibrahim-khan."

"How do you know my name?" the village headman gasped.

"Ghulam Dastagir told us. We've just now come from him."

"How did you know *his* name?"

"How could we not? He fathered the boy who gave his last breath in the sacred cause!"

"Who are you?" Ibrahim whispered. His body braced.

"Mohammed Jamal of the Achekzai clan. My uncle Abdullah—you've heard of him, of course—one of the greatest chieftains in the land. But I serve an even greater one: Wazir-sahib himself."

Wazir-sahib. Ibrahim gulped. Any big landowner might call himself "khan." Any man of high blood might call himself "sardar." But what kind of man dared to title himself *wazir?* A wazir was a king's chief minister. He was often more powerful than the king himself. After all a king wore robes, but his chief *wazir* wore armor. A king presided over ceremonies, a wazir gave orders.

"Forgive me," Ibrahim stammered. "When you say Wazir ...?"

"I mean Wazir Akbar Khan," the man declared. "Young lion of the Afghan cause. Implacable sword of Allah's justice. Mighty son of the mighty Dost Mohammed, our great and precious king. Wazir-sahib wants to meet you and your friend Ghulam Dastagir."

Oh. Ibrahim's limbs went warm for a moment. "Where is...?"

"Here in Kabul. The young lion has roared, the chiefs have heard, they're gathering. When you meet him, you will know why. Come now.

We must take you and your friend to Wazir Akbar Khan. Do you have a horse of your own?"

"Yes, sahib."

Aching with fear and hope, Ibrahim and Ghulam Dastagir said farewell to their friends who embraced them and whispered Quranic verses over them, abashed by their sudden grandeur. Who could have guessed that a pair of stray villagers they had taken in out of pity would be called to an audience with the famous prince about whom all of Kabul was gossiping, the man who made even the Engrayzee tremble?

The villagers rode through the streets, protected by a dozen mounted riflemen, gazing in sorrow and amazement at the many stores that looked plundered and abandoned. Smoke was rising from Shor Bazaar, where Alexander Burnes had lived and died. Smoke was rising from the other side of the river too, where the Qizilbash clansmen had their homes. A cannon roared from the hilltop palace once or twice. Gunshots kept cracking out. The streets were alive with the flittering urgency of people rushing to get to other places.

In one place, a crowd of ragged men blocked the entire street, having captured a string of camels. The merchant must have fled, or else he was lying somewhere dead. The beggars had pulled bags and bundles off the bellowing beasts and torn the sacks open on the spot. They were quarrelling over the goods now, over mirrors, spices, bits of jewelry. Another day, the mounted men might have scattered these looters and punished the ones they could catch, but today, grimly focused on another mission, they watched until they knew this blockade would not melt away, and then with silent gestures agreed on another route.

After a long canter through wreckage and deserted alleyways, the company passed through the Ghazni gate. Beyond this point, residential neighborhoods gave way to fallow fields and leafless orchards. Muddy roads criss-crossed a grim landscape. Every few miles, another fortress-like compound loomed up.

"Mahmood of the Barakzai." One of the mounted men pointing up the road, not to a man, but to a fortress. Evidently, it belonged to some lord of the Barakzai Pushtoons, the clan headed up by the exiled king. Ibrahim saw some hundred horses tethered amongst the trees around the fort. Grooms came flocking out to take charge of their mounts. Within the walls, countless men lazed about on cots or ambled along the walkways, chattering among themselves. Some wore bullet-loaded bandoliers. Others had shed their bullet belts and set aside their guns, evidently feeling safe enough here inside this fort; but their long-barreled Jezail rifles leaned in rows against nearby walls.

Servants led the villagers into a dark hallway filled with shoes. Ibrahim and Ghulam Dastagir slipped out of their own rude sandals and followed the servants into a room of dazzling size, where gorgeous red overlapping carpets covered the floors, and tapestries hung on the walls. The windows were fitted with shining glass and framed with oiled wood. At the far end of the room, a dozen men sat cross-legged on cushions around a dining cloth, feasting from platters of saffron rice.

One of these men looked up at the newcomers, and Ibrahim knew he was looking at the celebrated Wazir Akbar Khan. He appeared to be no older than Ibrahim himself and might even have been younger. A pristine turban wound tightly around his glossy black hair allowed some locks out to graze his shoulders. A jutting nose gave him a hawk-like look, but his round face and the cherubic shine of his round cheeks contributed a boyishness as well. When this young man looked up, so did all the others in the room. When he glanced from one of the villagers to the other, so did all his companions. Wherever his attention turned, so did theirs. He radiated power, this young man; all the others seemed like puppets attached to him by strings of unseen force.

One of the servants blared out, "The men of Char Bagh, my lord."

The prince said "Ah." Without rising, he gestured them closer. "Gentlemen." He spoke with polished courtesy. "Consider our house your house. We beg your pardon for starting the meal without you. Join us please."

He pointed to the place directly across the cloth from himself and the men in that spot quickly shifted position to make room for the newcomers. Hesitantly, the villagers settled down. The black intensity of the royal gaze discomfited Ibrahim. Since the prince was looking at him, every other eye was trained on him as well. Ibrahim felt like he was sitting next to a lantern, in a dark room filled with strangers, himself and his companion the only visible objects.

"You are Ghulam Dastagir," the prince stated. He addressed neither man in particular and waited for them to reveal which one belonged to this name.

"Yes, sir." Ghulam Dastagir cleared his throat. "And this is my countryman—"

But the prince interrupted him affably—he would do the talking. "Ghulam Dastagir, you have lost a son, we hear. Take pride in fathering a martyr. *Inshallah*, your precious boy is in paradise already, seated among God's most cherished favorites."

This declaration was followed by a moment of respectful silence. Ghulam Dastagir's permanent scowl released its grip enough to let his eyes uncrinkle.

"You charged a line of *sipahis* and eluded all their blazing bullets, people tell me. You dispatched one bastard with a single blow," said the prince. "This is true?"

"I don't remember. They murdered my boy," Ghulam Dastagir muttered. "My eyes were filled with blood."

"And properly so," said the prince. "Very properly so. Blood must be avenged with blood." He turned to Ibrahim. "You, sahib. You are the malik of Chil Bagh."

Ibrahim blinked. *Chil Bagh* meant "Forty Gardens." Should he correct the prince? Does one correct a prince? What if the prince was testing to see if he would a claim a grandeur he did not possess? "I *am* the malik of my village," Ibrahim hedged at last, but then, worrying that his hesitation made him sound evasive, he added, "It's a poor village known to *most* people as Char Bagh, sahib. We are famous for melons, grapes, and goats."

"I see." The prince nodded. He addressed his dinner companions. "Here are two of our real Afghans, Khan-sahibs. Stouthearted men of the countryside: honest, loyal, and brave. This is why the British will lose—men like these two."

A windy chatter of agreement rose from the prince's khans, like the wing-melody of pigeons rousted from a courtyard.

But the prince trained his attention on Ibrahim again, and the chatter ceased. "I am told you can read and write."

"Yes, sahib," Ibrahim confirmed, taken aback.

"Excellent," said the prince. "Our struggle requires scholars as well as warriors. Eh, men?"

The khans agreed. "Oh yes—indispensable—Scholars? Very important…"

"Tell me, sahib—as a scholar well-versed in the wisdom of the ancients—what do you say about these *farangis* who have settled upon our land like locusts, these foreigners who have driven my father from his throne and put a midget in his place, the accursed worm Shah Shuja?"

Before Ibrahim could say a word, Ghulam Dastagir blared, "What *could* he think? What gives these murdering bastards the right to choose our king? By what right do they even set foot on our soil without permission? On that count alone, we would hate the dogs, but they've given us so many other reasons too! Your father is the true king, Wazir-sahib. He will always be the true king. Our loyalty is wrapped around him like bark around a tree, eternal and unchanging. Long live Dost Mohammed Khan! Long may he live!"

The prince heard the man out. "Uh huh," he said, then returned his gaze to Ibrahim. "And you, Scholar? What is your opinion?"

Ibrahim thought of the malang, chained up in that underground cell. Guilt surged inside him so forcefully, he thought he might howl. He wanted to tear at his hair and scream. What did the prince want him to say? Something in particular, it seemed. Ghulam Dastagir's rant had not sufficed. What did he expect then—more fawning?

"Well, sahib," Ibrahim began cautiously, "we never knew such men existed until recently." Picking up the thrum of passion in Ibrahim's voice, the khans looked at him curiously. "They came to us this summer, for the first time, and what did we know? We let them live in a hut we had built for visitors. They gave us money, and we rejoiced, God strike us! Rejoiced at payments from those men! They said they were looking for special herbs, and we believed them blindly, so great was our hunger for their money. We never asked ourselves: are these men Muslims? Where do they come from? What could they really want? God strike us dead, half the blame is ours! All this happened, sahib, and then—then they did terrible things in our village… things I can't even bring myself to mention. Terrible things."

"When?" The prince's attention was like a needle now, poking into Ibrahim's story. The whole party leaned in to listen.

"The month of Assad," said Ghulam Dastagir.

"Or early Sunbula," mused Ibrahim. "Anyway, before we harvested the wheat."

"Go on," said the prince. "Terrible things."

"Yes, and our malang tried to protect us."

The prince raised an inquisitive eyebrow. "What malang is this?"

"The malang of Char Bagh," said one of his dining companions. "Haven't you heard of him, Akbar Khan? A poet of sorts. His book is floating around the bazaar."

"That's the one!" Ibrahim exclaimed. "But he's much more than a poet, good sirs. He is a sheikh!"

"The Malang of Char Bagh. Yes, I have heard of him," said the prince. "His pen name is Tempestuous Love or some such—correct?" The Prince lifted his eyes and recited two couplets in a croaking sing-song, "*Not all your prayers…nor all your piety or pleading … will alter by an ant-hair where your path is leading. Did you choose the hour of your birth on Earth? Do you think to choose the hour of your leaving?*"

Ibrahim's pulse skipped a beat.

"A man recited his verses to me last week," the prince explained. "They stuck with me. I have an excellent memory. He comes from your village, this malang?"

"Yes, he's ours. Those lines you quoted, Wazir-sahib—I have the original manuscript at home. I can make an accurate copy for you when I get back to Char Bagh and have it delivered to your lordship."

"What do you mean 'the original'?"

So Ibrahim told the story. The company listened raptly, their attention coming unstuck from the prince for those few moments. "That's the original manuscript," Ibrahim concluded, "the one taken down fresh from the sheikh's lips. We don't know where the sheikh hails from, but of all the villages in Afghanistan, he chose ours. Some call him the Wandering Malang, but he's a wanderer no more, sir. No more. He chose Char Bagh. We gave him land. And then the Engrayzee ripped him from us."

"What do you mean, 'ripped'?"

"They sent soldiers to our village and dragged him away in chains."

A palpable shock ran among the listeners. "Took him where?" one diner asked.

"Here," said Ibrahim. "He's here in Kabul, locked in a dungeon below Bala Hissar. That's why we came to the capital, sahibs—to petition the king for justice. But what king? Not till our feet trod upon the streets of this city did we learn the news: we humble Muslims no longer have a king! This creature on our throne is only a slave of the Engrayzee. So whom do we petition? When our grievance is with the Engrayzee, who do we turn to? I turn to you, Wazir-sahib," Ibrahim addressed himself earnestly to the young prince. "*You* are my king now. I plead with you, sir." And despite the turmoil that dimmed his gaze and made the room a twirl of confusion, when Ibrahim spoke those words, he saw something flutter in the prince's eyes, felt a tug in his heart like the one a fisherman feels when a fish has nibbled at his bait. He knew what he had hooked and went on playing the line. "You are my king now," he insisted. "Until your mighty father is restored, I look to you, as do all the suffering subjects of this tragic land, your sacred majesty—"

"No, no—" The prince shook his finger as if to scold Ibrahim, although he did not look at all displeased. "I am not the king, only my father's regent. Never use that title with me, lest the other khans suppose I have ambitions. Gentlemen! You all know I have no ambitions, correct?"

"You are the soul of modesty," his companions chorused.

"I am simply a patriot," the prince told Ibrahim, "seeking justice, seeking honor for my people. Justice and honor, nothing more."

"But how is justice to be incarnated except in you, your highness? Where else should we repose our hopes?" Ibrahim pleaded. "You say you seek to redeem the honor of your people, but you *are* that honor! We look to you for all our hopes. Help us! Only you can set the malang of Char Bagh free. Please, your sacred majesty—"

"Uh uh! I warned you," Akbar shook that playful finger again, then he looked about at his dinner guests, shining with pleased amusement. "What do you think, my friends? What do we see in these two men? Gentlemen, I give you—Afghanistan. Eloquence and purity! Courage! Can we deafen our ears to such a plea?"

"What sort of men would we be?" the dinner guests exclaimed.

"You fellows have touched my heart. This malang interests me. I will help you," the prince decided. "But you must help me as well."

Ibrahim responded with a heartfelt, "*Ba chishm.*" I would give my eyesight.

"You, Ghulam Dastagir." The prince turned to the big man. "A warrior like you in my service would lighten the weight upon my shoulders. Will you pledge your strength to me, Ghulam Dastagir?"

"A thousand times," the brute vowed. "Command me, sahib. My life is yours."

"You will record great deeds in the annals of our history," the prince predicted. "As for you, malik. You, who can read and write. Boon companion to the great Malang of Char Bagh. I need a scribe. I had a good one up north, but British bullets killed him on our way south. British—that's another name for these intruders. Can your village spare your leadership for a time? Will you pledge your pen to my service?"

"With my very eyes," Ibrahim repeated fervently. His head whirling, he tried to calculate what this offer (order?) might entail and how it might liberate the malang.

"Good," said the prince. "That being settled—please. The food is getting cold. Let's enjoy what remains of it."

Two boys came scurrying in with pots of warm water and towels. The men of Char Bagh washed their hands and began to feast from the nearest platters. Striving not to disgrace themselves with village table manners, they squeezed the rice into small clumps and lifted these delicately to their mouths, careful not to lose a single grain. As they ate, they uncovered chunks of baked lamb under the rice and tore these into smaller pieces with their fingers. The lamb was as soft as clotted cream, meat that even a toothless old man might have chewed. Ibrahim had never tasted such food. He sat with his head bowed, swimming in half-formed thoughts and powerful feelings. How destiny had played with him in this great and terrible year! He imagined telling Soraya about this place and then hearing her weave it into one of her phantasmagorical tales. The girls would shine with delight at a story featuring their father as a legendary hero. That is, if Soraya still had her wits about her enough to understand his report...if she had not sunk back to eating mud and trucking with *djinns*...And Khadija! How she would marvel to hear that he had dined with a prince! If she had not died of grief...and shame...Ibrahim's excitement clouded over.

After the meal, the prince's servants conducted the villagers to one of the buildings along the perimeter of the fortress walls, which served as dormitories and barracks. The front door was flanked by rosebushes. Ibrahim thought at once about the malang's words in the dungeon. *Before the seven rosebushes give up their petals your new friend will open the door for you.* But here he saw only four rosebushes, two on each side of the doorway, and none of them had any petals. The malang could not have meant these roses.

Inside, both men were given bedrolls of their own and shown where to roll them out. They were now just two more of several dozen retainers sharing one long room, a room with an enormous wood-burning stove at each end.

39

Khadija was sitting by a window mending a shirt when she heard the commotion down in the courtyard. Someone had come visiting, but who could it be at this late hour? Hope suddenly made her breathless. She dropped her sewing and hurried to the balustrade to look over. All she saw down there was Mullah Yaqub, the cleric from Sorkhab, leading his donkey to the stables while little boys tagged after him, grabbing at his shirttails and yammering to know why he had come all this way at dusk.

And why *had* he come? Soraya was out in the courtyard already, hopping in place and yelling, "Is it news?"

Khadija shrilled at him too. "Have you heard from Ibrahim? Have they found our dear Malang?"

The mullah looked up, his face haggard in the dimming light, but his body emanated excitement. "Well, salaam aleikum to you too, Khadija-jan. Thank you so much for asking about my health."

She felt the reproof and forced herself to be polite. "May Allah guard you, Mullah-sahib, welcome and forgive me. You must be tired. Boys, take mullah-sahib to the guest room, make him comfortable." This damned mullah! She had known him since childhood and was related to him in half a dozen different ways but still he demanded all the ritual observances. How easily his pompous dignity was offended!

She rounded up women and set the wheels of hospitality in motion, then made her way to the guest room where the cleric was already ensconced. From the dark hallway, she could see him in there already spilling his story to a rapt collection of men and boys.

"What are you telling them?" she demanded from the doorway. "Tell us women too."

"Big battle in Charikar," one boy shouted out, unable to hold back the thrilling news. "They killed them all!"

Khadija's knees wobbled. Behind her, Soraya gasped. Neither woman knew who had killed whom, but Soraya set a hand on Khadija's hip for support and leaned against her body to stand on tiptoe and peer over her shoulder. Khadija could feel the younger woman's warm breath on her neck, just below her ear.

"Who did?" Khadija said. She scarcely knew how to frame her question.

"We did," the Mullah blared out, sweating with excitement. "The Engrayzee had a fort in Charikar—it's ours now! I was passing by is all, I saw a crowd, boys, I stopped to look—I had no idea what was going on. The Engrayzee! Who would have guessed they had such a fortress there, such numbers—a hundred of them! More! Well, I saw a crowd, I plunged into it—and then it started. I don't know why. Suddenly, they were shooting—"

"Was Ibrahim there?" Khadija broke in. "Did you see him? I hope he's been eating! Was he looking well—"

"He wasn't there. Your Malang was hauled off to Kabul, your men followed him. But I'm talking about Charikar—like I said, I was there for a wedding, I had no idea—suddenly they were shooting, we were throwing rocks—bullets going zing, zang, this way, that way—I thought I was finished, by God—some men ran home for rifles—"

"And then what," Khadija said impatiently. "In the end? What happened finally?"

The mullah frowned. He wanted to wallow in his epic deed. "Long story short," he said grumpily, "we broke the doors down, rushed in and killed the dogs, a hundred of them. Only two got away."

"A hundred!" Soraya cried out. "How many's that?"

But Khadija zeroed in on the crucial point. "Two got away?"

"Traitors gave them horses," Mullah Yaqub huffed. "We killed all the rest. A hundred or more, I tell you! A mighty victory!"

But Khadija only glared at him. "Those two will bring the rest of their tribe down on us. You should have killed none of them or all of them."

"Those two won't get out of the mountains," the cleric swore. "The wolves will get them or the cold. I barely got back through the passes myself, it snowed so hard that night. And I came here at once to bring you the news."

"What news? We want to know about our men! You didn't even see him, you said. He wasn't there, you said."

"Well, I heard a rumor. That's what I came to tell you. Someone saw Ibrahim and Ghulam Dastagir in Kabul two weeks ago. Rejoice, they were alive and safe."

"A rumor!" Khadija wrung her hands, her heart palpitating. Soraya was pulling at her sleeve, but she ignored it. "Rumors can't be trusted. Who saw them? Two weeks—anything could have happened since then! Why even tell us news like that—"

"Trust in Allah," the mullah said.

Soraya was pulling harder, but Khadija didn't care. "It's hard, Mullah-sahib. It's hard to stay behind, helpless, totally in the dark." But the cleric had turned away. The men were bristling with discomfort. She could have stood up to their anger, but their embarrassment defeated her. She gave in and let Soraya draw her out of the room. In the courtyard, Soraya kept tugging at her. She pulled away but Soraya grabbed her hand. Khadija felt the warmth of those bony fingers. And still Soraya kept pulling. "What are you doing?" Khadija said. "Where are you taking me?" Soraya was pulling Khadija back toward the stables with all the bullish determination of a child. Khadija giggled but felt uneasy. Something was not right with Soraya. Something was wrong here. Maybe *djinns* had the girl again, maybe it was *djinns* who were trying to get Khadija into some dark corner. "What are you doing? Where are you taking me, Soraya?"

They were in the stable now. Soraya was breathing hard. The light in the courtyard had sunk to little more than a candle's worth, and here in the stable, it was too dark to see anybody's features. Khadija could make out only the general shape of Soraya's body against the mottled background of a cow. The large animal puffed out a warm, humid breath and lowered its head to its alfalfa. In the next stall, behind a mud barrier, two goats jostled and stamped.

"Why did you bring me here?" Khadija demanded in a sharper voice.

"You shouldn't have asked about him like that!" spat Soraya.

"What are you taking about? Who?"

"My husband, you shameless bitch with your hungry eyes! Who else? May the grave swallow you. Who else would I mean!"

"But we're all just dying to know—"

"I should be the one to ask! He's *my* husband! You crowd me out, you dance among the men, you let that nasty Mullah inspect every part of you—oh, Allah, why did I ever let you back in this house—"

"Let me! Oh, I like that! You begged me! Little Fool, I asked for news of him on *your* behalf. What's wrong with you? Ibrahim-jan—"

"*Don't* call him 'jan.' Have some shame. He's not 'jan' to you, he's Malik-sahib! My God! Even marrying you off doesn't stop you."

"So you take credit for my marriage! Oh, I suppose you should. I know how you pushed and prodded him and now you're jealous because I'm married to the greatest—"

"What else could I do? Him and you together all the time behind closed doors!"

"What closed doors? Have you lost your mind? Is Khushdil filling you with this slime? I'll forgive you this time, little one, but I swear if you ever dare—"

"Shut up, you thief! You shut up! Shut up! You can't threaten me. What door did you leave open *that* day when he came to your compound? When they dragged our poor, dear malang away to some horrid prison, and all you could think about was how to get my husband alone so you could do that thing with him."

"God strike your filthy tongue!" Khadija swung a slap against Soraya's cheek and a wet sound cracked out. It felt like slapping a frog. Soraya's head bounced to one side, but she recovered at once and came springing back. Khadija grabbed her wrists and held them, and braced against the lighter body. For a moment, the two women tilted and teetered from side to side. Soraya tried to pull her wrists free, and then to claw, but she failed in both: Khadija pushed her against the cow. Her sweating hands slipped off Soraya's wet wrists, but she kept pressing the woman bodily against the cow, pinning her there with her weight, feeling the slender, sinewy warmth of Soraya under her clothes, her breath… She flashed back to the memory of her breath on her neck in the guest room earlier…

Suddenly the fight drained out of Soraya and she went limp. She would have fallen had the pressure of Khadija's body not kept her upright. She shoved her hand between their faces to wipe her leaking nose. "You were seen," she said, her chin up-thrust. "Yell all you want, but you were seen, you liar, liar, you big liar. You're just a liar!"

Khadija stepped back aghast, letting Soraya crumple. "Doing what? Who saw me! Where? You tell me, Soraya. You better tell me."

"You were seen, you were seen," Soraya insisted, sing-song style, tauntingly. "The night he left for Baghlan. Everyone thought he was going straight to Ghulam Dastagir's, but he went to your house first. He was alone with you."

Khadija flushed with shame. All the animals were lowing and murmuring, shifting weight and rustling against the straw. The whole room felt moist with their breath. The warmth of the animals and the smell of manure filled Khadija's nostrils. Her gorge rose. Tears seared her eyelids. "He came to say goodbye," she whispered. "Do you begrudge me *that*, Soraya? Even *that*?"

"You were alone with him," Soraya accused.

"He came to tell me he would die to save my husband, if death is what it took. I let him tell me. How was that wrong? I listened to him. Then we said namaz together." Khadija bit her lips, glad for the darkness that hid her face from her beloved's wife.

"A man and a woman saying namaz together! That's just wrong!"

"Namaz is never wrong. Who claims he saw something more? Ibrahim came to my compound, he left my compound, that's all anyone saw." No one could have seen more than that. No one had seen, she was sure of it. She would defeat this assault.

Then Soraya let out a shrill laugh and said. "You stand there, pregnant with his child and lie?"

"Pregnant!" Khadija clapped both hands over her belly. "Pregnant? I'm barren! Everybody knows! How can you fling *that* in my face? How can you be so cruel?"

"You're pregnant! You are, you throw up all the time. You're pregnant, pregnant! How long do you think you can fool people? Your mouth can lie, but your belly don't. Your belly won't. It'll tell. Your belly will tell."

Khadija's fingers pressed against her own flesh. Then she knew. And yes, it was true. Knowing took no more than someone saying it out loud. Her body had already known. She was pregnant. If the thought had never entered her mind, it was only because she had never let it enter. She had shut her mind so utterly to any such thought so long ago. Pregnant was the one thing she knew she could never be.

Only now she was. Soraya stood there, still blazing out resentment—until Khadija fell into her arms and began to sob against her shoulder because there was no other shoulder to sob against. And still Soraya just stood there, not knowing what to do with her awkward arms, until finally—because her arms were tired—she rested her hands on Khadija's upper back. And then—because her hands were already in the neighborhood—she began to stroke Khadija the way she stroked the children when they were hurting.

It didn't last long. With Khadija, it never would. The malang's wife pulled away, and her sobs subsided. She pulled away and wrapped her arms around her own trunk as if against the cold, but really against the world, her usual armor restored. Into the darkness, she whispered. "It wasn't Ibrahim, dear child. Think about it. I'm barren. Everyone knows I am. Do you *really* think your husband could have quickened this poor womb of mine? Ibrahim is a good man, but he's just a man. *My* husband! Mine is the Malang of Char Bagh! *My* husband walks with his feet on the Earth and his head in the sky. He wades through clouds, he sees the face of Allah every day the way you and I see the sun and the stars. If I'm pregnant—even a wretched half-woman like me, *who could have planted this seed?*"

Soraya's eyes grew saucer-huge with awe. Her wonder shone in that dark room. "You're carrying Malang-sahib's child?"

Khadija said nothing, but now that Soraya had spoken the words, she knew they must be true. She was a vessel, Ibrahim could only be an instrument, this was Malang-sahib's doing, his miraculous child. Somehow, it must be true.

"You are," Soraya decided. "You're carrying *his* child!" The immensity of it made her voice tremble. The quarrel between the two women was forgotten, all quarrels were forgotten. Soraya's arms went circling around Khadija again to nestle her close and croon to her. For once, Soraya was the big sister. "The others will do everything to hurt you, but I won't let them," she promised fiercely. "Oh, Khadija, Khadija, I've been afraid of you all my life. How could I fear someone I love so much? I do, you know! I love you *soooo* much."

Khadija laughed through her tears. "We belong together, little one. Without you, they'll eat me alive. Without me, you're lost, admit it. Now dry those tears and put away your sulks. We need each other. Why should we ever fight? We each have a husband of our own—if they ever come back."

40

It was mid-morning, shortly after bread-and-tea, that Wazir Akbar Khan sent for Ibrahim and Ghulam Dastagir. The two men had spent weeks in the gilded cage of the Barakzai fortress, marking time while the malang rotted in his pit. They were glad, therefore, of the summons. They found the prince in the same big room where he'd been dining with the khans that first day, leaning against a fluffy cushion. "Ghulam Dastagir," he announced, "I want you to ride south as my messenger."

"A thousand times, your highness."

"I want you to meet with all the important Ghilzai chieftains down there. Don't worry, they won't harm you, they wouldn't dare: you'll be carrying my seal."

"I wasn't worried."

"I will give you the names of men who command respect. Find them wherever they are and deliver my message. Agreed?"

"At the glad sacrifice of my very eyesight, sir. What should I tell them?"

"Tell them nothing, just deliver a letter. But I want you to understand what will be in the letter. There's been some scuffling, you know, between us northern Pushtoons and those Ghilzai down south. I want to tell them, that's over with. We have a common enemy now. We must set aside old grudges and move as one nation."

"One nation." Ghulam Dastagir smacked his lips. "Common

enemy." From him, the words sounded like an oath. "I understand, Wazir-sahib. Yes!"

"The infidel is among us," Akbar pressed. "Until they're gone, we have no other quarrel. I will dictate a letter to Scribe-sahib here, he'll make enough copies for all the chieftains in the southeast. Can you write a hundred letters in a single day, Scribe?" He cocked a quizzical eyebrow at Ibrahim.

Ibrahim remembered his ecstatic midsummer days with Malang-sahib. "Yes, your highness. I can write fast."

"Excellent," said the prince. "Here is what my letter will say: 'The Engrayzees are coming through your territory soon. Let them pass unharmed.' Make every Ghilzai chieftain sign this promise. Understand, Ghulam Dastagir?"

But Ghulam did not understand. What game was this? He rested his large hands on his thighs and turned an injured gaze upon the prince. "Spare my son's murderers? Is that what you're asking? I should tell all the chiefs to spare my son's murderers?"

"Exactly." The prince stroked his silky beard, and his black eyes gleamed. "These bastard Engrayzee are ready to flee, my boys. The fear is in them now. They know who they're dealing with at last. I'm about to open negotiations with them, and if I can show them a crack of light, they'll run to it, the way roaches run to darkness. Such would never be our way, of course, we Afghans would stand and fight to the last man, but the Engrayzee are not like us. If they see a way to save their skins, they'll choose it, so I must show them a way. That's why I need guarantees from all the tribes along the southern passes. Without that promise—on paper—signed—a guarantee—the infidels won't leave. They'll crowd into Bala Hissar and fire their cannons into the city. Now do you see?"

"Let them fire!" Ghulam Dastagir shouted. "I don't fear their cannons, by Quran. I'll be the first to storm the heights. We are many, they are few! How many can they kill before we bury them?"

"Quite a few," the prince assured him. "Quite a few. But that's beside the point. Once the shooting starts, you're right: we'll storm their forts and none of us will count or care how many of our own go down.

We'll fight and kill until every last bullet is spent and every last Engrayzee stops twitching. By then many of our own will by lying still as well and we'll honor their martyrdom." He leaned forward then. "But if that happens, the Engrayzee will come back with a bigger force—more guns—more cannons... And the killing will start again. They have endless men in their own land, endless guns. And the Hindus will start gathering armies too, you can count on it. And the Sikhs will become four-testicled as well. And the Shah of Persia—no, no, we can put a stop to it *now* and we must! Ghulam Dastagir, I trust your warrior strength. The last man I sent south got his ears trimmed, but you won't let that happen to you. All men know your courage. I look in your eyes and I see rock hard resolve. But the task is now not just military. It's political too. You do as I command and leave the politics to me. Agreed?"

Ghulam Dastagir nodded heavily. "As you wish, sahib."

The prince went to the door and called for the Master of the Horse, and when this man appeared, he pointed to Ghulam Dastagir. "Equip this gentleman with our best mount," he ordered. "Give him saddlebags full of food that he can eat while riding—lamb jerky—plenty of pounded fruit-nut paste, a goatskin of good spring water—where he's going, the streams will be frozen and his journey is long. Ghulam Dastagir, you leave before sunset prayer, ride hard, and get to Abdullah Khan's fortress before midnight. That puts you at the mouth of Khurd-Kabul pass. Abdullah's men will show you where to go from there. Events are gathering fast, boys, we must move faster. Don't fail me."

Ibrahim studied the prince's profile and wondered at his confidence. Ghulam Dastagir might punch through where others had failed, but the southern Pushtoons would not relish taking orders from a northern Pushtoon, and even less so if those orders were delivered by a surly Tajik. Surely some diplomat with a ready tongue would have made a better envoy. Besides, what message would Ghulam Dastagir really spread? A man conveys a message by the way he talks, no matter what his tongue is saying. This man wanted to see the Engrayzee dead. Princes, however, don't take advice from village headmen, so Ibrahim kept his thoughts to himself. Perhaps, by sending Ghulam Dastagir, the prince intended to send two message, one on paper—"spare them"— and another more subtly conveyed: "Kill them."

Akbar shut the door on Ghulam Dastagir and turned to Ibrahim. "Come along, Scribe. We have a proper office in the back. Pens, paper, ink, everything you need. Let's get started."

Ibrahim retrieved his sandals and followed the prince into the recesses of the building. The prince kept chattering the whole way, just to hear his own thoughts it seemed. "I must write to my father. Oh, and my brothers. I have so many, God be praised. Brothers in Herat, brothers in Ghazni, brothers in Kandahar—phew! Everywhere. And uncles too, God be praised. What a curse!"

"Have you thought about the malang, sir?" Even to himself Ibrahim's voice sounded querulous.

"What about him?"

"He's injured, sir, and time passes. How long can he last in a dungeon?"

"He's part of my plan," the prince assured him without slowing down or glancing back. "Absolutely. A sovereign must always—here we are." He stopped at a doorway and took out a ring of keys. "What was I saying? Ah, the malang, yes. I'd not forgotten him, I assure you, but we must move in stages, Scribe—shifting, feinting, sparring as each moment requires —stick with me and you'll see miracles. Your grandchildren will tell the story—he united the tribes, they'll say—he drove the Godless from this land—and you'll be part of it! Once the foreigners are gone, rescuing your malang will be gnat's work! Do you think Shah Shuja can stand up to me for two blinks of an eye without his foreign helpers? We'll do more than rescue your malang, we'll elevate him, we'll shower him with gifts, we'll commission books from him—all in good time. Right now, we have the enemy to grapple with. Sit down, Scribe. There is your desk and your writing supplies. Ready?" Almost without a pause, the prince began to dictate. "*Respected sir! Beacon of your people! May Allah shower bounteous good fortune upon your exalted head—*"

Ibrahim clambered onto the desk chair and hunkered there as he would have done if he were sitting on the ground, for he had never used furniture like this before. He dipped the pen and began to scribble, struggling to catch up with the prince's voice. The two men worked without interruption until noon. Ibrahim had to write so fast he couldn't follow what the prince was saying or to whom. He just wrote. At last,

Akbar stopped dictating and wiped his brow. "Phew, that's thirsty work, Scribe! Now we'll have some tea." He clapped his hands and a pair of servants appeared with the tea service. While they poured, Akbar eased onto a platform piled high with cushions. "You probably wonder," he said to Ibrahim when they were alone again, "why I flatter the chiefs of Kohistan so warmly. What is to be gained, you ask yourself."

Ibrahim, who had wondered no such thing, rubbed his wrists to relieve his cramps. "It's not my place to ask."

The prince, however, wanted to explain. "The tribes are gathering from every direction," he said. "What a blessing, what a curse. Listen!" He raised his hand. Gunshots crackled in the distance, as it did every hour these days. "They're fighting all over Kabul, do you hear it? There's hard fighting in the passes too, and there's fighting up north—I know about up-north, I just came from there. Yesterday, the foreign leaders said to me, 'Akbar Khan, tell your chiefs to do this, tell your people to do that.'" The prince chuckled and wagged his head. "As if I can tell Afghans what to do! These *farangis*! They think if someone throws a rock, someone must have ordered that a rock be thrown. They know nothing about Afghans."

Ibrahim ventured an opinion. "They need to believe *someone* can start and stop the violence, Wazir-sahib."

The prince gave him an appraising look. "Very shrewd, village man. Shrewd indeed. We'll make a strategist of you yet. Yes, they need to believe there's someone they can talk to about all the trouble, so they talk to me. But you know what troubles *me*? I'll tell you in confidence, Scribe. The *farangi* is a wounded bear facing a tiger. The tiger grows in size and strength and ferocity every hour, every minute. Today, we love the tiger because we hate the bear. But once the bear is dead, what will the tiger do? *That's* what worries me."

Ibrahim nodded soberly. For days now, his body had been filled with the same kind of tension he felt back home when a storm of unknown intensity was coming. In Char Bagh, when the air darkened and people felt the wind quickening, they huddled around their elders, begging for ancient stories about disaster and survival. Another kind of storm was approaching now, and Ibrahim longed to be back in his tranquil village with Malang-sahib by his side, Ghulam Dastagir trailing behind, and his people celebrating his safe return. "You're right, sahib."

"Oh, indeed I am." The prince took a reflective sip. "Let me pose you a puzzle, Scribe. My father dealt these foreign bastards a crushing blow, shredded Robert Sale, their best general, at Parwan-Darrah, and then…that very same day! He rode into the British camp, yielded up his sword, and went into exile. Why do that directly after a victory?"

Ibrahim had heard speculation about this in the bazaar: bribes, betrayal, sheer cowardice. "It's a mystery," he said tactfully.

"It's not a mystery at all," Akbar countered. "The chiefs of Kohistan were sharpening their knives behind his back. They were planning to fall upon him from behind while he was driving out the foreigners. And all the other tribes had plans of their own too. I tell you, Scribe, in this country, nobody can turn his back on anyone. That's why—well. We should finish the letters. But here's a last point."

"My ears are open, sahib."

"Freedom is a fine thing. But every-man-for-himself isn't freedom. When every valley's a kingdom, when every patriarch is a king, when it's all against all, every men is a slave to chaos and chaos is the cruelest tyrant of them all. Chaos, Scribe! That's Satan's face on Earth. Write it down, it's worth remembering."

"Already written, your majesty," said Ibrahim as he jotted the epigram.

"At least, with the Engrayzee, you can sign a treaty. No one can sign a treaty with Chaos. Do you know why I tell you this?"

"I don't ask, Wazir-sahib. You honor me by your confidence."

"Well spoken, Scribe. But I have my reasons and I would have you know them. In days to come, men will question my deeds, I want at least one man to understand my true motives. You will be that man."

"You can speak freely before me, sahib. I'm a nobody."

"It's your best trait. You won't betray me, because you have no ambition—although I should check on that while we're on the subject: you don't want to be king, do you?"

"No sahib, I just want to liberate my malang."

"And you will. You'll do it, Scribe, because you're mine. God willing, so long as you pledge unwavering loyalty to me, your malang is saved. I need you by my side. I can't share my thinking with the chieftains. Chaos is already tickling their chins, you see. Bloody chaos, whispering to each of them, *you* could be king, *you* could be king, why not *you*?"

"Ten dervishes can share one blanket, but two kings can't share a country."

"Good one, Scribe. You know your way around words."

"That one, your majesty, was coined by Sa'di."

"He's good too. Pick up your pen. We have work to do."

41

Ibrahim was filled with misgivings as he watched Ghulam Dastagir ride away, man and horse diminishing to a speck and then vanishing into the distance. Would he ever see his friend again? Ibrahim had never felt close to the man and yet already missed him and feared for his safety. Thunderous rain fell in the days that followed, and snow must have fallen in the passes. Men had no business traveling in such weather, much less in mountains like the ones south of Kabul, where Ghulam Dastagir was riding now. To make matters worse, the prince was often gone on important business, and without his protective presence, Ibrahim felt insecure among all the Pushtoon lords and warriors. Fortunately, one of the prince's nephews took a friendly interest in Ibrahim. Unfortunately, this boy Sultan Jan was so young his beard had not even reached its full length yet. It was this soft-bearded boy who came to Ibrahim in the courtyard one day. "Wazir-sahib wants you to meet him in Kabul. He left directions. Can you read his handwriting?"

"Of course," said Ibrahim. The prince's unsigned note gave detailed directions to a building in one of Kabul's more crowded neighborhoods—a squalid area. The note told him to come on horseback, alone, and to make sure no one followed him.

Ibrahim saddled a horse and rode east. Weeks had passed since he had last seen the city, and those weeks had wrought tremendous changes. Kabul now thrummed with an atmosphere of bloodthirsty celebration. Everywhere he looked, he saw glowing faces. But everywhere, he saw beaten people too, skulking along timidly, ready to bolt into any alley, frightened to be outdoors, hurrying to get to shelter. Here and there, whole rows of empty stores showed blank faces to the world: they had been looted and their owners had fled. Sometimes, Ibrahim saw toothless beggars wearing robes of fur.

Recently, snow had blanketed the city; then the sun had melted some of that snow; then temperatures had plunged again, freezing the mud. Now, Ibrahim had to pick his way slowly lest his horse slip in an icy rut.

His way led right past the Grand Bazaar, so he stopped to visit Hakim Shamsuddin, but the hat merchant was not in. "He went home," said a neighboring hat and turban merchant. "It was last week, and he hasn't been back. Too much fighting, he said. He's going to lie low till all this blows over. Abdul Haq is gone too—he returned to Wardak."

"What about you?" Ibrahim asked. "Why are you still here?"

"What can a poor man do?" the other groaned. "I have babes at home. Food is expensive, and firewood too! It's so cold, wood is so dear! The woodcutters won't come into the city anymore. They're frightened. But it's worst for the tailors, I admit. The tailors have it worst. Trying to sew with freezing fingers."

"You're here because you need the money."

"I have no other livelihood, sir. No land, nothing else. If I can't feed my children, I might as well be in my grave. Alas, not many people shop for hats these days. If only I were selling guns. Did you want a hat, by any chance? A man can always use an extra hat."

"Not this man," Ibrahim apologized. "I'm a traveler and I have just this one head. May Allah be with you, merchant. I have business I must get to."

"Goodbye," said the other. "May you keep that one head."

Ibrahim followed the prince's directions to a narrow street he had never seen before. When he knocked at the designated door, a girl answered—a beautiful girl about the age Soraya had been when he married her. She had a scarf and nothing else covering her face. Shocked by the girl's bold display and embarrassed for her modesty, Ibrahim glanced about for male relatives, fearing that one might burst out of hiding at any moment and attack him for violating the privacy of this household, but he saw no one behind the girl. Ibrahim showed her Prince Akbar's note.

"I know who you are," said the girl. "I was told to give you the message that this is not the place. New instructions have been left for you. Wait here, I'll get them." She came back shortly with a sheet of paper folded in thirds and then folded in thirds the other way and sealed with wax. It bore no stamp. When Ibrahim broke the seal and read the note, he found it unsigned, like the other one. It gave directions to a house in another neighborhood, closer to the Lion's Doorway, the notch between two rocky ridges on the southwestern side of the city. It told him to commit the contents of the note to memory and burn it. Ibrahim asked the girl where he might find a fire, and she led him indoors to a coal-burning stove. He was astounded that the men of this household would allow such a girl to attend a stranger alone, inside the house, in a private room where a dishonorable man might do anything to her. She opened a hatch on the barrel of the stove and Ibrahim tossed both notes onto the coals. He watched until the paper burned to ash and the wax boiled away to smoke. Then he mounted his horse, and headed for the Lion's Doorway.

At the new compound, a man opened the door. "What is your name?"

"Ibrahim the scribe."

"You're expected." No sooner had he stepped inside the compound, then a girl came to him and the doorkeeper. She held her chador in her teeth to keep it in front of her face, but the cloth was so thin, he could see that she too was young and lovely. "This is the scribe," the gatekeeper growled. "Take him upstairs."

The girl led Ibrahim up a flight of stairs twisting through a narrow stairwell. On the way, Ibrahim noted how shabby the house looked. The chalky paint was wearing off and had rubbed away to bare clay in some places. Through a window at the first landing, he saw a small courtyard below. Three armed men sat on a bench next to a frozen pool. Among the shrubs lining the pool, he saw one stark rosebush. He kept following the girl up and up, his blood simmering at the sight of her buttocks moving under the heavy cloth of her dress, sensations that filled him with both shame and pleasure.

At the top, she stepped aside to let him into a tiny room. A narrow window facing south let in only a trickle of gray daylight. The only man in the room rose to greet Ibrahim. It was Wazir Akbar Khan. He opened his arms and embraced Ibrahim as close friends might do, as brothers do. "My scribe! The only man I trust! I'm glad you found me. I have a special job for you today. You're not to write down anything until I give the signal, but listen and remember the whole time. Memorize every word that's spoken."

"By who?" Ibrahim asked uneasily. "Aren't we alone?"

"Not for long. But don't worry, I have armed men downstairs. Sit next to the window there. If treachery breaks out, shout down to the courtyard and my men will come up. Beyond that, just listen and remember until I tell you to write."

They sat down and waited silently, each man immersed in his own thoughts. Soon, a knock sounded on the door, and Akbar said, "Enter."

A balding Engrayzee man came in, looking awkward and out of place in Afghan tribal clothes. He glanced from Wazir Akbar to Ibrahim and back again, then said something to Akbar in his native language, and Akbar smiled courteously.

"Mister Macnaghten." Akbar stood up and shook hands with the foreigner.

Three more men crowded in behind the first one. One was Engrayzee, another Afghan. The last man seemed to be Kashmiri, judging by his accent. All four wore nondescript Afghan pantaloons, shirts, and turbans. Except for the pink faces of the Englishmen, they would have gone unnoticed on the streets, and if they swathed their faces in their turbans in the style of the southwestern Pushtoons whose region was prone to savage dust-storms, no one would have looked at them twice. The Afghan said, "You were to come alone, Akbar Khan."

"This is my scribe." the prince replied. He might as well have said, this is my arm. This is my hat. This is my earlobe. He meant: I *am* alone.

The conference began. At first, the men spoke in the Engrayzee language, which Akbar Khan seemed to know. Only a few weeks ago, this would have dazzled Ibrahim, but nothing about the prince astonished him anymore. After a few minutes of the foreign tongue, they switched to Farsi. Akbar gave Ibrahim a subtle nod that meant: start listening.

The Afghan member of the other party said, "The Engrayzee knows you will keep your word, Akbar Khan, but he's giving up a great deal, and he doesn't see that you are offering very much at all."

"I am offering him his life," Akbar's long fingers stroked his beard into a sharp point. "I'll let him decide if that is worth a lot or a little."

"His life isn't yours to give," the Afghan countered.

"Under the circumstances, how can he assume it isn't?"

The men went back to conversing in the Engrayzee language..

Suddenly the Kashmiri demanded, "How can we be certain the Ghilzai will obey you?"

"Certainty belongs only to God," Akbar stated.

"That's a poor reply," the Kashmiri complained. "Lord Macnaghten is trying very honestly to reach an agreement with you. Do you wish to make a treaty with him or not?"

"Tell me again what he is offering. Be specific, please."

The Kashmiri conferred with the two foreigners in a whisper, then turned back to Akbar. "All British forces to leave Kabul by summer. You to receive a subsidy of 400,000 *rupias* a year for the next ten years. Shah Shuja remains on the throne, but with you as his prime minister. Shuja's army comes under your command. That is his offer. Tell me again what *you* are offering. Be specific, please."

"A written guarantee to let him and his people get out of this country alive. After you British depart, the court in Kabul to receive no ambassadors from the King of Russia. I believe that's a very generous offer."

"If it's yours to offer," said the Kashmiri. "Do you speak for the Ghilzai?"

"I have an envoy in the south at this very moment."

"When will he return and what will he bring back?"

"We must be patient. You know how the passes are in winter. "

The room lapsed into tense silence. Suddenly Macnaghten spoke to

Akbar in heavily-accented Farsi. "Yes or no I cannot say today. I must ask others, my people."

He whispered to his interpreter who now finished the Englishman's statement. "He expects a promise of safe passage from both Durrani and Ghilzai chiefs. In the meantime, he asks you not to discuss today's conversation outside this room. If you do, all offers are void. Shah Shuja won't tolerate every squalid commoner in Kabul knowing that he has been stripped of power. He has his pride, and you must observe his pride. Defer to him in public as if he's still king. Leave him that shred of dignity. Only on that basis will he cede power. Does Mr. Macnaghten have your word, Akbar Khan?"

"I can be trusted. Did I not arrange the privacy we enjoy at this moment? But you must be discreet as well."

"Mr. Macnaghten's discretion can be assumed," the Kashmiri declared stiffly. "He is an English gentleman."

"Mr. Macnaghten is one man out of four. The rest of you must pledge as well. And how can I be certain Macnaghten's people will keep their word? Once they are out of the country, how can I be certain they will pay the subsidy? Payments were promised to the Ghilzais as well, but those were cut off when it suited the English gentlemen. And what if Shah Shuja clings to his throne? What if he denies that you ever made the offer we've just discussed?"

"What are you suggesting?"

"I want your promise in writing, in Farsi. Write it down in English too, if you insist, and I will sign that too—but I must have it in my own language as well, to guard against double meanings and slippery interpretations. My scribe will write it according to your dictation and make two copies, one for each of us to keep. We will both sign both copies. Agreed?"

"So long as no one sees your document except you," said Macnaghten's interpreter.

"And you, of course," said Akbar.

The two sides glared at each other.

Then the prince produced writing material from a cabinet, and Ibrahim wrote down the agreement dictated to him, but every word made him cringe. He glanced once or twice at the prince, but Akbar looked blandly undisturbed as if he sold out to foreigners every day. The documents were signed, sealed in wax, and stamped with both the Englishman's ring and Akbar's. Then Akbar put one copy of the agreement in his own vest pocket. "You gentlemen must leave first," he instructed. "We'll leave later. We must not be seen together or in close proximity."

After the English delegation departed, Akbar tapped the pocket where he was keeping the paper and shook his head at Ibrahim. "Not a word about this to anyone," he warned.

"I am yours to command," said, Ibrahim, disheartened by the scene he had witnessed.

The prince saw his look. "Don't judge me, Scribe. It's not how it looks," he said.

At the Barakzai fort, Ibrahim said nothing about the events of the day, but that night he couldn't sleep. Pondering the prince's secret dealings with the foreigners wore out his brain. His mind drifted back to their exchange about the Ghilzai chieftains. The Engrayzee expected to get through the southern passes peacefully. Akbar's negotiation rested on that point. But that point rested on his envoys, at least one of whom was surely, even now, telling the Ghilzai tribesmen to load their guns and get ready, because the British were coming.

42

On a Thursday morning, Sultan Jan woke Ibrahim out of a restless sleep. "Wash your face and say your prayers. Wazir-sahib wants you in the city again."

"What's this about?" Ibrahim rolled out of his bedding groggily.

"Wazir-sahib is meeting the lord of the Engrayzees to sign a treaty. This is it, Scribe. The Engrayzee are surrendering today. They're going to leave. After this, it will only be a matter of how soon."

"Does this mean Ghulam Dastagir has come back? Did he bring the guarantees? When did he arrive?"

"He's not back. No one has heard from him. He no longer matters. The Ghilzai have sent some chieftains to speak for them. And Mir Musjidee's son has come from the north. Plus, the entire council of Afghan chieftains will be at the meeting, the highest lords in the land. Best of all, Akbar and Macnaghten will talk face to face, as monarch to monarch."

A sizable retinue of soldiers rode out of the fort that morning and streamed toward Kabul. A crowd of commoners had gathered at the Ghazni Gate. Silently, they watched the Pushtoon lords entering the city. It was a cold day, but a bright one. The sun shone on glittering fields of snow, and the horses' hooves crunched as if on crackers.

The men made their way to an ice-encrusted field between the Kabul River and the foot of Behmaru Hill. The two delegations had agreed on this spot because it was halfway between their respective hilltop strongholds. Neither side could fire into the meeting from the heights it held.

Both delegations arrived with troops of soldiers but left their armed men behind. Only political officials marched across the open terrain toward the meeting point in the middle of the field. As they marched, all the men held their hands in the air to show that they were carrying no guns, knives, or swords.

A balding, huffing red-faced man led the British delegation. Ibrahim recognized Macnaghten who had bargained with Prince Akbar in the secret meeting. Ten men accompanied him, and they included the second Englishman from that secret meeting.

On the Afghan side, Prince Akbar led the way, flanked by Sultan Jan and followed by Ibrahim. The Afghan delegation included the twelve chieftains of the High Council in Kabul, plus another dozen chieftains from various regions. Most of these men had one or two retainers with them, making the Afghan delegation three times the size of the British one.

The two sides stopped about five paces apart. Macnaghten clasped his hands behind his back, thrust his chest out like a small rooster, and strutted a few paces to the left and right. Then he turned to face Akbar, who was merely waiting.

"Well, well, Akbar Khan. I see you have all your ... lords here," the Englishman said in Farsi. Fleeting pauses punctuated his speech because in Farsi he sometimes had to search for a word. "I hope this ... delegation, has power to sign a ... treaty. Any agreement between us this day must ... bind, bind all people of Afghanistan."

"Macnaghten-sahib, we have come to this meeting in good faith." Akbar's voice was metal clanging on metal. "We have come here believing that when you English make a promise, you keep it. When you declare something to be true, your word can be trusted."

"And we have all the same hopes of you and your people," said Macnaghten. "Now. Here are my ... terms. In the first place, we require that a military ... escort, protect our march from Kabul to Peshawar next summer. This escort must include ... soldiers, from the army of every khan present here, and I insist that the chieftains themselves must ... accompany—"

"Pardon me. Stop." Akbar stepped closer to his counterpart. "Do you dare to speak to me of terms, Lord Macnaghten? Let us first settle the question of honesty. To me, trust is not merely a word. In letters exchanged between you and this council of chieftains, you have declared that you will take your puppet Shah Shuja back to India when you leave. You have given us to understand that you will leave hostages to guarantee your promises. You have agreed to restore my father Dost Mohammed Khan to his throne. This has been your public position, as every chieftain here assembled knows quite well."

"It's still our position, and it is just what we ... what we mean to do," Macnaghten assured him smoothly, glancing from side to side at his fellow Englishmen. "However, no agreement can be ... one-sided. We also have ... needed things. We demand certain ... guarantees. Now, then, as I started to say—"

"Just a moment, sahib," Akbar cut in dangerously. "This is still one of your positions? How many positions do you have?"

"One, of course. Only one. Do you try to ... insult me, sir? I place this proposition to you in good faith. I have approval from my Lord Governor in India. His ... authority, comes directly from the Queen. If you chieftains will just sign your names to these terms in one voice—"

"Do you mean to tell me you have not negotiated separately with any chiefs?" Akbar frowned.

"Separately?" Macnaghten giggled, but goggled at his counterpart. "Of course not! Well—as you know, sir!"

"Mister Macnaghten! Did you not summon me to a private meeting just last week in a building near the Lion's Doorway?" Akbar Khan demanded sternly. "My scribe was there, he will attest to it. Scribe Ibrahim! Step forward and tell the chieftains. Did this Engrayzee meet with me and dangle secret offers before me, thinking to tempt my loyalty away from the Afghan cause?"

All eyes turned to Ibrahim, who cleared his throat. No one had warned him the meeting might take this turn. In the heat of the moment, he could not puzzle out what he was supposed to do, other than to answer truthfully. His throat was parched. He nodded and then found his voice. "It is just as Wazir-sahib says."

"There!" Akbar turned back on the Englishman triumphantly. "My scribe testifies that you offered me—"

"For God's sake," Macnaghten hissed. "What are you playing at, Akbar? Think, man! What are you doing? Do not *do* this ... thing!"

The prince pulled a sheet of paper from a pocket under his cloak and waved it above his head for all the Afghans to see. "Here is the bargain this treacherous snake thought to strike with me. I made him put it in writing so I could show it to this assembly. Here is proof of my good faith with the Afghan cause. Proof that these Engrayzees can never drive a wedge between my countrymen and me. I want nothing they can give me, I want none of their secret bargains. They offer me gold, they offer me a throne—I spit on their gold, I spit on their throne!" Akbar thrust the offending document at Lord Abdullah, standing next him. "I want nothing but the good of Afghanistan! Unite under my standard, chieftains. Let us be one mighty nation! This man Macnaghten offers to make me Shah Shuja's prime minister—read it out loud, Abdullah-sahib!"

"Well it's true!" Abdullah Khan declared, staring in amazement at the document Akbar had given him. "It's right here with Macnaghten's signature, just as he says."

"You treacherous bastard!" Macnaghten swore. A clamor rose from all his compatriots on the British side.

"They promise him a yearly stipend," Abdullah announced, paraphrasing from the document, "a yearly stipend to betray his people—a fat stipend—"

"But I will never betray you, my chieftains," Akbar shouted. "I spit on their stipend. We are one nation! Do I speak for you? Tell me now, khans! Let your voices speak through mine, let me answer this invader with the thunder of all Afghanistan. Do I speak for the nation?"

Shouts erupted: "Yes! Long live Akbar Khan! Long live the lion!"

But Sardar Amanullah broke into the din, "Who else has he spoken to? Who else has the Engrayzee tried to tempt? Young Akbar is one— I'm another! Yes! He came to me as well, my lords, and I spat in his face right then and there! You can never split me from my brethren with gold, I said. Never!"

At this, scattered cries of "Long live Amanullah Khan" mingled with those in praise of Akbar. The prince frowned at the lord of Logar, but Amanullah seized this moment to shout, "I will bear your standard, Khans! As your leader, I will smite these infidels. I hereby appoint Akbar as my sword and my second-in command." The cries of "Long live Amanullah!" surged.

But Osman Khan's hand shot up. "I had no intention of taking anything the man offered, but yes, he wrote to me as well. I agreed to meet with him just to check the extent of his treachery. My fellow Afghans! I was offered Shah Shuja's very throne, but I turned it down. This throne, I said, is not yours to give! I slapped his very face!"

Macnaghten was trying to still the noise, moving his hands up and down in front of him as if stroking an invisible horse. "Quiet now. Calm yourselves. This is wrong. You're mistaken. Let us talk as … reasonable men."

"We are one people," Akbar roared. "Fellow chieftains, will you let *me* set new terms for this groveling dog? Do I speak for all of us?"

But the Afghan clamor had grown incoherent, some roaring the name Amanullah, others Akbar, and still others Osman. The whole crowd was gathering toward the center and they virtually encircled the English delegation now.

"Mister Macnaghten, in light of your treachery, we will have to set stricter terms," Amanullah declared. "Much gold! Much gold you will pay into our treasury—and we'll decide who replaces Shah Shuja, we Afghans will decide."

"In light of *your* treachery, sir, I can see no point in continuing this discussion," Macnaghten huffed, his face shining with sweat. With sharp elbows he tried to poke the Afghans back and keep a space open around himself.

"The Engrayzee is right for once," Osman cried. "We cannot make treaties with men like these. Lying is like breathing to them. My men intercepted a letter recently—written in Farsi—addressed to Mohan Lal, who served the late Alexander Burnes, may Allah forgive him. Akbar

Khan, your scribe has a good loud voice. Ask him to read this letter. Step forward, Scribe. Read this letter to the gentlemen. Loudly."

Ibrahim glanced at his patron, who looked lost. He knew nothing about this latest letter. In the absence of any signal from the prince, Ibrahim accepted the document. He scanned it quickly and his brain locked down. These were the most dangerous words he had seen yet. He must not read them to this crowd; but how could he refuse? If he didn't read it, someone else would. All attention was riveted on him. Mechanically he began to read: "*As previously agreed, you will receive no less than 10,000 rupias for the head of each rebel chieftain delivered to me at the British cantonment. For the head of the chief rebel Akbar, son of the Dost, former Amir of Kabul, the payment will be double—*"

The outcry drowned out Ibrahim's voice. Macnaghten was spluttering, "That's not—I never saw—who wrote that letter? Not official! It's unofficial. Sahib—I never—"

"It is signed," Osman Khan shouted. "Read the signature, Scribe!"

Ibrahim squinted at the unfamiliar name. "Jawn Connolly." Then he handed the paper back to sturdy Osman Khan. By this time the Afghan delegation had compressed the Engrayzees into a frightened clump.

"Who is John Connolly?" Akbar demanded.

"Macnaghten knows. Look at his face," said Osman. "You know all about this letter, don't you? As for offering double payment for Wazir Akbar's head—that's an insult, Mr. Macnaghten. Every chieftain standing before you has a head worth as much as young Akbar's. Nawab Shah Zaman? The people of Kabul have named him as their interim king! How can you offer a mere 10,000 *rupias* for the head of such a man? Amanullah Khan? Hamza Khan? You have insulted all these men! And me as well! But let's talk about another letter, written in Engrayzee. You think that's secret code? I have men who read Engrayzee as easily as water flows downhill. This one bears *your* signature, Mr. Macnaghten. You write to General Nott—"

"I never! Where did you get that?"

"—in Kandahar to say that you will keep the Afghans talking until he gets here with his troops. Keep us bargaining, you write, with false offers to withdraw from the country. When your General Nott gets his forces here—"

"This is an outrage! A lie!"

"—you'll be strong enough to burn our city to the ground. Burn it to the ground, Afghans! *This is what Macnaghten has decided to do. Burn our great city to the ground!*"

The Afghans were all screaming now. Macnaghten flushed redder than ever, picked at his buttons, kicked at the snow under his feet, shoved the Afghans crowding him. His own men kept trying to wedge between Macnaghten and the Afghans to form a wall of security around their chief, but the pressure had grown intense.

"Your spies have lied to you, Akbar." Macnaghten invested effort in keeping his voice unhurried, but his chest heaved with anxious breath. "These letters ... these forgeries. Troublemakers who don't want peace between our people—do anything to spread ... slander—just to keep us – spilling blood. Can't you see? This is work of ... evil men—I can't listen to such lies—I will leave—"

He turned his back on Akbar but bumped into Sultan Jan, who took him by the arm. One of the other *farangis* tried to wrench his leader out of the young Afghan's grasp, but Akbar himself took the Envoy's other arm. "He's trying to signal his soldiers," he warned. "Hold his arms down. Hold them down. He wants to betray us!"

Akbar and Sultan dragged the Englishman into the Afghan ranks. Sultan Jan had one hand over Macnaghten's mouth to keep him from screaming out orders. He and Akbar clamped the wriggling Englishman between them. Even though they were young men in the prime of their strength, they had trouble keeping that desperate animal still.

Macnaghten's friends were struggling toward him. One flung his coat open, revealing a pistol in his belt. "No weapons!" Akbar shouted. "We all agreed, and now look!" He pointed at the pistol. His arm was wrapped around Macnaghten's neck to stop him from breaking loose, but when he saw the pistol, he scrambled backward wildly, dragging Macnaghten along.

"Bastards! Nothing you say can be trusted," one Afghan cursed, and he pulled out a knife he had been hiding under his cloak. Within seconds, weapons had appeared in at least a dozen hands. Shots rang out and a man fell. The armed foreigners at the far end of the field began to pour across the open plain. Akbar let go of Macnaghten, who dropped to the ground like a sack of wheat. His head flopped on the end of an obviously broken neck. "Don't leave him there," Akbar shouted to Sultan Jan. "Drag him along."

Two Afghans swooped in to help Sultan. Gasping at the effort, they hauled the English leader's corpse along the ground, leaving a ragged rut in the snow as they retreated toward the river. The English troops were firing now, but so were the Afghans. A crowd of city folk had amassed along the field on the side near the river, and they began edging onto the field too. Some had sticks; others pawed through the snow searching for rocks to throw. The Afghan khans and their men reached the safety of the stone walls that edged the river bank. They jumped on the horses tethered there and galloped away, leaving Macnaghten's body to the crowd. Ibrahim looked back just once and saw men bent over the poor man's corpse, hacking at his neck with knives.

43

Rupert Oxley raked his spurs across the horse's flanks and bent low to its neck. One glimpse of the slaughter and he knew he must get back to headquarters, but others had preceded him. Approaching the garrison, he heard what sounded like the animal pit of some terrible circus. Inside, officers and enlisted men were scurrying every which way without purpose, everyone yelling questions.

Colonel Baldwin came tottering through the chaos like a drunkard. Rupert snapped to attention gratefully. "Lieutenant Oxley, sir. What are my orders?"

But the aging colonel just shook his head. "I don't know … What do you think?"

What did Rupert think? It wasn't his place to think! "Excuse me, sir!" He backed away from the colonel, feeling really frightened. He must go directly to Elphinstone then, get orders from the top. He elbowed his way up a crowded stairwell and along a corridor to the command center. No one was guarding the door. Anyone could bull his way in. Rupert did. The room was jammed wall to wall, but Rupert pushed to the front, where Elphinstone and his officers were sitting in council around a walnut table. The officers, however, were a random assortment of just anybody. Some of the usual high command were there to be sure: Shelton, Chambers, Anquetil; but also the likes of Captain Whitman and Sergeant Flannigan—men whose rank entitled them to no share in strategy, yet here they were shouting opinions as lustily as their betters.

General Elphinstone gestured in vain for silence. "All right," he rumbled. "Quiet now. Go muster the others. Tell everyone we must prepare to leave Kabul at once. No time to waste, no time. Let us put our backs into it."

Rupert stared. At once? What could he possibly mean? Talk of leaving Kabul had been buzzing about the city for weeks…but—leave at once?

Major Leech shouted over the din. Standing on tiptoe in the middle of the crowd, his face oily from effort and exhaustion, he waved a sheet of paper. "At once would be folly, sir—look at this letter from Akbar—I spoke to him. He promises an escort if we'll wait till spring. He won't guarantee our safety now. Read it, General."

Many voices shouted him down. "Akbar of all people!" "Good lord—" "Stake our lives on *his* guarantee?"

Elphinstone ran agitated fingers over his balding pate. His voice cracked as he tried to make himself heard. "You know, men, Wellington once told me—"

But Captain Whitman cut him off. "No more Wellington stories! No more lessons drawn from fifty years ago. Akbar is not Napoleon. For God's sake, you swing from side to side, General. After Burnes was killed you said 'wait and see, let us wait and see,' that was your whole plan. Now it's clear-out-by-New-Years-Day'! Get a hold of yourself."

"Well, well! Perhaps you're right, perhaps you're right," Elphinstone allowed, fumbling with a sheaf of documents. "We must consider all the circumstances, as you say." He squinted to see who had been so rude. "Best we disperse to quarters now, men. Let us sleep on this and see what the morning brings. Mustn't act in haste."

"Mustn't act in haste?" The words simply burst from Rupert. "Of course we must! Burnes is dead—Macnaghten—Trevor—murdered! The chiefs swarm all over Kabul, the natives hold the hills. Do you seriously say we should deal with this by *sleeping*? Sir?"

Rough hands jerked him sideways, someone rasped, "You're still a military man! Do you beg to be shot?"

"No, Shelton. No, no. Let him speak his mind," Elphinstone protested. "All sides, all sides. I must have good advice—what exactly are you suggesting, my boy?"

But Oxley had no suggestion. The commander-in-chief of all the

British forces in Afghanistan should not be wanting "suggestions" from mere captains. He felt stifled by the crowd, though gusts of winter were blowing through the door. Somewhere a chair scraped as Tommy Flannigan climbed upon it to wave some new sheet of paper soiled with mud and blood. "From General Nott," he grunted through bandages binding his wounded face. "He'll be here from Kandahar in days! If we can just hold out … Why not move into Bala Hissar until he comes? Behind those walls we could defend—"

"We should never have left Bala Hissar in the first place!" someone yelled.

"Too late for that, but we can go back, it's not too late."

"What!" came from some nobody in the crowd, "—and transport our women and children across the entire city? Through streets full of Afghans armed to the teeth—"

"Is that worse than making for Jalalabad?" Whitman snorted. "Over the mountains? In dead of winter? Damn it, listen to Tommy. We *must* try for the palace. We'll lose a few on the way, but the bulk of us should get through. We'll form a column of wagons—women and children in the center, sepoys on the outside—no, hear me! The fire will be deadly, but *many* of us should survive to the palace gates—"

At this, Elphinstone bestirred himself. "Bala Hissar? No, no, the Shah doesn't want us up there, he's been quite particular on that point."

"Who the devil is the Shah to keep us out? Who put that little man on his throne? Do we take orders from *him* now? By God, if we need his fortress, I say we take it! Shah Shuja!" Whitman leaned and loomed over Elphinstone, and the five ranking officers at the same table rose out of their chairs to restrain him if need be.

"You miss his lordship's point," Brigadier Shelton cut in. He was a handsome man with bushy, silver eyebrows and a considerable moustache. His voice carried to the furthest corners. "If the Shah shuts his gates on us, we'll be trapped against the walls—with cannon firing down from the ramparts—Akbar's men coming at us from below—it will be a slaughter. We can't make for the palace. It's too late for that. We *must* heed General Elphinstone. He's still our commanding officer, gentlemen."

Several of the younger men let out audible snorts, but Shelton frowned them down. "Still our commanding officer," he insisted. "We must gather what stores we need. Jalalabad is only ninety miles away. We'll spike what cannons we must leave behind. While we muster, we'll bargain with Akbar—he's a lying bastard, but whatever he will sign his name to, let's secure it."

"We're in this fix because you trusted Akbar in the first place."

"I never trusted him," snapped Shelton. "Damnable slander! I don't trust him now. I only say let's treat with him to buy time—so that we may leave Kabul when we're ready and not helter-skelter as the chiefs would have it." The din began to wane, people began to listen, lulled by his sonorous voice into hearing sense. "This city is a house of horrors now," he pressed on, "but the road to Khurd Kabul Pass is clear. Most of us will have to walk, but once we're in the pass, it's only ninety miles to Jalalabad. Sale will have fresh mounts for us there. He'll have food, carriage…" Every face in the room was pointed toward Shelton now. "The first few passes are daunting, but we shall wear our woolens. We shall bring English grit to the march. We'll survive, by heaven. I tell you, gentlemen, I do not mean to end my days in this accursed country, but if I must, I will sell my life dear."

No one cheered, but no one argued. Rupert felt faint with all the bodies pressing in from every side, too faint to speak his mind again.

"Excellent," said Elphinstone. "Excellent good sense, General. Let us gather our people, then, and make what bargains we can with the chiefs."

"But who will do the bargaining, m'lord?" General Burnett looked at Elphinstone apologetically. "You're hardly fit to, um, try the streets in your condition."

Who would bargain with the Afghans? No one spoke.

❧❧

Reeling out of headquarters, Oxley almost tumbled headlong to the yard. Behind him, the officers were still shouting, but the mob had made its decision—yes, mob: no other word for it. And he'd been a part of it,

God help him. His silence had fed the consensus to strike for Jalalabad, ninety miles away, on the other side of the mountains, instead of for the royal fortress merely three or four miles across the city. In the jostle and tumble of that suffocating room the scheme had sounded sensible. Now...?.

Thick clouds had swallowed up the sunshine, and the afternoon had turned as dark as an omen. Now the plan sounded mad, he realized. Absolutely mad! But if the others left, he must too. No one could stay behind. And Amanda—the memory of her brought him up short. Good Lord, she was stranded in that compound of hers, alone with her servants. What if the garrison forgot her? Who in that roomful of screaming officers had a thought to spare for one lone widow isolated in some corner of the city?

Rupert mounted his horse and left cantonments without a word to anyone. An hour later, he was banging on her door. His mind was shambling for thoughts, words, but he wasn't sure what he thought, what to say. Bring her away, was all he could fix upon. Bring her back to cantonments where the others were gathering. Safety in numbers, he thought, his heart moist with tenderness for the widow. Hard enough to lose a husband but to lose one at a time like this, in such a place!

A Hindu servant opened the door. "Sergeant Oxley," he said politely.

"*Captain* Oxley," Rupert snapped. Small of him to correct the man, he knew—what did rank matter now? Yet it rankled. "Is memsahib home? I must see her at once."

"Memsahib hope for you." The comment triggered flutters in Rupert's belly. She was hoping he would come!

Amanda stood up from her writing desk, pale as a tombstone. The room looked undisturbed. The chaos of the city had not intruded here, except for an occasional muffled roar. "What's happened?" she blurted, clasping her hands together in a knotted tangle of fingers. "It's something dreadful, isn't it? We've had nothing but stories. Such terrible stories! The commotion—"

"Whatever you've heard, the truth is worse." He would not soften the blow, it would do no good: she must know soon enough. "Macnaghten's dead, Amanda. The chiefs killed him." He brushed snow from his epaulets. "They're out for blood, and Elphinstone's gone to pieces. The city's swarming with tribesmen. You can't stay here. I've come to fetch you back to cantonments."

"And there we'll be safe?" she pleaded.

Her small voice twisted a knife in him. "There ..." He could not tell her of the plan, he felt ashamed, he feared the alarm he must give her. Drops of water fell from his sleeves and trouser legs, forming a puddle on her cement floor. He must not remain inarticulate. Suspense was the worst of agonies. Her face was draining of hope before his very eyes as he stood there. "We won't be staying there long."

"Why not?" she stammered. "What do you mean? Where shall we go?"

"We are to leave this country, it would seem." He could not bring himself to offer details, but she pressed for them.

"How? When? Where shall we go?"

His head drooped. "Jalalabad," he said. "And then Peshawar."

"Jalalabad!" she gasped. "But how shall we get there? It's across the mountains. Have we horses enough? Have we carriages?" Horror grew in her eyes as the implications dawned on her. He wanted to allay her fear, but how could he? Her fear was entirely justified!

"Most of us shall walk. But it's only ninety miles," he added hastily.

"In the snow, Mr. Oxley?"

"Please. Will you not at last call me Rupert?"

"Rupert. We shan't have...carriages to ride?"

"No, mum, but once we reach Jalalabad we can rest. General Sale will have fresh horses for us, hot food. We'll have carriages to carry you ladies in comfort from there. Only the first ninety miles will be hard."

"Ninety miles." Those were the only words she heard. Those were the only ones that really counted. He gazed at this soft, blond woman in her long skirts and thin blouse, hugging herself, her breasts squeezed between her forearms, that dear lock of stray hair dangling over her ear—he didn't want to picture her in the snow. He would not. But another image formed in its place: of the streets outside filled with raging natives, of a bearded tribesman snatching Amanda into his saddle and wrapping his cloak over her, of the mob closing in, howling for flesh…He shuddered and pity so brimmed in him that he almost made to reach for her, but he didn't want another slap.

"Ninety miles?" she repeated. "And it's *snowing!*"

"Only a little," he whispered. "We'll wear our warmest clothes. The marching itself will keep us warm. I shouldn't wonder if we work up a sweat!"

She walked to the window. Tiny flakes of snow blurred the outline of the trees in the courtyard. He followed her and set his hands on her shoulders. She did not shake him off. "Is there no other course?" she said. "Can we not stay here?"

"You would not say that if you had seen the streets. They've captured the commissary, they can starve us. They've taken the field outside the gates of cantonments. They can cut us off from water. They'll overrun us so soon as we weaken, and they will be merciless. I saw Macnaghten—I'm sorry to say it but I *must* say it: beheaded! We must leave while we have the strength. Not in haste, that much is settled. We'll gather ourselves properly and march out in ranks. But Amanda…" His hand dropped from her shoulder to her hip, and she did not move away. "Put yourself in my care. I'll protect you. I'll bring you out of Afghanistan alive and safe, I swear it."

"Do you?" She stayed where she was, leaning against the shutter, listless. He took her hand in his, and she let him, but said simply, "I should pack."

"I will saddle your horse," he agreed, "while you change clothes. We have a few minutes, though. You don't have to rush. We can still talk a little, here…alone…"

She didn't look at him. She kept her cheek pressed against the window frame, kept her gaze trained on the yard. He sensed the tension of her body. How to clothe his feelings in words? He swallowed. "I have something to say to you."

"Yes?" she said.

"I intend … I intend to bring you safe out of Afghanistan."

"Yes. You said so just now. You will do all you can, I'm sure."

"I am rough with words," he choked out. "I'm a soldier, do not despise me for that. I have not always been good, I know that, but I am trying to improve."

"I am very far from despising you." She stirred as if to create some distance between them; but since he didn't retreat, her motion only brought her back into contact with his front. And there she stayed. "You know I am fond of you, Mr. Oxley."

"Please," he pleaded, "call me Rupert. I am rough with words, but I know soldiering. Rely on me, Amanda. I want to tell you something.."

"I know. You mean to bring me out of this country safe and alive." She cast a glance over her shoulder, still touching against him, and he detected a smile hovering behind her blue eyes, but he didn't mind. If he could bring a smile to her lips at a time like this, he was glad to do it, even at his own expense.

"I must seem very clumsy to you. I know I do, I must sound comical when I say I will bring you out of this nightmare alive and safe, but you don't know what's in my heart. You don't know what I have inside me, Amanda. There is good in me. There is strength."

All traces of amusement vanished from her features. "I hope I don't seem to laugh. You have no idea how you comfort me. You're not so rough as you think. I have always found you brave. I do rely on you. I do. I will."

His spirits bubbled, his gut unclenched. "Amanda…" But the words clotted in his throat. Talking to a woman was harder than running a sword through a man! "So many men pour through this world without leaving a mark. I don't want to be one of those."

"And you won't. Now let me go and pack, my dear."

Dear? Had she said that word? He lost his head and pressed himself against her from behind, put his arms around her waist—she trembled but did not shake him off. "I have a worthy deed in me," he said. "I always thought I would come to nothing, because I was given nothing. I sulked through my life until I met you, Amanda. A man only gets what he reaches for and has only himself to blame if he reaches for nothing. I will bring you home. You'll see."

She turned, but not to escape his embrace. She leaned into his chest and accepted the encirclement of his arms; he felt the cling of her. "Hush," she murmured.

"You'll be proud of me," he vowed. "When we get to England. You'll meet my father and my brother. I will be so proud of you. And you of me."

"Oh, very proud." With her face buried in his shirt, her words were muffled.

He stroked her neck. "Will you say you love me?"

"I love you?"

"Ah!" He had spent such an agony of hours and days and months yearning for those words. Now he felt released, now he felt equal to any danger. "Go, my dove. Get ready." He untangled her hair gently from his shirt buttons. "Don't take much, only what you can wear—and nothing fripperous, just woolens and warm things. Boots, if you have them. It will be cold, my sweet. If we lose everything, it won't matter, we'll have each other, and that's everything."

44

Ibrahim rode in silence with the Afghan lords. The ruined city felt full of hidden eyes. The group diminished as each lord split away with his retainers, heading toward his own estates. By the time they reached the Ghazni Gate, Ibrahim was alone with Akbar and Sultan Jan. The three men reined up, their horses blowing plumes of wet nostril breath into the freezing sunshine.

"What now?" said Ibrahim.

"Now," said the prince, "we pray. Allah have pity on us. Satan is loose."

"And who set him loose?" Ibrahim lamented in a low voice. "Wazir-sahib, you were there to sign a treaty! Why the trickery?" In his agitation, he jerked at the reins and his horse commenced a nervous cantering.

"Blame Osman!" Akbar shouted. "Blame Amanullah of Logar! What were they thinking, those fools, pulling out *those* letters! Mine was enough to shame Macnaghten, I had the conniving bastard right where I needed him—"

"You never intended to forge a treaty," Ibrahim charged. "You went there to exalt yourself among the Afghan lords—"

"Scribe! Scribe! Do you think you're talking to one of your fellow villagers! Do you dare to spar with me?" Akbar wiped his sleeve across his nose. "This country needs one strong king! Without me..." His soot-black eyes flashed dangerously. "This country—"

"What country? What is 'this country' you keep talking about?"

Ibrahim demanded. "*My* country is Char Bagh, Wazir-sahib! Yes, I'm unimportant, Yes, I'm a nobody. Yes! Yes, but I came to you as a subject comes to his king because I saw greatness in you, and you let me down."

Akbar stared back at him with wounded eyes. "You and your's won't be spared once the lords start fighting. I did what I did for people like you, for villages like your's. Because someone must harness the tiger."

"Yes, I know all about the tiger, you explained. But it's loose now and who broke its cage open? My God, Wazir-sahib, what have you done?"

Sultan Jan spurred his horse past Ibrahim and slapped his face so hard, he jolted Ibrahim sideways on his saddle. The unexpected jerk on the reins made Ibrahim's horse rear. "You can't talk to Wazir-sahib that way, you wretched farmer!" Sultan Jan yelled tearfully. "By the Quran of God, I should kill you right here—"

"Stop that," the prince commanded.

But Sultan Jan had already wheeled his horse for another charge.

"Stop that! You stop at once! Stop!" roared the prince.

The youngster pulled back on the reins, his eyes red, bits of ice clinging to his flimsy beard. He was crying now. "I can't let him talk to you like that, my prince."

"Jackass! Today's the day I was going to unite all the Afghans. Do you think I want to watch one Afghan kill another on *this* day? On my behalf?" Akbar shook his head mournfully. "Give this peasant his due, Sultan, he alone speaks his heart to me. Honor his courage. Scribe, I should have done more listening when I had the chance."

"Allah knows best, your highness."

"I never wanted to hear anyone tell me I was wrong. It was my least kingly trait. I see that now." The prince scratched his cheek and stared at the hills. "A man sees things too late. Well, Scribe, I release you from my service. Pray for the country, go where you will. God alone knows what the rest of today will bring."

"And what will you do?" At the edge of his vision, Ibrahim could see Sultan Jan astride his horse, barely containing his violence.

"I suppose I will try to open new negotiations with the Engrayzee," Akbar Khan replied morosely. "This time..." He gazed into Ibrahim's eyes. "This time I'll bring the malang into it from the start. I always meant to keep my promise. If I get him out, I'll send word. If I don't..." The prince dug around under his cloak and brought out a bag of coins. "Take this money. If order breaks down totally, see if you can bribe the guards. Save your malang yourself. I can do nothing more for you, Ibrahim. God protect you now."

ಣಲ

Shamsuddin's family huddled indoors around a coal burning stove under heavy blankets, men, women, and children together wearing doom like an extra set of blankets. This was Ibrahim's first time in his friend's home. When he arrived, the women gave him room, none fleeing from his gaze, as if he were of the family, a generosity that brought tears to Ibrahim's eyes.

All that week, the city felt besieged, but the enemy was not outside the walls, it was inside and everywhere and it was anyone. Men ventured out only for essential supplies. Of the news, they knew only what they could tap from street gossip. Street gossip said the Engrayzee were lining up cannons on the slopes of Siah Sung—everybody should get into cellars if they had any. Street gossip said the Engrayzee were planning to burn the city down—everybody should get out of town, if they could. Street gossip said a new Engrayzee army was approaching, a hundred-thousand strong. Everybody should pick up arms. It was coming from the north. Run, run, everybody shore up the north. No, from the south, said the street. No from all directions at once.

Then one day, people came through the neighborhood yelling the most improbable rumor of them all. The Engrayzee were leaving. No one believed this one, but still, Ibrahim thought he'd better check it out. He climbed to the top of Behmaru Hill. From there a man could look right down into the foreigners' garrison and what he saw astounded him. A long procession was indeed moving through the back wall where cannon fire had knocked broad gaps. Hundreds of camels loaded with baggage, hundreds of horses and riders had already snaked to the river and beyond. Countless bullocks were pulling wheeled cannons and wagons piled high with supplies. Thousands of people were walking with enormous bundles strapped to their backs. Even from the hilltop, Ibrahim could see that many of the marchers were women, and quite a few were children. He closed his eyes and saw his own children, his dead son, his Khadija and Soraya among those marchers. A mob of shouting Afghans had collected in front of the cantonment and were throwing stones. Then the light started to fade, and snow started to fall, and Ibrahim could see nothing more. How did that ragged company hope to survive, marching away from shelter and into the mountains in this weather? Could they stay warm in some way that Afghans could not even imagine?

That night, in the healer's compound, the men sat up for hours after final prayers, talking in the dark about the strangers who had come to their land and had now, seemingly, departed. What had these people ever wanted in Afghanistan anyway? What had led them to suppose they could live and rule here, so few among so many? And what would happen to their puppet king? Was he still up in the fortress? Would Akbar take over? Would Dost Mohammed Khan return? Would the lords start fighting, the way the progeny of Emperor Ahmad Shah had done?

The next morning, Ibrahim made a decision. Since the prince had sent no word, and the Engrayzees were gone, he would set the malang free himself. He rode across the city on the horse the lords had given him and climbed the royal road up to Bala Hissar again. No one manned the checkpoints this time. He made his way unobstructed to the prison compound and banged on the gates. The same guard who had given him a dollop of money a month ago opened up and looked out with bleary eyes.

"Remember me?" said Ibrahim. "I was in your prison last month."

"No," the man shrugged. "Many people have been in this prison. Faces blur. I'm just the gatekeeper. If you're here to assassinate Shah Shuja, I'll open the gates for you, but I can't give you a gun. That you'll have to supply yourself."

"I'm not here to kill Shah Shuja."

"Good, because the cur still has teeth. I warn people, poke him if you like, but it'll be like poking a mad dog. Two went up there already and never came back."

"Are you sure you don't remember me? I'm the one who came looking for the Malang of Char Bagh."

"Ah, poor malang! Yes, I remember you now. Not your face, but your story. The malang was a strange man, a great man. I saw him once. He made me weep."

Was a strange man? The word sent a shudder through Ibrahim. "I'm here to get him out. Who do I see about it?"

"You're too late."

"What? No! If it's about money, I can pay. Isn't this still a prison? I can pay! Is someone still in charge ? Direct me to someone in charge!"

The gatekeeper poked between his teeth with a straw.

"What do you mean, 'too late?'" Ibrahim asked finally.

"The Engrayzee took him along. There was talk of putting him on trial in India. Him and the other ringleaders."

"Ringleaders of what?"

"Of all these troubles, all this fighting. They vowed not to let all this bloodshed go unavenged. This is what I heard They'll hang them all, I heard. Don't blame me, I'm just the gatekeeper. Anyway, there's no one left in this prison except Shah Shuja's personal enemies, and he didn't give a dot of dirt about your Malang of Char Bagh. Anyway, he'll be dead soon, if that's any consolation. Sooner or later, one of these assassins will succeed. Don't tell anyone I said so—not that it matters, the whole world is crumbling. I only stay because they still serve dinner here. Come inside if you wish, have some tea before you go, tell me the news from below. I can't leave my post, and it does get lonely up here."

Ibrahim turned away. The gatekeeper snatched idly at his sleeve. "What's the hurry, chief? Well, if you're going, go, but how about a bit of that money?"

It was only the enervated effort of a man enfeebled by a useless existence. Ibrahim rode back down and across the city to reach the Engrayzee garrison. Bric-a-brac lay strewn across the courtyard—bits of clothing, spoons, broken dolls.... "Malang-sahib!" Ibrahim yelled, running from building to building.

Beggars came trickling out of various buildings to stare, but seeing what they took to be just another crazed beggar, they returned to their commandeered shelters. Ibrahim galloped to Shamsuddin's compound. "They took the malang," he panted. "The malang is with the Engrayzee. They could be halfway to Jalalabad by now. I must catch up with them, plead with them, offer money. Thank you for your kindness, Shamsuddin-sahib, and forgive my rude haste, but I must leave you now."

The hat merchant begged him to wait until morning, and his family added their pleas, but Ibrahim shook them all off. At last, Shamsuddin's wife said, "Well, if you must go, we'll have to let you go, but not without provisions and equipment."

Out of their own meager stores, the family dug up warm clothes, a padded overcoat, and knee-high riding boots. They put a blanket under his saddle to keep his horse warm. They gave him a bag full of bread and a skinful of water. They made him pass under the Quran three times, even though Ibrahim was almost too frantic to go through that indispensable ritual. They gave him directions as far as Jagdalak and watched him gallop away on his black horse.

At first, Ibrahim kept his eyes trained for the landmarks his friends had mentioned. He wanted to make sure he was following the right road. It struck him that Ghulam Dastagir must have followed this same road to his unknown fate. A few miles from the city, the road brought Ibrahim to a makeshift bridge the Engrayzee had built across the river. It was broken in the middle and the jagged shards of it, cased in ice, dangled in the water. Down there, Ibrahim saw a cannon on wheels still harnessed to a dead horse. His fingertips tingled. He needed no more landmarks. This was the trail, all right.

Since the bridge was broken, he guided his horse down to the water's edge and cantered along the bank, looking for a ford. He found the same one the Engrayzees had used: he knew because two of them lay face down in the shallow water with ragged bullet holes in their backs. Both were clad in those red uniforms. The river had washed away their blood, and the skin, where it showed at their neck and hands, seemed to shine because a second skin of fresh ice had formed around their limbs.

The moon was rising. He entered the Khurd Kabul Pass and the trail began to slope upward. Soon, cliffs rose up steeply from one side of the road and the land dropped down steeply to the river on the other. The Engrayzee must have marched this way, the wreckage of their wagon train lay scattered as far as the eye could see. Some carts had fallen off the road and broken up on the rocks below where the river thundered. Other carts had overturned on the road itself for no obvious reason. Goods lay spilled and abandoned. Perhaps the wagons had come under attack from the cliffs above and the people had dropped their bundles and started running. But running where? With the river on one side and cliffs on the other, there were only two directions to go, forward or back, and neither way led to any shelter from the Ghilzai sharpshooters on the cliffs. And yet they must have escaped because Ibrahim saw no people. He saw dead horses, mules, donkeys, and even a few camels frozen into twisted shapes, their agony obscured by snow, but no people. Had the survivors piled their dead into wagons and hauled them along?

Yes, that was what they had done. He knew when he came upon an overturned wagon out of which eight bodies had spilled. They too lay where they had spilled, like the goods further back. Whoever had brought them this far could do nothing more for them.

A short distance up the path, he saw a woman about the same age as Khadija. Her hair was yellow. Her face, even her lips, were pale. Her eyes had frozen open, and he could see the moon reflected in each of those glassy green windows. She had died sitting up against a rock, her face, shockingly naked, turned toward the sky. Sprawled in front of her was a man he recognized. Okusley. He was hard to recognize, because his face was covered with blood and distorted by death. Engrayzees looked similar to begin with, and death blended them further, but this was Okusley all right, and he held a sword in his left hand. He had gone down fighting.

Ibrahim squatted in front of the woman and touched her square jaw. He could see a faint moustache on her upper lip. "W'Allah…" he whispered in wonder and disgust. How had it come to this? "What are you doing here," he whispered. Then he spoke louder. "Why did you come here?" Then he lost control and screamed at the dead woman, screamed at her. "Why? Why did you come here? This is not your country! Why did you come here to die?" The sound of his voice cracked against the cliffs on either side of him and came echoing back and died away. The woman had a hole in her neck, and the front of her dress was stained with blood. The wet, cold air felt heavy in Ibrahim's chest, a sensation almost indistinguishable from grief. He touched the woman's cheek, and though he shuddered, he forced himself to graze a finger lightly over her head, a gesture of caressing comfort. Corpses are unclean, but he felt he had to do at least this much for her: touch her. "Allah forgive you," he whispered. He should bury her, he thought: he should do at least that much. But he had no shovel, and the ground was covered with snow, and even without snow, this soil was probably too rocky to dig. And even without rocks, it was too frozen. The foreigners had done nothing for their dead except to carry them along for a while and then drop them, and he could do no more than they.

Walking back to his horse, he stepped on something that crunched under foot: a pair of spectacles. They belonged to Okusley. Without these on his head, he remembered, the man could not see. So Okusley had fought his final battle as a blind man, swinging his sword in the dark. Ibrahim pushed the spectacles carefully back onto Okusley's head and positioned the shattered glass in front of his eyes. He could do that much, even for an enemy. Then he mounted his horse and rode on.

Barely one *k'roh* further on, he saw another corpse, an Engrayzee soldier, his black moustache powdered with snow. He lay under a wagon that had rammed into the side of the cliff. Someone firing from above with one of those long-barreled rifles must have put a bullet through him. His horse had torn loose and his wagon had rolled on until it crashed.

Then Ibrahim saw another corpse. And then another. And another and another and another. And after that the landscape seemed littered with them. Some had been shot, some hacked up with knives, but many more had simply frozen, as if they had grown too tired to keep marching and had paused to rest, and had died where they paused.

He started to count the dead, but his count soon ran into the hundreds and he stopped, because the trail of corpses just went on, into the thousands, into the many thousands, and what was the point of merely counting them? In one place, where the road crested, he could see corpses behind him and in front of him as far as his gaze could reach, dotting the slice of landscape bisected by that road. The sight of children among the dead made him shut his eyes. Someplace nearby, water roared on its journey through rocky gorges, and all around him, he could hear wind whispering among the rocks, but there was no human voice— certainly no human voice.

45

He couldn't stop to look for the malang among the dead. If any Engrayzee still lived, they might have the living malang in their custody and he might still be saved. If he lay among the dead, Ibrahim would have all the time in the world to search for his body on the way back. He kept his cotton-padded robe belted tightly around himself, and the hat merchant's blanket wrapped over the robe, and yet he shivered. When fatigue overtook him, he tied himself to his horse's neck and slumped against the warm flesh to doze. From time to time, jerked awake by some sound, he stared about wildly, fearful that his horse had strayed, but there was nowhere to stray on that ribbon of road through the fifty-mile crack in the mountains.

Every so often, Ibrahim had to stop and let his horse rest. He fed it handfuls of hay from the larger of his two bags and from the other bag took bits of bread to keep himself nourished. While the horse rested, however, Ibrahim had to flap his arms and beat his hands against his thighs to stay warm, for the temperature was cold enough to freeze moving water. Indeed, wherever the road curved close to the gorge he could peek over the edge and see frozen waterfalls. Sometimes, if he listened hard, he could hear the water gurgling deep within the ice. Time passed unmeasured, some of it daylight, some of it night, and his dozing dreams mingled with fragmentary impressions of a landscape permeated by death.

Then he heard voices. Real ones. No dream could have yanked him out of slumber with such force. When he jerked upright, the rope binding him to his horse cut against his neck, so he loosened the cord to look around. The moon had set, but dawn had worn a patch of night sky thin. Against that glow, he could make out the silhouettes of mountains all around him, the taller peaks poking into the very clouds. Ahead of him the canyon widened into a valley and there, somewhere, he saw twinkles of light. A horse whinnied,. A gun sounded. A horse screamed and then—a hubbub of men's voices.

Ibrahim peered into the inky air. His horse still trudged along, careless of the danger posed by men with guns, stepping daintily over a frozen Engrayzee child, then picking its way up a rocky slope. From the crest, Ibrahim looked down and saw the skirmish. A group of thirty or forty Afghans had surrounded a handful of Engrayzee soldiers. The foreigners in turn had formed up around a sort of giant birdcage. The Afghans were circling the group and their cage on foot, hooting in Pushto, inexorably moving in.

Ibrahim rode toward the action. "People!"

A man separated from the circle of Afghans and ran toward him, calling out his name. His face was swaddled in a turban for warmth, but by his gait and voice, and by the size of him , Ibrahim recognized Ghulam Dastagir. "Dearest friend," he exulted. "Dear brother, I thought I would never see you again!"

"Ibrahim! Come quick—they have the malang!"

Ibrahim leaned out of his saddle to embrace Ghulam Dastagir but he snapped upright quickly and rode toward the fighting. Now he saw why the Afghans were only yelling, only brandishing knives, keeping their distance. In that big cage, the Engrayzee had a hostage: the malang, in fact. A dozen Engrayzees made a ring around the cage with their backs to it, facing outward, their bayonets swaying like scorpions' stingers, but two stood inside that circle with their bayonets poking through the bars and pressing against the malang's shirt. A single thrust from either would push steel between his ribs. The whole group looked like cornered cats, aroused to reckless ferocity by danger. They were fighting for their lives, and the hostage was their only card.

"Do they know who he is?" Ibrahim panted.

"The Pushtoons do. I told them," said Ghulam Dastagir. "They had heard of him already. These men are of the Safi tribe. They took me in. But the Engrayzees only know that we value this man, so they're threatening to kill him."

The Afghans were chattering in Pushto, breaking off occasionally to curse the Engrayzees. "Let him go. Let him go," one of them screamed, "or I'll kill every last donkey-fucker among you."

"We'll kill them anyway," murmured Ibrahim.

"That we will," vowed Ghulam Dastagir. "As soon as they release the malang."

"But they'll never release him if they think we'll kill them anyway. This way ends badly. Tell your friends, Ghulam Dastagir. We have to give them a way to live."

"It's too late," said Ghulam Dastagir. "Didn't you see the corpses strewn from here to Kabul? These ones will never believe we'll let them live, no matter what we do. They'll try to kill us first if we give them any opening. So we can't let up on them, Malik-sahib. It's them or us now, and we have all the power. They have only the malang."

"So they have everything, and we have nothing. I must talk to them."

"You can't talk to them. Are you crazy? You don't speak their tongue. They don't speak ours."

The sun had come up somewhere, diluting the blackness just a little. The Afghans looked weary but greedy. The Engrayzee soldiers looked haggard but deadly. If the standoff went on long enough, they might collapse, but they'd kill the malang before they went down. If they were down to one last deed, that would be the deed.

"Listen to me, men." Ibrahim's Pushto was rough and the tribesmen looked at him distrustfully.

"He's with me," Ghulam Dastagir assured them. "He's the headman of my village, the malang's first disciple." The tribesmen studied Ibrahim with tentative respect. "He's Wazir Akbar Khan's scribe," Ghulam Dastagir went on to boast, but the tribesmen burst out laughing at this one. Akbar Khan! Oh, those Kandahar Pushtoons! That lot plowed no soil in *these* parts. This was Ghilzai country!

"I've left Akbar's service," Ibrahim announced quickly. "He let the Engrayzees take away my malang. I put no faith in princes anymore. That's why I came myself."

"And what can you do?" one of the tribesmen scoffed. "We have them cornered and it's not enough. They can still kill the poor malang before we even get close to them. We've been puzzling over this for hours—how to break the stalemate. But perhaps," he added sarcastically, "you know a way that we haven't thought of!"

"I do. I have a plan. With all respect to your courage, let me talk to them."

"They speak gibberish. You *can't* talk to them."

In his clumsy Pushto, Ibrahim replied, "They only want to get out of here alive. For that, they need a hostage, but it doesn't have to be Malang-sahib. It could be me. I'll offer myself in his place. They'll accept the offer if they think I'm worth something to you men. So grant me one indulgence. Give me a show of respect. Make them think I have great value to you. Then, if they release the malang, let them depart in peace."

"But they'll have you," Ghulam Dastagir exclaimed in horror. "What will I tell everyone in Char Bagh? What will I tell your wife?"

"They'll have me, yes, yes, but Allah is compassionate, Ghulam Dastagir. He'll set me free in his own way. At worst, he'll admit me to the ranks of martyrs. If they let Malang-sahib go, you take my horse, it's a fine one I got from Wazir Akbar Khan. It will carry you both as far as Kabul. Take this bag of money, too. I don't know how much is in there but share it with these good tribesmen and keep enough to get yourself and Malang-sahib home. Take him home to Khadija. Tell her ... I send my greetings and will return as soon as God permits. But tell her I discharged my vow, I kept my promise—make her see that I did. I got her husband back to her. Tell her all this if God permits."

"Oh, sweet Ibrahim! Sweet Allah! Ibrahim, my good friend." Ghulam Dastagir dropped to one knee and began to kiss Ibrahim's hand. "If ever I doubted your greatness, forgive me. You are truly my commander, Hajji Ibrahim. You are loved by God, we put our faith and trust only in Him, I long to be as close to Allah one day as you are now, as you have always been. I see it now. I see that *you* are *my* sheikh. I know you at last and how can I bear to lose you *now*? Now that I know, how can I bear it? Oh my God!"

Ibrahim pulled his hand away from Ghulam Dastagir, glancing around embarrassed. The Safi men studied this interaction between the warrior they knew and the newcomer they had just met, and they were impressed. The Engrayzee looked on silently too, weighing what they were seeing. One by one, the Safi men stepped forward. Each one put a hand to his heart and bowed to Ibrahim, kissed his hand, and retired to the slopes. It was a spontaneous show of sincere respect, and it convinced the foreigners. They all fixed on Ibrahim now as he moved toward them with his hands in the air. The malang looked peaceful inside the cage, his head slumped to one side, his eyes half shut, his lips moving.

Ibrahim gestured toward the malang, then toward himself, and beckoned to the foreigners. "Let me be your prisoner." They only stared at him. Ibrahim moved closer, but they lifted their rifle barrels sharply and he stopped moving. "Be calm," he crooned. "Take me as your prisoner." These men looked beaten. Their uniforms were torn and their faces bled from assorted cuts. Their hair, once wet with sweat, had frozen. The closest one stared ferociously at Ibrahim and said something in a wild voice. He took a jerky step toward the headman, but his companions restrained him.

"Me for him," said Ibrahim. He set two pebbles on his palm and switched their places, then mimed himself and the malang switching places. "Me for him. Yes?" The foreigners stared at him intently. "The malang might die," said Ibrahim. He pointed to the malang and mimed collapsing. "Then what will you have?" He beat his chest. "I'm healthy, I won't die. You saw how those men kissed my hand. Take me."

"Die," one of the Engrayzees repeated. He knew that word. He and the others talked among themselves. After a moment, they beckoned Ibrahim forward and parted to let him step to the cage—which was actually a litter, he realized, designed to carry rich men's women. The tip of a bayonet touched his spine. He pulled the door open and touched his sheikh. The master kept on singing the qualities of God. The warmth of his skin sent relief through Ibrahim's body. He pulled the malang's arm, and the master came to his feet with all the docility of a child. Then he moved his lips close to Ibrahim's ears. He said something.

"What?" said Ibrahim.

"Shahnaz," the Malang whispered.

"Shahnaz? What about her?"

"Be kind to Shahnaz."

Why Shahnaz? But he couldn't ask, could not learn more. The Engrayzee were pulling the malang out of the litter now. They sent him teetering toward the tribesmen. Ibrahim yelled to Ghulam Dastagir. "He needs your help. Come and help him! Move slowly. Don't frighten the Engrayzee. Keep your hands up. Come quickly. Slowly though. Move slowly. Hurry."

He retired into the litter and from there watched Ghulam Dastagir's arms go around the malang. It was over, the malang was safe. "Stop with Shamsuddin in Kabul, shelter with him until the passes open." Ibrahim could not stop calling out advice, requests. "When you get to Char Bagh, tell Khadija—tell Soraya—tell my wife—tell everyone—"

"I will tell them all. Of your heroism. I will tell them," Ghulam Dastagir promised. "Let the foreigners go in peace," he yelled to the Pushtoons. "They have my master. Let the Engrayzee take him, he'll be safe. Allah will keep him safe."

Snow was beginning to fall again. Ibrahim's eyelids felt like cast-iron pots He had been riding across ice and fighting his way over snow-choked passes through almost two sunsets and moonrises without pause. Through black spots, he saw Ghulam Dastagir help the malang onto the horse and walk the horse into snow swirls, up toward the passes where a ribbon of road strewn with corpses ran through the gorge. Ibrahim's work was done; he had no further reason to stay awake. People who fell asleep in weather like this did not usually wake up again, but Ibrahim didn't care. He waited for the foreigners to lock the door.

But instead, they pulled him out of the litter. They tied his hands behind his back and poked their bayonets to prod him forward. With Ibrahim in the lead, the group moved south, leaving the heavy litter behind. By midday, however, they had gone only a few *k'rohs*, because they were all so broken, all so spent, every one of them. They called a halt at that point. One of them untied Ibrahim's hands and pushed at him. They didn't need him any more. He was now more trouble than he was worth. Ibrahim understood what was coming. Now they would kill him.

He lifted his shoulder against the expected blows. These men who had lost everything, who had no food, no shelter, no safety, could still have one thing. They could have revenge. But they had only his one body to punish for all the thousands they had lost on the road between this lonely spot and Kabul. This would be long and it would hurt. One of the men pushed him from behind, and he stumbled onto the rocks but picked himself up at once. He'd make them work for it. He'd not let them get their satisfaction easily. But the first blow didn't fall. He looked back. The man who had pushed him just stood there making a pushing gesture and muttering. What were they waiting for? Did they not realize how helpless he was? Perhaps they were even weaker. The foreigner raised his voice. He kept repeating the sound, "Goh! Goh!"

Then it dawned on Ibrahim. They didn't need him anymore, *so they were releasing him.* At that, he didn't want to go. Such an abundance of human compassion from these people overwhelmed him: to relinquish vengeance, when vengeance was the only nourishment they could have! It took greatness of soul! He wanted to wrap his arms around these men, wanted to embrace their knees. Confused by his own emotions, Ibrahim tottered forward, his cheeks burning despite the snow.

The foreigner watched him, too spent to care, and then suddenly his face erupted. Gore and bits of bone came bursting out from the place where his nose had been. He pitched forward. A bullet had come through the back of his skull and out the front. Ibrahim heard men whooping in Pushto. Afghan horsemen were circling in on him and the foreigners. The Engrayzee immediately squared up. Six of them dropped to one knee to form a line, the other three stood behind them. All pointed their muskets at the enemy, disciplined to the end, ready to shoot—but their guns were empty, they could not shoot, they had no bullets, no powder; yet none of them flung up his hands to surrender. They waited to engage the Afghans hand to hand. But the Afghans didn't have to come that close. They had bullets, they could fire from afar. And the bullets came in, one and two at a time. The Engrayzees dropped one and two at a time. One man crawled away on his hands and knees, but a rider chased him down and clubbed him till he stopped moving. Then a bullet hit Ibrahim in the shoulder. He yelped and grabbed his arm, staring at the blood spurting out of him. A horseman was bearing down. He flung up his good arm and shouted, "Allah-u-akbar! I was their prisoner. I'm not one of them. Don't shoot!"

The Pushtoons stared down at him from their cavalry heights, faces wrapped in turbans. They looked like those marauders who had descended upon Char Bagh years ago and carried off eight precious women. But at least they were not foreigners.

One of the men dismounted and crouched next to him. "What's your name?"

"Ibrahim. I'm from Char Bagh. It's a village in the north."

"I've heard about Char Bagh." The other spat snuff and leaned down again. "That's where that famous malang comes from. You're from there too?"

"The foreigners took him! I came to save him, I'm the malik of Char Bagh. My companions got him away from the infidels, but I fell prisoner to them."

"No longer, my friend: you're safe among your own now."

He spoke more words, but Ibrahim blacked out and didn't hear them. Ibrahim knew nothing of being slung over a horse and taken to a village deep in the Hindu Kush mountains, many hours journey from the highway. He knew nothing of lying bundled in sheepskin blankets and lamb's wool coats, wracked with fever. He scarcely knew that the women of this Safi tribe fed him hot broth, nursed him, drew him back from the edge of death. There he lay throughout the winter months, recovering his health while the people of Char Bagh mourned his death.

By spring, he was strong enough to walk about, but the village was still snowbound, and the tribesmen want him to stay, because they thought his presence brought them luck. After all, his village had produced the great malang. So they told him there was no point in trying to get back to Kabul now: he'd never make it.

But at last the snows had melted and the flowers had started blooming. The roads had opened up and caravans were moving freely once more. The time had come.

"Stay, Malik-jan. Be our permanent guest," the head of household begged him.

"I would like nothing better," Ibrahim responded, "but I have family in a land my own, I have a village that looks to me for guidance. My heart longs for my own soil."

His hosts relinquished him then; they gave him a horse piled high with gifts of mutton jerky and tasty baked goods, not to mention embroidered cloth and a woolen prayer rug. With these gifts, they sent the malik of Char Bagh on his way.

46

When he recognized the mountains of Char Bagh, Ibrahim caught his breath and wiped moisture from his eyes. Then he gave his horse's ribs a gentle dig, but the tired animal kept to its dogged pace. Why tears, Ibrahim wondered? Surely, what he felt was joy. The slopes were covered with crocuses and purple burdocks and the wind against his face brought a flavor of sage-pollen to his nose and throat. When he smelled the river, he thought his heart would break. Every river smells different, and this one, the river of his childhood, gave off an aroma of wet gravel, cattails and moss, a scent of sand and willow pollen, a memory of summer afternoons spent swimming with the other boys, of standing in irrigation ditches to plaster up the dikes, of harvesting the alfalfa.

Ibrahim rode to the river's edge and dismounted. He tied his horse to one branch of a fallen tree and crouched by the water to perform his ablutions, splashing his face three times, washing his hands to the forearms, washing his feet. He took off his turban and skull cap and passed his wet palms over his hair until he felt the cool moisture on his scalp, then took out his little prayer rug and performed his afternoon *namaz*.

At sunset, when he reached Char Bagh, a crowd of children saw him coming, whispered amongst themselves, and bolted for home, chattering like birds. Ibrahim rode through the gate formed by his own compound and tethered his horse, intending to go directly up to the malang, but his family poured outdoors to greet him. His girls grabbed at his legs. Soraya rushed into his arms, but decorously let go after three quick neck kisses and started scolding Ibrahim for being gone so long, mingling wails of gratitude with shrill complaints.

Ibrahim had planned to comport himself with dignity; he tried to keep his back straight, and to pat children's heads, and to smile in every direction with benign self-possession, but emotion got the best of him. He started hugging indiscriminately. As the homecoming whirl mounted to a frenzy, some fat person waddled into his grasp. Her girth was all in her belly, and he had to lean over the lump to get close to her. Only then did he realize he was embracing Khadija. He squelched the impulse to kiss her lips and kissed only her neck, choking out her name. Whereupon, with a start he realized she wasn't fat but pregnant. She was pregnant. The blood drained from his face, and his mind began to riot. Praise God was his first thought. Of course, of course. She whom all the world had considered barren! But then: horrors, the scandal! Did the village know? Had she been disgraced like Shahnaz, had they made her suffer? Did Malang-sahib know? Why else would he have spoken of Shahnaz as he stepped out of the cage? He meant Khadija really. How could Ibrahim face his sheikh now? His gaze slid down to Khadija's belly and back to her glistening brown eyes. "Is it—?"

"Yes," she declared. "It's Malang-sahib's child."

"Malang-sahib's?"

"Yes. It's a miracle. All praise to Allah."

"All praise to Allah," the others echoed in a ragged chorus. They spoke what should have been joyous words but with the longest faces Ibrahim had ever seen. A terrible suspicion struck him.

"Where is Malang-sahib right now?" No one answered him. At that moment, he knew, and the tears he never would have shed in public over any private sorrow came spouting out. The household started crying with him in simple compassion. "Allah!" the women keened. His wife came into his arms, whispering, "Life be upon you, Malik-sahib, life be upon you."

They wept in the courtyard and then went indoors and wept some more. The village had mourned the sheikh when they buried him, but the headman's homecoming gave them all a second opportunity. Visitors poured through the compound and lamented and departed. By the time

Ghulam Dastagir came over, night had fallen and the tears had run dry. Ibrahim felt lifeless inside but was glad to see the companion of his great journey. Ghulam Dastagir told him the simple, tragic story.

The sheikh had taken a beating in Bala Hissar prison and had fasted relentlessly during his imprisonment. By the time the Engrayzees took him along on their doomed retreat, he was already famished and feverish. On the way home, Ghulam Dastagir had wanted to stop in Kabul, but the malang would not hear of it. "I can't be late," he said. "I have to meet my friend."

Ghulam Dastagir thought he was talking about Ibrahim and assured the great man that his "friend" was not in Char Bagh but would follow later when he could, and so in fact they were in no great hurry.

"You're in no hurry. I have an appointment to keep," the malang insisted.

"But the passes are blocked with snow," Ghulam Dastagir protested. "We can't get through."

"The passes were blocked yesterday," the malang said. "Today they're open."

This was impossible, of course, but Ghulam Dastagir decided to push on from Baghlan and let the malang see for himself. Once they reached an impossible barrier he wouldn't protest against turning back and finding shelter in the city. Such was Ghulam Dastagir's plan.

So they set off from Baghlan on mules in bitingly bright weather. The snow was deep and soft in the gorges and hollows, but it held up well on the path where earlier traffic had stamped it down. This earlier traffic kept nibbling at Ghulam Dastagir's peace of mind. Who could have come this way in dead of winter? It must have been quite a host to stamp the snow down so thoroughly: dozens of men, scores of bullocks, camels, horses, donkeys. Ghulam Dastagir watched for this crowd around every bend, worrying that it would be, not a caravan but an army. He also kept expecting the snow to deepen over each rise and block the path, but the route remained open and they kept moving.

When they reached Char Bagh, the malang went straight to the mosque and performed a silent *namaz*. Then he went to Ghulam Haidar's house and asked for Shahnaz, of all people. Instead of raining the expected curses down upon the girl who had started all the trouble, he stroked her humbled head and said, "You will tend the rosebushes around my grave."

After that he asked Ghulam Dastagir to take him home, but he collapsed on the way. Ghulam Dastagir carried him up the final slope and laid him down in the house Char Bagh had built for him. His wife Khadija knelt by his side to warm his hands with her own, but the malang never opened his eyes. He just lay there breathing softly, and then more softly, until he was not breathing at all.

Even though the ground was cold and hard, the village dug a grave for him the next day, not among all the common graves but on a hilltop above the cemetery, where they would have room to erect a shrine. Just this week, the village had transplanted seven rosebushes to the soil around the great man's grave, and Shahnaz had begun to tend them as charged.

No one noticed how these words startled Ibrahim. The next morning, after bread-and-tea, he made his way to the sheikh's grave, accompanied by Ghulam Dastagir and Ghulam Haidar, and counted the rose bushes.

Seven!

Ghulam Dastagir was busy discussing the mausoleum they ought to construct as soon as the weather warmed up a bit more. What kind of monument did the headman favor? Should they enlarge the guest house? Surely, the malang's final resting place would attract a stream of pilgrims during the summer months. What did Ibrahim think?

The distracted headman muttered some answer, but his mind was back in that dungeon with Malang-sahib. *Before the seven rosebushes drop their petals you must*...what was it he must do? See his friend Shamsuddin. That's what it was. He'd forgotten, he'd hurried through Kabul without stopping, driven by his hunger for home. Now he regretted his haste.

Khadija gave birth to a son at the end of Saratan. It was a hard delivery that left the mother wounded, but Soraya helped bring the boy out safely. Mullah Yaqub came from the bigger village to whisper the obligatory prayer in his ear. After an all-night conference, the household decided to call the baby Azizullah—"Dear-to-Allah."

Dandled by two mothers, the little boy grew long and fat and cheerful. Khadija began to recover her shape. Ibrahim's gaze was drawn to her increasingly, began to cling to her. Now that Malang-sahib had broken the spell, might she not bear another child? Many more perhaps? Sons, even? Indeed he looked at her now and saw a fountain of fertility. She caught him looking once and returned his gaze for a blistering instant, her lips dimpling in a guarded smile. She must be nearly thirty years of age now. How could a woman so old still stir desire in a man? This yearning went beyond lust. It was a longing touched by grace. He wanted her to bear his heir.

The malang had known about this all along. *Your yearning will end...* In that dank and lightless cell, he had practically asked Ibrahim to marry Khadija after his death and raise the son he had planted in her womb— what else could he have meant? But only if he fulfilled one condition, a penance lighter than a feather. "Go back to Kabul and express your gratitude to Hakim Shamsuddin." That was all he had asked, all it would take to gain his forgiveness and his permission to possess Khadija for life.

The day after the last of the wheat was harvested, therefore, Ibrahim sent for Khadija. She handed the baby off to Soraya and went up the stairs. Ibrahim pointed her to a soft mat, and she took the honored spot uneasily. "What's wrong, Hajji?"

"Nothing's wrong. I've been thinking of a trip to Kabul—my dear."

"God watch over you!" she blushed. "Must you go now?"

"It won't be as hard this time. I know the way. But yes, I must go before the first frost. Men were kind to us there, and we never expressed our gratitude properly."

"And you want my advice about the trip." She gave him a pleased smile.

"I do, but that's not why I called you up here now." He bowed his head, feeling curiously shy, and the silence dragged on.

"Should I get some tea?" she asked at last.

"Soon. Let us settle our business first." Desire made his voice thrum.

"What business, Ibrahim-jan?"

"Khadija-jan." He mustered a frown. "I worry that people might mistreat you in my absence. Everyone knows you're under my protection, but is that enough? And Azizullah is fatherless. How can I allow that? The son of my sheikh! In sum—to make a long story short—I will come right to the point. It's best to be direct, I think. So long as we understand each other. Do you see? Well, then, good, that's settled."

"No, Malik-sahib. I don't see. What's settled?" Her gaze liquefied him.

"About you and me. Mullah Yaqub can take care of it quickly next time he's in Char Bagh. It should be done before I go. That way, I won't have to worry while I'm traveling. Because what if something should happen on the road, God forbid? Azizullah would be left without my inheritance! But if you're my wife, he becomes my son."

"Your wife?" she stammered.

Warmth flooded his face right to the top of his ears His eyes met hers and a feeling washed between them, but he did not move. He must cage himself a little longer. He had not earned forgiveness yet. "Yes," he gruffed. "My wife. The compound on the hill will be your house, Soraya will queen it down here, and I will split my time. You and Soraya get along, don't you...dear?"

"Yes," she trembled, "but on this...I cannot speak for her..."

The headman went to the door and stuck his head out. "Soraya! Come up here."

"Oh! Ibrahim, no! You should talk to her in private first. Just the two of you." Khadija started to rise, but Ibrahim waved her down again.

"I want both of you together. Stay where you are, woman."

Soraya came into the room, a piece of embroidery still in her hand. She glanced suspiciously from her husband to Khadija and back.

"Soraya, my dear," the headman said. "You do love Khadija-jan, don't you?"

Soraya caught her breath and just like that her eyes brimmed with tears.

"Soraya-jan—"

"You're going to marry her!" she croaked.

He felt rebuked. "I should, you know. It's best," he said. "It's best I do. Sheikh-sahib's son must have a father. This way the land and the water will be all one inheritance."

"Oh yes, it sounds very 'necessary'," sniffed Soraya. "What a wise malik you've turned out to be! How wonderful when the thing you want is the thing you *should* do. How *nice* when duty *forces* you to take what you've wanted for years and years and—"

"Hush!" He glanced at Khadija, who sat with her hands clenched in her lap. "Come here," he cajoled his fragile wife. "Come sit beside me."

She succumbed to his wheedling and settled next to him with the delicate caution of an injured little rabbit. Khadija remained across the room but all the emotion in the chamber was flowing between the headman and her. Their unity made Soraya the outsider. She drew her knees up and rested her chin on them and pouted.

"Nothing needs to change," the headman assured her. "You will see. Our prophet peace-be-upon-him said 'take two wives if you can treat them equally,' and I intend—"

"I know what you intend. You always have the best *intentions*, Ibrahim. You *intended* to save the sheikh."

The barb made him flinch, but he knew she spoke hurtfully only because she was hurting herself, and knowing this sweetened his heart with pity. He took her hand. "You must stop interrupting me, Soraya. You don't know what I'm going to say. Listen more."

"I'm no good at listening," the girl moped. "I have a fever. I'm burning up."

"But my dear," he said, "your hand feels like ice."

And Khadija came over to feel Soraya's forehead. "You don't have a fever."

Soraya tossed her head. "When is this marriage?"

"Soon," said Ibrahim. "I'm going to make a trip to Kabul and we must complete the ceremony before I go."

"To Kabul!" Soraya turned a stricken gaze on her husband. "Again? But you just came back. And you were gone so long the last time!"

"This will be a shorter trip. Going and coming takes twelve days, add a few more for my business—I should be back in three weeks, if Allah wills it."

"But *must* you go now? Why?"

"I made a promise to Sheikh-sahib. Don't inquire further, this is a private matter between him and me, and my honor is at stake. Just accept it. I must go and come before the rosebushes on Sheikh-sahib's grave lose their petals."

The solemnity of this silenced Soraya and she stood up.

"Where are you off to?" Ibrahim demanded.

"The well." Soraya wrapped her long head scarf around her body like a shroud, but her face radiated none of the mad look she got when *djinns* were troubling her. "I need water."

The water that turns to wine when Love does the pouring. Ibrahim felt a pang. Was he misinterpreting the sheikh's words? Perhaps the sheikh wanted him to stay right here with his women. "Soraya, you can't run away from this conversation."

But Khadija asserted herself. "For pity's sake, Hajji-sahib, let her go. She wants to think about this without your will pressing down on her. Let her go."

Soraya wafted from the room as silently as a shadow.

"It's hard for her," said Khadija, "Don't worry, I'll talk to her, I'll ease her mind, and she'll recover. We will all be happy. You will see."

"If God wills. You're still recovering yourself, I know, from giving birth...." Ibrahim looked at her breasts, looked at her belly, and then lower.

"I'm quite restored," Khadija said. She had taken Soraya's spot next to him and she leaned toward him until he could feel her breath on his face. "Ibrahim. The night I married your brother—during the very ceremony that made me his wife, I saw you—"

"I know." If he let her finish the thought, he might lose control.

"And I knew." Already her breath was resonating in his ears like a music that his blood was dancing to. "Already I felt your son inside me—I wanted—"

"I know. Me too. From that first night. That first glimpse."

"Thirteen years ago!" She grazed her finger across his cheek and lips.

He pulled back. "Someone might see."

"Let them see." Her voice was low and slow. "We're engaged now."

He could bolt the door and have her: she would turn this plain room into heaven as Soraya had never done—but it would be wrong. He did not yet have permission. He must go on yearning until he had done what his sheikh had asked; he had asked so very little! Ibrahim disengaged himself from her fingers, which were already insinuating themselves into his clothes. "What we did that day... "

She pulled back. "Nobody knows about that day. Nobody saw."

"Sheikh-sahib knows. We piled up a debt to him that we can never repay, Khadija, and yet in his compassion the sheikh has given me a way. He told me how to cancel the debt. He said I must go to Kabul and see a man. That's all he asked. I don't know why, but if I do it, I come back to you forgiven. After that, requiting my desire in you won't take me away from my sheikh, it won't take me further from Allah, it will only bring me closer. If we wait till then."

Khadija bit her lips. "I remember that day like a fever dream. I sometimes think it didn't happen. I've put it out of my mind. I can't think about it."

"Mullah Yaqub is coming next week," said Ibrahim. "We'll have the ceremony while he's here. Then when I return from Kabul... "

"So much can happen to a traveler!" she murmured anxiously.

"God is compassionate," he assured her. "Trust Allah."

ℰℭℛ

When he called a meeting to discuss his journey, some of the village elders shook their heads. "Why so soon! Men lose their souls in cities."

But Ibrahim pressed his case. "Brothers, now that we know merchants in the capital, we might sell our products there. The Kabul bazaar is bigger than you can imagine. We have excellent goat felt that blanket makers there will want to buy. We can grow cotton, now that we have so much water. Our pine nuts will fetch a good price in the city. What do you say, Ghulam Dastagir? Will you come with me?"

Ghulam Dastagir shook his head. "I've had my fill of cities. In a year or two, if I'm still alive, I might visit my son's grave. If you go now, visit him for me, Malik-sahib, but think hard about going right now. This might be a bad time. I hear rumors."

"What rumors?"

"That the Engrayzee are coming back with another army. Mullah Yaqub heard it from his people in Baghlan. Everybody says they're coming back."

The elders cocked their head to see what their young leader thought of this.

"Rumors," said Ibrahim. "I can't change my plans on account of rumors." Already one of the rosebushes had lost one of its petals. He had no time to lose.

47

Ibrahim traversed the passes alone this time. It still took him six days to get to Kabul, yet the trip seemed shorter, now that he knew where he was going. Along the way he kept hearing Engrayzees, Engrayzees, but he never saw a single redcoat. Several strangers warned him against going on to Kabul, but he ignored them. When he reached the capital, the city seemed quiet. The streets were crowded, certainly, but Ibrahim's memory of the place bore the stamp of furious mobs boiling through alleyways and foreign soldiers running for their lives, and nothing like that was going on now.

In the Grand Bazaar, men were drinking tea and trading gossip. Ibrahim made his way to the hat merchant's store. He could have gone to Shamsuddin's home, but he didn't want to presume on courtesies extended to him during the war. Besides, the hat merchant spent most of his time in his shop, and indeed, there he was now, rotund as ever, resting his back on a hump of pillow while a boy massaged his feet.

Abdul Haq was there too—the man never seemed to have any business elsewhere. "Scholar-sahib!" he exclaimed. "You drop upon us like some hero from the Book of Kings. We had given you up for dead, yet here you are, home from the smoky battlefield, covered in reputation! Where have you been all year? People keep asking about you and we tell them he's vanished—you make liars of us all. Come in, papa, tell your story! List by name the giants you have slain. Tell us what countries you've explored. Describe the plants and animals there, and the customs of the people."

Ibrahim laughed and stepped into the store and wasted no time delivering a formal speech of gratitude for all the generosity the two men had showered on him. And with that speech, he completed the atonement he owed his sheikh. It felt curiously flat, strangely unimportant, much too easy; but who was he to question? He took a seat and began recounting the horrors he had witnessed in the Hindu Kush mountains. All of Kabul had heard the stories, but they never tired of hearing more. Shoppers and bystanders tarried to listen, and a few actually climbed into the stall. Hakim Shamsuddin shooed them out, but they came creeping back, and gradually accumulated into a sizable audience.

Once, a flurry of raucous noises elsewhere in the Grand Bazaar made Ibrahim break off, but his listeners urged him on. "Never mind the rowdies," said Abdul Haq. "It's been like this all year. Order is a water pot, once shattered never mended. Thugs roam the streets these days. Ignore them."

Ibrahim took up his tale again. But a boy at the edge of the crowd tried to break in with some urgent news. When Ibrahim described how the last of the Engrayzees were killed, he did manage to cut in with, "Not the last of them! One got away! He told his kin and they're back with murder in their hearts. They're planning a massacre."

Hakim Shamsuddin growled at the boy to quit spreading his alarmist rumors. "Every day, you hear these stories, sir. They've hit Shor Bazaar, they've burned Siah Sung, they've killed ten thousand in Behmaru—it's never true. When people are afraid they invent stories. Then their own stories come back to them and they consider it evidence! A few of the Engrayzee are back, it's true. They're here to collect hostages and haul away their puppets. Dost Mohammed Khan is coming back, I hear, and the Engrayzee are here to negotiate his return. that's all it is. They lost a war to us. Do you think they've forgotten?"

"So you don't think they're seeking revenge?"

"God forbid," cried Abdul Haq. "They might want revenge, but they wouldn't dare! Fifty thousand of them marched out of Kabul and only one made it to Jalalabad! Who can fail to learn a lesson from a beating like that? And we're the same Afghans here, we're still ready. Hundreds of them, thousands upon thousands of us—no, no, Ibrahim-jan. Rest easy. We frighten them. That's why they've brought so many soldiers. When I pass one on the streets, he barely has the courage to look me in the eye. Honestly, I feel sorry for them."

"You mean there are redcoats in the city right now?" said Ibrahim.

Shamsuddin cocked his head. Beyond the immediate hubbub and clamor, shouting could be heard. A man screamed, his voice rising to a womanish pitch. "Listen to those bastards!" said the hat merchant. "We've got our country back but how do we now protect it from our own?"

"Thugs!" Abdul Haq complained. "Bandits! Rowdies!"

"What are they fighting about?" Ibrahim asked.

"Gold. Goods. Women. Who knows?" The hat merchant spat. "Ten years ago, a man could travel to Bokhara with a camel load of carpets and fear no harm. These days—" He broke off to glare at the troublesome boy who had come scurrying back. "Can't you see your elders are talking?" He turned to the others. "Gentlemen, look at this younger generation! When I was a boy—"

But the boy shouted, "Run, you goddamned old fools! The Engrayzee are attacking the Grand Bazaar. They're here right *now*! Run!"

"Why, you—give me that squishy peach there, Ibrahim-jan." Shamsuddin threw the rotting fruit at the boy, barely missing a pedestrian. The peach splattered and the boy dashed out of sight. "And stay away!" Hakim Shamsuddin yelled.

But the hullabaloo had grown louder as if a fight had broken out just a few lanes over. Shamsuddin rose from his shopkeeper's nest and went to investigate. The idlers in front of the shop sniffed at the air. "What's that smell?" said one. "Is it smoke?"

Just then, a scuffle burst through the row of stalls visible at the end of the lane. No one could see quite what was happening down there, only that awnings were coming down and people were wrestling and scrambling. Within one shocking instant, however, all the idlers and lay-abouts turned into a mob, coming like brushfire, coming in such desperation they plugged up the lane and began punching at one another to get through, trampling each other in their haste.

Fear radiated ahead of the moving mob, fear ignited all along its path. The gawkers in the hat store jumped to their feet. Some heaved out the back and some into the lane, but all found walls of people charging at them, running from some danger no one could see.

Ibrahim dove out the rear but found himself in the narrow aisle between two rows of stalls that faced in opposite directions, an aisle just big enough for one skinny person to run through, but this was choked with people who had come out the back of all the stores along its length. Ibrahim raced back through the hat store and into the front lane again.

Even if the Grand Bazaar had been empty, it might have taken him half an hour to get out of the maze from here. Today, it was literally impossible. The lane was plugged with people and filling up with smoke. Ibrahim could see flames at both ends. Trapped between two sheets of fire, screamers tore at the walls that hemmed them in. The people closest to the flames had caught fire. Ibrahim retreated in panic, past Shamsuddin's store, through another store, into a second crowded lane, punching and bulling with his shoulders, forging on with no idea if he was headed out of the bazaar or into it. The lanes in this area were covered, so he could not see any sky. Smoke seared his eyes, but through his tears he had an impression of men on horses, men in red coats, blocking the only way out. The crowd kept surging at them, they kept firing guns, and bodies kept dropping and piling up. People clawed to get over those mounting mounds of corpses, but soldiers were hacking them to pieces as they emerged.

But all of that seemed far away to Ibrahim and impossibly out of reach. His back was so hot! His shirt felt ready to burst into flames, but at least back here in the blazing depths, a man had room to move freely. At head level, the smoke was too thick to breathe so he dropped to his knees. And there, as he crouched close to the dirt, he saw a boy, the same boy who had warned of the Engrayzee attack. The poor little lad's clothes were on fire. Ibrahim wanted to save him, even though he had no idea how to save himself. He crawled toward the motionless body, and the closer he came, the hotter he felt. Ibrahim thought the boy was crying, for his mouth was moving. But when he got close enough to hear, he discovered that the little fellow was singing, actually. And he wasn't the urchin who had been annoying Hakim Shamsuddin earlier—this boy was Karim!

"I thought you were dead," Ibrahim exclaimed, wrapping his arms around the singing boy. "Oh, you're hot, you're *so* hot. I must find you some water."

He rose to his feet with the boy in his arms. Everyone else was intent on getting out of the burning bazaar; so traveling further in was easy. Ibrahim wondered why everyone didn't go this way, since it was so easy. The crowds parted to let him through. But the boy he was carrying was not Karim, he suddenly realized. How could he have made such a strange mistake? This was Ahmad in his arms, his own dear little son Ahmad. How could he have failed to notice? And he wasn't dead or even seriously hurt! He was simply asleep. And even in his sleep, he was singing, this precious son of his, this heir of his, a smile clinging to his lips.

Ibrahim was alone, now. All the other people had rushed away. Here in the heart of the Grand Bazaar, he found a bathhouse. He knew it would be here. Why else would he have brought Ahmad to this spot? The little fellow needed some cooling off. The malang stood in the open doorway. No surprise there. Of course he would appear when he was needed. "Come inside," he beckoned. "Come in. Now at last you will see water."

"Am I forgiven?"

"You have been kind. You're forgiven."

Ibrahim moved toward his sheikh. The man unwound the turban from his head. It was made entirely of water and yet held its shape. Ibrahim handed his son over to the malang, who wrapped Ahmad in the cool blue liquid, gently winding the shimmering turban around and around him until he was entirely enveloped.

"Malang-sahib," Ibrahim exclaimed. "Where did you get this wonderful turban?" *

"I got it from the blue sky above and from the stars at night," the malang replied. "The Friend left it in the world for you and me to find."

"Oh," sighed Ibrahim. "When will you take me to see the Friend?"

"I am doing so now," said the malang. "Stand beside me. Look out there."

Ibrahim moved next to the malang. Inside the bathhouse, he no longer felt hot, although he could still see flames. They were licking over his body as if he himself had been transformed into fire.

The malang pointed toward the lanes jammed with turmoil, toward the shops blazing and burning. "What do you see?"

"I see the bazaar," said Ibrahim.

"Look again!" the malang commanded, and again he pointed. "What do you see?"

The people were all on fire. The shops were on fire. The merchandise was on fire. The ceiling was on fire. The very dirt seemed to burn. "I see fire."

"What do you see?" the malang cried a third time, pointing imperiously, and his voice filled the universe. Again, Ibrahim looked— the bazaar was gone! The fire mounted and roared, white heat interlaced with flickering reds and blazing yellows, and then the heat dissolved all colors, dissolved red into orange, orange into yellow, yellow into pure and colorless light.

Ibrahim understood. "I see only God."

The malang wrapped him in water and drew him into the light, and Ibrahim's yearning ceased at last.

Epilog

It took a few weeks for Char Bagh to hear the dreadful news—how the foreigners had returned to Afghanistan with an even bigger army than before, how they'd swept into Kabul and taken revenge for their losses by burning down the Grand Bazaar.

Everyone knew that Malik Ibrahim had friends in that bazaar; but that didn't mean he was dead. A man does not spend all his time with friends. He might have gone to the mosque that day; or he might have had business somewhere else. So the village waited for news; but the news they awaited never came. What did come were reports that at least ten thousand people had perished in the flames of the Grand Bazaar. No one could know if Ibrahim was one of the martyrs, for most of the corpses were burnt beyond recognition. Those at the heart of the bazaar were reduced to a few fragments of bone. And if Ibrahim had escaped the fire, where was he?

But slowly, the village accepted the loss of its headman. From the compounds where his wives still lived, a keening began to sound at odd hours of the day or night, now from one, now from the other, sometimes from both, permeating the village with unearthly sorrow. At last, the village gathered at the mosque to perform funeral prayers for Ibrahim. The ritual felt hollow, since they couldn't bury the poor man's body, nor even his bones, nor even his ashes, but that alone made the *namaz* especially fervent. Mullah Yaqub presided, of course, and many people from Sorkhab took part. Afterwards, hundreds stayed to eat and mourn and tell stories about the soon-to-be legendary headman and his mighty deeds. Char Bagh was able to host a worthy funeral feast, God be praised, because the water from the mountainside had made its fields so bountiful. Not even the eldest elders could remember such prosperity; and all the credit went to the visionary Malik Ibrahim, who had recognized the malang for what he was, and befriended him with the generosity that makes a good man great, binding him to Char Bagh with marriage and devotion.

Ghulam Dastagir did not make his move until the 40-day period had elapsed. Normally he would have waited at least a year, but these were unusual circumstances. When Ibrahim was alive, his two wives had lived in separate compounds, but now that their husband was gone, they lived together, sometimes in one compound, sometimes in the other. Their children moved with them, the three girls and little Azizullah, who was the child of the great malang. Elderly step-uncle Agha Lala stayed in the lower compound, and so did a number of other male relatives of Ibrahim's and of Soraya's... One of Khadija's cousins from Sorkhab, a young fellow with a mere shadow of a beard, had now moved into the upper compound, which used to be malang's; and so had the eldest of Asad's ox-like sons...nominally therefore males anchored each compound, but still, the whole village regarded the widows' situation as precarious.

One week after the second communal reading of the Quran for Ibrahim, a delegation of women from Ghulam Dastagir's compound came to visit Ibrahim's two widows. By this time, winter had closed the passes already, and the valley was cut off from the outer world, which gave a sense of urgency to the visit, for two women with children could not be left to their own devices. If they came to harm, it would shame the entire village. Ghulam Dastagir was now the biggest landowner in Char Bagh, and he had only one wife. Marrying two women at once would certainly mark a novelty in the annals of Char Bagh, but a man must shoulder the duties imposed on him by Allah.

His courting delegation consisted of three younger women and two crones who added weight and dignity to the group. The presence of the crones signaled that this was no mere social visit but an embassy seeking to launch negotiations for an important marriage. The crones were

Ghulam Dastagir's aunt Shireen Gul and his step-mother Bibi Jan. Ghulam Dastagir's wife stayed home.

The women were escorted to the sitting room near the front door of the compound. Both Khadija and Soraya came to sit with them. Khadija was suckling Azizullah, who was over five months old now, praise God. Girls swarmed in with tea, candies, nuts, raisins, and cookies to make the guests feel welcome.

For the first hour, the visitors merely reminisced about the tumultuous events of the past year, picking through the stories for tidbits not yet dulled by retelling. The widows listened largely in silence, shrouded in an air of tragic dignity. Then Shireen Gul got down to business. "Khadija-jan," she said (oh, she knew which of the women to address). "My heart grows faint with sorrow every time I think of you and sweet Soraya alone in these big compounds, struggling to manage double households, no man to call upon for lifting and loading, no man to open the door when some stranger comes knocking. We all fret and worry about the two of you. We all would love to see the two of you made secure. I will not allow the torment you are suffering to endure, not so long as breath still animates this wrinkled flesh of mine and I can do one single thing to ease your difficulties."

"Oh, auntie, do not fret for us!" Khadija assured her. "When you weather such catastrophes as we two, your skin hardens against the storm. Come back in spring and you'll find the two of us just as you see us now, God willing, a little more wrinkled, but who's to care? Thrice-widowed as I am, how can I fuss about appearance? What man would want a hag like me except as a sort of servant?"

"God forbid, God forbid, Khadija, my dearest! Of your hundred blossoms, not a one has withered yet. As for Soraya-jan! Well!"

"Yes, she's a pretty prize, isn't she?" Khadija smiled fondly at the younger woman, her one-time co-wife and sister-in-law once removed. "But she too has survived terrible losses. She's tougher than she looks— aren't you, my dear?" She smiled again at Soraya. "She'll survive this storm too, never fear—if Allah wills it."

"Survive! There is more to life than surviving. Now, my nephew Ghulam Dastagir—"

"He has a nice wife," Soraya noted sweetly. "Really. She is *so* nice."

"One wife! A man like him, a lord of such proportions, a man with land enough to feed a multitude should support more than one wife! And he stands ready to do his duty. After all, our Prophet, peace-be-upon-him-and-his-descendents—"

"Ghulam Dastagir is a stalwart man," Khadija declared. "In this house we have nothing but respect for him. My husband, God-bless-and-forgive-him—oh, I scarcely know whether to call him my husband or my brother-in-law—forgive me, Soraya-jan! I'm speaking of our dear Malik Ibrahim—he regarded Ghulam Dastagir as a brother."

"Ghulam Dastagir is like a mighty elm," his step-mother proclaimed. "How fine it will be to draw you pitiful widows under his sheltering arms!"

"He owns so much land," Khadija noted.

"And he has the strength to cultivate it all, with the help of his tenant-farmers, God be praised! And very soon, of course, the men will name him our new malik, and then you two will be able to say, 'We are the wives of the malik'."

"If he marries both of us," said Khadija, "what a tremendous landowner he will be. Quite rich enough to stand eye to eye with the Khan of Sorkhab. After all, his lands will then be joined to *our* domains."

The old woman blinked. "Your domains?"

"Yes," Khadija explained. "When Ibrahim Khan married me, he became master of everything the malang owned which I had inherited, of course, because I was Malang-sahib's widow. Now that Ibrahim has been gathered to God, all his property and all the malang's property belongs to us widows and our children."

"But—but you're women," Shireen Gul spluttered.

"Khadija consulted with Mullah Yaqub," Soraya said, with a quiet confidence no one had seen from her before. "We're permitted to inherit."

"It's true," said Khadija, transferring the child to her other breast. "Mullah Yaqub says we inherit one-eighth of the estate—Soraya-jan and me. The girls share one third amongst them. All the rest belongs to Azizullah. In the end, of course, we will transfer *all* the land to him. It will not be divided. Never."

"Of course, when Azizullah grows up," Soraya mused, "perhaps he'll seek one of Ghulam Dastagir's daughters as a bride. Then—unless Ghulam Dastagir's wife gives him another son—his lands and ours will all be combined into one gigantic estate." She clapped her hands in sudden delight. "What a big, big landowner Azizullah will be!"

"If God wills it," Khadija added prudently. "Oh, just think of it— Malang-sahib's boy and one of your mighty Ghulam Dastagir's girls — joined! What an heir *they* will produce! Surely Ghulam Dastagir would favor such a match. Let's talk about the possibilities. Who might Azizullah marry?"

The five women from Ghulam Dastagir's household simply gawked, unable to absorb so much astonishing news or to formulate a proper response. At that moment, perhaps, as they gazed upon tiny, gurgling Azizullah, they felt some inkling of the future progeny that would flow from the seeds already in this room, the warriors and politicians, the calligraphers and poets, the professors, doctors, engineers, diplomats, and so many others who would trace their ancestry to the legendary Malang of Char Bagh, raised by the widows of his devoted student, the great Malik Ibrahim.

Finally Bibi Jan managed to gasp out, "How could you listen to Mullah Yaqub? He's only telling you these things because he wants these properties for himself. Two women, on their own, managing estates! How could that be? Good heavens, that Mullah is a conniving one. Where did he get this fantastic story? Women owning property! It's unheard of!"

"He got it from Allah's revered Quran. It's right there, Bibi Jan. That great Khadija whose name I bear—the wife of our Prophet, peace-be-upon-him-and-his descendants—*she* was a woman of property before she married our dear Prophet. Malang-sahib himself once told me so."

"Don't try to back me down with Quran, you—you woman. You can recite verses all day long but at the end of it, you will still be a pair of helpless, defenseless women, living on your own, without men!"

"Not true! This is a man." Khadija pulled her son away from her breast and held him up. He gurgled and beat the air with his tiny fists. "A little one," she admitted, "but with God's favor he will grow bigger every day. And we do have Agha Lala."

"He's eighty years old! And senile!"

"And yet, he's still a man. Not that I've checked between his legs, but anyone who claims he's not a man will have to prove it."

Soraya half-hid a smile and slapped at Khadija's arm, reveling in the domineering wit, the cocky confidence of this co-wife of hers, this big sister.

"And my cousin's nephew Mahmoud is living in the compound on the hill and Asad's boys, and, well—in short, we have almost too many males in these households. No need for the village to fret over our safety. Go home and tell Ghulam Dastagir we thank him for his concern, we appreciate his compassion, we love him as a brother, but we have accepted our sad destiny: to live out the rest of our lives as pitiful widows, devoted to the memory of the men we both loved so much, and to the toil and glory of raising the only son of the Malang of Char Bagh, who is the final heir of both Malang-sahib and our great malik."

"But the water—"

"Will belong to him." Khadija gave her son an affectionate kiss.

"You mean to you!" Bibi Jan accused.

Khadija gazed at her soberly. "No, my dear Bibi Jan. To him. We will manage these properties for him. When the heir comes to manhood, he will have it all."

"And if marauders come one day?"

"We will depend on the entire village to protect us," Khadija crooned. "Surely the men of Char Bagh will never stand by and let the Malang's son be harmed? Oh, not a single hair of his head. Surely not! Allah forbid! We trust in Allah and in the goodness of the people of Char Bagh."

The master of the household and the future owner of all the water in the village of Char Bagh and much of the land let loose a melodious burp. The startled women looked at the little fellow. At that moment, another sound caught their ears. Frogs? Could it possibly be frogs? Now? In the dead of winter? Here, in the middle of the compound? How could that be?

Then they realized what they were hearing: it was the unbroken rumble of the Sorkhab River gushing through its channels, even under the thick cap of ice it wore at this season. No one could remember hearing the river from this spot before, so deep inside the compound, so far from the river banks, even though the sound must have been there all along, for the water never stopped flowing, the water never did stop rushing through Needle Gorge, rushing down the endless slopes to join with other streams and other waters, rushing down to join the mother of all waters, the great ocean that was said to encircle all the land, somewhere out there in the vast world beyond the four sweet gardens of little Char Bagh.

ॐ